3/16

S. M. PARKER

Simon Pulse

New York London Toronto Sydney New Delhi

SIMON PULSE

An imprint of Simon & Schuster Children's Publishing Division

1230 Avenue of the Americas, New York, New York 10020

First Simon Pulse hardcover edition March 2016

Text copyright © 2016 by Shannon M. Parker

Jacket illustration copyright © 2016 by Simon & Schuster, Inc.

All rights reserved, including the right of reproduction in whole or in part in any form.

SIMON PULSE and colophon are registered trademarks of Simon & Schuster, Inc.

For information about special discounts for bulk purchases, please contact Simon & Schuster Special Sales at 1-866-506-1949 or business@simonandschuster.com.

The Simon & Schuster Speakers Bureau can bring authors to your live event.

For more information or to book an event contact the Simon & Schuster Speakers Bureau at 1-866-248-3049 or visit our website at www.simonspeakers.com.

Jacket designed by Regina Flath

Interior designed by Steve Scott

The text of this book was set in Electra.

Manufactured in the United States of America

2 4 6 8 10 9 7 5 3 1

Library of Congress Cataloging-in-Publication Data

Names: Parker, S. M., author.

Title: The girl who fell / by S.M. Parker.

Description: First Simon Pulse paperback edition. | Summary: "When new boy in school, Alec, sweeps Zephyr off her feet, their passionate romance takes a dangerous and possessive turn when Alec begins manipulating Zephyr"— Provided by publisher.

Identifiers: LCCN 2015029214 | ISBN 9781481437257 (hardback)

Subjects: | CYAC: Love—Fiction. | Psychological abuse—Fiction. | Dating violence—Fiction. | High schools—Fiction. | Schools—Fiction. | BISAC: JUVENILE FICTION / Social Issues / Dating & Sex. | JUVENILE FICTION / Social Issues / New Experience. | JUVENILE FICTION / Social Issues / Violence.

Classification: LCC PZ7.1.P366 Gi 2016 | DDC [Fic]—dc23

ISBN 978-1-4814-3726-4 (eBook)

To all the girls struggling to find their voice

The End

I pick up the landline, dial Mom's cell. It takes too long to connect. There is only the static silence of a dead line, and that's when I know I'm not alone.

I drop the phone onto its cradle and eye the door, my car keys on the floor in my path. In seconds I calculate how my body will need to scoop the keys as I run from the house. I move just as a metallic snap echoes from under the house.

The breaker.

In the basement.

Someone has thrown the main switch, pitching me and this house and my escape into blackness.

Fear roils in my blood. Becomes me. I kick around for my keys but with each sweep, I am losing time.

I reach for the island, my eyes adjusting, carving light into the shadows. The smell of spearmint bleeds through the air, through my memory, as my senses conjure the last time panic joined me in this space. And how my fingertips reached for the knife set even then. But the block of knives is gone now. The counter cleared. I open a drawer, rifle for utensils, scissors. My fingers meet with the smooth wood of inner drawer and nothing else. I fumble around the sink, but even Mom's pruning shears are missing.

The phone rings and I freeze from the impossibility of its sound. A second ring sears through silence. I wade across the black, remove the handset, place it at my ear.

I pray that it's anyone besides him.

Terror climbs the ladder of my spine. My voice, reluctant. "Hello?"

Silence.

Then the dial tone cries *beep beep beep* and I hang up, quickly dial 911. But he's quicker.

The line falls dead again.

He's in the basement, where the phone line enters the house.

But then, no.

He could be outside. At the junction box.

All at once the woods outside feel too hungry, haunted.

My body tells me I need to flee, protect. My brain tells me to fight, engage. I tuck into the forgotten corner of the laundry room, quiet as my fear, and wrap my hands around the butt of my field hockey stick. I hold it tight against my chest, a weapon.

I try to reverse my breathing. Make it soundless. Make it so I cannot be found. The darkness is a comfort, a cloak. I blend into it. For anonymity. For safety. There was a time when I feared darkness. As a child. Alone.

Not now.

Darkness doesn't have fingers that twist into my flesh. Darkness can't stalk me. It can't drive me into the shadows because darkness is fleeting. Not like the threat before me.

Chapter 1

The Beginning:
Three Months Earlier

I've got one foot in this world and one in the next.

Stuck in the limbo of being a high school senior. Here, but dreaming of next year, of college and freedom. Freedom from hall passes, curfews, field hockey pressure, and conjugating French verbs in a gray classroom on the most beautiful day of autumn. I twist a ringlet of my too curly hair and stare at the lone sugar maple in the courtyard outside room 104. It's early October and most of the leaves have already fired into reds and golds. One mad burst of flame at the end of a growing season. Just like senior year.

A pale yellow finch settles onto a high branch and twitches its head nervously. I watch it scan for what? Predators? Its mate? An early acceptance letter from Boston College? Around me, the room fills with the muffled sounds of students shuffling in. Conversations hush and quicken. The metal legs of a dozen chairs scrape the floor as the teacher writes "Learning Target for *Français*" in flawless cursive on the whiteboard just as Gregg fills the seat next to me like he's sliding into home plate. His chair glides a few inches closer and he's in my face, all shoulders and cologne.

"Bonjeer, Zephyr." He winks. "Looking good," he tells me, like he tells every girl on the planet. Even so, a blush pushes onto my cheeks, like always. It's embarrassing how easily I embarrass.

Gregg Slicer is my oldest friend and a legend at Sudbury High for being the best ice hockey player in the history of our school. And I mean The. History. Colleges from all over the Northeast have been scouting him since our sophomore year. Today he's wearing his red mesh number 17 hockey jersey and even though I can't see the back, I know it reads SLICE in oversize white block letters. Everyone in Sudbury, New Hampshire, calls him Slice because the boosters have invested a fortune marketing "The Slice on Ice." We take our hockey seriously in these parts. So seriously that Gregg's parents even call him Slice. Me? I'm the sole holdout for refusing to feed his ego.

"Did you—" I start, but he's talking to someone on his opposite side, someone I don't recognize.

Mrs. Sarter begins in hitch-pitched French, *"Bonjour mes étudiants. Es-vous bien?"*

Bien on a Monday? I don't think so.

Her teacher-speak fades into background noise as I consider the identity of the new student sitting next to Gregg. I lean back and catch a glimpse of the boy's neatly cropped, golden brown hairline. Huh. I study the collar of his blue oxford shirt, rumpled slightly. But Gregg's wide frame blocks a clear view. *When did Gregg's head get so big?* I lean forward, glimpsing New Boy's footwear. Faded black Converse. Long legs. His jeans are an Abercrombie shade of worn denim. His fingers drum a tune onto the broad part of his thigh. I fixate on the song he's tapping. Old-school rock? Black Eyed Peas? Something from the *Grease* soundtrack?

Next to me, Gregg opens his textbook. The room fills with pages being fanned, the collective hunt for *chapitre huit*. I flip open my book to a random page, but keep my eyes cut to New Boy. There's something about the boy's elongated fingers, the

4

steady, sure rhythm that's coursing through to his fingertips.

When Gregg drops his pencil and bends to retrieve it, New Boy turns my way, stares at me across the void. His eyes flicker cinnamon brown, like newly minted copper pennies. He shoots me a casual head toss and my breath catches in my throat. Just as Gregg blocks him again.

My head fills with New Boy's face. Smooth as honey skin. Searing gaze. My cheeks flush, and I'm certain I'm the color of a pomegranate.

"*Mademoiselle Doyle?*" Mrs. Sarter calls, louder than necessary. My eyes snap to the front of the room.

"*Oui, professeur?*" My voice crackles over the foreign words.

"*Nombre dix, mademoiselle? Quelle est la reponse?*" She rattles her throat. Never a good sign.

Number ten? What is the answer to number ten? I search the pages in front of me. There's a picture of two teenagers at a sidewalk café, each wearing a colorful beret. The word bubbles above their heads tell me they're chatting about homework.

"*Mademoiselle Doyle?*"

I scan the page, but can't find a *nombre dix*. I'm lost. Totally lost. I look up at Mrs. Sarter and know she's expecting more from an honors student, even though French is hands-down my worst subject. "U-uh . . . ," I stutter. The room falls quiet. The clock marks mechanical seconds. *Tick. Tick. Tick.* I swear I can hear the steady rise and fall of New Boy's breath, the smile that lifts slightly along the corners of his mouth. Then I hear the admissions board at Boston College, asking me about my goals and aspirations and why I want to attend their institution. Their questions are all in French-that-sounds-more-like-German, unintelligible and alien. My nerves shatter.

My weak voice spills into the still air. "Uh . . . *Je suis* . . . *Je suis* . . . stuck."

The classroom skitters with laughter. In the front of the room, Jeremy Lang repeats my words: "*Je suis* stuck! Classic!" Mrs. Sarter winces with disappointment and reprimands him. She does this in lowly English, and her scrunched expression makes me think it physically pains her.

Suzanne Sharper's arm flies into the air, pole straight—the answer practically bubbling off her overeager lips. Mrs. Sarter calls on Suzanne and nods at her correct *la reponse*. She turns to the whiteboard, writes the answer in measured purple strokes.

Gregg leans over and whispers, "Page eighty-four, genius."

"Right." I flip to that section of my book.

"Way to have your head in the game." He flashes me his press-popular smile, now twisting with a smirk.

"You could have helped me out."

He cuts his eyes to the front. "Who says I knew the answer?"

"Pa-lease." Gregg speaks French better than Mrs. Sarter on account of his dad being French Canadian. I straighten in my chair and smooth the pages of my book. Gregg slips me a small rectangle of a note, a makeshift business card. He's printed FRENCH TUTOR across the front using the red Sharpie marker he carries for autographs. He's scrawled his cell phone number on the bottom right-hand corner. I snark a glance at him and his self-satisfied grin. Then I can't help the way my eyes move beyond Gregg to find New Boy's profile.

I pull my attention away. What am I doing? I tuck Gregg's fake business card into the pages of my textbook and find number ten. I put my finger on it as if to physically plant my brain in this lesson even as the sentences morph together, indecipherable. My insides collapse into a warm sensation. Can a crush take hold this quickly?

Lizzie likes to say I "crush without the mush," which is her headline-clever way of reminding me I steer clear of deep commitment in the boyfriend department. Unless you count my two years in a junior high nonrelationship with Matt Sanders, which I don't. Or going to the senior prom with Zach Plummer when I was a freshman and being embarrassed by his drunk self all night.

But since my dad ditched me and Mom this summer, Lizzie's worried my inability to commit may have more to do with burgeoning abandonment issues. "Crushing is safe," she said. "It only involves one person . . . you. And you can be in control."

I prefer to believe my preference for remaining romantically unattached stems from the fact that I have a carefully mapped-out plan for my future, and there's no point in hijacking that with unnecessary dating drama now. The best boyfriend in the universe will be at Boston College. With me, next year. See? Perfect. Hooking up with a guy in Sudbury will only anchor me to a place I've wanted to escape since I was a freshman. So why can't I help but wonder . . .

If New Boy smells like oranges . . .

Has a British accent . . .

Plays sports . . .

Has secrets he'll tell only me?

When the bell rings, I jolt.

"Twitchy much?" Gregg jokes while gathering his books.

I stuff my books into my bag, stand, and force myself not to watch New Boy. I take one last look at the maple tree outside. The finch is gone. A spiral of panic swirls in my stomach. Nothing seems grounded lately.

And then Gregg's voice: "Zee, this is Alec." I turn and New Boy appears from behind Gregg like a shadow.

My heart quickens. The classroom goes fuzzy around the edges, as if my brain is only capable of taking in this one boy and nothing else. I try to appear calm. "Hey."

"Your name is Z?" he asks, with a distinct lack of British accent.

My pride ruffles. "Zephyr, actually."

His eyes throw an apology. "What does it mean?"

"What does Alec mean?" I counter. I'm aware my reply is obnoxious, but that question has always annoyed me.

"It means 'gentle breeze,'" Gregg says. "But I called her Zipper until we were about seven."

I redden.

"Her parents were hippies." Gregg knows my family story almost as well as I do.

I think of my mother, stuck in her unmovable fierceness, and my father, God knows where right now, and I don't see a shred of hippie. "They were young," I clarify. They were only nineteen when I was born. I can't imagine having a kid *next year*. Talk about hijacking college plans.

"Well, it's a cool name," Alec says. Damn if my blush doesn't deepen. But something else. Does his face redden too?

"Alec's transferring from Phillips Exeter," Gregg tells me.

My eyebrows knit. "To *here*?"

Alec laughs. "You don't approve?"

"No. I mean . . . it's just . . . why would you do that?"

"For Sudbury High's world-class foreign language program." A smile plays at the corner of his mouth.

"Sorry, I just meant . . . Exeter is such a better school."

Gregg laughs. "How long are you gonna dig this hole, Zeph? We've got a meeting with Coach."

Alec's gaze dips to my chest and I flatten my bag against me like a shield. He lifts his eyes quickly, a blush definitely blooming. "Do you play? Um . . . field hockey." It's impossible not to see his feet shift with embarrassment.

That's when I remember the emblem on my sweatshirt, the two field hockey sticks crossed in an X. Duh. I clear my throat. "Um, yeah. Forward."

"Zeph's the captain of our field hockey team," Gregg says.

"Cocaptain."

"Still, the best Sudbury's seen," Gregg adds.

Alec's eyes widen. "Impressive."

His acknowledgement sends a shiver racing across my skin, like heat and ice tripping over one another.

"You playing this weekend?" Gregg asks.

"Thursday's our last game of the regular season."

"I'll be there," Gregg says as if this is news. He's never missed one of my games. "You coming to Waxman's kegger on Friday?"

"Probably." Ronnie Waxman has a kegger every weekend. It's pretty much the apex of Sudbury's social scene.

"Come. You can help me show Alec around."

Alec is cute and new. He won't need a tour guide. "Sure, but keep in mind, this is Suckbury. You're likely to be disappointed by local customs."

Alec draws up the softest of shy smiles. "I don't know, I thought French would be lame."

My heart hiccups.

"Look, we gotta see Coach. Let's roll." Gregg slaps Alec's back before he slips out the door. The classroom empties except for me and Alec, and Mrs. Sarter wiping down the board as if it's an aerobic workout.

Alec takes a step back and motions for me to go ahead. "Ladies first." He lowers his head as I pass, like I'm royalty. It makes me wonder if chivalry is standard private school curriculum.

Just as I'm through the door, I hear, "Zephyr actually?"

I spin to face Alec. I should respond with something brilliant but my voice betrays me.

"It was nice to meet you." Alec's damn shy smile softens his every beautiful feature.

"Thanks." *Thanks?* I can only imagine what Lizzie would say if she were here. *Not the most memorable first impression, Zee.* I manage a nod and dart down the hall thinking Alec's *Zephyr actually* was both adorable and clever. A dangerous mix.

When I get outside, Lizzie's waiting for me in the courtyard, sitting at our picnic table. Her cropped hair looks ice white in the sun as she hunches over the small spiral-bound notebook she clutches with two hands. She flips a page, reviewing the shorthand reporter code I have yet to break. This is her process, the way she decides what story will appear on the front page of the school's *Sudbury Sentinel.*

"This seat taken?" I sit, and swipe an impeccably julienned carrot from Lizzie's lunch bag.

Lizzie lowers her notebook with a sigh. "This place might kill me, Zee."

"Dramatic much?"

"I'm serious. There is exactly nothing going on at this school. Unless I'm expected to use my professional genius to dissect the nutrients in the caf's tater tots or dig into the bizarre—and might I add—disturbing flirting rituals of some of Sudbury's faculty."

"Please spare us that."

Lizzie smiles, her face softening. "I need to get out of here."

"You and me both."

Lizzie and I have wanted to be free of small-town Sudbury

since we met in fifth grade. She's always had plans to be a reporter in a big city. At twelve, she wore a fedora, complete with a tab of paper that screamed PRESS in orange crayon. While other kids played tag, Lizzie taught herself shorthand.

Me? A marine biologist working off the shores of Cape Cod. Or Cape Town.

Lizzie peers over her New York cool black-rimmed glasses. "I hear Sudbury's snagged itself a transfer student." She squints, scans the crowd in the quad.

"Alec. He's in my French class."

Her mood perks. "You met him? Any scoop there?"

"I'm not trained in human observation the way you are, Lizzie." I pop the top of my Sprite and it hisses with release.

"Oh come on. There has to be something."

I take a short sip. "He's friends with Gregg. Plays hockey. Moved here from a private school."

Her smile winks. "But you weren't paying attention, right?"

"I guess some might say he's cute."

"'Cute' does not a headline make, Zee. Rumor has it he got expelled from his posh school for having a girl in his room."

"I met him for, like, two seconds. It didn't really come up."

Lizzie stretches out along the table. I envy the way she's always seemed so comfortable in her own skin. "But he's nice?"

"Like I said, our conversation wasn't deep. He could be a total player for all I know."

"News flash: All guys are players. It's called having a Y chromosome." Lizzie arches her neck toward the sun in a way I never could. Not without feeling everyone's eyes critiquing me. "Perhaps we should investigate. See if this boy is crush-worthy."

"Not interested."

"In him or any crush?"

"Come on, Lizzie. I've got, like, zero time for any of that. All that matters is getting my ass to Boston next year."

She turns to narrow her eyes, study me. "Maybe. I mean, I get it. But we're here now and he might be an attractive prospect. He could help keep your mind off some things."

I shoot her a look, one that warns she's going too far.

"I'm on your side, Zee." She throws up her hands. "I just don't want you to shut out opportunity now because you're thinking a thousand steps ahead about how your heart might get hurt."

Lizzie's been dating Jason since sophomore year. He's a year older and attends NYU. He comes home a lot, or she goes to New York. Each time they meet up it's like no time has passed between visits. I can't imagine getting lucky enough to share that depth of trust with another person. "And how is Alec an opportunity?"

"I'm not talking about Alec, Zee. I'm talking about taking chances. Making this year a little more than doing time." Her voice softens. "It's our senior year, our last chance to do whatever we want without consequences. Promise me you'll at least be open to different. Whatever form it takes."

I cringe at the thread of pity I hear in Lizzie's voice.

And her words don't leave me for the rest of the day. All through the grueling sprints of field hockey practice I can't wrestle free of Lizzie's advice: embrace different. But she doesn't get how hard *different* has been without Dad. I've kind of had my fill of different for a while.

Ugh. Maybe I have turned into a sad abandonment cliché.

Chapter 2

By the end of the week nothing matters except winning our game. There's no room to think about crushes or Dad disappearing or Mom trying to hide how her world has detonated into a thousand shards.

"Huddle up!" Coach's sharpened-knife voice slices through the locker room, and we quickly round into one. I breathe in the scent of lemons and too much bleach, and the adrenaline skulking about, readying to be set free. The room smells like I feel. Bottled, reined in. I need air. And the space to run.

And then Coach's speech: "This is it, ladies. An entire season—an entire career for some of you—is waiting for its punctuation mark. Will it be a period? That small dot at the end of a sentence that the reader glazes over? Or will you leave this season with an exclamation mark? A long streak of ink that proclaims you as victors, unbeatable!" Coach doubles as Sudbury's freshman English teacher.

We bang the butts of our sticks against the concrete floor until Coach's hands quiet us.

"Focus hard. Feel your youth. Use it."

It's her mantra. We all know it by heart and I am suddenly thankful for the things I can count on.

As if she knows what I'm thinking, she scans the room and I watch her trying to stamp this moment into her memory, fix it there like a photograph. Or maybe that's me.

Coach's face reddens then in the way I'm used to, all the blood rushing to her rallying call. "The word 'lose' does not exist! Not in your wheelhouse! Do you understand?" Her words ricochet off the cement walls, their echo washing away the bleach and the lemons. Leaving room only for the pulsing adrenaline. "Get out there and win!" My heart resets, beating with the pregame intensity I've known in all of my four years at Sudbury. When we raise a collective cheer, our pooled enthusiasm climbs into me, shares my skin. It feels familiar and safe.

The room thunders with the beat of a thousand sticks smashing against the cement floor. I gather my gear and slam my locker, the sound of its tinny, hollow screech singular amid the noise. A sound I won't hear again after tonight. Unless we win. Unless we make it to the playoffs. And in this moment I realize I'm not willing to let go of Sudbury. Not yet. No part of me wants tonight to be my last night in this uniform. I tuck my mouth guard under the strap of my sports bra, feel the weight of a hand patting me on the back. Then another. I grab my cleats and in a terrifying flash I realize I'm not even sure who I'll be without my teammates—without field hockey. I draw that fear down, deep into my core.

I'll use that fear to win tonight.

Prolong the season.

Cool air sweeps over me as I exit the gym, the bright lights of the distant field marking our arena: a rectangle of cropped grass, regulation lines, and more hope than any space should be able to contain. It feels odd to realize I'll miss even these lights, these electric eyes that have been watching over me for four years. My stomach dips with unexpected sentiment just as I hear Gregg's call.

"Wait up, Five!" I turn, even though my jersey says 23. When I was a freshman, five wasn't available so Gregg suggested two numbers that add up to my lucky number. I've been 23 ever since.

Gregg jogs to me, his smile moon-wide.

"Hangin' around the girls' locker room, huh? It's kind of a creeper move."

"Funny." He bends into an almost-bow. "I'm here to carry your cleats."

"Come again?"

"It's an epic night, Zeph. I thought I might have the honors." He reaches for my cleats and my game shoes look small in his palms. A wash of gratitude feathers over my skin.

We head toward the field, my feet bare except for socks. It's the only way I've ever walked to a game. Ever since the first time I played for Sudbury when I was running late and the Junior Varsity coach yelled me out of the locker room before I had all my gear on. I scored two goals that night. Got promoted to Varsity three games later. The cold pavement seeps through my socks and licks at my toes, but it only energizes me. Baseball players aren't the only ones who hold on to their superstitions like lifelines.

"You psyched?" Gregg asks.

"Um, kind of petrified."

He thrusts out his arm, stops me short. "Why?"

I stare into the washed blue of his eyes and my worry forces itself out of my rib cage. "This could be my last game for Sudbury. Or my last field hockey game ever. What if I fuck it up? What if we lose?" There are so many unknowns next year. What if I'm predisposed to bailing on all that's important to me—like Dad? What if I let the team down? "What if—"

Gregg pulls an imaginary zipper across his own lips and I quiet. "Remember our school talent show in second grade?"

My voice almost left me that night, too scared to speak to an auditorium audience. "I remember."

"You wore that Groucho mustache and told a bunch of knock-knock jokes. Remember your closer? Knock-knock . . . ," Gregg prompts.

"Who's there?"

"Tanks."

"Tanks who?"

"No, no, no," he mimics. "Tank you!" He bows for an imaginary audience. "You had the crowd laughing their asses off."

The memory paddles up in me like a friend visiting.

"You were a star that night, Zipper. You'll be one tonight."

The eight-year-old me visits when she hears Gregg's nickname. She tells me I've got this.

Gregg bends his tree form to nudge my shoulder with his and we continue to the field. Our shadows march forward in front of us. Straight. Determined. Together. Just like our plan for Boston next year.

A sudden flash of pom-poms and cheer cascade by us.

"Cheerleaders?" Gregg says. I shrug.

Lani Briggs, head cheerleader, sidles up to Gregg's opposite side. "Hey Slice."

"Lani. What brings you and the crew out tonight?" I can hear Gregg flashing her that killer smile.

"Football's loaning us out since, you know, the field hockey team hasn't gone to State in, like, forever."

"Jinx much?" I mutter under my breath, and Gregg elbows me.

"That's cool. Good to see so much support," he tells her.

"Maybe we can meet up after?" Lani asks, her full flirt dialed high.

"Maybe."

"I hope so," Lani coos just before she bounds forward to join her clan, her red and white pom-poms raised over her head.

"Gross," I tell Gregg.

"Lani?" He laughs. "Please. I'm not man enough to handle her stimulating conversation."

"I'm not sure it's conversation she's looking to stimulate."

"Get your head out of the gutter, Doyle. You've got a game to win." We reach the sidelines and Gregg hands me my cleats. "You'll rock this, Zeph."

I lace up my cleats and watch the football cheerleaders line up on the opposite side of the field. I snug my mouth guard around my teeth and squat in a final stretch.

Coach calls for us to take the field and I assume my position as right wing forward. Gregg's unmistakably deep, "Bring 'em hell, Five!" reaches me from the crowd. Then the ref's whistle blows a split second before I hear wood crack against the hard round ball. I run deep, open the face of my stick, ready for a pass. I bend low when the ball comes my way, trap it under my stick and snake it down the length of the field. I reach scoring position without a defender, no one blocking me, but it's not my shot to take. Lyndsey is set in front of the goal and I flick the ball to her, where she instantly hammers it into the corner of the net, putting Sudbury on the scoreboard first. Lyndsey and I crash into each other with a full-body high-five, riding on our wave of adrenaline. The cheerleaders sing out a practiced chant, which makes tonight seem bigger than all of us. That surge carries me through the rest of the game, through the fatigue and frustration, until the ref's whistle blows for the last time and he raises his arms in a win for Sudbury.

The cheerleaders sound out a victory cheer as my team smashes together, bound as one in our exhaustion and elation. I feel grounded here in the middle of a hundred heartbeats. Cocaptain

Karen nudges me and we call the team into a straight line to high-five the Clinton Colonials. With each hand I slap I wonder why I've always wanted to leave this town so badly. Has it really been that bad? Because right now, in this moment, the thought of leaving Sudbury sits uncomfortably upon my bones.

Lizzie meets me at the end of the line, puts on her old-timey newsman voice. "You're a star, Doyle. Front page news, see."

I laugh and pull out my mouth guard, jiggle it in my loose fist. "Front page, huh?"

"The frontest."

Gregg joins us. "Way to go, Five. It's playing like that that'll get a Boston College scout scrambling for your number."

I scoff. "As if. I'll be lucky if they let me sit on the sidelines to watch their games."

Lizzie knits her eyebrows. "Maybe it's because I know exactly nothing about college sports, but why is it such an impossibility that you could play for Boston College?"

"Because those girls are amazing. They are, like, the best of the best."

Lizzie bursts a short laugh and looks to Gregg.

He shakes his head at me like I'm dense. "You're a captain who just took her team to State, Five."

And that's when it hits me that the girls playing for the Boston College Eagles were playing for high school teams before they got to college. Hope spikes in me and it's almost too much to want.

"Zephyr!" It's my mom. At the bleachers, waving.

Lizzie pulls up her notepad. "I should go see how the Clinton coach spins this loss. I'm hoping for lots of expletives, but we probably both can't get that lucky tonight."

Gregg tosses his chin toward the corner of the field. "I'm gonna roll with Alec. Catch up with you later?"

My eyes follow his nod, find Alec. He's alone near the net, waiting for Gregg. Watching me. He gives me a shy wave and I raise my stick casually. Like him watching me is nothing.

"Tell your moms I say hey." Gregg pats me on the shoulder and jogs toward Alec.

I go to Mom, her face too small to hold a wider smile. "Oh Zephyr! You were amazing! I'm so proud of you, honey!"

"You should be," Coach says from behind, catching me off-guard. "You played one hell of a game, Doyle."

"Thanks Coach."

She nods and asks Mom, "Does she get her athletic talents from you, Olivia?"

Mom laughs. "I'm the definition of uncoordinated. Zephyr has her father to thank for her physical skill."

Mom hugs me to her. It's odd how easy it seems for her to talk to Coach about Dad. Mention him in this offhanded way like he comes up casually in all our conversations lately.

Coach raps on my stick, tells Mom, "You make sure she rests up, Olivia. Tonight is only the beginning."

Mom beams, pulls me tighter. "I will."

"I'm grateful," Coach says before heading over to the other players, their parents. But I'm the one who's grateful, for Coach including Mom in our team's success. It's a mission Mom doesn't take lightly. After devouring an enormous banana split at Fernalds, we head home where she tells me to shower and head to bed. "Like Coach said, you need your rest."

I oblige her the shower, but I spend half the night texting Karen and some of the other players. We're going to State and sleep is the last thing any of us seem capable of.

Chapter 3

The following night I go to my dresser and grab the woolen socks that are standard armor for a fall party in New Hampshire. Only days ago I would rage against the idea of attending yet another lame party at Ronnie Waxman's, but tonight feels different.

My full-color Boston College catalog sits on my desk. I trace my finger along its spine. Like always, I imagine I'm the girl on the cover, walking the brick path to the arched entrance of an academic hall, books rested on her hip, the photographer catching her on an up-step so that she looks like she's floating. *Soon*, I think. *Soon*.

Except . . . *except* . . .

Lately I've had a harder time imagining I can really be that girl . . . self-doubt Lizzie would attribute to parental issues.

When I sit on my bed to fasten my boots, a soft knock sounds on my bedroom door. For a dumb second I wonder whether it's Mom or Dad.

"Come in," I tell Mom.

She opens the door slowly, Finn forcing his wide doggie body through the crack before pushing his soft head into my shins. I feel for his ears, that sweet spot that makes his back leg flick quick as a jackrabbit.

"Hey Sunshine. Do you want to join me for pizza before you leave?"

Finn's head lifts at the mention of pizza, and his enthusiasm tempts me down the hall.

In the kitchen, Mom's setting the table, still wearing her fitted navy suit. She's a state prosecutor with meticulous grooming skills, never a hair or fact out of place. I wouldn't want to go up against her in a courtroom. She's fierce and forward in a way I could never own.

She sets out knives and forks, folded napkins. She's even poured two glasses of milk. Dad's the eccentric artist type—writes graphic novels for a living—and is way more relaxed. When he lived here, we'd stand around the island eating pizza right out of the box, sneaking Finn the crusts. I take a seat, slide a slice onto my too-formal plate. Finn drools at my side.

"I noticed the Boston College catalog in your room." Mom wrestles a slice onto her plate. "When's the application deadline?"

"Not till January." I don't tell her that I've applied early decision. Fact one: I can't wait until spring to know my academic fate. Fact two: I can't have Mom checking in every day to see if I've heard. I play with the crust of my pizza, knowing Mom's approach. She knows the application deadline but wants to talk about something important, something more important than Boston College. I imagine this is how she warms up her witnesses, gets them comfortable with some safe, calming chitchat.

She blows on her slice. "I talked to your father."

She doesn't even try to camouflage these explosive words. The words I have longed for and dreaded since my eighteenth birthday, the day Dad left with a note as his explanation: "Zephyr's an adult now and there are things I need to do besides being a parent." That wasn't his whole message, but it's the part I remember, the part that hurt most.

I stare at Mom, unable to conjure a simple *and* . . .

"We're going to meet for drinks. Tonight."

"You're *meeting* him? As in *seeing* him?" I want to scream, *Where is he? Where has he been? How can he all of a sudden be in a place that's close enough for you two to meet up?* In my brain four months spreads itself out like a distance. Four months means equator far away. Off-our-radar far away.

Mom's fingers move to the middle of the table and pick expertly at the yellow leaves on the centerpiece lipstick plant. She's been vigilant about perfect houseplants lately, as if pinching away dead foliage will exert some sort of order in our Post Dad Universe. "I know it must seem out of the blue, but we have a lot to talk about, Zephyr."

I tense in my chair, slip Finn my slice. He slinks to the corner to indulge. I can't help but wonder where Dad's been eating his dinners and if he's been alone. Does he have a girlfriend? Another house? A new kid on the way?

She wipes her hands on her napkin, reflattens it against the table. "He wants to talk to you, Zephyr."

"It's a little late for that, don't you think?" The words bite with all the anger I've stored.

She looks at me hard. "No. I don't. I don't think it's ever too late. I didn't have the luxury of talking to my parents or even knowing them."

I soften, knowing Mom's parents were killed in a car crash when she was an infant. "I know. But this is different. Dad *chose* to leave. Does he expect me to just forget him ditching me? That note?"

"Those are questions you'll have to ask your father." Mom reaches for my hand across the table. "I think you need to be really careful about dismissing your father, Zephyr. You can be angry at him. You can be upset. But in the end he's the only father you'll ever have."

I look at her, searching. Doesn't she know that I know that? It's why his leaving hurts so much.

I hear Lizzie's horn outside and practically jump for the door. "I gotta go." I bring my plate to the dishwasher and knock Mom's pruning shears from their perch at the sink's edge. The dull *twang* of them hitting the metal echoes in our quiet house.

I give Mom a quick kiss on the cheek. I don't tell her to have fun, like I would if she were going to her gardening club or meeting a friend. I can't find a combination of words that would be appropriate in this beyond bizarre situation. I mean, a twenty-six-letter alphabet has its limitations.

I fold into Lizzie's passenger seat.

"How's Olivia?" she asks.

"My mom is officially jenked. Apparently she's having date night with my father." I pull my seat belt across my chest and hope it's enough to keep my insides from spilling out.

Lizzie twists to face me. "So wait . . . what does this mean exactly?"

"It means that my parents are the last thing I want to talk about."

She gives me a hard stare. "But your dad is back, right? You don't want to talk about that fairly major event in Doyle family history?"

I press my head to the cold glass of the passenger door, hoping it will freeze still my racing thoughts. "I don't know if he's *back* back or why he's here. I can't even process."

Lizzie lets out a low sigh. "You still up for going out?"

"God yes. Anywhere. Please."

Lizzie drives and I watch the dark blink past my window. By the time we arrive at the party, we have to hike to Ronnie Waxman's house because cars already pack both sides of his private road. The October air sings crisp and I pull my scarf from my pocket, wrap it around my neck.

Lizzie links my arm in hers. "Be prepared to be treated like royalty."

Sovereign is the last thing I feel. "What for?"

"This place is crawling with jocks, and you just captained your team to State, girl. That makes you an A-lister."

"Hardly."

"You'll see."

As we approach Ronnie's house the rap is deafening. I'm grateful it absorbs the ache in me as we walk across his enormous, flawlessly groomed backyard, the earth thudding with reverberating bass.

On the raised patio, two kegs are positioned on opposite sides, like always. I don't drink. Control issues.

"Captain Fantastic!" Shane Taylor calls. He's manning the keg, handing out cups. He fills one, passes it to me. "You drink for free tonight, Zephyr Doyle." Shane swims in his own smile.

"Thanks."

He raises his cup in a toast. "Legendary."

"Told you," Lizzie says, nudging me.

"Right as usual."

Someone walks behind me, pats me on the back. "Great game, Doyle."

I look at Lizzie and laugh. "When did students at Sudbury start giving a shit about field hockey?"

"It's not the game, Zee. It's the fame. Everyone wants to be affiliated with a winner. Tonight, you're a winner."

Lani bounces in front of us and I have to take a step back from her energy. "Great game, Zephyr."

24

"Thanks."

But Lani's looking past me. "Is Slice here?"

"No clue."

"Oh. Okay. Well . . . Can you tell him I'm looking for him when you see him?"

"Will do."

"Okay, see ya!" Lani cheers and bounds off.

"Being ignored by Lani Briggs could be the biggest compliment of my life," Lizzie says.

"Hah! If I could be so lucky." I search the crowd. "I do suspect Gregg's behind this jock marketing campaign, though."

"Yeah, well, he's here somewhere. Nowhere else to go in Suckbury."

"I know, right."

We duck into the house, where I dump my beer and fill my cup with water to disguise the fact that I'm a total party dork. The rooms are packed and the music is too loud, and when Lizzie tells me she needs to use the facilities, I need air. "Meet me outside when you're done." I have to scream to be heard over Rihanna. Lizzie nods and I head out to our spot at the edge of the lawn, turn my back to the evergreens and feel comfortable hiding in the shadows. I like the distance. From here, I spy the already-wasted football team pooled around the kegs and the girls fawning. And Alec.

He leans against the house, three girls hanging on his every word. I can see their smiles and their too many hair flips. I lean forward, pulled by warped interest.

"Hey!" Gregg appears behind me and I jump. Cold water splashes over my wrist. "Man, what is with you lately?"

I blot the water off my skin with my jacket sleeve. "What do you mean?"

"You were jumpy in French class too." I smell the beer on his breath, recognize the way his words stumble out slower than usual.

"Don't sneak up on me and I won't jump."

"So . . . o . . . rry." He bats his eyes. "Forgive me, Zeph?"

"Always."

He takes a sip of beer, looks out into the crowd. "Where's Lizzie?"

"Bathroom break. But Lani's looking for you."

"Yeah? How come?"

"Probably because she's in love with you."

"Not my type." He swigs another sip. "So how are you enjoying your fame?"

I fan my arm around my deserted space. "I prefer the side-lines."

"Not comfortable with stardom? Inconceivable. How is it that we're friends, again?"

"Hilarious." I throw an eye roll.

"Well, I think you had an amazing season."

I shift my feet, uncomfortable. I'm not the hugest fan of compliments, something Gregg knows. "I had help."

"Oh right. I forgot that you're blandly ordinary and your team pretty much carried you." He smiles over the ridge of his cup.

"Your accuracy is impressive." I nod toward the house. "Looks like Alec's making friends." Two of the girls have moved closer to Alec. "So is it true he got expelled for having a girl in his dorm?"

"Fact. Why? Is that important?"

"Not to me. Lizzie's writing an exposé."

"Classic, right? One of the most interesting things to happen here didn't even happen here."

"Classic indeed." I take a sip of water, the cold shocking my insides. "How long have you guys been friends? I've never heard you mention him before." My curiosity about Alec surprises me.

"His peeps moved here last year. We share ice when he's home on break but I'm one of the only dudes he knows in town."

"Bummer for him," I say, and laugh.

Gregg puts his arm around me and squeezes. "Enough about Alec. How about you? Things cool?"

I lean into him in our comfortable way. I know he's asking about my home life. Olivia. The Missing Link that is/was Dad. I pull in a deep breath, prepared to blow the entire update his way, get his take on the unfolding madness. "Olivia's meet—"

But then my words are stolen.

Gregg's mouth presses onto mine, evaporating sound between us. His cheek stubble pricks against my skin. He thrusts his tongue between my lips and it meets mine, furiously searching. I pull back, shove my palm against the thick ridge of his collarbone.

"What was that?" Shock ripples through me in a way I thought impossible only moments ago. Gregg tilts his head and settles it onto my shoulder.

"Go out with me, Zeph." A plea whispered into the crook of my neck.

I slink out from under the weight of his drunk head and he scoops me to his tree trunk chest. My feet dangle in midair. He pushes "Zeph" into my ear. Half of me shivers from the intensity of being held by his strong arms. The bigger half of me can't believe this is happening because it's Gregg. My friend-since-preschool-Gregg.

"Put me down."

He eases my feet to the grass.

My voice falls soft. "You kissed me."

"I know. It was a little more one-sided than I'd planned."

"*Planned?*"

"I—" he starts, but something rustles behind us. Lizzie.

"You two look cozy," she says.

Gregg staggers backward, looking as disoriented as I feel.

"Sober much?" Lizzie laughs, showing no signs she saw the kiss. The kiss that was planned. Oh god.

Gregg stares at his empty hands. "I-I need to grab a beer." He turns quickly, heads toward the patio. I pull my sleeve over my hand and blot my mouth, wishing I had a stronger drink to wash away the taste of Gregg—Gregg, who's practically my brother.

Lizzie arches her eyebrows. "Is it something I said?"

"No, I think he just . . ." But I don't know how to process the last two minutes, let alone make an excuse for Gregg's behavior. I grab Lizzie's beer, swig a sip, and shove the cup back into her hand.

"Whoa. What's gotten into you?"

"I think I want to bail." I can't drink enough to forget that kiss, but maybe Gregg will. Maybe he already has.

"We can leave if that's what you want. Things have to be pretty messed up for you right now."

Major understatement. "I need to go."

On the drive home, Lizzie doles out supportive advice about the recent development with my parents in the way I've come to depend on, but tonight I only half listen. I'm too floored by Gregg's kiss to focus on much else.

I retreat to my room and lock the door. Lying on my bed, my brain cyclones with thoughts of men and boys and boys and men. All making the wrong choices.

Gregg's kiss haunts me all Saturday morning, so I ditch my homework and run. A lot. Just like I always do when too many issues creep up that are beyond my control. When I return to our long dirt driveway I stop to stretch against the pole that is supposed to hold up a green Ashland Drive sign, but the lonely metal rod stands as bare as the surrounding trees.

A twig cracks in the far distance. A deer, probably. The quiet of our forest is a comfort after the chaos of Waxman's party. A bit of thankfulness surges in me for Dad deciding to buy so much property. But then I remember that this wooded seclusion and me and Mom wasn't what Dad wanted after all. Or is it? A chill licks my insides as I reach for the mailbox, duck my hand into its mouth, and retrieve the stack of letters. All bills. Some with Dad's name.

Inside the house, Mom's sitting at the kitchen island studying *Gardeners' Supply Catalog*. My skin drips with a heated layer of sweat. All I want to do is take a shower, but Mom asks me to sit. Instead, I stretch my hamstrings. Again.

"I wanted to fill you in on my dinner with your father last night. He misses you, Sunshine."

I miss him too. The words are hard enough to admit inside the protected shell of my brain. I can't imagine giving them to the world.

"He wants to be in your life again. And I hope you're open to the idea."

"Well, I'm not. I'm still pretty pissed off."

"Language." She gives me a manners-reminding stare and stands. "Having a relationship with your father is important. More important than anything going on in your life right now, whether you can see that or not."

"It's pretty hard to see past him bailing on us." And can you even start over with your own father?

Her face hardens with thought. "Maybe it's time you start

focusing on what your future will be like if you can't welcome some forgiveness."

But how can I when my brain is busy obsessing over all the reasons my father didn't think me worthy of sticking around?

"You should know he has an apartment in Concord. For now."

An hour away. Then . . . "For now? What does that mean?"

Mom gathers her catalog and stacks it with the others. Her "future gardens" as she calls them. "It's a little early to say, but that shouldn't be your main concern. You need to focus on the relationship you want to have with him. You're an adult now, Zephyr."

Being reminded of my eighteenth birthday shifts the walls inward, devours oxygen. "Mom, I can't see him. Not now. I can't deal with hearing about why he left or why he's back." My heart's still breaking over the why he left part.

"Zephyr—"

"No, Mom. If you see him, that's fine. That's between you and him and whatever."

Mom folds her arms across her chest like she's holding in all the rest of the stuff she wants to say. But she keeps it locked in. Instead, she tells me, "I know you'll do the right thing."

The weight of her expectations crumbles me. I've always done the right thing. She expects me to make good choices but I don't even know what good choices look like after being abandoned by my father. His note had the edges of a serrated knife, tearing through the bond we'd once shared, carving out Before and After.

I escape to the shower and when I get out, I text Lizzie that I'm not feeling great, which isn't a total lie and it's enough to excuse me from tonight's limited Sudbury social scene. I bury myself in English and trig for the rest of the weekend, and obsess over why Gregg hasn't answered my "You around?" text.

"Do you think things are still cool between us?" I ask Finn, who's stretched out on the bed next to me, his head on my pillow. I nuzzle close to his face. "Do you think Gregg was too drunk to remember the kiss?" I interpret Finn's slobbering lick across my lips as a definitive no.

Chapter 4

By Monday I'm practically crawling out of my skin from Gregg's silent treatment. I can't even name the last time I went a day without a text from him, let alone an entire weekend. Does he hate me? Blame me? I'm so preoccupied with bracing myself for seeing him in French last period that the last thing I expect is Alec waiting for me at my locker. "Uh . . . hi."

"Hi yourself." He must read the question in my eyes because he says, "Mind if I walk with you? I thought it might be good if we started over. Our introduction wasn't exactly epic."

"Yeah, not my finest moment."

"It's all good. I'm in a position to be very forgiving considering you and Slice are the extent of my social connections in this school."

I hate the way my heart dips when I hear Alec mention Gregg.

Alec wiggles his French textbook before letting it hang smoothly by his hip, a gesture I try not to notice. "I've been studying."

I grab my own book and slam my locker closed. "Yeah?"

The corner of his mouth turns up. "In an attempt to master the language as you have."

A laugh betrays me and slips right past my lips as we move down the hall.

"Seriously though, it's intimidating to be in an AP French class when I've never taken it before."

"You've never taken French?"

"Nope. I've studied Latin since, like, the third grade. I can tell you anything you want to know about noun declension. Impressive, right?"

I try to force back a growing smile, but it's hard to tame.

"But French, now that's tricky. As you so brilliantly displayed last week."

"I wasn't exactly paying attention."

His eyes widen. "Distracted?"

"Bird watching."

"Lucky bird."

Huh. "So how did you get into this class? If you've never taken French before?" I ask as Mrs. Sarter's room comes into view.

"I scored high on the placement test. I used my Latin and a lot of educated guessing. Who said dead languages are useless?"

Dead languages. Like the dead silence between me and Gregg. I shake the thought from my head.

We enter the classroom and take our seats at the back. I open my book, pretend to review. Gregg's homemade card for free French tutoring flutters to the floor. And that's when I see him in the front row, chatting it up with Suzanne Sharper, his charm turned on high. Mrs. Sarter calls the class to order and Gregg twists in his seat, like he's supposed to be in the front row. Like he's always been in the front row.

Gregg successfully ignores me the rest of the day, despite my best efforts to catch him coming out of class or run into him at lunch. It's like he's changed all of his patterns just to avoid me, an observation that makes my stomach coil. I remember the same sinking feeling in the weeks after Dad left, the way I'd search for him in the aisles at the grocery store or through the windows of passing cars. I don't want Gregg to slip away like Dad did.

I need advice.

I text Lizzie to meet me outside for lunch and she's already at our picnic table when I arrive. She starts her interrogation before I'm fully plunked down across from her.

"So are you finally going to tell me what's up? You've been acting weird all day."

"Have I?"

She wrestles a handful of Junior Mints from their box. "You thinking about your dad?"

"What? No. I mean, yeah, I guess, but no."

"Then what?"

"More like who." I pop the top of my soda, trace its metal rim with my finger. "Gregg, who."

"Slice? Is he okay?"

"He's fine. At least, I think." I hesitate. It's unsettling spilling my private bits, even to someone I trust as much as Lizzie. But what choice do I have? "He kissed me. On Saturday. At Waxman's."

"He *kissed* you?" Lizzie practically yells. "That's why you two were acting so weird. Zee, oh my god! It's about time."

I stare at her, dumbfounded.

"You cannot be shocked. He's been in love with you since junior high."

"He has not."

"Zee, I'm a reporter. I get paid to notice these things."

"You're the editor of the school newspaper. No one pays you."

She waves off the technicality. "Slice loves you. Everyone

knows that. And you guys would be incredible together, an unstoppable force of hockey on the ice and field." She ghosts her hand along an imagined, overenlarged headline. "Hockey Couple Zee and Slice, Twice as Nice." She frowns, considering. "Okay, needs some work."

"I think there's a bigger problem than your headline." I swallow hard. Gregg is strong and kind and all the things any sane girl would want in a boyfriend, but he's practically family. "I just can't like Gregg like that, you know—I don't *like* him like him."

"You're not interested in being swept off your feet by one of the most popular guys in school?"

"It's too weird, Lizzie. He's like my brother. You know, if I had a brother."

Lizzie steals a sip of my soda and contemplates. "Yeah, okay, I get that."

"Why would he do this? It's beyond bizarre. I mean, our families have been friends forever." My face rushes with heat.

"Complicated."

"Right? And now he's avoiding me. Even moved his seat to the front of French class. Told Mrs. Sarter some bullshit excuse about not being able to see the board. But he never misses a puck flying at him at breakneck speed. Doesn't need glasses for that."

"Ouch. What are you gonna do?"

I shrug. "I have no idea."

"You have to talk to him. Drive to his house. Confront him. You guys can get past this. I'll even go with you if you want."

"Yeah?"

"Of course. This will all blow over, Zee. And this could be a good thing." She pops a mint.

"How do you figure?"

"It's probably healthy that you're dealing with a little boy drama instead of the relationship chaos imploding over at *chez* Doyle."

"I can assure you that getting kissed by Gregg does not feel healthy."

"Okay, maybe the Slice thing is bizarre, but it'll make for a great story when we're years away from this crap town."

Just as she says it we look at each other, realizing maybe clearly for the first time that we won't be together next fall. This is the part of limbo that we don't talk about, how our individual futures don't include each other. It physically hurts to imagine my life without Lizzie, but I never imagined my life without Gregg, and yet here it is, my life, with Gregg conspicuously absent.

Lizzie clears her throat and nods at the space behind me. I turn, my heart quickening, expecting—hoping—to see Gregg. The sun hangs directly behind the approaching silhouette but even after one short week, I know his shape, the rolling lope of his stride. Alec looks haloed in the brightness as he moves closer. I raise my hand to my forehead to shield my eyes as he peers down at me.

"Hello, Zephyr actually."

"Hey." I don't have to see the smirk plastered across Lizzie's face to know it's there.

Alec reaches to shake Lizzie's hand. "I'm Alec. Residential new kid."

"Lizzie. Smartest girl in school."

"Always a good person to know." Alec points to the building across the courtyard. "I was on my way to meet Coach. Thought I'd say hi. Do you guys always eat out here?"

"When the weather's nice," Lizzie says. I see her skilled observer gaze sizing Alec up. "Why?"

"The caf's a little overwhelming when you've got no one to sit with." I find myself intrigued by his vulnerability.

"You miss your friends?" Lizzie asks.

"I miss things being familiar. It's not easy starting at a new school senior year."

"I'll bet." Lizzie gives a sympathetic nod. "But your girlfriend will visit, right? That'll help."

He grins. "No girlfriend."

"That's not the rumor going around," Lizzie says. I nudge her on the thigh, a move Alec registers.

"Do you believe everything you hear?" Alec asks.

"No, that's why I'm fact-checking. The story is that you got kicked out of school for snogging a girl in your dorm room."

"Snogging?" Alec laughs.

"There are a million different words for it. Pick another, if you'd like."

"Like I said, don't believe everything you hear." He gives the table a quick knock and throws me a soft smile. My stomach twitters. "I gotta run. Coach will kill me if I'm late."

"So you made the team?" I ask.

"That's what they tell me."

"Congratulations," I say.

"Thanks." That blush deepens across his cheeks. "I only hope ice hockey is as good as field hockey in this town." He turns to Lizzie. "It was nice meeting you." Then, to me. "See you in French, Zephyr actually?"

I nod. "See you."

Lizzie waves.

Alec jogs to the granite steps, takes them two at a time before disappearing into the mouth of the school.

Lizzie needles my thigh with her finger. "The new kid has a pet name for you."

"Funny."

"He looked pretty sincere to me." Lizzie tosses a trio of mints into her mouth, her smile growing wider. "I don't think it would kill you to investigate hanging out with him. He seems nice. We could all go out together, maybe. Jason will be home next weekend. What do you say?"

"Maybe." But it's a big maybe. I think Lizzie found something special in Jason, and there are only so many Jason and Lizzies in the world. Up until a few months ago, I thought my parents had that same kind of steel cable connection.

I raise my face to the low sun and close my eyes the way I've watched Lizzie do hundreds of times. I try to push away the fear of anyone watching me and relax into the wash of yellow light that paints the backs of my lids like a canvas. On it, my mind draws Alec and his smile, the way it speaks of a secret. It's easy to be distracted by him, for sure. But then Alec morphs into my dad, grinning, happy. Popping out of his art studio with his next idea for a character from another galaxy. I dart my eyes open, fully aware of how dangerous blind faith can be.

Chapter 5

Saturday morning I hang in bed studying for my upcoming trig test. Finn seems content to lounge next to me all day, but by noon stir-craziness beats inside me fast as hummingbird wings. I can't deal with the silent treatment from Gregg and I need to head over to his house. But first, a run. To clear my head. Prepare for The Talk I'm pretty sure we need to have.

I lace up my sneakers and grab my iPod. "Sorry Finn," I say when his pant becomes *please, please, please.* "You wouldn't be able to keep up with me today." Or any day, for that matter. Finn's a mixed breed, but the girl at the shelter called him a Couch Retriever since all he ever did was sleep. "I promise I'll walk you later."

I jog the quarter-mile length of our dirt driveway and check the mailbox for an envelope from Boston College. Nothing. I channel my disappointment and head into the woods, running carefully over the grooved ruts of the path, the ground already hard with the coming winter. My thoughts crowd with Gregg's kiss, and I struggle to find the words to make us right again.

After nearly four miles my brain shuts off and all I feel is the breath passing in and out of my lungs. It's the best kind of inner quiet, the kind where every other problem in the world falls away.

When I reach Gosland Park I take a break before heading home. I settle onto a swing and pedal my feet off the ground. I float above the earth, back and forth until my body cools. I lean way back, extended. My eyes study the unobstructed blue of the sky, as vibrant as a spring wildflower. I breathe the color deep into my lungs, knowing December will soon rob me of this hue.

"Zephyr?" My name carries on the wind, like a whisper, like birdsong. I'm in such a fog, I think I imagine it. Until I hear it again.

I squint, see Alec leaning on the swing set pole, one hand crooked into his side.

I sit upright, dig my toes into the bark chips to brake. "What are you doing here?"

He plucks an earbud and lets it drop around his neck. "Out for a run." I take in his fleece, his running sneakers, the horizon of sweat that hangs at his hairline. "Clears my head." He takes the swing next to me, pushes off before tucking his feet under his body like a child. He surveys the park. "You come here a lot?"

"Sometimes," I lie. "I used to come here when I was a kid." It was special then. Now it's an escape.

He stares at the far fields, where tiny kids in blue shirts play T-ball against tinier kids in red shirts. "Would it be dorky to want to ride the seesaw?"

I laugh. "Totally."

"Wanna be a dork with me?"

I stare at him, registering this unexpected request. "Sure." I stand. "Why not?"

"Not exactly a ringing endorsement, but I'll take it." Alec smiles as he invites me to mount the board first and then slowly lifts my side of the seesaw into the air. My legs dangle with the freedom

40

and I can't help the way my toes kick out, happy. He straddles his end and calls, "Just so you know, I plan on having kids someday, so no quick movements."

"Got it."

He climbs on, shimmies forward to balance us. We catch an easy steady rhythm and the floating sensation makes my whole body soar. I'd forgotten how weightless seesawing could make me feel, like a world of problems can be brushed away through bristles of moving air.

"My dad used to take me here every Sunday. We'd tell my mother we went to church, but really we just ate donuts." I'm surprised at how easy this personal memory rises into the space between us.

"Is that your flaw, then?"

"My flaw?"

"You come from some donut-worshipping cult and I should be afraid. Very afraid."

I laugh and the sound rises along with my body.

"Do you still do that with your dad?"

I shake my head, float downward.

"I don't think I've ever been to a park with my dad. Not even when I was little. He's too serious for such nonsense." Alec's face contorts like he's mimicking a familiar stern expression. "Not sure he's ever even eaten a donut, poor guy. If it's not made of bran or cabbage, it's not worthy of his gullet." I wrinkle my nose. Alec laughs. "Exactly."

"Is your dad glad you're home? He'll be able to go to all your games now, right?"

A flicker of sadness drops over his face before disappearing. "My mother's the one who got me into hockey. Probably thought

41

the coach would be a good role model, seeing as my dad was never around."

"Are your parents divorced?" It seems like such a simple question to ask a stranger, even though I can't bring myself to ask my mother or father if that's what's coming for them. My body rises and my ponytail bounces just as I peak, then instantly begin to fall.

"Nah. They're more of the *live separate lives* type of people. My dad works in Singapore. Tries his best to get home for Christmas. He Skypes sometimes, when he can remember he has a family."

"That's kind of awful." I plant my feet on the ground before pushing hard.

"Not really." Alec floats buoyant toward the sky. "Not when it's all you've ever known." His face retains a kind of peace at this statement and I bite back envy. Will I ever be okay with Dad leaving the way he did? Or is my family's situation harder to understand since Dad never seemed distant or unhappy? Just one day he was gone. My stomach drops, but not from the seesaw.

I dig my heels into the ground at my next landing. "I should go."

"Is it something I said? Perhaps it's the potent stench of my runner's cologne? And the fact that you've had the pleasure of being downwind?"

"Nothing like that." I nod toward the sandbox and reach for an excuse. "There are a couple of kids giving us the stink-eye. I don't mess with playground politics."

He laughs, gives me a shy smile. "Drop me down." I do. He dismounts carefully and holds the seat to counterweight my descent. It's another gallant gesture and my stomach tumbles.

I look toward the darkening sky. "I should run home while there's still light."

He agrees and we walk in silence until we arrive at the park's metal gate. He reaches for the latch, lifts it free. "It'll get better, you know."

I narrow my eyes. "What will?"

"Whatever's going on between you and Gregg."

"How did you . . . ?"

"I didn't know for sure. Not until just now. But you two haven't been exactly chatting it up in class lately."

Even he's noticed Gregg avoiding me all week. "Has he . . . said anything about me?"

He surveys the ground at his feet. "Gregg talked about you a lot when I met him. I thought you were his girlfriend, but he said you guys were just friends. Best friends, I think he said."

My heart wells with loss. "The best."

"Did you guys ever date?"

"No. Why?"

He shrugs. "I just thought maybe that's why there's tension now."

"No, nothing that dramatic."

"Then I'm sure whatever's going on between you two will work out. It has to. Good friends are hard to come by."

He's right. Spot-on right.

He swipes the toe of his sneaker into the dirt, creating an arc. "Can I ask you something else?"

"Sure."

"Would you meet me here tomorrow?"

"Yes." I'm surprised by the commitment.

Surprised?

No, scared.

Chapter 6

The crow of a rooster wakes me. It's close; in my ear close.

I open my eyes and fumble for my phone, knowing it's Lizzie. For a long time it was a game to see if I could keep her from messing with my ringtones. But she always got to my phone somehow. Now I can't imagine being surprised by her selections.

Finn lifts his plump head from my pillow, clearly displeased with the disruption to his slumber.

LIZZIE!—in all caps, of course—blinks on the screen. I silence the rooster with the practiced twitch of my thumb.

"Morning." The word rumbles low and scratchy, a storm scraping the sky.

"I'll need reinforcements at work today."

"M&Ms or Junior Mints?" I sit up and Finn lets out a gruff sigh before repositioning himself at the foot of my bed.

"It's feeling like a Tootsie Rolls day. It's just me and Shorty so I'll need a big bag. Party size." Shorty is the middle-aged manager of Too Cute Shoes, the dumpy discount footwear place where Lizzie earns the cash to visit Jason. "What are you doing?"

I prop my pillow and pull back my shade. A blast of too bright light hurtles into the room, illuminating my wall of photos like the trained light in a museum. There's the picture Lizzie took of me and Gregg in the lunchroom last year. We are both laughing, his two fingers in a peace sign behind my head. I drop my gaze to my bureau, to the framed photo of us when we were five, Gregg pushing me on a swing at Young Ones childcare center where we got bused after our half days of kindergarten. I remember how we'd play king and queen and pretend to live in our castle under the slide. He kissed me then, too. A peck on the lips because we were married and that's what married people did. It's almost impossible to believe my view of marriage and trust was ever that simple.

"I'm heading over to Gregg's."

A beat of silence. "Do you want to wait? I can go after work. You know, if you need support."

I do need the support. I have no idea what I plan to say, but, "I think I should go alone." It's never been hard to talk to Gregg. I've never had to prepare to talk to Gregg. I draw hope into my lungs that this time will be no different.

"Okay, come by after. With chocolate."

"You bet."

I shower, get dressed, and head out on my mission. I drive for nearly two hours and never even enter Gregg's neighborhood. I start to understand why Dad took the easy way out via a note.

By the time I arrive at the park, Alec is waiting. Heat rushes to my face as he watches me pull into a tight parking space. Honestly, no one can understand the curse of Irish skin unless you live in it. I turn the keys, keep my eyes cut to Alec and his casual lean against his shiny robin's egg blue antique Mustang. He's wearing that secret smirk that I've come to expect.

I wave. He nods. I move toward him, suddenly self-conscious

about my body. My too long legs. My too curly hair. My nose that's just this side of crooked. Why are effortless good looks always wasted on boys?

"Hey," he says casually.

"Hey." I go for casual too, hoping it doesn't sound like I practiced this one-word greeting in front of my mirror a hundred and three times after hanging up with Lizzie this morning.

"You're right on time. Two o'clock exactly."

"I'm punctual," I say.

"Punctual says a lot about a person."

"What does it mean when a person shows up early?"

Alec just smiles, in a way I can't read.

So I look at his car. Cars are easy. I know cars. Dad used to leave issues of *Classic Car* magazine on practically every surface. He gave me and Mom quizzes when we were driving and he'd see the oncoming chrome grill of any car manufactured before 1972. I've been dragged to enough car shows to know this model anywhere. I swallow back the sadness that rises when I think of the July issue of *Classic Car*. The one that came right after Dad's note. The issue that prompted Mom to cancel the subscription altogether. I can't tell her the magazines keep coming, how I hide them in the back corner of my closet along with some of his other things.

"Sixty-seven fastback. With a three-ninety, right?" My voice inadvertently takes on the tone of grease monkey mechanics, men with toothpicks wiggling between their teeth. Why can't I just be normal, be myself? But that's the thing about meeting Alec here today—just seeing him makes me think there might be a whole other normal for me, one I don't even know yet. I shift on my feet, my toes nervous with this uninvited newness.

46

"Um . . ." He laughs. "Unexpected."

"What is?"

"A girl who knows muscle cars."

A blush heats my face like wildfire combing underbrush. "My dad," I say, as if that's enough of an explanation.

He nods, but doesn't press for details.

I feel a sudden need to thank him. For not prying. For not pushing.

"I'm glad you came," Alec says.

"Yeah?"

He reaches a tentative hand toward me and I take it. His fingers spider around my own.

His eyes ask, *Is this okay?*

No, I think. *It's crazy. Holding hands at the park with a boy. Like a sixth grader.* I spread my fingers, let them relax enough to pull away.

But then I see his blush and remember the way he listened without judging and reassured me things would be okay with Gregg. My fingers reposition, locking against his.

He smiles. "Seesaw? Or shall we shake it up a bit?"

"Feeling brave enough for swings?"

His laugh validates me in a way that baffles. "A fine choice. Oh wait. I almost forgot." He drops my hand and I'm shocked by how the cold pierces in his absence. My fingers feel different from the rest of my body now, not fully mine anymore. I shake the nervous energy down through my arms and shove my hands into the front pockets of my jacket.

I think of excuses to bail as I watch Alec jog back to his car, pop the trunk with its vintage squeak.

"A picnic," he calls, holding up a wicker basket.

His enthusiasm makes me nod, bite on another smile. And stay.

We walk together and I scan the familiar grounds, the monkey bars, the rickety swing set. "I used to think swinging was the closest you could get to flying," I say. "When I was a kid I'd close my eyes and pretend." All the while knowing Dad was there to catch me if I lost my wings.

"That's how I feel when I'm on the ice. Like skating is the closest thing to flying." Alec nods at his basket. "You want to swing first or eat?"

"I could eat."

"Yeah? It's not lame?"

"Not lame."

His smile beams as quick as a child's and I feel myself drawn to his innocence. He sets the basket onto the ground, removes a checkered cloth, and we float out the corners into a perfect square. "I'm glad you came."

"You mentioned that."

He blushes. "Five minutes in and I'm already redundant. What a lame date."

My gut dips. This cannot be a date. I cannot do complicated right now.

Alec looks at me softly, his eyes apologizing. "No . . . sorry. I just meant . . . it doesn't have to be a date. Not if you don't want it to be." He drags his fingers through his hair. "Christ, I sound like an idiot. What is wrong with me?"

"What do you mean?"

"I sound like a twelve-year-old around you."

I chuckle.

"It amuses you that I'm a bumbling twelve-year-old?"

"No," I say, laughing.

"All I'm trying to say—as inarticulately as is humanly possible, apparently—is that I'm glad you're here." He looks down, bashful. "Shit, that is actually the third time I've said that now." He unwraps a tuna sandwich and hands me a square. "I might not be displaying it so brilliantly at this moment, but I think you're easy to be with. I like talking to you."

"I'm sure you know lots of people who are easy to be with. I see you talking to people in school all the time." I bite into the soft bread and taste the unexpected crunch of celery and red onion.

"School chat's easy. It doesn't have to mean anything. I miss real friendships, you know?"

"I can't imagine moving to a school without Lizzie." And Gregg, I almost say Gregg.

"It's been the hardest part. Leaving the buddies I was tightest with." He takes a bite of his sandwich, settles back onto an elbow.

"So why did you leave your school?"

He squints against the sun and finds my eyes. "Why, Zephyr actually, that's a fairly sly way to ask if the rumor is true."

I feign indifference. "You don't have to tell me if you don't want to."

He sits up, looks off into the distant ball field. "The true part? I had a girl in my room after lights out, which was an expulsion-worthy offense."

This revelation translates to Complicated with a capital C. I should have gone to Gregg's instead. Worked things out with him. What am I even doing here with this other boy?

He meets my eyes. "The tricky part is that this girl was my roommate's girlfriend. She was there with him. Not me."

"Then how come you got expelled?"

"I took the blame for it, said she was with me." He picks away the crust along his sandwich. "Honestly, I didn't even really think about it. I knew my buddy couldn't take the fall. He was on scholarship and would've lost everything. I figured I'd be fine, since colleges only want me for hockey, not my grades."

Okay, so not totally complicated. It's more — "Selfless," I say.

Alec pulls two bottles of water from the basket, opens one and hands it to me. "Not entirely. I mean, he would have done the same for me. Besides, I'd been wanting to come home for a while and saw my chance."

"I can't imagine ever wanting to be in Sudbury."

"That's because you've always been here." He takes a sip of water. "And it's not Sudbury, really, I just missed home. My mom. Or . . . I miss the way she used to be."

"Used to be?"

"She was softer when I was a kid. That probably sounds ridiculous."

"Not really."

His eyes lock on mine, hint at trust. "Since my dad's been working overseas, my mom's all aggressive and hyperfocused on her company. My coming home hasn't changed that. Not like I'd wanted it to."

"My mom's been the same way since my dad split. Like she's overcompensating." This fact is out of my mouth before I realize.

"No small burden. When did your dad split?"

"In June." *On my eighteenth birthday* echoes in my head. When the kitchen smelled like lemon basil because Mom took cuttings from her plant to make my favorite pasta sauce. "He wrote a letter to my mom saying he couldn't do it anymore." The minute the words are out I want to shove them back into silence.

50

"Did he write to you?" Alec asks.

"No." It is a hard word. A hard truth.

"Shit."

The air feels hollow then, like it did that day. Like breathing is no longer an option. "I used to think my dad was perfect. Until he wasn't. You know?"

"I do." His eyes throw me a soft smile and it feels like he really might know.

"My mom's been trying so hard to hold it together that I think she'll shatter. It makes me nervous about leaving for college next year. I mean, what if she loses it? Has a breakdown or something?" I don't tell him how I'm *really* afraid I'll never even get into college because I fear I'm deeply flawed and that's why my own father didn't want to stick around or at least give me a letter explaining why he left.

"I think we can make ourselves crazy thinking about all the what-ifs."

"Yes. Exactly. That's exactly what I'm doing. But somehow it feels easier to stress about the future instead of really looking at the past. Like maybe I don't want to see what was there."

"That sucks, Zephyr," Alec says, and I'm surprised by my laugh. "What?" His eyes brighten.

"Nothing, it's just . . . well, you're right; it does suck. It did suck. Everyone's been saying they're sorry and it'll get better but no one's ever called it out for what it is. Sucky." I take a drink, trace the open top of the bottle with my finger. Marvel at how easy it is to expose my private thoughts to Alec. "And now my dad's back and that's sucky too."

"Like *back* back?"

I shake my head. "He's somewhere. My mom's talking to him

I guess." I hope he doesn't hear the way my voice cracks, falls through that sad space.

"Have you seen him?"

"No. I can't."

"I get that."

His three words are so much bigger than just three words. They are a space in which I am understood by another person. No questions asked.

"I'm glad you told me."

I'm glad too. And relieved. And relieved. Listening to Alec talk about his family is different from talking to Lizzie, whose dad was killed in Afghanistan, or to Gregg, whose parents are the definition of Happy Couple, completely devoted to their six kids and each other. Alec's dad has been making a choice to be away from his family. Same as mine.

Empathy exchanges between us like a pact.

When we're finished eating, Alec extends his arm and offers me an escort to the swing set. He effortlessly guides my body into a slung rubber seat and I am a wave carried on his current, surprised by the warmth his breeze of a touch sends through my body. He steadies the chains with his outstretched arms while straddling my legs. Our knees are only inches apart. If I moved the tiniest bit they'd be touching, connected. Just thinking about it sends a fear-filled bolt of electricity through me. I draw in a deep breath to steady my nerves but my senses fill with the sharp mixture of his sweat and cologne. Somewhere in the distance a toddler screeches. And then sound gets pulled into a tunnel and all I can hear are the words falling across Alec's lips.

"Can I tell you something?" He holds the chains, his chest and arms closed around me. "Promise you won't laugh?"

"Promise." My nerves cause laughter to tickle across my lips.

"You promise you won't laugh, but you laugh while you're promising?" He shakes his head in mock disappointment but then catches my gaze, holds it. He is looking in me. Through me. He doesn't even blink. It's all I can do not to look away.

"I couldn't stop thinking about you after seeing you here yesterday. Wait, no, that's a lie." He rubs at one of the metal links with his thumb. "I couldn't stop thinking about you after you didn't know the answer to *nombre dix*." His jaw bites back a laugh, but one bubbles right over my lips.

"Ah, so *that's* why you wanted to meet up today. You need French pointers."

He squats in front of the swing, rests his forearms across his thighs. "Please tell me you don't have a boyfriend."

"I don't."

"Okay, wait. Are you telling me that because I told you to tell me that, or do you really not have a boyfriend?"

"No boyfriend."

"Girlfriend?"

"Not like that."

He considers. "See, now that's strange. I would've thought you'd have a million guys falling over you, based on your French prowess alone. It's a highly effective mating technique, you know."

I smile. "I wasn't aware."

"Check out Discovery Channel sometime. Butchered French is a primal mating call."

"Very funny."

"Seriously though. How can you not have a boyfriend?" The air falls still around us.

"I haven't met the right person."

Alec smiles. "Until now. You're supposed to say . . . *until now*."

"Oh, is that what I'm supposed to say?" I push the toe of my shoe into his and he presses back.

We are touching shoes.

The tips of our shoes.

I can see this. Know this.

So why does it feel like bees buzz under my skin, whirring a demand to touch more of him? I pull my foot away. It leaves me empty in a way that is new. The craving to touch more of Alec is beyond intense. And I want to push it away. Tame it.

Alec plucks a square of bark mulch from the ground and turns it between his fingers. "This has never happened to me before, you know. It's like they say, about attractions being chemical and all. Okay, maybe that does sound Discovery Channel primal. Forget it."

But I can't. It's as if he's in my head. Humming under my skin.

A soft breeze guides a curl across my cheek and Alec moves to catch it. He tucks it behind my ear, brushing my lobe with his fingers. Something inside my chest skips, like there's a heart racing inside my heart.

"Would you go out with me?"

He can't even know how his words paralyze. They tie and bind with a commitment I can't give after living in the aftermath of my father bailing. Or the mess that is my relationship with Gregg since his kiss. I can't do complication.

"Alec, I . . ."

Alec's face waits on my words, patient and forgiving even though he appears to sense what I'm going to say. A small boy scrambles into the swing near us, reprimanding his mother's offer of help. "I do it!" he shouts at her.

Alec smiles at the boy's independence, his fierceness, and that is when the word slips out of me. "Yes."

"Huh." Alec lets out an enormous sigh, threaded with laughter. "I wasn't exactly expecting a yes after that enormously elongated hesitation, Zephyr actually."

"Me either." My cheeks redden. His blush reveals understanding.

Alec moves behind me and gives me a gentle push. My feet leave the ground. My legs extend.

When I return to Alec, he catches my hips and holds me, suspended for the briefest second. His fingers lock onto each hip. A spiral of heat climbs inside me, pours into my blood, coats my skin. My whole body alights. Then, he whispers furtive words in my ear: "I used to space out in Latin all the time."

He lets go. My insides curl.

I return to him with a gentle swoop. He grabs hold. "I'm not so bummed about being the new kid at Sudbury anymore."

I swing.

"Not since I found a girl who digs muscle cars."

Swing. And I smile.

"A girl I'm with and might already miss."

Swoon.

I am lost on the cloud of his words until the little boy screeches. He's figured out he can't swing without his mother's help so he gets down, scrambles toward the sandbox at the opposite side of the park. I watch him angrily hurl a red pail onto the grass when his mother lifts his wriggling body and starts toward their car. Then we are alone—the approaching dusk our only company. I curse the day for not being longer. Stretching out for miles like a summer afternoon.

When I see the wafer moon begin its rise over the ball field,

Alec halts my swinging and twists my seat. He rubs the length of my fingers, follows each to the tips where they are wrapped around the cross of the chains. His touch lights my flesh, fire coaxing more heat.

"I have to go," he says.

My body jolts. Go?

He slips his phone out of the front pocket of his jeans, checks the time. "I have a preseason game tonight."

Tonight. Dinner. Mom. Oh shit . . . Lizzie. A visit to Gregg's. All the things I spaced on today.

"I wish I could stay." Alec takes a tentative step closer, whisper close. I smell his familiar cologne, that faint waft of mint. He brings his hand to my face and brushes the gentle rise of his knuckles along my jaw. My breath catches as he spirals a long strand of my hair around his finger. His touch drops to my neckline and I pull back. The heat of him too intense. His face flushes red and he spins me so that he's standing behind me. I wait for him to push me one last time, but his hands slide along my shoulders until he gathers my ponytail, moves it to the side. Heat tightens my stomach into a fist.

The autumn air licks my neckline with a crisp draft. Every inch of me wants to feel his lips on the curves of my neck—soft and unhurried. And every inch of me thinks I should leave. Now.

But my flesh tingles. And begs.

I lean into him. He lifts my hands high on the chains and closes my fingers around the spot where he wants me to hold on.

"You smell like vanilla," he tells me.

You feel like a dream. I don't even know the me who thinks these words.

His hands trace along my outstretched arms, his broad palms

56

smoothing over my coat but feeling closer, like warmed lotion against my skin. I allow my back to press into him, this stranger, this boy. My breath seizes as he cups the warmth of my neck. There is a spiraling ache between my legs, foreign and demanding. It is the same ache that tells me to run.

But I don't.

I turn my head. I let my lips meet his. Alec's mouth tastes of spearmint and flight, without a hint of complication.

Chapter 7

Driving home from the park, laughter bursts from me so free and light—a laugh I can't remember laughing since Dad left. Somehow, Alec's made me feel like me and someone wholly new at the same time. Like I've stepped out of my own shadow.

Parts of me think it's absurd. Meeting Alec, having a picnic, making out. But other parts want to do it again.

And again.

I turn onto Ashland Drive with my phone in my hand, ready to text Lizzie for an emergency meeting. But when I pull up to the house Gregg's truck is parked out front. My hands squeeze tight around the steering wheel and my breath goes shallow. Even though this is what I've wanted—Gregg and me going back to normal—I can't help my stomach from knotting.

I park, slip my phone into my pocket, and enter the kitchen where Gregg's sitting at the island, thumbing through one of Mom's fall bulb catalogs. His posture rests easy, like it's the most natural place for him to be. There's a small stack of dog treats on the counter, and Finn is alert at Gregg's feet, gazing up expectantly. Gregg was with me when I got Finn from the pound and Finn adores Gregg. Then again, who doesn't love Gregg?

He looks up. "I let myself in with the spare key. Hope that's okay."

"Yeah, of course. Any time. You know you're always welcome."

"Am I?" He closes the magazine, slides it toward the middle of the island.

"Look, Gregg—"

"Don't. I shouldn't have kissed you. I get that. You're not into me."

I lean against the island, bracing myself. "I don't want what happened to change anything."

"It has. It sucked, Zephyr. Not the kiss . . . your reaction to the kiss. And then being blown off."

"But I texted you. I wanted to talk the next day."

"That was a pity text and you know it."

I fix my posture straight. "How am I the enemy here?"

He lets out a long breath and softens his voice. "You're not. Look, I'm trying to admit I made a mistake."

"O-kay."

"I screwed up. I got the timing wrong."

But it's more than timing; it's chemistry. I know that after kissing Alec.

"I know you have your plan for next year and I hope that still includes me."

"Of course, Gr—"

He holds up his hand. "No need to go all fangirl over me." Gregg winks. "Look, it's done. I just need to hear we're cool."

"We're cool. That's all I ever want us to be."

He raps his knuckles on the butcher block counter. "Good. So you'll come to my game tonight? Preseason opener." He smiles that perfect smile. "You can't break tradition now."

My heart leaps at the chance to restore balance. "What time?"

"Seven. We're playing Hampton."

I nod approvingly. "Rivals. Nice."

"Those wannabes? They wish they were good enough to be called our rivals." He stands, starts toward the door. "So you'll be in my cheering section?"

"You bet."

"That's my girl," he says, and I bristle. Gregg pets Finn and sneaks him a parting treat before heading out the door.

The whir of his engine fades as he drives off and I text Lizzie that I'm kidnapping her for the rink.

We find seats on a midlevel bleacher. "So Slice was cool?" Lizzie says.

"Totally cool. It was so nothing, just a drunk kiss." I neglect to tell her that I never got my sorry ass over to his house, or how I spent my afternoon instead.

Music pumps from the speakers around the rink as the two teams pour onto the ice, gliding into position. My eyes go directly to Sudbury's goal. Even though I can't see Alec's face behind his goalie mask, I keep my eyes fixed on his alert body, made wide with protective hockey gear. The ref drops the puck and bodies scramble. Alec wards off attempted goals with his blocker and his leg pads, his movements as slick as the ice under his skates. The crowd roars each time he deflects a shot. I bite down on a secret smile. Just thinking about being at the park with him warms my body from the inside, like a furnace, even though it's about two degrees inside this tin stadium.

Lizzie buries her cheeks into her mittens to ward off the cold. "So how long were you at Slice's today?"

"Where?"

"Earth to Zee. You said you'd visit me at work. I had to endure a six-hour shift with Shorty. Alone. Without chocolate of any kind. It was cruel and unusual. I texted you a million times."

"I totally spaced. I left my phone in my car."

Sudbury scores and everyone in the bleachers stands and hollers. Me and Lizzie do the obligatory stand, but we're not the hooting types.

"I went for a run," I lie. "Cleaned my room." As much as I want to tell her about Alec, it can't be here.

A whistle reprimands. Lizzie's shoulder prods mine. She points her multicolored mitten toward the penalty box. I see the large white letters on the player's back: SLICE. "I bet he's trying to impress you. You know, by being the bad boy."

"Stop."

"What? It's scientific fact that girls are attracted to the bad boy."

I roll my eyes, which gets a laugh. The only person I want to look at is the boy guarding the net. I watch Alec's broad shoulders defend the goal and can feel the ghost tickle of his touch.

When the final buzzer echoes throughout the stadium, I startle out of my trance. Sudbury players raise their sticks in victory as they skate toward one another and an odd flicker of pride flutters within me. I glance at the scoreboard over the net. Visitors 2, Home 8. In hockey terms, it was a slaughter. The whole crowd cheers and stomps their feet against the metal bleachers like it's a rock concert. I pull my scarf tighter and stand.

Lizzie yanks me down by the hem of my coat. "We can't go now. We have to congratulate Slice."

"Right . . . yeah." Nerves mount. Alec didn't exactly invite me and I don't want to look like a creeper for coming. Lizzie hops down the four rows of bleacher seats, me in tow. The players remove their helmets, almost in unison. Each head drips with sweat, their cheeks apple red. I can see Gregg's bright smile from where I'm standing, nearly twenty feet away.

Alec's still on the ice, leaning against the frame of the goal. He picks up a plastic bottle and squirts water into his mouth, across his face. It gives me a chill just watching him. Then Gregg is standing in front of me.

I startle. "Hey."

"Glad you made it."

"Great game," Lizzie tells him.

"Thanks." Gregg raises a towel to his face and wipes at the sweat. "I don't think we can lose now that we've got Alec in the goal crease."

My stomach flutters at the mention of his name. This cannot be normal.

The team shuffles past us toward the locker room, the crowd thinner, the air quieting. That's when Alec makes his way off the ice and right to us.

The smile on Alec's face is slightly crooked, and contagious. He nods a hello to Lizzie. Then to me: "I didn't know you were coming."

Lizzie shoots me a look just as Gregg knuckles Alec on the arm. "Let's hit the showers. I smuggled in a six-pack."

"Sounds good," Alec says, his eyes dropping from mine.

Gregg turns toward the locker room and Alec follows, but soon doubles back. Alec is so sure and steady on the thin metal blades of his skates. He holds out his hand, asking for mine. My breath comes in slow, thin bursts until my hand locks with his. Then, when we're connected, the entire world falls away and it is just me and Alec. Zephyr Doyle and a beautiful boy. I almost laugh at the surprise of it all. Instead, I take in his hair, how it's dark with sweat and disheveled. How his lips glow plum pink, the exact color of his frozen cheeks.

Alec leads me to the side of the rink. I look back and see Lizzie with her mouth hanging open. I know I should stop whatever is about to happen, but I don't want to. The entire stadium—and everyone in it—fades away as Alec leans his hips into mine. His chest is enormous, covered in protective plastic. He moves toward me and his pads press me against the Plexiglas. Still, I can feel his heat.

He burrows his face against my cheek and plants a quick kiss. His lips are ice. "Were you here for me?"

"Maybe."

He winks at me in a way that makes my pulse dance.

Then his lips touch mine in a hovering butterfly kiss, so soft and ethereal I find myself leaning in, begging for more. But there is only air when I open my eyes. Alec's back fades as he jogs off to the locker room. I see him push open the door. And there's something else. A movement, a blur of color. Gregg.

He moves out from behind the refreshment stand and shuffles across the hall to the locker room. He shoots me a contorted look that tells me we are so not cool.

"Do you mind telling me how *that* happened?" Lizzie sputters.

I'd managed to convince her to get into my old Volvo and drive to a nearby neighborhood, away from the rink and my unintentional love triangle. I keep the engine running for heat. A tiny dog yaps at us from behind the window of a small tan house.

"Alec and I hung out this weekend. And again today. At the park."

"Wait. While I was at work? Did you blow me off for a guy?"

"Not intentionally. And I feel bad, but I didn't want to tell you about Alec until I knew it was something."

"And is it something?"

"I think so." I feel the rush of red color my face.

Lizzie leans in, fans her hand for details.

"He asked me to go out with him."

"Old school. I like it. And I assume by that kiss you said yes."

A nod. A lip bite.

Lizzie rolls down her window and I hear the wafer rustle of dried leaves skittering across the asphalt. The wind is cool, promising winter. She sticks out her hand and surfs the still air. "I'm happy for you, Zee. It's just unfortunate Slice has to get hurt."

"I feel bad about Gregg but he admitted he never should have kissed me. Besides, you're the one who told me to embrace different."

"I did, but this is still so very un-Zephyr. You jumping in, following your gut, or your loins."

A guilty smile blooms across my face.

Lizzie laughs. "You look like you're in love."

"I'm in something, Lizzie. I didn't know I could feel like this."

"Already?"

I nod.

"For reals?"

Another nod.

She slumps back in her seat. "Whoa. This is huge. Front page news in the Zephyr Chronicles."

"Funny.

"I'm not trying to be funny. I'm just . . . well. Surprised."

"How do you think I feel?"

"By the looks of that smile, I'd say pretty dern good."

"Maybe it won't go anywhere. I don't know. How can anyone know, right? I just... damn, Lizzie. I just really liked kissing him."

"Obvs." She winks. "Let us go to Fernalds. Frappes are on me. To celebrate the millennial shift that is your interest in pursuing actual coupledom."

On the drive across town, my thoughts curl around Alec. I worry this has already become too complicated.

Because I can't unsee the hurt look on Gregg's face.

Chapter 8

On Monday, a pink carnation pokes its head out of the grill of my locker. At the base of the bud is a small note tied with twine. "Good luck on the field!" I pluck the stem and scan the row of lockers, searching for flowers in my teammates' lockers. But the other lockers stand sickly pale. I bring the flower close to my nose and it smells of something so outside high school that I'm immediately back at the park. I blush and tuck the bloom into my chem textbook. I wish the flower could just be a flower, but instead it makes me wonder what Alec sees in me, and if this is what I need right now.

I hate that trust seems harder to hold on to lately. I try to push my doubt down, try not to question this. At least, not for today.

Alec's already in his seat when I get to French class, looking more beautiful than any boy really has a right. Gregg's in the front row, chatting up Suzanne Sharper. He doesn't even bother to toss me a wave.

When I slide into my seat, Alec moves the toe of his sneaker to touch my shoe. Our simple, electric connection. This time I don't pull away.

"So Gregg's still sitting in the front row." I pull out my books.

"Secret crush on Mrs. Sarter."

"That must be it."

"Whatever his reasons, I like that it's just the two of us."

A definite perk.

Alec taps his pencil against my textbook. "Favorite country?" he asks, picking up where we left off on our phone call last night.

"Australia. It's a country and a continent. Plus, there's kangaroos and deadly box jellyfish."

"Favorite tree?" Alec prompts.

"Birch. The bark looks like peeling paint."

"Favorite food?" he asks.

"Chocolate chip cookies. No explanation needed. Least favorite food?"

"Cranberry sauce." His face contorts. "Gross texture."

Mrs. Sarter clears her throat, turning us to the front of the classroom. Alec pushes his toe harder against the tip of my Uggs, his foot nuzzling into mine. It is an effort to focus on verb conjugation.

I don't wear my cleats onto the bus headed for southern New Hampshire. I've never competed in a state championship playoff game, but it turns out my superstitions don't just claw at me during regular season. I heed their warnings. Listen to their whispers. Try to do everything the same as the last game.

But there is no Gregg to gallantly carry my cleats, escort me to the sidelines. There will be no Lizzie in the stands. Alec never hovered around the edges of almost every thought the way he does now.

In fact, everything seems different today. Even the sanctioned skipping of last period so our bus can make the hour drive and be on time for an afternoon game. I think Coach feels this energized difference because she begins the ride with an impassioned speech that makes her voice raspy. I'm not sure if it's one of these things or a combination, but the afternoon passes in a blur. The opposing Warriors play too fierce, too strong. I lap the midfield a hundred times or more, trying to track the ball but can't reach it. All I can do is block and cover. And it's enough. We win 6–5, the tension leaving us only after the final whistle blows and we move one game closer to the state title.

This is what I wanted. Keeping a toe in field hockey. Prolonging the good parts of Sudbury High. But a part of me is missing. The Gregg part. Tonight was my first match he didn't watch and I can't deny the difference it made in my game. I scanned the stands too many times. Missed a couple of key passes that Coach reamed me for. It wasn't my best night.

When the bus returns to school, I decline invites to the afterparty. I tell my teammates I'm not feeling great and hope they'll accept that as an excuse for why I played like shit. I have to get my head straight before the next game so I shower in the locker room and head straight to Gregg's.

It's just after seven when I pull up to his house, see his enormous green truck in the driveway. The garage's spotlights burst on, interrogating. Cowardice rattles within me. I want to turn around, drive far away, but then I am trapped by Mrs. Slicer's Suburban pulling in behind me. Within seconds, Mara and Quinn, Gregg's youngest sisters, scramble out of their seats and run toward me.

"Zee Zee!" Mara yells, scaling my side to perch on my hip bone. Quinn, a year older, pretends to be too mature for such nonsense. She is dressed in a peach tutu and ballet flats, her fire-red hair slicked into a severe bun.

"Zephyr, how nice to see you." Mrs. Slicer bookends her hands on my cheeks and leans in for the kiss. Her lips stay on my brain for a second longer than I think a kiss should last, but it's always been like this. Like she's trying to press her love right through me. "You are looking as gorgeous as ever."

"So pwetty." Mara burrows into me.

"We've missed you around here." Mrs. Slicer turns to the SUV, opens the tailgate. "Gregg tells us your team's competing in the playoffs. Congratulations."

I hope that's all he told her. "We've got a great team. We won our first game in the series. Today, in fact."

She pops her head out from behind the back of the car. "Today? But Gregg's been home since school let out. Did he know you were playing?"

I shrug. It's the question I've come here to ask. That, and to apologize for kissing Alec at the rink—something I'd never wanted Gregg to see.

Mrs. Slicer looks confused. "He must not have known about your game." She shakes her head as if to clear it. "Things have been so nuts around here planning for Anna's wedding that we're all a little off."

Anna. The older sister Gregg got but I always wanted. "I get it." I slide Mara off my hip. "Let me help you." I throw a bag over each shoulder and take the third and fourth bags in my hands.

"I hewp too." Mara squeezes a stray box of Frosted Flakes to her chest and runs inside.

"Oh, you don't have to do that," Mrs. Slicer says, but her tone betrays how much she appreciates the help. It's no small gig buying groceries for a family of eight. "You can just set them down in the kitchen. Slice is probably in his room. Head on down."

I do. I slip off my grocery bag garments and head to the lower level of the house. The floor with the enormous game room, double doors out to the pool, and Gregg's bedroom at the far end.

His door is closed. I stand in the hall, my heart pounding against my rib cage. I squeeze my eyes shut, think of Waxman's, the way Gregg hugged me so hard he lifted me from the ground. I think of his kiss and it seems dreamlike. Did it really happen?

But of course it did, because we are left dusted with a layer of ash from the fallout.

I call up my nerve. "Come in," Gregg says in response to my knock.

I open the door slowly and he plucks his earbuds free as he registers my presence. His face falls. Plummets. Bails and leaves the stratosphere.

"What's up?" Gregg stands but doesn't extend his customary invitation to sit on the edge of the bed.

The bed, where we played countless hands of gin rummy and talked our throats sore. The bed is now a line between us, dividing what used to be and what is.

"I missed you today." The words are out before I can think if they're the right ones.

He runs his fingers through his thick mass of strawberry hair. "Yeah."

I take him in, his straight shoulders, serious height, and the constellation of freckles across the bridge of his nose. Any girl would be crazy to complain about a kiss from him. But I'm not any girl. I'm his best friend.

He turns away, winds his earbuds around his iPod and places it on his desk. I can't see his eyes when he says, "So you're kissing Alec now?"

"God, Gregg. I'm so sorry about that." I should have taken more control of the situation. Stopped Alec before Gregg had any chance of seeing us together.

Gregg faces me, his eyebrows raised. "You're sorry for kissing Alec?"

I drop my gaze to the floor. "No." The admission is a disgraced whisper wrapped in shame.

"Didn't think so."

"I'm sorry you had to—"

"Do you know what I'm sorry about, Zephyr?" Gregg harpoons me with his pointed gaze.

I shake my head. I know and I don't know and I don't want to know.

"I'm sorry you didn't want me to kiss you. I'm sorry you didn't kiss me back the way you kissed Alec. I'm sorry that kissing you is something I've been thinking about since we were twelve years old and we found that rope swing by the quarry."

I remember that summer. I'd borrowed his shirt to swim in because we hadn't known the quarry would be full of water. I fell asleep in the late afternoon grass and he got a sunburn on half his face. Because he'd been on his side the whole time I'd slept, watching me rest.

"Gregg . . ." The word thin as wind. I take a step closer to him.

"Don't." He thrusts out his hand to stop me. "You've known this dude for all of, like, five minutes and you're sucking face with him at the rink. In front of everybody? Jesus, Zephyr. You've known me your whole life and you don't have enough respect for me to take that shit someplace where I don't have to see it?"

"Gregg—"

"No. You don't get to come here and ask me to pretend everything is normal. I can't just show up at your game like none of this happened. You can't have it both ways, Zeph. That's not the way shit like this works. You made your choice and I get to make mine."

His words steal air from the room.

"I think it might be better if you weren't here right now."

I force my feet to move, my heart not to shatter. At the door, I tell him, "I'm really sorry. I never meant to hurt anyone." I hope he hears the truth in the apology.

When I leave Gregg's, I feel a strange need to see Alec. Be propped up by the security of his arms. I pull into Gosland Park and call him.

"We won," I tell him, forcing my tone bright. "But I played like hell. I'm feeling pretty beat up. Any chance you're free?"

"I wish. But I'm wiped. Coach had me at special practice, blocking shots from a machine all afternoon. I wish I could have been at your game instead. I'm bummed I missed it."

"Yeah, no . . . that's cool." I bite at the skin at the edge of my thumb. Silence hangs.

"You gonna be okay?"

"Fine. Yeah." I squint at the abandoned swing set.

"I'll make it up to you. Promise."

"It's nothing," I lie. "I'm beat too. Like I said, tough game."

"But you won." His voice rallies with support.

"We did."

When I get home, Mom is all cheerleader. She actually squeals when I tell her we're one game away from winning State. Finn greets me with his usual enthusiasm, always convinced I'm a winner despite my failures. I decline Mom's offer to celebrate by going out for dinner and retreat to my room. I snuggle with Finn on my bed and the quiet of the house drums in my ears. It is a pulsing soundlessness that taunts me with all that I've lost with Gregg. With my dad.

I bury my head in Finn's velvet fur and wonder how anyone is supposed to trust another person with their heart.

Chapter 9

I am grateful for the demands of postseason field hockey. Today's practice was grueling enough to obliterate the stress I've been feeling over Gregg. I run off the field and grab a towel.

Karen pats me on the back as I wipe the sweat from my forehead. "Good form, Doyle. Glad to see you back." I can easily picture Karen being a high school coach someday. She tosses me an orange slice and I suck at the meat of the fruit and let the juice slake my thirst.

Now I need a shower to soothe my sore muscles after running six miles, playing a full scrimmage. I head toward the bleachers and the pressure to win State strangles like a snake tightening. It's been eleven years since Sudbury's held a field hockey state championship. The stress makes my shoulders ache, until I see Alec leaning against the stands.

He comes to me. "You looked awesome out there." He nudges my hip with his. "Even better up close."

"Ugh. I'm a sweaty mess."

"Doesn't bother me." He takes my hand. "Do you have plans now?"

"I need a shower."

"Hang out with me instead. I've been worried since you sounded so down last night."

"I'm better. Too exhausted to be bummed out."

"You played great today." He squeezes my hand tighter. I feel a trickle of guilt for not clarifying that my sadness yesterday was purely Gregg-related. "You'll win State, Zephyr actually. I know you will."

I smile at the nickname. "I wish I had your confidence."

He scoffs. "Don't let my manly exterior fool you; I'm a mess on the inside. Same as everyone." He kisses the top of my head, his lips leaving a shadow of warmth. "I believe in you, even if you can't right now." His words soothe like balm. "Hang with me. We can be messes together."

I straighten and take one last look at the field. "I want to, but we've got our final game tomorrow. Coach wants us to rest up."

"You don't need rest; you need to keep your mind occupied. You need someone to keep you from stressing about field hockey." He smiles that coy smile. "And lucky for you, I just happen to be that guy."

"You are, are you?"

"Convince me you're not going to go home and obsess about the game and I'll leave you alone." He catches my smile and points at my lips. "Hah! I knew it. Hang out with me and I'll help you keep your mind off things. Besides, I could use some help with my French homework."

"You must really need help if you want me to be your tutor."

Alec laughs, tickles my palm with his finger. "So I'm invited over?"

I nod, biting my lip.

He turns me to face him, raises his hand to my mouth and runs his thumb over my lower lip. I release the bite. "No, don't. Bite it again." He bites his own lip in demonstration. I mimic him. He caresses the indent, the part of my lip that's pulled in by my teeth. "I love the way you do that," he tells me. I only hear the word *love*.

When I arrive home, Finn greets us, his tail wagging so fast it kicks up a breeze. I bend down to pet his head and he pushes his plump body against my leg.

"Finn, this is Alec," I say. "Alec, Finn. Shake on it."

Alec leans down to Finn and extends his hand for paw. Finn stares at him with his oil-black eyes.

"He's not much into tricks, but he usually shakes." I give Finn's head another quick pat and close the door behind us. "Mom! I'm home!"

"In here!" she calls. Mom's standing at her desk when we enter her study. She's wearing one of her severe black suits that scream *tough day in court*. Her desk is piled with papers and miniature repotted houseplants. I can't figure how she keeps anything straight.

"Mom, this is Alec."

She steps forward, firmly shakes his hand in the way lawyer moms do. "Nice to meet you."

"It's a pleasure to meet you, Mrs. Doyle."

Mom crosses her arms and looks Alec up and down without moving her eyes. It's a seriously enviable trait. "Alec . . . Alec," Mom says, as if trying to place him. "Are you hockey phenom Alec Lord? The Alec that Rachel Slicer raves about?"

"Mom!"

Alec blushes. "Mrs. Slicer is too kind, ma'am."

Mom raises an eyebrow, signaling that Alec's *ma'am* has impressed the hell out of her. "Well, any friend of Gregg's is welcome in our home."

"Thank you. I'm glad to be here."

"We've got French homework to finish, Mom."

"Are you hungry? I've got lasagna warming."

I'm starving but I look to Alec, who shakes his head. "We're good for now. We'll just be in my room." I conjure noncha-lance.

"Door open." Mom removes a random transcript from the pile of rubble on her desk, though her fingers set on it like it's the exact document she wanted.

I grab Alec's hand and guide him down the hall to my room, Finn following behind.

"So this is the inner sanctum?" Alec looks around, spies the carnation lying out on the table next to my bed. He runs his fingers over the flower's pink edges just beginning to brown. "From someone special?"

"It's a theory."

He laughs and I give a quick glance into the corners of my room, scanning for stray underwear or snotty Kleenex, but the space screams *neat freak*. I grab a change of clothes from my bureau. "Be right back." I slip into the bathroom where I slap on pit stick, wash my face, and try to calm the train wreck that is my hair.

When I return, Alec's at my closet, surveying the clothes on hangers. "Your clothes aren't just color-coded, they're arranged according to length, aren't they?"

"Maybe." I blush.

He laughs. "The world is a ball of raw chaos. We have to impose order when we can."

"Something like that."

"I get it," he says, filling my room with his presence. He picks up the Boston College catalog and thumbs its pages. It is a cataclysmic collision of my two worlds. The only other guy I've had in my room is Gregg, but Alec is so not Gregg. He pats the bed and I sit next to him. Our knees touch and power the world with electricity. He pushes his knee deeper against mine, volts surging. "Is this next year?" He taps the glossy maroon cover.

"Hopefully."

"The only choice, right?"

"How'd you know?"

"An educated guess from a fellow control freak." He returns the catalog to the exact spot where he found it on my desk. "I assume you applied early. Have you heard anything?"

I study him, wondering how he can name my secrets so easily. "No, despite checking the mail, like, three times a day."

His face pops with an impressed smile.

"I'm a little obsessive."

"You're smart and driven. Smart and driven people make precise plans for their future."

"Then what are your precise plans?"

"University of Michigan."

"Michigan?" God, that's far away.

"Go Blue." He forces a fisted cheer. "I kind of don't have a choice."

"Everyone has a choice."

He snarks. "Not this kid."

"How can that be?"

Alec straightens, lets out a breath. "My folks met at Michigan. They were business majors so I need to be a business major."

"You don't look too psyched."

"Probably because I want to be a chef."

"A chef?" That I did not expect.

"I have talents that extend beyond the tuna fish sandwich, Zephyr." He fingers the fringe of my bedspread. "I've never told anyone that before. The only places I feel right are in the kitchen and on the ice. Not very manly, is it?"

"Does it have to be?"

"It does when you have parents like mine. They won't pay for school unless it's literally all business at Michigan. Then it's architectural planning and development with Mom's corporation. My life's planned."

"I'm sorry." The words seem too lame.

"At least Michigan has an awesome team. The hockey coach came to a bunch of my games at Exeter, though that could be off the table now."

"How come?"

"I guess I didn't really think it through in the moment, you know . . . taking the fall for my roommate. At the end of the day, getting kicked out of school doesn't make me the perfect candidate for any college. I'm not sure if my game is good enough for Michigan to overlook my expulsion record. The pressure's kind of on for me to kick ass at Sudbury."

"Couldn't you call Michigan's coach? Tell him what really happened? How selfless you are."

Alec scoffs.

"What?"

"Maybe I need you to go for me. Be my advocate."

But I'd be a terrible advocate because a greedy hope bubbles up in me. That his expulsion will mean he might stay in New England next year. "Maybe it will all work out. There are plenty of other colleges."

"Sure, but not for me. No Michigan means I go straight to

work for Mom's business. I don't have a lot of choices, Zephyr. My parents have made that very clear."

My stomach curdles. I can't imagine my parents controlling my future.

He reaches for my hand, and Finn sits upright, watching us from the doorway. He barks one quick burst that makes me jump.

"You okay?" Alec says.

"Yeah, it's just that he never barks." I turn to Finn. "What's gotten into you, boy?"

"He's protecting you, claiming you as his. I can't blame him."

A blush rises along my neck, runs to my cheeks.

Alec catches my chin, holds it. "I like it when you blush." He moves his mouth close. His fingers brush my cheek, disappear into my hair. He holds me in place, freezes me until his lips are on mine. When he pulls away, I try to remember to breathe.

"I like too much about you." He floats these feather words between us, his mouth hovering so close. He kisses me again, sliding his tongue through the valley of my lips. I move into him, finding his tongue with my own, kissing him deeper.

I pull away because I'm afraid I won't be able to if it goes on much longer. And I'm even more afraid of what that means. "We should stop." I spy the open door and turn on the bed, bend my leg between us. "With my mom just down the hall and all."

Alec sits straight, smoothes his hair. "Right. Sorry. I mean, sorry if I made you uncomfortable. I'm not sorry about the kissing part."

I smile and Alec runs his thumb over the flesh of my bottom lip. He pulls my forehead to his and we press into one another. "Favorite drink," he says.

"Cold or hot?"

"Cold," he whispers.

"Raspberry lime rickey. Supersweet and fizzy."

He pulls away. "Where do you get one of those? A soda fountain in 1952?"

"And you want to be a chef?" I mock outrage. "How can your restaurant be successful if you don't plan on having lime rickeys on the menu?"

"It's a beverage choice I'll now have to consider thoroughly."

"As you should," I tease.

"Thank you." He cups my ear, strokes my lobe.

"For widening your beverage horizons?"

"No. For believing in me. For thinking I'll have my own restaurant someday."

"I'm sure you can have anything you want."

"You make me feel like that's possible." Alec raises my palm to his lips, kisses the tender skin.

My insides race with belonging.

He shakes his head quickly, like he's trying to dislodge the heat between us. He gets up, ventures to the corner of my room, crouches in front of the turntable. "Old school vinyl." He thumbs through the albums.

"I have a thing for the art on the album covers." The best covers from the sixties are pinned to my wall. "And the scratch. I kind of think the needle is an instrument, part of the band."

"The sign of a true connoisseur." He sets the needle onto the record in the player. The hollow scratching joins us. Then the music starts, Joan Armatrading's "Whatever's For Us."

Speaking of love

You ask how much you should give

It's a question I can't help asking myself as Alec reaches for his

French book and opens it onto the bed between us. Finn watches his every move.

"So . . ." Alec says.

"French?" I suggest.

He draws his hand to his chest. "Why, Zephyr. How forward of you!"

I shove at his knee and he laughs. We manage to review the last few weeks of work, with Alec stealing a kiss for every correct past participle and two kisses for every incorrect conjugation. I suspect he throws a few. When a burned smell reaches us from the kitchen, Mom comes in to inform Alec it's time to go. I walk him to the door where he tells me, "You'll be great tomorrow."

"Tomorrow?"

He plucks his finger off the tip of my nose. "See? I told you distraction was best."

He's right. Field hockey and friend drama are the last things on my mind.

Later, as I slip under the covers, Alec's spearmint scent lingers on my comforter and I pull it close to my face, breathe him in again and again.

Chapter 10

By the next afternoon, I'm crawling out of my skin in anticipation of the state championship game, the final game of my high school career. I can't remember one thing my teachers have said all day and I refuse to let even Gregg's cold shoulder bring me down.

Alec left a mock menu in my locker this morning. "Restaurant Grand Opening: Everything from A to Zee." There was an old-timey soda fountain picture on the cover. Inside, lime rickeys were listed in every size and availability, all with unique pricing. I carry the menu in my game bag now. For luck.

Having Alec with me in this unique way gives me strength as I ride the bus south to Concord, the town where, apparently, Dad now dwells. I can't help but wonder if we drive past his neighborhood or if he knows we're coming. But for the first time in months, I don't question what's ahead. It's like Alec's absorbed some of the doubt that's haunted me and I'm glad to be rid of its shadowy weight.

When I reach the field, the sweet scent of grass fills my head and my muscles remember their mission. My brain knows what it wants. Nothing less than victory. And it feels, miraculously, within reach.

The referee drops the hard white ball in the center of the field and time slows. A whistle sings just as the two center forwards battle for control of the first play. Sticks bang and beat against one another until my teammate gains control. I sprint for the pass and tuck the ball under my stick's head. But within seconds, I'm being guarded by a nymph. I'm twice her size, but she's quick. And cunning. She hovers the butt of her stick inches from mine, no matter how expertly I try to jog the ball away from her. She steals the ball and runs it to the opposite end of the field. She bends low, sends the ball so close to our net, where Karen stops it with her oversize glove.

Sudbury works the ball to the opposite side of the field, but with effort. By the time I'm set to score, the nymph flits out of my blind spot and hops the ball over my stick. She attempts another goal that Karen thwarts. My breathing comes heavy. Every muscle engages.

Nearly an hour into the game, lights buzz on overhead like mosquitoes. Chants construct walls of sound, the rival crowd so much louder than our supporters. The autumn air nips at the tips of my ears and feels too cold as I breathe the shock of it in and out of my overworked lungs.

By halftime, we're tied 0–0. Near the end of the last quarter, the game is still scoreless. I feel drained. Only a few minutes remain on the clock. We're facing possible overtime and all I can think of is splaying myself out on the cold grass and never running again for the rest of my life. Exhaustion spasms my thighs as Coach gathers us for our last time out.

"It's us or them, girls," Coach tells us. "One team has to bring home the trophy. That's the way this works. What you do in the next string of minutes will determine which school will hold the state title. Understand?"

We nod collectively as Coach continues.

I know the high of winning and I want it for me, our school, Coach. I let her last pep talk propel me back onto the field with renewed energy.

Within seconds, a hard *thwack* sends the ball within reaching distance of Karen. She runs to it, smacks it down the right sideline, and another forward gets control. She keeps the small ball magnetized to the end of her stick. I summon my last bit of strength to sprint to the opposite sideline and position myself for the pass. It comes. Hard. The ball soars over the cropped grass and I halt it with my stick.

I draw it back.

One arm straight.

One elbow bent.

I fix my shoulders.

I swing hard and hear the *whoosh* of air as the stick cuts through the atmosphere. My forearms ripple with a sting and the *thwack* echoes against the silenced crowd. I watch the ball rise on wings, heading right for the enemy goal.

Their goalie stretches to reach with her oversize glove, but the ball soars into the upper right corner of the goal box. The net absorbs the spinning orb before spitting it onto the quiet grass, where it stops rolling with all the finality of the end of a sentence.

The final air horn blows. The game is over. The end of my field hockey days for Sudbury. Our supporters explode with cheers and I am lifted by a dozen arms, hoisted into the air so that I'm flying inside and out. Beyond the madness, I see Karen between our goalposts, raising her stick above her head like a bar, pumping it fiercely with two hands. She runs toward me and I swallow this feeling, how it tastes like sugar and pride.

The fatigue in my muscles washes away and my adrenaline convinces me I could run a marathon. When we line up for our good-game high-fives, pride pulsates through me and I'm convinced there is no greater high in the universe.

From within the crowd I hear Lizzie's distinctive ranch-hand whistle. I spy her on the sidelines with her camera, her hand corralling the team into a group shot.

"Gather up, ladies!" I call, and they do. We pile onto and around one another and scream out "Champions!" at Lizzie's prompting. We are a mob. A mass. Connected in our triumph. I raise my stick over my head. Someone thrusts the game ball into my other palm. I hold these pieces above me as my teammates raise me above them. Lizzie's camera follows me upward, her repeated flash leaving dots in my eyes—smaller, brighter versions of the field lights that have borne witness to our hard-won victory.

When my feet return to the ground, Lizzie tells me, "You are now without question the most bestest field hockey player I've ever been best friends with. It's my working headline." She pulls me to her before her face contorts. "Even if you do smell ripe."

"It's an unfortunate side effect of greatness."

"You were awesome out there, Zee. Really."

I can't stop the smile sprinting to my face. "It felt great. A tough game, but an unforgettable one for sure."

"Not a bad way to end a career." Lizzie scans the photos on her camera's display screen. "Yours and mine."

That's when it hits me that this is the last game of mine she'll watch. The last time she'll write up a story about my team. The thought jolts me with loss. That, and . . .

"Have you seen Gregg?" I wipe the sweat from my forehead with my sleeve and scan the crowd.

She looks at me, her eyes soft. "It's his loss, Zee."

My heart plummets to my stomach.

Coach calls for me to get my hustle on. "Chop, chop, Doyle!"

I thumb toward my classmates loading onto the bus. "I gotta ride back with the team. I'll text you about the party at Karen's."

"Figure out the details and just come pick me up. After you shower, obvs."

"Will do." I turn, but before my feet carry me away, I move closer toward her. "I want you to have this." I jiggle my gift in a loose fist.

Lizzie extends her palm, onto which I slide my saliva-filled guard.

"A small trophy. To mark the end of an era."

"You are gross, Zephyr Doyle." She hooks my mouth guard across the V of her hoodie like some perverse medal. "You make me so proud, little grasshopper."

"Thanks Obi-Wan."

My smile reaches Coach before I do. The bus literally rocks from my teammates clanking sticks in beats of victory. Adrenaline surges. I'll never have a night like this again and all I want to do is capture this rush, bottle it.

We plan to celebrate in style. Karen's parents have opened up their house to the team and our fans. Heated pool. Catered food. And even though I'm psyched that Lizzie will be there with me, I can't help how the sadness of absent Gregg wiggles into this night.

I approach the door to the bus as a figure steals out from beyond the headlights.

I'd know the shape anywhere.

His steady gait.

His broad shoulders.

86

My heart sprints as if I'm on the field again.

Alec walks to me. "You rocked it, Zephyr actually."

"You're here?"

"Wouldn't have missed it." He pulls me softly off to the side. It's almost too surreal: his support, his tousled hair, his beautiful tallness. "See me tonight. To celebrate." He strokes my cheek with his finger and I press my face into the tenderness of his touch.

"I-I can't. I already made plans."

He scowls softly, his disappointment making him even cuter. "With who?"

"The team has this huge celebration bash planned. I told Lizzie we'd head over after I showered."

"Be with me instead." He steps closer to me, his breath so close to my neck I can feel its signature heat. And I smell the spearmint hovering on his words.

"I can't." I couldn't.

"You can."

I laugh. "If only. Maybe tomorrow?"

Alec nods, smiling. "Tomorrow." He steals a quick kiss on the cheek before Coach hollers again.

"Thanks for coming." I board the bus and it lurches into gear. I wipe the fog from the window with my palm and that's when I see him.

My father.

Standing under a parking lot spotlight, hands in his jacket pockets, watching our bus start out on its return trip to Sudbury. I press my hands around my eyes, against the glass, trying to magnify this one person among a crowd of people. But then I don't need to focus or wonder if he can see me. My father brings one hand free of his jacket and gives me his signature wave, a sideways thumb held steady . . . steady. Until he raises it quick and firm into a thumbs-up.

My heart wrenches. It is the same signal he gave me a million and four times from across the playground when I jumped off a swing or when he watched me compete in junior high track meets. My own thumb twitters with a response, but I tuck it into my fist.

The bus lumbers out of the parking lot and I can't help watching my father's figure become smaller with distance. Until darkness erases him. Music booms and my teammates sing and scream, but inside my brain the world is silent. And filling with anger. Does he think he can pop back into my life whenever it's convenient for him? Whether it's what I want or not? He had to know his presence would rock me. And then my anger reaches out, grabs Mom. Did she tell him to come because she couldn't be here?

The ride home is too long. It is long enough for my anger to fall into confusion. Over why Dad wants to be a part of my life again. And then anger again at him leaving in the first place and allowing any of this sadness to drape over my insides like a permanent shadow.

By the time I see the WELCOME TO SUDBURY sign, I realize I've become *that girl* again—the one from summer who doubted she had any worth at all if her own father couldn't see a reason to stay with her. I hate that my father has this much power over me still.

I drive home and stop at our mailbox. I tuck my hand inside and pull out a few bills—all addressed to Dad. I crush them into a ball, toss them in my backseat. Then there is only a card. With two stick figure people walking hand in hand along a beach. The drawing is crude, the shoreline just a thin swipe of ink. I open the card and read:

I dig hanging with you.

A.

I stare at the two outlined figures connected on paper and feel that same connectedness with Alec. How can he know exactly what to say? Even when he's not here? I clutch the card and know he's the only person I want to process my father's skulking with.

I drive the long, dark road of our driveway and am surprised to see Alec's car waiting in front of our garage.

He steps out just as my headlights wash the side of his perfectly polished car, its chrome gleaming in the starlight.

I roll down my window. Alec leans in. "I know you have plans and you can tell me to go, but you looked so happy after the game, I just had to see you again."

"I'm glad." Alec's presence, the high of our win, the card in the mail . . . these things lift me again. I open my door, climb out.

"I feel like I'd be a really shitty boyfriend if I didn't at least try to celebrate with you tonight. Besides, your voice is all low and sexy from all that cheering, so there's that." He wraps his arm around the small of my back like a hook, pulling me to his hips. When his lips are on mine, I feel the beginning breath of that rush, that adrenaline that built just before scoring.

"I just got your card."

"I thought . . . you know, this way you wouldn't be totally disappointed if your acceptance letter didn't arrive yet. *Yet* being the operative word."

His thoughtfulness swallows me. "Can you hang out?"

He looks around. "Tonight? As in now?"

"Yeah, I kind of feel like staying in."

"What about your plans?"

I shrug. "Not really in the mood anymore."

"But you're in the mood for me?"

"Kinda." I bite on a smile.

"Consider me honored."

He gathers my Adidas bag and field hockey stick from my back-seat and we meet Mom in the kitchen. She looks gorgeous. Her long blond hair has been blown out into soft waves. She's wearing a periwinkle blue dress and it makes her skin glow. It's been a long time since I've seen Mom wear anything but a dark suit.

"You look nice. Are you going out or coming home?"

"Out." She urges me with animated eyes. "Well, did you win?"

"We're the official state champs."

Mom pulls me into her arms, hugs me tight. "Oh Zephyr! That's incredible!" She looks to Alec. "Did you go to the game? Was it wonderful?"

"Zephyr scored the winning goal."

Mom releases her hug, puts me at arm's length to study me. "You didn't! Oh, it kills me I wasn't there to see it. You know that, right?" Mom had to meet with a client at the state prison. The timing of those things is pretty precise.

"Lizzie's covering it for the paper. She'll make you feel like you were there."

Mom pulls me to her again. "I can't wait. And there'll be photos too, I hope?"

"Lizzie's thorough."

Mom squeezes me, whispers in my ear. "I'm so proud of you, Zephyr." Then she finally releases me. "I'm meeting up with people from work, but I'll only be an hour or so."

I take in her outfit again. And the three new plants on the counter, a bag of potting soil waiting at the laundry room door.

"Where are you kids going to celebrate?"

"Karen's," I say, too quickly.

"Oh, that sounds like fun!" Mom can hardly contain her joy,

but I don't think it's because of my win. Not totally. "Be home by eleven."

Alec squeezes my hand. "I'll make sure of it," he says, so quickly a conspirator in my lie.

"Good. Thank you." Mom looks around frantically for her purse. I spy her bag on the island chair and hand it to her. "You don't mind that I'm going out? I could stay if you wanted to do something special."

"Nope. We're leaving for Karen's in, like, five."

"Okay, good. Great. I want you to enjoy this night, Zephyr. You trained so hard for this." She turns to Alec, says good-bye.

"It was nice seeing you again, Mrs. Doyle."

Mom kisses me on the head then, pulls me in for another deep hug.

When she leaves, the house falls quiet. Too quiet. "I'll be right back," I tell Alec. I run outside and catch up with her.

"Mom . . . ?"

Mom turns, looking so beautiful. "Yes?"

I want to ask her about Dad. If she told him about the game and why she didn't warn me. But seeing her smile, the way she looks—confident, happy. "Have fun," I say instead. Mom winks at me before heading to her car.

I dip back into the house, where Alec's waiting. I go to him, my lips finding his so quickly. His hands pull my hips to his. Hard. I kiss him harder, for an eternity of minutes. It is an effort to pull away.

"I'm so glad you're here. This is just what I needed. A night in. Something quiet. No drama." I kiss him again, quickly this time. "I need to call Lizzie. Let her know I'm bailing on Karen's."

He takes a small step back, rakes his fingers through his hair. "Yeah, of course."

I text Lizzie and she calls two seconds later. "What's up?"

"I've decided to stay in. Alec's here."

"You're blowing me off for Hockey Boy?"

"I'm not blowing you off, Lizzie. I just . . ."

"Don't be that girl, Zee. You need to be out with the team. You're the captain."

As if I didn't know. As if the stress hasn't been enough all season. "Cocaptain, and I wanted to celebrate, Lizzie, I did. But . . ."

"Something happened. What happened?"

I turn away from Alec, fidget with the dish towel folded under Mom's pruning shears. "My father was at the game."

"Holy shit, Zee. You doing okay? Do you want to talk? I can be over in, like, fifteen minutes."

"Thanks, but it's cool. Alec is here."

I hear the weight of her sigh. "Yeah, okay. I'll tell Karen you weren't feeling well."

I tack on another "thanks" before hanging up.

Alec gathers me to his chest and I feel safe. "I'm sorry your father hijacked your win. That's really lame."

I pull back. "He didn't." I'm surprised by how quickly I leap to Dad's defense. "It just left me feeling kind of lost I guess. Like I don't know what to do."

"Do you have to do anything?"

I search his eyes.

Alec caresses my jaw. "Right now, right here, you don't have to do anything or decide anything. You can just be. With me, of course. That's my caveat. That you *just be* with me."

"Bossy," I tease. But it's perfect. I want to just be with Alec. Free of any doubt or drama.

I toss my Adidas bag onto the laundry machine and tuck my

stick into the forgotten corner of the laundry room. I take Alec's hand to lead him to my room.

I watch him stretch out onto my bed, prop his head against my pillows. He kicks off his sneakers and they thud onto the floor, one before the other. He crosses his legs and even his socks are cute. Finn sniffs around his Alec's toes, his ears flat back in a way I've never seen.

"I don't think your dog likes me." Alec holds out his hand for Finn to sniff. Finn backs away.

"It just takes him a beat to warm up to new people. I'm not sure he had the nicest owner before we got him." I kneel next to Finn, which feels easier than joining Alec on the bed. I pull Finn's head to my chest. "But now you're loved, aren't you? Who loves you more than chocolate?" I kiss him on the nose. "That's right, I do. I love you more than anything."

When I stand, I pin Alec's card and the "Everything from A to Zee" menu to my wall collage, careful to place them far away from any pictures of Gregg. "How'd you get to be so thoughtful?"

"I never thought I was, really. I think you might bring out the best in me."

I blush, bending to tousle the red fur on Finn's head. "I have to change. I think I might stink." I step out of my sneakers, line them up with my other shoes.

"Don't let me stop you."

I turn at the suggestion in his tone, a new blush already painting the rounds of my cheeks. "You mean, like, here? In front of you?"

He sits up, crosses his legs, balancing his elbows upon his knees. "Are you offering?"

My room shifts Arctic cold. I raise my arms across my chest;

spy my bedroom door that's cracked open. Part of me wishes Mom was still home. "Um, no. Definitely not."

Alec stares at me, stares through me. He walks across the room, shoos Finn out the door before closing it. He grabs my hips from behind, presses his lips to my ear. "I would never want to make you feel uncomfortable, Zephyr. I just want to be around you. Is that okay?" He spins me to face him and the entire world falls away.

"Of course."

He kisses me on the forehead, returns to the edge of the bed. That's when he drops his eyes to my legs, to my thighs. "But is it weird that your legs kind of drive me bananas?"

I let my nerves release with a laugh.

"Really. They are kind of awesome." He raises his gaze, finds my eyes. "You're kind of awesome." He waves me to him, wraps his arms around my waist, presses his head against my stomach. Then, almost in a whisper too quiet and personal to hear, "I didn't see you coming."

I bend to kiss him and his hands caress my calves, first one leg, then the other, his fingertips brushing softly over my skin, up my thighs until he stops just before the hem of my shirt. It is almost impossible to breathe.

Alec moves back, runs his fingers through his hair. "You can't do that."

"Do what?"

"That." He points his finger up and down the length of me. "You're too . . . God, I don't know. I can't even think straight. You need to take, like, five steps back at least."

I move to my dresser, intoxicated by his fumbling. I grab a bra, folding it into a small square that I can palm.

"What's that?"

94

"Just a bra. I need to go change."

A shyness shades over his face. "Can I ask you something?"

"About my bra? Um . . . why does that make me nervous?"

He shakes off his inquiry. "Yeah, no. It's stupid. Forget it."

I laugh, now curious. "No. What? Now you have to ask. It'll be all weird if you don't."

Alec blushes, looks down at his socks. "It's just . . . well, there's this thing I've always wondered about. Like if it can really be done."

"Okay, now I'm officially curious."

He blushes deeper. "I can't."

"Just say it." He looks too cute. Too lost.

"Okay." He pulls in a deep breath, steadying. "Can you do that thing where you take off your bra through your arm hole?"

Hah! That? "All girls can do that."

"Really?"

"Of course."

"Would you show me?"

"Show you?"

"No, it's stupid. I told you it was stupid."

Maybe it is. Or isn't. I don't know. "It's . . . well, it's a little more complicated with a sports bra."

"Yeah, that's okay. Forget it."

I watch Alec look around the edge of my bed, unable to make eye contact with me. He is sweet in his embarrassment and I feel almost bad for him. I reach through one arm, pull out the strap. "Is this what you meant?"

Alec lifts his head, his face an ocean of heat.

I pull out the other arm. Nerves hum over and under my skin as his eyes stay fixed on me. It is an effort not to turn away, keep myself from being on display. But I don't. From under the front of my shirt, I tug the bra down over my hips, wriggling it free.

It takes Alec a beat to find words. "You might be the coolest girl in the universe."

"It's that easy?" I say, trying to pretend it was easy.

He smiles. "Might be."

I drop my sports bra into the hamper. "Okay, now can I change?"

Alec stands, moves behind me. "Please don't." His hands round my hips and he presses his long body against my back. I reach my hands to cover his and he breathes out a noise that is both heavy sigh and small moan. My pulse thunders. "Thank you, Zephyr."

"For what?"

"For trusting me enough to do that in front of me."

But I liked it. The rush.

Alec steers me to the edge of the bed, moves out from behind me and takes a seat. My heartbeat ricochets against my chest. I force myself to breathe.

Alec takes one hand, pats the bed next to him with the other. I slip beside him. He moves me deeper onto the bed until his legs curl around mine, his arm draping over my stomach. "Is it okay if we just lie here together?"

I want that. To just lie here.

Alec's fingers mine my hair, excavating curls until his lips discover my neck. He presses kisses like stamps and I let whatever hesitation I may have float away for these few moments.

"I think I might be falling for you, Zephyr actually."

He whispers to the deepest part of my heart, the part I didn't even know was there until now. A secret even to me. I hold him there. In this place that is the beginning of everything.

Chapter 11

I wake and fumble for my buzzing phone. A text from Alec.

Miss u

I'm about to respond with the same just as Mom knocks, walks in. She sits on my bed, picks up Baba, my ratty stuffed lamb, and balances it on her lap. "Did you have fun at Karen's last night?"

I study her to see if this is a trap, but she is somewhere else entirely. "We did."

"And Alec? You like him?"

"He's nice, but why do I get the feeling Alec's not why you're here?"

"Always so perceptive." She nudges my calf. "Look, Zephyr. You should know your father is coming by today. He has to get some things from his art studio and I didn't want you to be surprised when you saw him."

This is the last thing I expected Mom to say after our talk. "I was already surprised. At last night's game. He was there you know."

Mom shakes her head in a way that tells me she did know. "I told him about your game. I didn't think he was going to show up."

"You shouldn't have said anything. I wasn't okay with seeing him. I told you that."

"Zephyr."

"No Mom. We had a deal. It's fine if you want to see him but I'm not ready."

"How can you be certain unless you—"

"I know, believe me. Dad being at my game last night totally freaked me out and I'm still trying to deal." Or at least catalog all the questions I need to ask my father.

"You'll have to face him sooner or later."

I throw my legs off the bed and stand. "I'll take later."

"You're being selfish."

The whip of her words cuts deep. "*I'm* selfish?"

She reaches for my hand, but I yank it from her reach. Her back straightens the way I know it must in the courtroom when she's arguing a case. "I don't need this, Zephyr. I've been trying my best to hold this house together and now we have a chance to heal and move on and you won't even entertain the idea of talking to your own father."

"Dad bailed on us, Mom. On *both* of us. I'm glad you two have started to move on or whatever, but I'm still kind of stuck on the fact that my own father woke up one morning and ditched me, without a word. Remember? He wrote *you* the note, not me." I pull on a pair of leggings. "Sure he waited until I turned eighteen, but when did he really want to leave? Since I was twelve I bet."

"Zephyr—"

"I'm not going to see Dad just because he's coming over to get some stuff he left behind. I'm the stuff he left behind." I push past her.

"Where are you going?"

"Out. I need to be gone when he comes."

Mom follows me to the kitchen. "Zephyr, don't leave. I don't want you driving when you're upset."

"If he's coming, I can't be here."

I slip out the door. I don't care that I'm still in my pajama tee as I drive through the back roads of Sudbury; I let the tears come — for Mom's ability to heal faster than I can, for Dad's leaving and even more for his coming back. For Mom calling *me* selfish.

I stop at the park and turn on my phone. A text from Lizzie: U doing ok?

Not even close. But I was. When I was with Alec last night.

My fingers hover over a response to Lizzie, but I call Alec instead. He invites me over, no judgments, no questions asked. Something like a deluge opens in me as I drive to his house and the stress of the past months breaks open. I want to feel alive for me. No one else. No parents, coaches, or teachers. No college admissions board. No one but me.

Alec meets me at his front door and draws me to his chest when he sees my tears. He rubs my back, whispers hushing words. He guides me, uses his thumb to wipe away a tear. "Your eyes are green," he says, searching. "Bright green."

"That happens when I cry."

"Okay, I don't ever want to see you cry, but how is it you can you look this beautiful when you're upset?"

"Hardly. I'm still in my pajamas."

"Is it weird that I like that? Sort of cool to see a secret side of you."

I blush. I can't help it. "Is your mom home?"

"Nope. Just me. Is that okay?"

Yes. I guess. Maybe. I nod.

He takes my hand as we walk up the stairs to his bedroom. His room is painted marine blue and he has one of those perfect bed sets like you'd see in an L.L.Bean catalog. Bed. Matching end tables. Desk and chair too. He watches me inventory his things. "My mom picked it all out. Remember, I didn't really live here until a month ago. My dorm room was a bit more . . . well, relevant."

"No, I like it," I say, but it's weird that the walls are missing photos, ticket stubs, hockey swag.

"Sit." He coaxes me to the bed so that my head rests on his lap. He strokes my hair and doesn't ask me to speak. The quiet is a welcome relief from Mom's expectations and the thoughts crowding my head. I close my eyes, drift under his touch for a wash of uncountable minutes. "I'm glad you called."

"I just couldn't be at home anymore, you know?"

"Why do you think I saved up for such a nice car? It's the best thing to escape in." He caresses my cheek. "Do you want to talk about it? The reason you're crying?"

I sit up, take in his tenderness. "I really don't. I'm sort of done talking about it. Thinking about it."

He nods. Understands.

"Do you ever think—"

"Yes." He winks.

"Funny," I say.

"Do I think what?"

"Do you think it's weird that we've just met?"

"Ah, yeah. It kinda scares the shit out of me."

Oh god. Me too. "Scares you how?"

"It freaks me out that I think about being with you a lot and we hardly know each other." He releases a long breath. "And because I've never felt anything close to this before."

"What about your other girlfriends?" I want to know how many. Has he loved someone before? Will he laugh at my inexperience?

"The few girls I dated at school weren't really special, just . . . I don't know, there, I guess. God, that must sound shitty."

"No, I get it."

"Yeah?"

"Yeah." All my crushes before were just for fun. Now I find myself running to Alec after fighting with Mom, needing him.

He brushes my lip with the calloused tips of his fingers. I've come to love the roughness there. "I'd make things at your house better if I could."

"And I'd help you go to culinary school if I could."

"That might be the nicest thing anyone's ever said to me."

"Really? That's sad."

He narrows his gaze. "Why sad?"

"Because you should have people saying nice things to you all the time."

"I think I do now. I have you."

"You do." I lean in and we kiss slowly. Until we don't. Alec rolls me onto the bed, his hips meeting mine. His knee spreads my legs, makes our bodies fit. His hands move along my stomach, up my shirt. Alec's fingers cup my flesh as he lets a heavy breath escape. I steal back, out of reach.

Alec pulls away. "You okay?"

I sit up, dazed. "Yeah, fine. I just . . . I don't know. . . ."

"I don't ever want to push you, Zephyr. Is this"—he moves one finger under the lip of my shirt, paints across my stomach with the slightest brush—"okay?"

I suck in an ocean of air. I want this, even if I'm afraid of what this is. But then a voice inside me tells me I've been afraid for too long. And being with Alec doesn't make me feel vulnerable or scared. Being here makes me feel alive in a way I didn't know was possible.

I pull him to me and he moves against my skin. Everywhere.

My fingers grab, my body trembles. I give over to the sensation of finding my body under his hands, closing my eyes to what feels like floating, flying, dreaming.

"Yes," I tell him. The word is mist, our breath pooling into vapor.

When I return home it's late, but Mom's not home. I grab a bottled water from the fridge and climb into bed. When I close my eyes again, Alec is with me. I smell him on my hair, my skin. I know it's him when my phone rings.

"Favorite book," he asks.

"*To Kill a Mockingbird.* Because guilt and innocence are in all the wrong places. Favorite poem?"

"There once was a man from Nantucket—"

"Stop!" My hushed laughter explodes.

"Yours?"

"*Leaves of Grass,* because I'd love to feel large and contain multitudes. Favorite movie adaptation of a book?"

"*Princess Bride.*"

"Mine too!"

"You're breaking the rules of the game."

"Right," I say. "What's your one reason?"

"The stable boy's got serious game. You?"

"Duh. Because it's a kissing book, Fred Savage."

We both laugh until I hear the metallic grind of the garage door opening. I don't want Mom to know I'm awake. "I gotta go," I tell Alec.

"As you wish."

I turn off my light and pretend I'm asleep, cowardly avoiding Mom. But it's Lizzie who wakes me the next morning, plopping down onto my bed and yanking the covers down. "Wakey, wakey,

Sleeping Beauty. I need pancakes and you're coming with."

"When did you get here?"

"Two minutes ago. Let myself in."

"What time is it?" I scrape crust from my eyes.

"Almost eleven. The Blueberry Muffin's gonna stop serving breakfast soon and I needs me some carbs."

I slip from my covers and pull on jeans and a top.

"You didn't call yesterday. I've been worried about you," Lizzie tells me.

I corral my curls into a ponytail. "Ugh. I had a shitty fight with Olivia. It was a whole thing."

"About your dad?"

"What else? It's all beyond bizarre. Can we just not talk about it and get something to eat? I'm starved."

"We can and we shall." Lizzie ushers me out of my bedroom and I'm glad Mom's not in the kitchen waiting to ambush me. I notice all the ailing plants are cleared from the sill and it strikes me that Dad might have taken them, though gardening has never been his thing. Over the summer, Mom let all her heirloom houseplants wilt slowly, turning kaleidoscope shades of yellows and browns as they battled against her erratic watering.

I focus on the stack of mail on the island, which I rifle through.

"Any news out of the Commonwealth of Massachusetts?"

I eye her. "No, why would there be?"

"Please. You don't think I know you already applied to Boston College? You? Miss I-Have-My-Whole-Life-Planned?"

"You make me sound like a predictable loser." I pick at a heavy white envelope. At first I think it's another note from Alec, but it's addressed to Mom. The script glitters with gold ink.

"Ease up, Zee. I think . . . never mind."

Lizzie at a loss for words? "What? What do you think?"

"I think your dad leaving messed you up more than you let on and you want to feel like you have some control over your future. I think it would be weird if you *didn't* apply early to Boston College. I would've done the same thing if I were you, and I wouldn't have told anyone either."

"Really?"

"Yep. No one needs to have the whole world processing their rejection. I mean, not that you'll get rejected, you know, but I'm just saying . . . some things should stay private."

"I should have told you." I tap the thick envelope against the lip of the counter.

"No worries. I didn't tell you I applied for an internship at *The New York Times*."

"You did? When?"

"Doesn't matter." She waves away her words. "I'll be competing with college students, college graduates. I'll never get it."

"You might. You're fairly awesome."

"Yeah, well, ditto. Guess we both crave validation from the big, bad world." She nods at the envelope. "What's that? An invite to the ball?"

"Anna's wedding, I think."

"Who?"

"Gregg's older sister." I toss the card onto the pile of mail, unopened. I hate not knowing if my dad will be there, if I'll have to see him before I make the choice to see him. "We've had a 'save the date' card on the fridge for months. She picked New Year's Eve of all days."

"Way to hijack a holiday."

"I know, right?"

"It's been said love makes people do crazy shit, Zephyr."

"If you say so." I grab my coat and catch a new addition to the family calendar. "Dinner with Jimmy." Date night for Mom and Dad. Every Monday. I pull the door tight behind me.

The Blueberry Muffin is packed when we arrive, with a line of at least a dozen people waiting in the freezing cold.

"Oh, this sucks." Lizzie's breath crafts a white cloud just beyond her lips.

I shuffle my feet for warmth. "Do you want to bail and go somewhere else?"

"There is nowhere else. That's why everyone's here."

"I can wait," I say, just as I hear a tap on one of the front windows. I see a hand waving. I look behind me, but there's no one. I peer closer and see it's Lani Briggs, waving us in.

Lizzie shrugs. "It's better than waiting." But only just. Lizzie seems to forget Lani's wholly unlovable enthusiasm as she pushes us through the crowd to her table.

When we slide into the booth, there are two steaming plates of pancakes, eggs, and sausage waiting, an order I recognize as the Lumberjack Special, though Lani's alone. And, come to think of it, I've never actually seen Lani eat.

"Mind if I grab one of those sausages?" Lizzie asks, unwrapping a fork from the rolled napkin place setting.

"Have at it," a voice says from behind us. My stomach drops realizing we've just crashed a breakfast date.

With Gregg.

Lani and Gregg?

Gregg takes a seat next to Lani, plucks his coffee mug from in front of me.

"Maybe we should—"

"Wait in the huge line?" Gregg interrupts me. "That's lame. Eat with us."

"Really?" Lizzie says. "It's cool?"

"Totally. We'll never finish all this food." Lani pushes her plate to the middle of the table.

"Don't mind if I do." Lizzie spears the coveted sausage with her fork.

Gregg smashes a mound of egg onto an English muffin like all of this is perfectly normal.

I shift uncomfortably in the hard booth, deserted by my appetite.

"I heard you pulled off a miracle at State." Gregg drizzles maple syrup over his egg muffin in crisscross stripes like nothing's been different between us the last few weeks. As if he didn't kiss me, tell me I'd crushed him by kissing Alec . . . or, apparently, started having breakfast dates with Lani Briggs.

"Zephyr scored the winning goal," Lizzie mumbles from under a mouthful of food.

Gregg catches my gaze, holds it. "The only goal, eh Five?" He reaches behind Lani, pulls a folded copy of the *Sudbury Sentinel* from the windowsill.

"My article! Zee, have you even seen this?" Lizzie doesn't wait for my answer, but points to the picture of my team on the front page. We are a heap of bodies and grins and mouth guards and victory. I am just off center, my smile larger than my face, my hands clutching my stick, the game ball.

I am sucked back into that moment and can feel the sweat on my skin again, taste the high of that collective win. Gregg waves his red Sharpie over the article, a request.

I throw an uncomfortable laugh that comes out louder than intended. "I'm not signing it." I'm not even sure he's serious.

Gregg dangles the pen. "Come on, Five, you'll never be as famous as you are now. Sign it. For me." It's his two final words that get me. What wouldn't I do for Gregg? And if this one small gesture starts us back on the road to normalcy, then I will sign a thousand signatures.

I take the pen and pop its top. The thick scent of ink overpowers even the sausage. I feel too much pressure to think of something witty or meaningful to write, so I just sign my full name. *Zephyr Marie Doyle.* The red looping ink bleeds into the newsprint, making my signature thicker.

"I don't want to see this on eBay," I tell Gregg as I pass the pen and article back to him. He gives me a wink and I don't know what it means. Are we okay now? He's dating Lani so now I can have Alec guilt-free?

"You should have been there," Lizzie tells him. "Zee's goal rocked."

I pop a cube of cantaloupe into my mouth, force my teeth to chew. I want to ask Gregg why he couldn't put all this stuff between us aside and watch me compete in the playoffs. A month ago I could have asked him anything.

"Gregg was with me," Lani says, squeezing Gregg's biceps in a way that makes the fruit in my mouth hard to swallow. "Cheerleader party. You know, to celebrate the start of hockey season."

I want to gag, but Gregg lifts his orange juice and pins his stare on me. It seems impossible that he can be three feet away when a universe wedges between us. A canyon crammed with all the things we aren't saying.

"Sounds like it was a blast." Lizzie's tone tells me she's aware of the tension sharing a place at our table.

107

The waitress appears and I recognize her as Steph DeLuca, a sophomore girl on the JV field hockey team. She barely registers my presence; her gaze is glued on Gregg's face. I watch her carefully. Her eyes flicker over Gregg's broad shoulders, the number on his sleeve.

"C-can I get you anything else?"

"A refill of OJ?" Gregg raises his empty glass.

"Sure thing, Slice. It'll be on the house." Steph flirts the cup from his hand and retreats.

"You've got fans everywhere," Lani says.

Gregg laughs it off. He's used to it, after all. "Hey, we're going go-cart racing after breakfast. You guys wanna join?"

"Go-carts?" Lizzie says.

"What, too childish for you?" Gregg teases.

"Um, no. Go-carts are the ultimate level playing field. I can kick your all-star ass," Lizzie says.

"Challenge accepted," Gregg says.

Am I the only one who thinks this is completely surreal?

"It'd be great if you guys came," Lani directs her words at me.

"We're so there," Lizzie says.

"Sounds fun." The lie grates over my tongue.

"Great," Lani says, though her tone makes me question if I'm totally welcome.

Steph brings Gregg's orange juice, along with the bill. Lizzie and I reach for cash, but Gregg waves us off. He sets a generous tip onto his overturned paper placemat and pulls out his trusty red Sharpie to write: "Steph, stay fierce. —Slice/17."

Lizzie and I slip into her car. She turns over the engine, cranks the heat. I watch Gregg open the passenger door for Lani, hold out his arm to help her into his giant truck.

"There is a good chance I will slip into a food coma, so be prepared to take the wheel," Lizzie tells me as she searches the radio stations.

"Maybe we shouldn't go, then."

She cuts me a look. "Why?"

"If you're not feeling well . . ."

"Don't put this on me, Zee. If it's too weird for you, you're gonna have to name it." Lizzie backs out of the parking lot. Gregg waits for us before pulling onto the main road.

"You *don't* think this is a little weird?"

"Gregg and Lani? Yeah, it's odd. I mean, she's not exactly known as a brilliant conversationalist, but whatever. He's moved on. So have you." She merges onto the road, the rear chrome bumper of Gregg's truck reflecting the bright sunlight. "You have moved on, right?"

"There was nothing to move on from." I stare out the window, wondering what Lani and Gregg are talking about, if they're holding hands.

"The kiss was meaningless."

"Yes, Lizzie, why are we rehashing this?"

"Not rehashing. Just trying to establish a clear timeline of factual occurrences." She brakes for a red light, stops directly behind Gregg and Lani. "You're digging on Hockey Boy, right?"

"Totally."

"I assume he's the one helping you process all the Jimmy and Olivia chaos?"

"Yeah, he's been great."

"Good."

"Good."

In front of us, Lani casts her arm over the lip of Gregg's bucket seat. She slides next to Gregg and takes his chin in her hand. She rotates his head, kisses him on the lips. For a long time. Like, until-after-the-light-turns-green long time and Lizzie has to beep. Lani pulls away from the kiss and turns toward us. But it's not Lizzie she's staring at. It's me.

Lizzie gives a quick, short laugh. "Now that kiss looked like it had some meaning."

"Gross. Can we please move on?"

"I thought we already had."

I did too. But I hate the way Gregg never bangs Lani's go-cart when we're on the track, despite him purposefully crashing into me and Lizzie about a hundred times. I see the small ways he protects her, watches out for her. And all I can think about is how he used to watch out for me. Maybe even without my realizing it.

When I get home I almost call Alec a dozen times, but I don't press send. Mostly because I can't wrap my head around my own thoughts and no one needs to see me be this kind of mess.

Chapter 12

Mom's left a note on the island the following morning. In her perfectly symmetrical script:

Zephyr, I'm sorry. I've handled this all wrong.

Can we talk after work tonight?

Luf,

Mom

"Luf" was the way I'd spelled "love" on a Mother's Day card when I was six. Mom and Dad have signed their notes to me like that ever since. It is our secret family handshake. But now the word looks like a promise that's been broken. I leave the note and head to school, where Alec, my beautiful escape, is leaning against my locker, a small smile pulling at the corner of his lips. When I reach him he gives me a quick peck on the cheek.

"I hope that's okay," he says. "We haven't really discussed the rules on school PDA."

"It's all good."

"Great." He steals another peck. "I thought I'd hear from you yesterday, you know, to tell me how things went with your mom."

"I should have called, but Lizzie woke me up for breakfast and then it turned into a whole thing with Gregg and Lani and go-carts. I didn't even get a chance to talk to my mom."

"Gregg, huh? So you guys have patched things up."

"I guess so. Who knows. But I did discover Gregg's dating Lani Briggs, which makes exactly zero sense. I mean, have you ever talked to that girl? There's not a lot going on in that head. Why would Gregg date her? It's beyond weird."

Alec laughs.

"What?"

"You're not dating Lani, so what does it matter?"

He's right. It doesn't matter. It's none of my business and affects me exactly zero. So why am I letting it? "You're so right. Excuse the mini rant."

"Well, I'm bummed I missed go-carting with you. But I did the next best thing."

"Yeah? What's that?"

"I stayed in and pined away for you."

"Funny."

"And bought this." He hands me an envelope. "I'm glad things didn't blow up with your mom. I—"

"Zephyr!" Someone shouts, followed by a lot of someones. A dozen upperclass girls from the field hockey team run at us, nearly knocking me over.

Karen surveys Alec up then down. "We interrupting something? Were you two sucking face?" I laugh, wishing I could be as bold as Karen, bold enough to say whatever was on my mind.

"Just heading to class," Alec says.

Karen links her arm in mine. "Well, Zephyr gets a pass from study hall. We're surprising Coach in the gym and we need our captain."

"But—" he says.

"No buts. And no boys allowed," Karen adds.

"Come on Zeph!" Melissa Hines shouts.

"Yeah, yeah, yeah, let's go, go, go," Samantha Railey chants.

A cloud of whooping starts, sounding like a human engine.

I look to Alec. "I really should go."

"Yeah, no. Of course." He thrusts his hands into his pockets. "See you in French."

"See you." I throw him apologetic eyes as my teammates steer me down the hallway.

We barge into Coach's office, where she looks impossibly small behind her desk, not the big presence she is on the field when she's yelling at us.

Coach eyes us suspiciously. "What's all this?"

Karen bursts, "We came to tell you how much we love you."

Coach's eyes narrow. "Where was that love when I made you run sprints with your goalie gear on?"

"Bygones, ladies," Melissa says.

"We really do love you, Coach," Samantha says. "And some of us won't be here next year, so we wanted you to know we couldn't have won State without you."

"Or Zee." Karen hugs my shoulder.

I lean into her. "Right back at you."

Coach stands, adjusts the whistle that perpetually hangs around her neck. "It just goes to show you how hard work and dedication will pay off. Remember that next year. It's been an honor to watch you grow into remarkable women."

"Thanks Coach," a few girls whisper.

As she talks, I know my time with the team is over. I mean really over. This moment makes me see that every relationship I have is in flux, which is by far the strangest part of senior year limbo. I won't have Coach watching over me next year, pumping me full of confidence for my work on the field. My stomach unstitches with the pull of a dark, distant thread. That string that's tied to the ache I feel when I think about Dad leaving. I take a deep breath and shove that murkiness down to my feet.

Coach comes to me and gives me a small hug. When she releases, I feel her familiar claw-grip penetrate my shoulder. "You've been a real leader this year, Doyle." I nod, but it's hard to reconcile this emotionally charged coach with the hard-ass I've known. "I want you and Karen to accept the trophy for the team on Alumni Weekend."

Alumni Weekend is this huge fall event in Sudbury, when alums come back to town and the football team plays on Saturday and there's a parade the whole town turns out for. It's the Super Bowl mashed with the queen's visit, Sudbury style.

"You should do it," I tell Coach. "It's your team."

"Don't fool yourself, Doyle. This team belongs to you and Karen."

The girls throw up a low hoot, thundering the concrete wall with their palms.

"Okay then. I'd be honored."

"Me too," Karen says.

Maybe it's the closure I'll need before saying good-bye to all the parts of Sudbury I never thought I'd miss.

When I return to my locker, I realize I'm still holding the envelope Alec gave me. I tear open the flap and remove the card. It's bright white with a simple, small cupcake in the middle. The cupcake is decorated with a smiling clown, complete with a pointy hat. The caption: "Life is better with a sugar buzz on." The word "sugar" is crossed out and Alec's written "Zephyr" instead. I bite my lip and beam.

I flip the card open and there is a heart scrawled next to his initial. I study the lines of the heart, how he drew it for me, and I'm unable to tame my smile, even when Lizzie sneaks up from behind. "Heavy," she says.

"Where did you come from?"

"I saw you walk by the common room. I was covertly researching teen study habits for a new piece I'm writing and thought I'd see what had you skipping study hall." She nods toward the card. "I give Hockey Boy mad respect. An old school card *and* the proper shout-out to sugar."

The faint heat of a blush colors my cheeks and I wave the card in front of my face like it's a hot day in July instead of a chilly November morning.

"He seems pretty great."

"He is. I mean think about it. Alec had to go to a store. Pick out a card. Search for the perfect one. Modify it so it was even *more perfect*. That might be the definition of 'pretty great.'"

"I already gave him a shout-out. No need to sell me on him."

I tuck the card back into its envelope and can't help having an Alec buzz on.

"I guess this means you're definitely not hung up on Slice dating Lani?"

"I told you, I never cared about that."

"Okay. Just as long as you're sure."

• • •

When I see the back of Alec's head in the hall on the way to fourth period, I race to catch up to him, dodging students in my quest. I grab his arm and he slows enough for me to lean into his side. "Hey there."

"How was your coach?"

"Good. Sappy." I shake my head. "Whatever, look—"

He jerks his arm away. "I gotta do a thing before calc, Zephyr. I can't be late." He turns too fast, doubles his stride down the hall. I watch the back of his head disappear into a sea of students. A body slams into me and a tall kid apologizes. I wave it off, aware only of a small bit in my middle sinking with more force than gravity.

At lunch, I search for Alec but he's nowhere.

"Earth to Zee." Lizzie's voice reaches me from the valley of some outlying place. "You look like you're on a totally different planet."

"I need to talk to Alec." I didn't imagine Alec pulling away from me, did I? "I think he might be mad at me, or annoyed or something."

"I'm sure everything's fine. He just gave you that card, like, this morning."

"True."

But Lizzie's eyes hang on me. I avoid her gaze and hate the questions that fill my head.

When Alec arrives late for French he has a hall pass. He and Mrs. Sarter exchange hushed words as he hands it to her. I find myself leaning forward wanting to know where he was, what teacher wrote the excuse for him. But he doesn't give me any clue. He doesn't even look at me, keeps his legs tucked squarely under his desk. I could physically reach over and touch his knee but his forced posture defends his space. This I'm not imagining. He bolts as soon as the bell rings. I don't even have my books gathered before I see his empty chair. Just like Gregg's.

I feel totally abandoned.

And I can't go home. I know Mom's apology is waiting for me there, but I can't get my head around Dad's return or their Monday night dates or any of it. Not enough to talk to Mom openly, the way she deserves.

Not while all I can think of is Alec feeling so far away. I am rudderless without field hockey to fill the afternoon hours, so I disappear into the town library, try to catch up on the work I've let slide. I'm not nearly done when the library closes at six o'clock. I check my phone and there are no texts, no missed calls. I pull out of the parking lot for home, but drive to Alec's instead.

He answers the door, steps outside onto the stoop with me. His hair glistens from his post-practice shower. "What's going on?"

"Are you mad at me?"

He rubs his arms for warmth, looks out at the dark, stagnant neighborhood. "Not mad. Disappointed, maybe."

I search for an answer in his eyes. "Why?"

"You ditched me this morning. I gave you a card, Zephyr, and you didn't even stick around long enough to open it. It was like . . . like I didn't matter or something."

I think back to this morning, Karen and the girls pulling me away. "That was the team, not me."

He looks at me hard. "You could have asked them to wait."

"I didn't realize . . ."

"Look, I get it, they're your friends." He tucks a stray piece of hair behind my ear. "But I'm your boyfriend. At least, I think so, right?"

"Yes, of course! Please don't doubt that."

"Do you know how nervous I was to give you that card? And then you just walked away?"

"I'm really sorry. I felt like hell all day if that's any consolation. I knew something was wrong."

"I'm not a big fan of hashing out my private issues in front of other people."

"I get that."

"Do you?" He searches my face, finds my eyes. "Do you get how much I'm into you, or how much it killed me when you blew me off to hang with Slice? I thought you needed help with your mom and then I find out you're go-carting with another guy . . ."

"And Lizzie and Lani. And it wasn't my idea. I would've rather been with you."

"Ever since we met at the park, I've been freaking out that you dig on Slice and you're only with me as . . . I don't know . . . a placeholder or something."

"Uh, no. You couldn't be more wrong."

"I'm not sure I am wrong."

"There was this thing between us but it meant nothing. Noth. Ing."

"What thing?" His eyes narrow.

I force a dismissive tone. "Around the time I met you, Gregg kissed me."

He steps back, releases a burdened laugh. "That's what all that tension was between you two?"

"Only because it was a mistake."

"Zephyr, you can't even know . . . God, just hearing you and Slice kissed makes me insanely jealous."

The world trembles as I watch Alec flush white. "I didn't want to kiss him."

"How can I know that?"

Are we really fighting over something so ridiculous? "Because Gregg's kiss was wrong. It only lasted for, like, two seconds before I pushed him away."

"You can't know something's wrong in two seconds. It had to last longer than that."

"Maybe, but not much. I swear." Then, because his posture straightens, recoils from me, I draw up an enormous betrayal. "Gregg's tongue felt awful—like kissing a brother. I had to rinse my mouth out with alcohol." I hesitate a step closer. "You're the only one I want to kiss. Most times I never want to stop kissing you." There it is. All out there.

Alec sighs, softens. "This is so messed up."

"What do you mean?"

"Now you know what an insecure mess I am. Shit, Zephyr, I'm making you explain something that happened before we were even dating. That's nuts."

"It's not. Don't you think I wonder about your old girlfriends? But I don't ask because it will make me insane."

"Really?"

"Duh." I smile.

He leans in with a soft kiss but I pull him closer, my hunger for him rising. He twists me with his kiss, my back bumping against the door's brass knocker with a dull ring. His hands quickly explore my body, the ridges of my hips, the layers under my jacket. But just when my head has emptied of all its worries and there is nothing else but Alec, his touch disappears, leaving me fevered and wanting.

He finds my ear, fills it with his words. "You're sure it's okay when I kiss you?"

"So sure." My focus is singular: I want to go inside with him. Go to that place only he can take me.

He pulls away. "But don't you worry it might be too much?"

"Too much?" My words squeak into the air between us, barely strong enough to hold themselves upright.

"This." He moves his finger between us. "I told you this scares the shit out of me. I don't know if I—"

"It scares me too. All the time."

He searches my face, reads my sincerity. I watch his lips as he says, "You should go."

Go? "Go?"

He signals toward the house. "I've gotta do some stuff. Just like you . . . this morning."

My senses blink back to reality. The impervious granite block under my feet turns liquid. "I said I was sorry." It is a frail attempt to bring him back, have him lasso me with his arms.

"I know, but I need to be careful with you, Zephyr."

I pull breath into my lungs, but it's labored, struggling. I search his eyes for tenderness, but all I see is hurt. So similar to Gregg's, but the ache to heal Alec roars primal within me. The need drums desperate. "I would never hurt you."

"But don't you see that's the problem? I'm scared you can hurt me without even knowing it."

Sickness swirls my middle.

"I really do have to go." He gestures to the door and I step aside. Alec disappears into his house, the lock bolting his only good-bye.

I scramble down the steps, into my car, holding back the tears until I'm out of his cul-de-sac. I want to make time for him now, give him everything. Make it right.

Driving away, my brain explodes with questions like *How do girls do this?* Handle relationships and friends and insecurities? Or do they? I think of all the drunken drama sessions at parties, all the tears in the girls' bathroom at Sudbury High.

I am tortured by a fear that tickles up my spine:

I'm not good enough for him.

I don't know how to do any of this.

I'm a terrible girlfriend.

Chapter 13

I almost *want* to vomit, bring up the sick and purge this stir of anxiety. I wasn't even lying last night when I told Mom I wasn't feeling well and avoided having to reconcile. I got zero sleep thinking about Alec and he's the only thing my mind can focus on now, despite Mr. Frank's earnest attempts to convince us that the Pythagorean theorem is education's most significant piece of information. I crouch over my trig text. Triangles morph into a maze under my unfocused stare.

Time mocks me, slowing down on purpose, like it can sense how much I need to see Alec, make everything right with us.

When I hear a familiar laugh swelling just outside the open door, my attention darts to the hallway where Gregg's walking by, flanked by adoring underclassmen, his arm strung around Lani. I strain in my seat searching for the particular edges of Alec's hairline. I could get up. Get a hall pass.

But Alec isn't with Gregg's pack, and my body deflates against the stiff plastic seat. I bite at my already raw thumbnail, practicing my apology to Alec the way I rehearsed it in my head—and in front of my mirror—an obsessive number of times last night. I only hope my words are good enough. They have to be good enough.

Oh god. What if *I'm* not good enough? It's the same question that's haunted me since summer.

Sick rumbles deeper in my stomach. I need Alec to tell me we're okay. I need his hands on my hips, his breath mixed with mine. I want that closeness back and I want Alec to know I'd never jeopardize us on purpose. By the time the bell rings I have a headache that weighs a thousand and nine pounds. My skin shivers with nerves as I walk to his locker.

He's swapping out books, Lani leaning against the wall next to him. God, why is she everywhere now? I shift on my heels, readying to turn, when I hear Lani squeal my name in a pitch that could deafen a dog. Alec sees me and our eyes catch, but not long enough for me to read his, know what he's thinking.

"We were just talking about hockey parties," Lani announces with her usual cheerleader perk.

"Yeah?"

"I'm sort of in charge of getting hotels for the after, after-parties. You know, for the hockey team and cheerleaders."

"I'm aware of the tradition," I say. Enigmatic Alec stands across from me, giving nothing away.

"So fun, right?" She flirts her curtain of blond hair, gives me a wink.

Alec slams his locker. "Just let me know what the other guys are doing and count me in."

As he turns to walk away, my words stretch to reach him. "Will I see you later?"

He twists to me. "Do you want to see me later?"

"Am I missing something? Are you two . . ."—Lani needles her finger between us—"hooking up?"

123

Alec stares at me, stares through me. "Zephyr means way more than a hookup."

Is that forgiveness?

"Bummer." Lani's fake pout morphs into a fake smile. "I mean, good for you, Zephyr, but I'll have to tell the squad that Alec Lord is off the market."

I cringe at her mouth forming his full name, how it feels like an invasion. "The whole squad, huh?"

"Squad-*zz*. Soccer. Football *and* hockey." She reaches for Alec's forearm, gives it a squeeze that makes my insides burn. "Your Alec has a serious fan club." She makes pouty lips and treats us to a finger-fluttering wave before she bounces off down the hall. Literally, bounces. I'm relieved when Alec's eyes don't follow her.

"Why do I have a sudden need to take a shower?"

Alec's face fills with intrigue. "Alone?" He wraps his hand around my waist as the hall empties.

I'll be late for English but I don't care.

"It's good to see you, Zephyr."

"You too." I don't have the words to tell him how much. "Am I forgiven?"

He pulls me closer. "I'm not big on grudges. Besides, I'm madder at myself for being an insecure ass."

"You heard Lani. You could have any girl at this school."

"I don't want any girl." He cups my chin. His eyes lock on mine, clutching my heart. "Don't you get it? You're more than I deserve." My knees weren't built to withstand the kiss he gives me.

I pull away gently, press my forehead to his. "Just to be clear . . . hanging out with battalions of cheerleaders isn't tempting?"

"Not even slightly." He squeezes my earlobe with a delicate

pinch. Even that small gesture makes my skin blaze. "Why? Are you jealous, Zephyr actually?"

"Not at all." A lie.

"Good. There's no need. I don't want you to have any insecurities. I've got enough for both of us." He trails kisses along the hard line of my clenched jaw.

I breathe him in.

"Speaking of which . . ."

"Yes?" I tease him with a lifted brow.

"Yesterday kind of made me realize that I'm not totally comfortable with you hanging out with Slice."

"Gregg?" How are we talking about Gregg?

"The one and only. In particular, the Gregg who kissed you and probably still wants to."

Alec's grip tightens, pulling me against his pelvis. The rush is raw and immediate. The fog of his touch is almost too much to see through, but a small voice manages to scramble up and into air. "I can't just suddenly stop being friends with him."

"I'd never ask you to do that. Just . . . hang back a little."

"But why?"

He locks our hips. "Because I'm not sure I can take it—worrying about him kissing you again."

"That's ridiculous. He'd never. Besides, he's with Lani now."

Alec presses his cheek to mine and whispers. "Please don't call my insecurities ridiculous."

I pull back. "I didn't mean—"

"I know. Look, I get it. I know my fears are stupid. But it doesn't help them go away." Alec kisses me just under my ear, the skin so tender in that spot that my spine shivers. "Can you do this? For. Me."

My legs weaken.

"So you can hang with him but I can't? How is that fair?"

"It's totally different. Slice doesn't want to make out with me." He smiles, bites at my lip. "Or at least he hasn't tried yet."

"Yet, huh?"

"Look, I'm not proud of it, but it wrecks me, thinking of his hands on you, or him thinking about having his hands on you. I wish I were a stronger or better person, but I'm not."

I know exactly what it feels like to want to be better, more. For him. A familiar word bubbles up inside of me: yes. "Okay."

"That's my girl." He moves his mouth against mine so gently his skin feels like faded cotton, warm and inviting. I fall into his kiss, my tongue in a liquid smooth search for his rhythm. For him. For more.

The dull metal thud of a locker slams somewhere in the adjacent hall, making me break away. A teacher clears his throat behind us and moves us along.

Only a month ago I would have been mortified by a teacher seeing me so close with a boy. Now I want the whole world to see.

Mom's crisscrossing bittersweet vines into a thick wreath when I arrive home from watching Alec's game. Neither of us says hello. I go to the fridge where Mom's pinned Anna Slicer's wedding invitation next to the paper turkey I made in first grade. Great. I've got a little over a month to figure out how I'm going to duck out of that Gregg-filled soiree.

I pull out a bag of grapes when Mom says, "Are you feeling better?"

"Much."

"Okay enough to hear that I'm sorry for calling you selfish?" She nods toward the empty chair across from her and I sit.

"I'm sorry I stormed out." Finn scoots across the floor, rests his head on my sneaker. I reach down and scratch between his ears. "Did you take him for a walk? He looks tired."

"No. He's been sluggish all day."

"Hmm." I give Finn a tender pat along the length of his head and he lets out a low sigh.

"Zephyr." Mom clears her throat. "It wasn't okay for your dad to show up at your game like he did and I told him so. You need to see him when the time is right for you. I support that."

"Thank you. That means a lot."

"But with Thanksgiving coming up, I wanted you to know that if you want to hike, I'll go with you. Finn, too. Or"—she hesitates, pinches two vines steady between her fingers—"maybe you want to do something else?"

I roll a grape along the ridge of my palm. Every Thanksgiving morning since I was old enough to make the climb, Dad and I have hiked to the top of Mount Vernon. Mom always stayed behind, joking about how she was thankful for the quiet. She'd pack us Thanksgiving Stuffers, her special sandwiches made of stuffing, turkey, and cranberry—like eating leftovers before the meal. Climbing made my breath ragged and my mind would empty of everything as Dad and I ascended the narrow pine-needled path that led to the icy crunch of the mountain's summit.

And as much as I wish I could hike with my father like any other year . . . "I don't think I want to hike."

"Maybe this Thanksgiving we'll keep it simple. Start making new traditions." Mom's voice cracks and I hate how Dad's changed everything and I don't know how to put the pieces of our family back together. Worse, I don't know if all our pieces will even fit back together.

"New traditions sound about right."

"Is that really what you want?"

I nod. "I think it's the only way it can be. I mean, we can't do stuff the way we've always done it and pretend like Dad didn't walk out on us." I see Mom begin her side of the argument, but cut her off. "Even if he is back."

"Okay." She looks satisfied. For now. "And maybe we can check in with each other more. About this or anything. I don't want you to pull away before you leave for Boston."

"I can do that."

"Look, Zephyr, there isn't a parenting handbook on this so I'm kind of out of my element, but I do know that I want you to be happy. And strong. And I think you're at serious risk of regret if you don't at least try to see your dad at some point, listen to what he has to say."

"I know." I do. Of course I do. It still doesn't make that first step any easier.

Chapter 14

Alec has been slammed with hockey practice and homework all week, but he's found time to call every night to wish me sweet dreams. Even sweeter is the way he's managed to leave me tiny gifts, despite his grueling schedule. A pyramid of Hershey's Kisses on the seat of my car, an origami bird left at my front step. I didn't tell him how I crushed it during my rush out the door that morning.

It's crazy how badly I'm dying to see him. And awful how much I wish I hadn't made plans for a movie night with Lizzie.

Now Lizzie lazes on my bed, waiting for me to pack clothes for a sleepover. She taps her finger against the maroon cover of the thick Boston College catalog. "I don't see the fascination with this place."

I pull on a shirt and my sneaky brain reminds me how Alec watched me slip out of my bra when I was standing almost in this exact spot. And how I liked it. More than a little.

"Earth to Zee."

I'm pulled back to the now. "What's up?"

"Boston College. It's so . . . boxy."

"Boxy?" I snort.

"Yeah, the buildings are all square and institutional." She

shudders like she's physically offended. "It's wicked confining. I mean, how's college any different than Suckbury?"

I move to the side of the bed and wrench the brochure from her hands. "You are under no obligation to visit me in my boxy dorm room at my fine, boxy establishment of higher learning. Oh, and when I'm summering in Hyannis Port with the Kennedys you shouldn't feel obligated to visit me there, either."

"Oh, I'm coming to the Kennedy Compound. That place is scandal central. I'd write an exposé that would bust my career wide open."

"Rise to fame at the expense of others?"

"Name me a journalist who's done it any other way." Lizzie snickers and goes to my bureau, paints one eyelid with a deep shade of purple I didn't know I had. "I assume you haven't heard yet."

I shake my head. "You? Any news about the internship?"

"*Nada.*"

"So what's the plan if you don't get in?" Lizzie asks, dabbing more color onto the applicator. "What's your Plan B?"

I swallow. Hard. Dad always said the way to reach your goals was to have a Plan A and only a Plan A. Plan Bs are just a way to keep you from attaining Plan A. I've never had another plan other than studying at Boston College's Morrissey College of Arts & Sciences. Living in one of America's oldest cities. On my own. That's what all the studying and good grades have been for. I can't imagine my life taking an alternate course. A not-so-small part of me collapses into that raw vulnerability.

"I'll apply to a bunch of places, just in case." My words fall flat and unconvincing.

I wriggle on my favorite jeans and watch Lizzie's reflection in the mirror, how suspicion draws over her features. Before she can call me out, though, my phone rings with Carly Rae Jepsen's "Call Me Maybe." Lizzie plunks down onto my bed, picks up Baba and pulls at the nubby balls of his remaining fur.

Hey, I just met you and this is crazy, but here's my number so call me may— I dig my phone out of my bag, see HOCKEY BOY pulse on my screen and press accept. Lizzie grins at her latest handiwork.

"Hello?"

"Hello, Zephyr actually. You miss me?"

"Who is this?" I bite my lip, smiling.

Alec laughs softly. "I need to see you tonight."

I blush. My entire body tingles. I look at Lizzie and mouth, *It's Alec.*

"Yeah, got that."

"You with someone?" he asks.

"No one special." I smirk at Lizzie and she rolls her eyes.

"So, tonight?"

"I told you we're having a girls' night."

"I need to see you. I'll die."

"Dramatic much?"

Alec laughs. "Just for a few minutes. Please? I'm at that Waxman kid's house."

I hear a whoosh of noise. "Tomorrow," I whisper. "Promise."

"Look, a bunch of people just stormed the room I'm in. It's kind of hard to hear. Come see me. Just for one kiss."

What can that hurt? "Just one."

"Can't wait." I hear the smile in his voice. "Wear something sexy."

"See you soon." I flick off my phone and beg Lizzie with my eyes. She huffs. "Fine. We can stop by and see him."

My body zings with an electrical current. I never imagined I'd be this girl.

I shake off my jeans and trade them for a skirt and pair of knee-high boots.

On the way to the party I ask Lizzie, "How can you and Jason stand being away from each other?"

"It sucks sometimes. Most times. But what's the alternative? Give up my life and live his life? No thank you." She turns onto Waxman's road and has to double-park because the street is already jammed. "Besides, it's always better when we see each other after a break. We have more to talk about."

Lizzie puts the car in park and I want to ask her if there was ever a time when it killed her to be away from Jason. But I don't. Just in case she's never felt the way I do now.

"I'll wait here. I'm not really in the mood for crowds."

My hand is already on the door handle when my phone rings. Kurt Cobain's sultry voice tells me, *Come as you are, as you were, as I want you to be*. I shoot Lizzie a look of quiet admiration and tell Alec I'm just outside. "Hurry," he urges.

"I'll be back in ten minutes," I tell Lizzie.

"Tell him I said hi."

"Will do." I pop open the door, the sharp, winter cold air surprising my lungs, and my bare legs. Dubstep beckons from within the house. I go inside, my entire body zipping with the promise of seeing Alec. I spot him seated at the large dining room table, his posture easy against the high-backed chair as he surveys a game of quarters.

His gaze settles on me as I walk into the room and his smile grows, lighting his eyes. He cuts a quick glance to the room behind him and throws a nod. The corners of my mouth twitch up at this secret communication. Alec gets up from the table and I make my way through the crowd, following him. I'm halfway through the throng when someone grabs my forearm. I stop short. Gregg.

"Remember me?" he asks.

"H-hey," I stammer.

"We met once or twice."

I look down at my arm. "Let go."

His fingers lift immediately. "There are other things—other people—in the world besides Alec, you know." He takes a short swig of beer.

"You're drunk."

"Or maybe I'm the only one willing to tell you what you need to hear. *In vino veritas.*" He raises his glass.

"I'm confused. You're calling me out for hanging with Alec when you're the one who *chose* not to speak to me for the longest time? And then we saw you at breakfast and you acted like everything was okay?" It's surprising how much anger that stupid breakfast can boil in me even now. I turn from him, move through the crowd to Alec.

Alec grabs my hands, spreads my arms open, drinks me in. "Damn." He leans in, kisses my neck, strokes one finger along its length. "I never thought it was possible to miss someone's neck." His words purr into my ear, so soft against the noise booming from the other rooms. "Where's Lizzie?"

"She's waiting outside. I've got ten minutes."

He plays up dejected eyes. "Sad news."

"It's better than not seeing you at all."

"Too right." He adjusts his stance, moves the toe of his sneaker against my boot. "I saw you talking to Slice."

"Yeah, it was nothing."

"Exchanging words is never nothing."

"Nothing important."

"Did he mention me?"

I nod.

"What did you say?"

"I told him I was here to see you. Only you."

He kisses me on the nose. "Thank you."

"For what?"

"I don't know. For coming." He gives a shy laugh. "Or maybe, for choosing me."

"It wasn't a contest."

He bites gently on my earlobe. "How about I prove to you that you made the right choice?"

"You can do that in ten minutes?"

He raises his hand to trace the crease of my smile, the way my lips run into the swell of my cheeks. His eyes fire. "Maybe I'll surprise you."

Oh my. "Consider my interest piqued."

He smirks a devil's grin and directs me into a spare bedroom.

He pulls the door shut behind me. "You look beautiful." He opens my coat, runs his palm over my neck, my collar bone. My body faints against the door. His hands rest at my waist and his fingers tuck under the band of my skirt. My breath shuffles out in erratic bursts. He pops the clasp.

I grab his hand. "Not here."

He plucks my hand away. "Why not?"

"What if someone comes in?"

His lips meet my neck. I dissolve when I feel the heat of his breath on my skin. "Don't worry, I locked the door. Now stop interrupting me, I'm up against a serious deadline here."

A small laugh trickles out as I relax. His mouth hovers between my face and neck and I wonder if his kiss will land on my jawline or my lips. His hands find my shirt, float over my breasts. He pushes up my top, exposing my bra. He smoothes his lips over my chest, making my breathing heave, forcing my hands to fumble in the softness of his hair. He crouches and nestles his head against my stomach, lowering until his mouth finds my skirt.

My eyes dart open to the dark room as his teeth open my skirt's side zipper slowly, methodically. I feel the metal open, catch by catch. Then he's slipping the skirt down over the spiked rise of my hips and letting it drop to the floor.

I should tell him to stop. I want to tell him to stop. But I don't want him to stop. Not yet.

I step out of my skirt. He guides me to the bed.

He kisses me, reclines me onto my back before his fingers brush the inside curve of my knee, the soft length of my inner thigh. My back arches. My hands search for fabric, anything to steady my whirling head.

Oh god.

And then, he stops. My breath is ragged, wanting. Alec stands over me, studying me. He hooks a finger through the spaghetti string of my underwear and tugs. "Do you think you need these?" There's a laugh sitting under his words, but it's mixed with something darker. A desire for more?

My body stiffens. Does he want to have sex? Here? Now? I am so not ready. I shuffle back on the bed. Suddenly, the music outside our door is too loud. The pressure too great. "Alec, I can't . . ."

"Can't what? Feel good?" He steadies me, studies me. "That's all I want for you, Zephyr. I'll stop if you want me to . . ."

"No." The word is out before I can stop it. And I don't want to take it back.

Alec plays with the side string of my underwear. "Would it be all right if I took these off?"

I nod because anticipation wins out over fear.

He tugs and my hip wrenches toward him with the force. Material splits. One side, then the other. Ecstasy floods through me in a flash of endless, soaring white. He slips the material from my body. I watch him ball the severed cotton in his palm and tuck it into his back pocket.

He crawls slowly over my body, lies next to me. I feel his fingers at my temple. The way he softly brushes the curls from my forehead. "I want more than ten minutes."

"What?" My head is spinning. My mouth dry.

"Our time's up. Your friend is waiting."

Lizzie. Shit. The real world. Part of me wants to cancel my plans and stay here forever. And the whole of me pulses with the echo of Alec, the want I have for him.

"Do you think it would be okay if I helped you dress?"

I nod, wanting his hands on me still.

Alec is so delicate as he guides my legs through my skirt. He helps me to stand, fastens the clasp of my skirt. "You go out first," he says. "I'll hang back for five."

He opens the door and a jolt of bright light spills in from the hallway. Muffled conversations fill my ears. I hear chanting, a piercing squeal. Then the laughter. A house full of laughter.

My knees quiver and I have to concentrate on putting one foot in front of the other. Until I am almost outside. Until Gregg bumps into me. He sidesteps, registers my flushed face.

"Seriously, Zephyr?"

Gregg stands before me, judging me. But I don't care. I am trapped by the undertow that is Alec and how I want it to drag me under and bury me with its force. I didn't know a person could make another person feel like this. And I won't let Gregg make me feel guilty about it.

I move past him and step outside. The cool night air eddies around me as if I'm drunk. Through my haze I spot Lizzie's car, engine running. Inside the cabin the dim overhead light seems too bright and I squint against its glare.

She snickers. "I see our little pit stop was worth it."

"What do you mean?"

"I mean, you have total sex hair."

My fingers rise to my hair, try to smooth down my curls.

"Did you . . . ?"

"No! God Lizzie!"

She gives a short laugh and shakes her head.

By the time we reach her house, I can almost think clearly again. Lizzie gets a phone call from Jason and chats with him as she unpacks an enormous bag of snacks onto her kitchen island, filling a mixing bowl with gummy worms and M&M's. I head to the bathroom.

I lift my skirt and search my hipbone for the pinch I feel there. There's a cut.

Thin as a whisper but warm and fresh red.

Alec's watch must have nicked me.

I press my finger across the cut and it reopens. The tiniest red river of blood.

Alec has marked me.

I let go of a small grin, one so secret I'd only show it to the mirror. And my reflection returns the smile, proud of this new version of me made more alive by Alec.

When I join Lizzie on the couch, my phone buzzes. A text from Alec: Ten minutes isn't enough.

Chapter 15

I'm grateful Lizzie has plans with Jason today. She drops me at my house so I have time to shower and change before heading to the mall with Alec. He needs a new pair of sunglasses and the process is akin to picking out a prom dress. There are *a lot* of choices. When he finally finds the right pair, we get ice cream and talk about hockey, next year, his signature take on pesto sauce, how much he envied Lizzie being my overnight host. I fear there aren't enough minutes in the universe to share all the things I want to share with Alec.

When we get to his car, I pull out my phone.

"Who are you calling?"

"Just texting my mom to tell her I'm on my way."

"Cool." He studies his rearview mirror until he can pull out of the parking space.

Mom responds immediately: Be safe. And then a heartbeat, a moment, before another text: Thank you for checking in.

"Everything okay?" Alec asks.

"Perfect. Favorite card in the deck?"

"Ace. It can have two different meanings, depending on the game you're playing. Favorite song?"

"'Down to Zero' by Joan Armatrading. This one line, *'There's more beauty in you than anyone.'* It sort of wrecks me."

"There's more beauty in you than anyone."

I smile. "That's not the way this game is played and you know it."

"Couldn't help it. Seizing the moment and all."

"I might be able to find it in my heart to forgive you this once."

"As you wish."

Alec holds my hand as he drives and I'm left wondering if I'll ever find the words to tell him how he's unearthed the deepest part of my heart. Created it, really. When he turns into my driveway he pulls over at the mailbox. "I believe this is your stop."

"Hah! You know me too well." I pop out of the car and open the box, its creaking metal latch echoing in the dark woods. The box is empty, though I thrust my hand in to be sure. How is it possible I haven't heard from Boston College yet? Tyler Grinnel heard from Penn. Amy Gettes was accepted by USC. Where's my letter? But then maybe it's wrong to want more than I have.

"Anything?" Alec asks when I duck back into his car.

"No, and I'm getting seriously frustrated." He puts the car in gear but I steady his arm. "Not yet. I want to say bye without my mom creeping at the window."

He returns the car to park and pops his seat belt. The heater spurts out waves of warmth. He pats the side of his seat and I move closer, inhaling the sweet smell of his skin and cologne. "I had a great day with you."

"Me too."

"Next time we'll go out to dinner. I like to sample restaurants, get ideas for"—he sputters a laugh—"for the restaurant I'll never have."

"Don't say never. A business degree will help you run a

restaurant. That's something, right? You can go to culinary school after. Your parents won't have a say then. You'll see."

"I wish that were true." His words clutch sadness.

"You can make it true. It's your life, not theirs." I snuggle closer, drape my arm over his waist.

"Maybe."

"Not maybe. You can. I believe in you."

Alec takes my hand in his. His one finger draws down the length of my ring finger. Then again. Even this small touch, this odd exploration, seizes my attention. "How did I get so lucky? Let me take you out Wednesday. Our own Thanksgiving, just the two of us."

Sounds perfect. But there's something about Wednesday. . . . "That's the start of Alumni Weekend."

"And that matters why?"

"It's Sudbury tradition. The school band does a parade thing and then there's an athletics ceremony before the football team plays our school's biggest rival. A lot of people who graduated come back to watch."

"And are there alumni you want to see?"

"Not particularly."

"And you don't love football?"

"Ah, no."

"So then why can't you spend the day with me?"

Why was I planning on going to the ceremony? Lizzie and I hate it every year. Literally spend the entire time talking about how much we hate it. "I guess it's just tradition."

He bites lightly at my bottom lip, his breath mixing with mine. "Make a new tradition with me."

His words echo Mom's. And I want new with Alec. But . . . "I promised Lizzie I'd go."

"Sure, but if you're with me we can do a little of this." His hands glide under my shirt. His lips press along my neck.

"Yeah?" My breath is too faint.

"Yeah."

Yes. Yes. "Okay."

He leans his forehead against mine. "Good. Boston College may not have made up its mind, but I can't get enough of you. You're mine Wednesday. No friends, no school. Just the two of us. I promise I'll make it special. You'll forget all about Alumni Weekend."

I already have.

He puts the car in gear and we slowly drive toward my house. When I get inside, the air is so still I can hear the hoot of a barn owl outside the kitchen window. I grab an orange and pad to my room, calling, "Mom! I'm home!" There's no response. I flash forward to next year, returning to my dorm room after a party, no parents to check in with. The intoxicating freedom makes me want Alec with me at Boston College more than ever.

I flop on top of my comforter and it's impossible to say how much time passes before Mom pops in, sits on the edge of my bed. "Hey Sunshine, did you have a good day with Alec?"

"I did."

"Are things getting serious with you two?"

"We were at the mall to buy sunglasses, Mom."

She cuts my attitude with a glare. "It doesn't matter where you go, Zephyr. Only that he treats you well."

"He does." The best.

She pats the curve of my shin. "Good. That's what matters. You deserve that. Every girl does. And no need to rush things." She stands to leave and I can't help feeling like I only got half of a parental speech, that if Dad were home this conversation would have gone differently and included a lot more rules. My brain doesn't know whether to feel sad or relieved.

"Oh, almost forgot. I need a favor," Mom says.

"What's up?"

"I know you're invited on your own and can bring a date, but I'd like you to be my plus one for Anna's wedding."

"You're not going with Dad?" The question is not one I wanted to ask, and the very question I've wanted to ask for weeks now. How much is Dad back in her life? What's the new protocol? The new boundaries?

Her eyebrows raise. "No. I'd never put you in a situation like that, Zephyr."

"Well, I don't have to go."

Mom looks startled. "That's unthinkable. You adore Anna."

"I know. I do. But I want you to be happy too, Mom." I shrug. "So if you want to take Dad I'll stay home."

"I wouldn't hear of it. And it would break Anna's heart."

"Okay then, but no dancing." I want to be a part of Anna's big day, see all her little sisters dressed like princesses. Her day isn't about Gregg or me or Alec or rogue kisses.

"Deal."

"The no dancing clause is non-negotiable."

"You've made your terms clear." Mom laughs. If I played the One Thing game with Mom, I'd tell her that her laughter is the one sound I've missed the most these past months.

When she closes my bedroom door, I kick off my boots and curl into my covers just as my phone plays.

I kissed a girl and I liked it—

I grab for it. "Hey."

"Favorite time of the year?" Alec says.

"Spring. Renewal and all . . ."

"Worst memory?"

The question startles me and I hesitate for a beat, which is against the rules of the game. Dad's leaving sucked, but it wasn't the worst thing.

"My dog dying. The one I had when I was a kid. She was hit by a car and I was the one who found her."

"God, that's awful."

"What's your worst memory?" I ask.

"How about something lighter? Favorite letter in the alphabet?"

"S. It has the potential to go on forever."

"I hope we have that too." Alec's words draw around me, hold me with their promise.

I dream on the possibility of forever with Alec on my drive to school on Monday. Maybe this thing between us can be sacred and lasting. Maybe nothing can break it. The thought absorbs me until I meet up with Lizzie at lunch, her stare already boring a hole in my skull as I approach our table. "So you're blowing me off?"

"It's good to see you too." I grab an apple from my bag, shine it against my jeans. "Lizzie, you hate Alumni Weekend." I bite into my apple, regretting sending her that text last period.

"That's not really the point. We made plans, Zee." She slumps back in her chair, aimlessly rearranges the tater tots on her plate.

"You know I love hanging with you, but Alec has something special planned and I don't want to bail on that for some lame school tradition. He's my boyfriend. I want to spend time with him."

"I get it, Zee. I have a boyfriend too, remember? And I manage to still hang out with my friends and keep my commitments."

She abandons her fork and the metal *thunks* against the plastic cafeteria tray before she crosses her arms over her chest.

"Don't be mad, Lizzie. It's just different for me."

She narrows her eyes. "Careful, Zee."

"No. I just mean . . . well, it's all new with Alec, and you and Jason have been together for years."

She leans forward, aims her words. "Jason and I have managed to stay together because we have our own lives outside of our relationship."

She doesn't understand. I don't want a life separate from Alec. I don't even want time separate from Alec. But I don't say that. "I know. I'm still figuring all this out."

My words seems to release some of her steam and she unbinds her fierce posture. "You do realize it's our last Alumni Weekend before we're alumni. And that I'm going to visit Jason and his family in New York for Turkey Day. I won't see you all break."

"We'll catch up when you get home. I promise."

"Sounds like a consolation prize. Besides, aren't you supposed to represent the field hockey team during the awards ceremony on Wednesday?"

"Shit. I forgot all about that."

"You forgot?"

Completely. Coach will be furious if I miss it. I can't miss it. So when I meet up with Alec in French class and mention this small but somewhat important commitment I'm locked in to, it kills me to see the color fade from his face.

Alec sighs. "Yeah, okay. If you can't get out of it. It's just . . ."

"What?"

"I made plans when you said you'd be free."

Ugh. "I'm so sorry. I seriously forgot all about it."

"Could you make an excuse? I promise it will be worth it."

I cringe, already hearing Coach's screams. "I can't. I'm the captain."

"Cocaptain. And you were the cocaptain, past tense. Field hockey's over now."

He's right of course. Still, his words kick up a flutter of fear in me. How can such a huge part of my life be over with unrelenting finality? And am I ready to move on?

Mrs. Sarter claps her hands and bellows out a too-cheerful French greeting. Alec leans over and whispers, "Our date's important to me."

I stare at the board and try to listen to the French babble Mrs. Sarter is laying on us, but I cut my eyes to Alec. His black Converse with the scuffs on the toe. The fray of his jeans where they rub at his sneakers. My mind bends to the class when I daydreamed over his citrus smell and the secrets he'd tell only me. And now that I know him I want even more. His secrets. His touch. My curiosity leaps thinking about what he could have planned just for me.

And that's all I can think about, even as Wednesday morning arrives and I ready for my mystery date with Alec. Drying my hair, I remind myself that accepting a trophy in front of a random crowd is meaningless. What matters is winning State, and we did that. Karen or Coach can trot out the trophy for the citizens of Sudbury to clap over. Still, there's a rumbling in the pit of my stomach telling me I'm missing out on something. Something I wouldn't have missed for all the world before Alec.

But that was before Alec. A lifetime ago.

Then, as if he senses my doubts, he texts: On ur way?

I check the clock. Eleven thirty. Out the door now.

Hurry. It's torture waiting.

I laugh. My stomach flitters with a lightness. Extreme much?

Stop texting and get over here!

Yes, sir.

Me likes it when u call me sir. ☺

I grab my keys.

When I arrive at Whites Pond, the horizon is a blanket of ivory. We only got a dusting of snow last night but the sky is bland and crisp, stretching like a sea until it reaches the stand of lodge pole pines framing its northerly side. I see Alec skating on the edge of the ice, over the shallow end where little kids swim in the summer. I walk to the lip of frozen water and Alec skates to a stop in front of me, his sharp blades spraying a crest of shaved ice between us.

"Good morning, Zephyr actually. Wanna join me?"

"I didn't bring my skates."

"No need." He coasts to the bank and pulls a white box from the snow. He removes a pair of figure skates, holds them up for me to see. "I come prepared."

I giggle my disbelief. "Are they my size?"

"Yep. Custom purchased." He places them in my hands.

"How do you know what size shoe I wear?"

"Ah, Zephyr. When are you going to realize that nothing about you goes unnoticed?" He pulls off his fleece and sets it on the snow. "Go ahead and sit. Put them on."

I slip my foot into the hard leather of the skate and Alec kneels before me. He positions my blade between his knees and pulls on the laces, starting from the bottom and tightening his way to the top of my ankle.

"How do they feel?"

"A perfect fit." But it's the tender way he's dressing me that feels too good.

He laces my other skate before pulling me upright. I lean into him and put my lips to his. It is a shock to feel the warmth of his mouth in the thick winter air.

His skates start their metered slide and I follow next to him, possibly overaware of how sexy his legs are as they pump into each glide. But I really am powerless over the staring, which is exactly how I manage to practically skate on top of the two hay bales. I swerve wide to avoid them at the last possible minute, but then I notice the third one, the one draped with a white tablecloth. Alec guides me onto one of the bales, as elegantly as if he's pulling out a chair at a restaurant. He takes a seat across from the makeshift table and produces a basket from under the cloth.

"Another picnic?"

He sets out a thermos and two mugs. "Too predictable?"

"Predictable can be good." The deepest part of me needs predictable. Needs to know that the things I rely on—the people I rely on—will be here tomorrow and then some.

"Consider this my small thanks for believing in me. No one's ever done that before." He pours two mugs of hot chocolate and I take a sip. Alec sets two croissants onto plastic plates. "One's chocolate and one's almond."

"Chocolate, please."

He grins, slides that plate in front of me. "I know it's not a Thanksgiving feast on top of a mountain the way you're used to."

Tears creep up behind my eyes for his remembering the details of my holiday tradition with my father. "It's perfect. No, it's beyond perfect."

"I wish it could be more. Next year will be even better. We'll plan it together."

"Next year?" I round my hands along the outside of the mug, my palms warming.

"I hope so." His eyes send me a pleading gaze. "Is that too much pressure?"

"No." The word, a whisper.

"So it's cool to tell you that nothing really mattered BZ?" He winks. "Before Zephyr."

"Catchy. And totally cool." I bite on my growing smile, one which Alec returns. It's the same for me. Alec stops me craning my neck to stare at the past. And he's made me feel worthy of Boston College. The campus is no longer some shadowy nirvana that only people with perfect families can access. He makes me feel like I belong. Here. There. Wherever I journey in between.

The minutes slip away as we skate together across the lake. The sun sits low on the horizon by the time I notice how cold I am. We duck into his car and my fingers crave the heat blowing from the dash. Alec pulls me close, lays me on his lap. I stare up at him as he strokes my hair. The windows fog instantly and I catch Alec's hand as he reaches for the defroster.

"Don't. It's like being in a cloud."

Alec's fingers fall back into my curls. "How do you always know the perfect thing to say?"

"Hah! I think the same thing about you."

He laughs. "So we should just hang out in our cloud and say perfect things to each other?"

"That would be heaven."

"Favorite day of the week?" he prompts.

"Sunday. It even sounds lazy." I cherish this familiar game that has become so much more than a game. The words seem simple, but they build a trust that feels deeper and stronger than anything I've ever known. "Favorite flower?"

"Tulip. It's kind of the only one I know." He laughs. "Favorite indulgence."

You. "My handmade back scratcher. For all those hard to reach places. Favorite time of day?"

"Midnight. The bridge between one day and the next. Favorite spice?"

"Pepper." I bite my lip and smirk. "It's kind of the only one I know."

He bends to kiss my forehead. "Well, we'll have to change that."

He asks me for my keys then and jumps into the cold. I watch him in the rearview mirror as he starts my car. My stomach drops. Is the day over? Something like regret washes through me, but why? And then as Alec ducks his body back into his seat, I know. He raises his hands to the vent, rubs them together furiously. I study his hands and know I want them on me in all the unexpected ways he's explored me before. I feel robbed of his touch and the loss makes me shudder.

"Cold?"

"I'm fine," I say, because how can I tell him that I crave his physical attention, that I feel lost without it?

"Follow me to my place?"

Favorite question? That one.

On Alec's couch, I stress about trying to appear casual as he cooks dinner, but when he returns to his living room, he looks dejected.

"It's ruined."

"What?"

"I made eggplant parmesan but . . ." He sits, hangs his head in his hands. "I swear I turned the oven off. I just left it in there, you know, until we got back. I was going to heat it up."

"It's okay."

"No, it's not. I promised you dinner out, but then I wanted you to taste one of my dishes, show you I'm not crap at cooking. Turns out, I am."

I rub at his back. "You can't stress over one burned dinner."

"It's not just one dinner. It's *your* dinner." He pulls away quickly. "And please don't tell me what I can stress over."

I raise my hands in surrender.

"Sorry, I didn't mean that." His tone is softer, but a vein at his temple throbs.

"I don't need a big meal. I'm kind of craving popcorn."

He lights. "Yeah?"

I nod.

He leads me to the kitchen where we microwave popcorn together. When the smell of the hot kernels permeates the kitchen I realize I'm starving.

With a huge bowl in hand, Alec and I return to the living room and I pop a kernel into my mouth. I resist scarfing the entire bowl.

He picks up the remote, navigates to Netflix. "At least I can't screw this up."

"You didn't screw anything up."

"Says you." He selects a movie called *Love Actually*. "I saw this title and thought of you."

"What's it about?"

"Um, if I had to guess?" He throws me a delicious smile. "Love."

"You make that leap all by yourself?"

Alec laughs and grabs for my free hand. He turns it palm up and traces the lines there. Slowly, tenderly. I watch Alec as he studies me, learns me. He concentrates his stare, clears his throat. "I don't really know what love is, but I think it might mean being happier than you've ever been in your life. I could probably Google a more articulate definition." His one finger follows the long line spanning my palm before looking up at me, his eyes darkly fevered. He spiders his fingers into mine, brings our clasped hands to his chest and rests them, together, over his heart.

"I'm so happy when I'm with you too."

Alec breathes a heavy sigh. "You're not just saying that because I've made it all awkward?"

"No. Of course not."

"And you're not just pitying me because I'm a shitty cook who can't even do something nice for his girlfriend?"

"Stop."

"Seriously, Zephyr. What do you even see in me? I'm some pathetic jock loser who got kicked out of school and will probably be blacklisted from any decent college. I have zero choice for my own future and I'm completely incapable of showing you what you mean to me."

"I love you, Alec." The words are out before I can stop them. Still, they feel right. Hanging in the quiet space between us. "You don't have to prove anything to me."

He presses his temple against mine, his face so close. "For real?"

"Nothing's ever felt so real." My love for him is a deep blue love. So blue it is black. Like an ocean under the ocean. The beginning and the end.

He purrs his cheeks against mine until his lips find my mouth.

"I love you too. So much." He kisses me and it is somehow new, weighted with this bold promise between us. When we pull away, my head is light. Alec nudges me closer and I want him to lay me on the couch. I want to feel his weight on top of me. I want to hear him say those three words a million times while the sun rises and sets around us. He slowly removes the bowl from my lap and my skin readies to be touched, explored. It is the height of anticipation how much I want to melt into him in this moment, so when he reaches for the remote I feel cheated.

"Let's see if anyone in the movie has it as good as us." He cuddles me closer, pulls a blanket over us.

This should be all I want. A movie with an amazing boy. A boy who loves me. Loves. Me. So why do I want so much more than a movie? How is it that I ache for his kiss, his breath against my skin? I want his fingers to bump over the small cut his watch made. I want the surge of heat he brings when we're alone.

I try to push away the tick of resentment as the movie's opening music starts.

Chapter 16

Thanksgiving is impossibly weird. Mom feels it too, like the pulses of all of our movements are different, hurried and slowed all at once. Mom overcompensates by talking too much and too fast. I want to tell her it's okay. That silence is okay. That I feel Dad's absence the way she does. That I miss him. But I don't say anything because my brain is a record scratching over the sounds of yesterday. The music of Alec saying *I love you*.

My phone vibrates and I pull it from the pocket of my hoodie just enough to read Alec's text. Happy T-Day.

Happy T-Day to you, I respond.

It's just u and ur mom today?

Yup. In this unexpected way, I feel closer to Alec knowing his father won't be at the Thanksgiving table either.

Try 2 have fun.

Before I can respond his next message pops up, one that seizes my breath. I want u all 2 myself this weekend.

Oh. I swallow hard as Mom bumps my hip to persuade me away from the swing of the stove door. She opens it, bends to baste the bird that looks way too big for just the two of us. The rush of oven heat campfire-warms the back of my legs. I pull out my phone while she's not looking.

Done.

Mom wipes her hands on the dish towel, surveys the overflow of food. "Set the table, Sunshine?"

I fetch the linen napkins and the plates from the sideboard, one less setting than our usual holiday table.

Mom finished her traditional bittersweet centerpiece with its twisting vines and tiny orange berries and it sits in the middle of our table now. I'm surprised by how this preserved tradition comforts me. She brings over the turkey, nods toward the carving blade.

I pick up the knife. Mom passes me the giant carving fork. I stare down at my hands and a memory tiptoes inside of me. Dad's hands holding these same utensils, wielding them in a way that orchestrated all our holiday meals. He was our family conductor. The person in charge. Can he be that again? I don't know if that's what he wants, if that's what I want.

Mom pours me wine.

"Did you mean to do that?" I ask.

"The drinking age in Canada is eighteen."

"We're not in Canada. Hence, Thanksgiving."

She shoots me a look. "I'm perfectly aware of what country we are in, but you are old enough to vote now so it only stands to reason that you are old enough to taste alcohol. I'd rather you try it with me than with your friends."

"Mom." I laugh.

"Could you at least humor me so I can make a proper toast?"

I raise my glass, the red wine painting the clear edges with its wave of liquid.

"To Zephyr and a lifetime of possibilities. To Boston College and all that it entails."

"Here, here." I silently toast a lifetime of possibilities with Alec.

Mom's glass *clinks* mine and I fake a sip. I dislike even the smell of red wine.

We eat while the food is hot but there is enough to feed a family of six. The leftovers heap over the tops of our storage bowls as we pack the fridge with all the dishes we couldn't possibly finish. I'm stretching Saran wrap over a container of yams that I know will get tossed in a few days. Mom unties her apron. "Not a bad feast, huh?"

I nod. It was great, except for how much I miss my father and our traditions. I feel like calling him tonight and am about to tell Mom so when she announces, "So I'll just go and freshen up and we'll leave for the Slicers?"

"What?" My head jolts from my task, the plastic wrap clinging into a puckered mess.

Mom removes her apron, folds it neatly even though I know she'll throw it in the laundry bin. "Pie Night. I want to change before we go."

Pie Night is an annual engagement for Gregg's family and mine. Mrs. Slicer bakes, like, a dozen pies every year and spreads them out on their dining room table—the sweetest buffet imaginable. Only I hadn't thought we'd be attending this year. "Um, are you sure you want to go?"

"Why not? We go every year."

My palms start to warm. "Yeah, I know, but new traditions and all."

She waves off my concern. "It wouldn't be Thanksgiving without Rachel's pies. Besides, it'll be good to catch up with her and Nathaniel, hear about the wedding plans."

Mom must see my face blanch because she adds, "You don't have to endure the details. You and Gregg can escape to the game room, like always." And then Mom disappears down the hall, humming.

I stack the rest of the leftovers, trying to decide whether I should tell Mom I feel sick and can't go. But by the time she returns to the kitchen, I realize I really want to go to the Slicer's. I want to see if Lani's there and if Gregg's making new traditions of his own.

Awkward. A bird carries this feeling on its wings as it crashes over and over against the window panes of my brain. Like that bird, I am stuck. In Gregg's basement. I stare out the French doors and see the pool where we swam almost every day this past summer, every summer since I can remember. When I hear Gregg's heavy footfall on the stairs behind me, I turn and he stops short. He's alone. "I didn't think you'd come."

"It's tradition."

He throws a short, bitter laugh. "Like Alumni Weekend? You didn't have a problem blowing that off."

"Now you're mad at me because I missed Alumni Weekend?"

He plops down on the couch and throws his feet onto the over-size coffee table. "I couldn't give a shit about Alumni Weekend, Zeph, though your coach may feel differently."

"It's likely." I move to the opposite side of the couch, sit on the arm. My feet press into the soft cushion. There's something about the warmth of the basement, the familiarity of my surroundings. Hanging out like we used to suddenly becomes all I want to do in this moment. I want things to be easy between us. Like before. My phone vibrates in my pocket but I ignore it. "I—"

He holds up his hand. "Wait. Whatever you're about to say will probably make me forgive you for being so out of touch lately, so can I just say that I've been really bummed that you barely even look at me anymore. What happened to us, Zeph? You get this boyfriend and suddenly our friendship isn't worth your time?"

"Gregg—"

"No. Seriously, Zeph. Some stupid drunken kiss was not enough to make you completely dis me."

"Things got complicated." My phone pulses again. I flick it off.

Gregg laughs. "Believe me, I know. I kissed you and then you fell for another dude. It's a story as old as time. It's lame. Who needs to rehash it?" He gets up, goes to his record player and selects Blind Faith's *Blind Faith* album. Older than old school. Gregg's the one who turned me on to vinyl. Claims iPods killed the rock star.

"But since you're with Lani now none of this even matters, right?"

He looks at me hard. "Lani has zero to do with this." He returns to the couch, sitting closer now. "I wouldn't have done it, you know. If I'd known. I'd rather have friend Zephyr than no Zephyr. So while I retain the right to be utterly annoyed by your assholery at Waxman's the other night, I do think I could muster the strength to call a truce in the spirit of Thanksgiving. Now that I've said my piece and all."

"Yeah?"

"Fuck. Of course, Zeph. I'm not the asshole."

"But I am?"

"I believe I've made my thoughts clear on this subject."

"But can't you see how you've basically done the same thing? Telling me"—I deepen my voice and do a shitty Gregg impression—"that 'you made your decision and I can make mine.' And apparently you've chosen Lani." I shift in my seat. "You were the one who blew me off first. You stopped coming to my games. You moved your seat in French. You were the one who changed, Gregg. Not me."

"Hah! Saying you haven't changed is like saying that kiss wasn't a mistake. I admit I went into a kind of self-preserving hiding, but how can you claim to be innocent in all of this?"

"Not totally innocent, but I don't deserve to be called an asshole. Unless I can call you one too."

The music swells around us. "Fair enough. It's exhausting fighting with you, or whatever it is we've been doing. I hate it, Zeph."

"I do too."

"Then why are we acting like total shitbirds to each other?"

"Like I said, things got complicated. But I could do a truce."

A shade rolls up over his features, revealing something like relief. Or gratitude? "Well, then at the risk of sounding completely corny on this day of giving thanks, I'm glad you came. I didn't think you would." He shakes my leg at the calf. "Now because I really need to change the subject . . . What's the news from Boston College? Are they begging for you yet?"

"No one's knocking down the door."

"They will."

"I'm not so sure anymore."

"Why? What's up?" And the tender way he focuses on my answer reminds me of all the other times I trusted Gregg enough to confide in him. Instances that can't be forgotten just because of some stupid kiss.

"I'm afraid Boston College won't want me because of my dad." It sounds so stupid when I say it that I'm afraid Gregg will laugh, tell me I'm an idiot. But he doesn't.

He doesn't break his gaze. "What does one have to do with the other?"

I have known the answer to this question since my father left his note behind like a footprint. "If I wasn't important enough, vivid enough, special enough to keep my own father from moving on to something else, how can I possibly expect the admissions board at Boston College to see me as anything other than a dull wannabe of a human being?"

Gregg breaks then. His chest cracks. I can see it in the way the force hunches him forward. He grabs my hand and swallows it between the sandwich of his massive grasp. "Christ, Zeph. Is that what you think? That *you're* flawed? How could you even believe that for a minute?"

A nervous laugh bursts. "You just called me an asshole a few minutes ago."

He smiles. "Well, that's different. That was my bruised ego lashing out." He squeezes my hand tighter. "Zephyr, your dad left because he lost his shit or something. Whatever it is had exactly nothing to do with you."

I wish just one atom of my existence could believe that.

"I've been thinking about this a lot lately. Ever since Jimmy split."

"You have?"

"Of course. It would be impossible not to. Here's the thing. Olivia and Jimmy got married when they were our age. You came along a year later. Imagine becoming a mother in the next few months. Imagine spending the next twenty years of your life raising that child. You'd love him or her and your life would be great but . . ."

"But what?" In my mind I've been the "but" in the middle of the junction of Dad's life. Zephyr: love her, but.

"His life might have gone by too fast. Maybe Jimmy needed

to be a kid again for a while. It's not an excuse. It doesn't make it right. But he's not a monster, Zeph. He's never been that."

"He was selfish."

"We're all selfish sometimes." His finger strokes my thumb, a metronome of affection. "And maybe that's why he's back. To set things right."

"How'd you know he was back?"

Gregg nods upstairs. "Please. Your family is pretty much the talk of our family. There's a lot of love for you here."

And I feel it. The multitudes of love.

Gregg inches back in his seat, releases my hand. "Did that weird you out?"

"No, not at all." He should know that even though I didn't want to kiss him, his words and his hand holding are perfect. "I'm really glad I came tonight."

The music drums between us.

"Zephyr. Don't ever for a minute think that you aren't the most special person on the planet. Boston College will want you. They'll prove me right. You'll see."

Tears of thankfulness well up in me and I can't think of the right words to tell him how grateful I am for his fierce belief in me. But then I remember I don't need words. Tonight has reminded me that with Gregg, I can just be.

By the time the night is over, I'm exhausted. I crash on my bed and pull out my phone. Finn settles into a ball at my feet.

Two missed calls. Four texts.

The first text: Call me. ☺

The second: U still eating?

The third: Where are u?

The fourth: Call. Me.

I don't even listen to my messages; I'm too eager to pull up Alec's number.

"Where have you been?" he asks quickly.

"Um . . . having Thanksgiving with my mom."

"I want you here," Alec says, his voice heavy.

I look at the clock: 10:16. "Now?" I hear Mom rattling around in the kitchen, likely trying to squeeze Rachel Slicer's chocolate cream pie into the fridge. I don't know how she has the energy to do anything when I'm so tired.

"Tomorrow. Five o'clock."

"Ooo . . . kay." I grin. "What's with the formality?"

"My mom's visiting my aunt for the night. I'll have the house to myself. Which is why I need you here."

"Well then, I need to be there."

"Good." I hear his smile in the word. "Because I love you, Zephyr."

My heart leaps. My body hums.

I have so much to be thankful for.

Chapter 17

If I could crawl out of my skin to get to Alec's house faster, I would. I've been on a high since last night and the only person I want to share it with is Alec. I brake for a light in the center of town and the red bulb seems brighter, crisper. Everything seems sharper thanks to Gregg's bolstering words.

My headlights brush Alec's garage doors just as his front porch light flickers on.

Alec jogs to my car, opens my door. "Why does it feel like forever since I've seen you?"

"Because I'm just that magnetic?"

When I get out, he pins me against the car with his hips, flirts his mouth to mine. "That is an understatement." He bites at my bottom lip. "You ready?"

I swallow hard, a lump suddenly blocking my throat. Ready for what?

Alec guides me into his warm house, through the living room and kitchen until we reach a set of sliding doors at the back. "I wanted to start here, considering our origins." He looks at my clothes, one long gaze over my jacket to my boots as he opens the sliding door a crack. "Unless you'll be too cold."

The frosty air whistles into the hot room and it steals some of my anxiety. "Outside is good."

He ushers me through the door. The sky is littered with stars and the air drafts cold into my lungs. "Over here." He leads me to a jungle gym, a smaller version of the one in the park, but only just. It offers monkey bars, a rope ladder, and a twisting slide. Lights poke out of the house's windows like yellow eyes, but the lawn is fenced off from the neighborhood and we are alone. Alec settles me onto the wooden slats of the platform. He hovers over me, a growing shadow in the dusk.

"I don't think it's a good idea to make me wait to see you." He moves the tip of his sneaker to meet the side of my boot. A rush surges, like always.

"Shall I rearrange the holidays then?"

"Yes, please. They are terribly inconvenient."

"I'll see what I can do."

"That's my girl."

"Your girl, huh?"

He stares at me. "I hope so."

I shift my back against the post, a blush deepening on my face.

"My shy girl," he adds.

"A little."

"Yet another thing I like about you."

"There's a list?"

"A list I've only started."

"So smooth."

He recoils as if I've slapped him. "Why would you say that?"

"I don't know. I didn't mean it in a bad way. I'm just nervous. Forget it."

"Forgotten." He stretches his leg so that his foot nudges my hip. My hand covers the curve of his shin. "Does it make you nervous that you touching my shin makes me crazy?"

"No," I lie.

He nudges his leg closer, stares at me for an eternity. A car drives slowly through the cul-de-sac before its engine fades. Otherwise, the early evening is calm. Quiet. Holding its breath for us.

Chilled air spirals around our bodies. I draw my coat closed at my neck.

"Please don't." Alec opens the collar of my jacket, separates the sides. He lets the back of one finger slide down the trail of my exposed neck and my lungs surge, push out toward him. Cool air floats over my skin, making gooseflesh rise. He hears my breath catch and withdraws his hand. He floats above me, half hanging from the bar above us. Disappointment floods through my veins, which he senses somehow. A Cheshire grin lights his face. "You like when I touch you."

So much. God, too much. My insides skip and I throw a nervous laugh. "I do."

"Would it be weird if I asked you to say it?"

I force the words out, my nerves tripping over their own edges. My insides blush with the admission. "I like the way you feel. Next to me. Your hands. All of it."

He nudges his knee between mine and I open my legs enough to let him in. The seams of our jeans rub together.

"I want to go slow if that's what you want."

It is. And isn't. "No."

Alec's fingers drop to find my neckline. He cups the curve of my neck, lets his thumb travel my tapering collarbone. I tilt my head back, giving him more room, more permission. His fingers glide to the V of my peacoat. He reaches inside and with one hand, he unbuttons two . . . then three buttons of my shirt. I try to look down, but he catches my chin, moves my gaze back on his. His fingers are so delicate I can hardly feel him at all. Instead, I feel the coil of desire twist between my legs.

He gently slides my jacket, my shirt down off my shoulder. I feel the cool air lick the slope of my chest. I wonder if my skin glows in the fading light. I wonder if he likes it. I arch my back, begging for him to touch me. But he doesn't. He leaves me like that. Exposed and wanting.

"Is it too cold?"

"No." The cold is a rush.

He sits next to me. Lies back. Props himself onto an elbow and stares at me. I try to breathe. I study his long body, the lean, rippled muscles that peek out from between the lip of his pants and his fleece that has hiked up just that little bit. I want to run my fingers over that band of skin, but I'm afraid I won't do it right.

His eyes drop to my chest. He breathes in. Stares. Breathes out. Stares. "Can I see you? Out here?"

"I'm right here." Even though I know what he means.

He rests his hand against his own chest, gazes at mine. "I want to see more of you. Just a little. Just for a second."

"Uh, no." I dart my eyes around the yard.

"There's no one here."

"I can't." I'm not even comfortable being on display when I'm fully clothed.

"You can." He shoots me a measured, steady glance. "It's only a matter of if you want to."

I let out a shaky laugh. "I don't want to."

"Okay," he says as he crawls to me. He lingers his lips to mine.

"But you should know that I want to see you. That I've never wanted anything more."

The electricity of his words melts me. My hand drifts to my bra, but then stills. Alec sees my hesitation.

"Only if you want to, Zephyr." He looks around. "It's just you and me. I'd do it for you. Anything you asked."

And then it visits again, that fear that I'm not good enough, that I don't know enough to make Alec happy.

I hold my breath, readying. My fingers slide my shirt to the side and roll the cup of my bra under my breast. The air greets this bit of my nakedness. Alec watches my face and I force myself to study his, to not look away.

And the thrill is deep. Like skinny-dipping. The raw, unlawful act of exposing your private bits to the air. I bite my lip, hard.

"God, I love you," he says.

A screech in the distance pulls my attention, asks me: What are you doing? This can't be right. I fold in my shoulders trying to hide, but Alec slips toward me with the confidence of a hunting snake. He holds his head steady just in front of me, right in front of my naked breast, but he doesn't touch me. I reach for his hair then, wanting him to cover me, protect me. My chest rises and falls with heavy breaths. I comb my fingers through his hair, trying to pull him closer.

He hovers. His hot breath teases me. I lean into him. The heat between my legs has become a voice and it's screaming inside of me. And just when I think I can't take it a moment longer, he reaches me. His hands explore my body and I pull him closer, deeper.

By the time we get to his bedroom I'm shaking. We lie on the bed floating somewhere between excitement and exhaustion. Alec's body is pressed up against mine, our shirts off. He strokes my hair at the temple. "I'll miss you," he whispers.

"I don't have to leave for a while."

He tucks a curl behind my ear. "No, I mean next year. When you'll be hundreds of miles away."

"I don't know anything for sure yet." Like how I'll survive without seeing him every day.

He kisses me on the cheek. "I love being with you, Zephyr actually."

I look through hooded eyes, flirting even now. I want to tempt his tongue to mine, tempt his tongue to my chest, my neck, my arm, my . . . I press into him harder, wrap my legs around his.

He drops his head into my shoulder. "Don't. I'll devour you right here."

Devour? A flush of want heats my skin.

"You have no idea how you make me feel."

But I do.

"I want to show you something." Alec reaches for his bedside table. I hear the wood slide of the drawer. "Here." He hands me a letter. I see the Michigan return address, know what it is. Hate that it is here, now, in bed with us.

I don't want to open it. I don't want to read the words. I unfold the paper and I know it makes me a shitty person, but I pray he got rejected. Gregg's words revisit, justify: *We're all selfish sometimes.*

But Alec didn't get rejected from the University of Michigan. The proof is in my hands.

He watches me read. "Crazy, huh?"

"Not totally crazy. I mean, you kind of knew, right?" I force a smile. It kills me I haven't heard from Boston College yet.

"What's wrong?" he asks.

Sadness haunts my face, cracks my words. "Nothing. I'm really happy for you."

He strokes my cheek. "So why do you look like you're about to cry?"

I sit up, pull a pillow to my chest. As if a square of feathers could protect my heart. "It just seems so real now. Everyone's hearing about their plans for next year and . . . I don't know . . . what if I'm the loser who gets left behind?" Gregg's pep talk is lost to me in this moment and I am rudderless again.

"You're not a loser, Zephyr, and I would never leave you."

My exhale sobs, my words rush. "Well"—I shake the paper—"this letter doesn't exactly inspire a lot of hope that we'll be together next year. They want you there in July, Alec. July. That's half a year away. It might as well be tomorrow. God, how can this all be happening? I was fine last night, you know. I was actually dumb enough to believe Gregg when he said I'd hear soon, that I was worthy of Boston College. But I don't have a letter. You do. You know what your future holds. All I know is how far away Michigan is. It's so far, Alec. On another planet far."

"Zephyr?"

I pull in a deep breath, try to calm my rampage. The silence of Alec's room battles with the cacophony in my head. "Yeah?" I whisper.

"What do you mean about last night?"

I stop, stumble. "What?"

He repeats the question with a hard stare, his posture suddenly too straight. "Did you see Gregg on Thanksgiving? You said you were with your mom."

"I was, but our families have this tradi—"

"You were with him last night?"

I search his eyes. "Not like that. I mean, yeah, I was at his house, but I wasn't *with* him with him."

"Is that why you didn't answer my calls?"

"No." I reach for him, but he stands, begins to pace the room. "I was going to tell you but then we went outside and everything was so perf—"

"Did you have your phone turned off?"

"Yes, but Al—"

"Did he try to kiss you again?" He bends to pick up my shirt off the floor, rounds it into a ball and hands it to me.

"God no! It wasn't like that." I scramble to the edge of the bed, shimmy my top on.

"You need to tell me if you're into him."

"I told you, he's like a brother to me. It couldn't be anything more. Ever." And then. "And he's with Lani."

"That's supposed to make me feel better?" he says, sarcasm dripping. "How do I know you weren't taking your tits out for *him*?"

"What? *No!* God, I would never."

His laugh comes hard and quick. "Are you sure?"

What's happening here? "I don't want anything to do with him that way. This is so nothing to freak out about. You have to trust me."

"Trust you?" He runs both of his hands through his hair and pulls at the back, locking his head between his stiff elbows. The muscles in his arms bulge. "How can I? You're over at his house without telling me, hanging out, doing fuck knows what, lying and telling me you're with your mom."

"I *was* with my mom."

He turns on me, quick. "You should have told me you were going over to his place. You should have answered my calls." His voice is almost a whisper now as he paces the floor. "You promised you wouldn't see him and you did. Then you keep it a secret. How do you think this makes me feel, Zephyr?"

"You asked me to hang back, Alec. I did. I barely even talk to Gregg anymore."

"You've justified all this in your head already, haven't you?"

"What? No!"

"If you really loved me you would ha—"

"I do love you." I reach for his arm, but he shrugs me off.

"I need to be alone."

"Are you kidding?" What about our perfect night? The night to ourselves? God, what have I done? "Gregg is so not anything to me. You have to believe that."

"You should have been honest, Zephyr. Half truths after the fact don't count."

"You're right. It was stupid. I should have told you right when I got here."

"No. You should have respected me, told me yesterday. I opened up to you. I came clean about my insecurities." He gives a harsh nod toward the door. "I have to think."

"Alec, please . . ."

He points to the door. "Go."

The one word is a punch to my gut, knocking the wind out of me.

I gather my coat and slip down the carpeted stairs, out the front door. The spotlights blare, accusing me in their own way. Tears bite against my skin but I brush them away as I start my car, wondering if I'll ever see clearly again.

It is an ache to breathe.

• • •

Somehow I manage to drive home, though tears obscure my vision. Maybe that's why I'm slow to realize Finn's in the middle of our dirt drive, spinning in circles, looking disoriented and lost out here on his own. Did Mom leave the back gate unlatched? I jump out of the car, kneel to him and he whimpers. His eyes are glazed, remote.

"You look like I feel, buddy. Come on." I take hold of his collar, walk him to my car where I have to help him jump into the front seat. He collapses in a heap.

"You scared out here all alone?" I slip behind the wheel and scratch his head. "You'll feel better when we get home," I tell him.

And I want this to be true for both of us.

Chapter 18

I bring Finn into my bedroom and set him onto a nest of blankets on my bed. He folds lazily, curls into himself. I fetch water, but he refuses it. I crawl onto the bed, wrapping his body with my own, and stroke him along the white patch that marks his breast. An occasional gurgle spills from his insides.

"Did you get into something, boy?" I nuzzle against his soft head. "You'll be okay. I promise."

I stroke his legs, down to his snow white paws. His fur is so soft and soothing that I close my eyes. When I do, I think of Alec.

It's impossible to stop picturing Alec in his room, his defensive posture turned away from me. He was so honest about feeling threatened by my friendship with Gregg. So vulnerable and trusting. Why didn't I just tell him I was going to Gregg's and that he had nothing to be jealous of? Why didn't I tell him Thanksgiving night on the phone? Tell him everything?

But I know. I know and I don't want to know. That parts of Gregg live in that deep, secret space within me too. Last night made me realize that.

I text Alec: Please talk to me.

An alert from HOCKEY BOY pops up almost immediately

and that's something. It is a fragile wisp of hope and I cling to it like a lifeline. Then, I read his response. I need time.

How much?

Crickets build a symphony in the silence. I refresh my phone maniacally, this whole thing making me mental. It's a miracle I fall asleep, but the morning doesn't bring me the text I'd been hoping for. I am greeted only by the sun, strangled by sadness.

I roll over in bed, lacking the energy to pull myself vertical, let alone shower or get dressed. I feel hollowed and vow I'll never keep the truth from Alec again. If I haven't lost him already, that is.

Finn shares my agony; he remains as mopey and withdrawn as I am.

Until I hear Alec's engine, thick with power as it approaches the house slowly over our rutted driveway. Even Finn's ears perk. Alec's car sounds like forgiveness. Like a second chance. I jump up, pull on a clean hoodie, and smooth my hair. I run to the kitchen. The engine purrs louder. Closer.

My pulse races faster than I can make my limbs move. I'm breathless by the time I reach the door, an apology wrapped in a promise hanging from my lips. I hear the cut of the engine, the whine of the heavy car door opening and then the slam of it closing. I grab at the kitchen door handle and yank it wide as a bloom of cold air rushes in.

My muscles freeze.

My head scrambles.

My heart drops.

"*Gregg?*"

"Zeph." He gives me a wink. "Nice bed head."

My brain empties. I'm only vaguely aware I've stepped aside to welcome him in when he crosses the threshold. I stare at the car in the driveway, Gregg's father's old truck. The engine too much like Alec's.

Fading hope shrivels me.

I close the door slowly, taking a deep gulp of the winter air. Finn greets Gregg with a slow but eager tail wag.

"What are you doing here?" My words are tight. Because he is not Alec. He's not the forgiveness I crave.

"Thought we could go for a drive up into the mountains like we used to."

"I can't," I say, too quickly.

He holds up his hands, surrender style. "Whoa, it was an invitation, Zee, not an attack."

My head is a mess. "I know. It's just . . ."

"What's going on?"

"I'm kind of in the middle of this thing with Alec."

"Alec's here?"

I shake my head.

Gregg pulls up a seat at the island. "Then I fail to see how your 'thing' with Alec affects me and you hanging out. You and I aren't complicated, Zeph. I thought we established this on Thanksgiving. That was you at my place, being my friend again, wasn't it?"

"Yes, but I made this stupid mistake and Alec and I got into this huge fight and we're kind of at a critical place right now."

"How does your 'critical place'"—he makes air quotes—"have anything to do with me?"

"Because you were the mistake." I stride along the edge of the counter hearing how awful that sounds. "I mean, not *you*, exactly, but hanging out with you. I didn't tell Alec and he's so hurt."

"Wait. What? You're not allowed to hang out with me?"

When he says it like that it sounds impossibly horrible. "No. It's just that Alec's really jealous."

"Of what?" His stare is laser sharp.

"Of you. He's jealous of you."

Then Gregg's face breaks open in a laugh. "Me? That's a good one. He's the one who got the girl, Zephyr, not me. Maybe you need to remind him of that."

I'd remind him if he'd talk to me. "It's just that you and I have all this history together. Alec feels . . . well he's not totally comfortable with us hanging out since I told him how you kissed me."

I should have just slapped him; it would have been kinder.

"Since you told him I kissed you? Huh. Well, all right then. There's that." Gregg stands, his palms pressed against the edge of the island. He taps the side of his thumb on the counter the way I've seen him do countless times before.

"Well you can tell Alec that my visit was an innocent one. I just came to tell you something but now I'm afraid it falls under the traitorous *too much history* category you two have so deftly established. I thought—stupidly it seems—that you might like to know a letter came from the coach at Boston College, basically offering me a spot on the team."

"What?" A shocked puff of air. "I didn't know you were accepted."

"I'm not, technically. I have to apply. But it looks like they want me. That's why I came over. Because you're still the first person I want to tell news like this to."

I pace my side of the island, trapped. I smell the fresh earth in the room with us, freshly potted rosemary, too happy.

"I guess it was too much to expect a congratulations, maybe even a hug. Or, I don't know, let's just think wild for a minute and maybe, just maybe, you could choke out an *'I'm happy for you, Gregg.'*"

"I am." I am. But Gregg here now, Gregg in Boston next year. It's all just bad timing. "I'm so ridiculously happy for you and I want to celebrate with you, but it can't be today."

"Why not?"

"I just . . ." God, I don't even know. "I just need a little space right now."

He plants his thumb at his chest. "You need space from me?"

"I know it doesn't make any sense and I promise I'll work it all out and everything will be fine, but for now . . . do this for me. Please."

"If that's what you want."

"It's just the way it is. For now," I add quickly.

Gregg neatly tucks the chair under the lip of the island before walking to the door. "I'd try to duck out with dignity but I think we both know that's not going to happen." He reaches for the doorknob.

"Gregg . . ."

"Bye, Zephyr." He disappears outside before I can take another breath. Finn whimpers at the closed door, Gregg on the wrong side.

I slide my back down the length of the wall and Finn comforts me as my bottom finds the floor. I'm grateful dogs never know when we don't deserve their affection.

When the sound of Gregg's truck disappears, I run down our road. I reach the mailbox and the weight of this moment siphons oxygen from the atmosphere. I flick my fingers over the door and open it quickly as if the metal is hot.

I remove the contents. Two items.

A cable bill.

And a letter for me.

But not the one I've hoped for. This square envelope is thick with weight. There is no return address so I know the sender instantly. I rip at the flap, tear the card free as the envelope falls to the ground, a scattered leaf among pine needles.

I gobble up Alec's words. In his handwriting. All for me.

There is never enough time with you, Zephyr Woyle. Love, A.

I scramble for the envelope, inspect the postmark date. Three days ago.

Before I disappointed him.

I bolt into the house, find my phone. I pace my room as Alec's voicemail picks up. Just hearing his outgoing message is enough to shatter me.

Then, the beep.

"Alec, it's Zephyr. Your card came today and it's perfect. You are perfect. I don't want to leave this on a voice mail, but needed to tell you that Gregg stopped by this morning and I told him we couldn't hang out. That was it. I wanted you to know it happened, even though nothing really happened because I don't want to keep anything from you ever ag—" A heartless *beep* severs my call and I am not entirely sure if the message was sent and cut off or if rambling-long messages don't get sent at all.

I am too full of cowardice to redial.

But in this moment I know why Mom let Dad back into her life. I would do anything to have Alec back.

Chapter 19

Lizzie calls me early Monday morning, before I'm even dressed for school. "I have news. Meet me before homeroom."

"I'm not going to school." It's a lie. Sort of.

"Why? Avoiding your coach?"

Shit. I forgot about Coach. She'll want to ream me for missing the trophy presentation and I can't take someone else hating on me right now. "Not feeling great."

"Okay, if I can't tell you in person, the news must slip over the wire: I got the internship." She waits a half beat before adding, "At the *New York* freaking *Times!*"

There is a skip somewhere deep in my chest. Like this accomplishment of Lizzie's has happened for me too. "Lizzie, this is huge!"

"My dad's the one who got it for me. I asked for a favor from one of the guys he worked with . . . over there." Lizzie's father was an embedded reporter in Afghanistan. Lots of guys from the platoon he was assigned to still keep in touch with Lizzie and her mom. "It's not like I earned it."

"Of course you did! Anyone can do a favor, Lizzie, but you're *worth* doing a favor for. Don't believe for a second you didn't earn this."

"You think so?"

"I know so." I swallow hard because Lizzie is leaving me. And because I have no idea where I'll be next year. That's when it hits me that her accomplishment isn't mine at all. "You better not turn into a Yankees fan or anything."

She laughs and it sounds different, like parts of her are already gone.

"So, when does it start?" I almost choke on the next part. "When do you leave?"

"Right after graduation."

"In *June*?"

"Change is all around us, Zee." The line falls quiet—but not the comfortable quiet of years together. The air, along with our future, has shifted. "I plan to do a feature story on you discovering some insanely relevant aquatic life form someday. That is, after I spend quality time fetching coffee for the *actual* writers."

"You're going to be a rock star." I hate the jealousy creeping in, filling the cracks carved by my growing insecurities.

"I'll settle for being employable at the end of the internship."

"You'll never have to settle. You'll see."

When will *I* see? When will I know what my next years will look like? It physically hurts having this little control over the outcome of my life.

I wish I were a better friend, someone who could feel joy for Lizzie without thinking of what I want for me. But I'm not. My head clutters with this new trifecta of abandonment: Lizzie in New York, Alec going to Michigan, and Gregg bound for Boston. Quicksand tugs at my feet. I'll be stuck in this town with no future. No friends. It will be as lonely as I am now. Or worse, and that I couldn't stand.

We say our good-byes and my bedroom walls breathe in, shrinking. How can four years of careful planning and calculated extracurriculars result in my entire future hanging on the decision of one school's acceptance board? How did I give over so much control?

I move to the bathroom to splash water on my face, brush my teeth. I coil toothpaste onto my brush and a hint of mint rises. It settles inside me, waking that part of me that Alec owns. The part he brought to life. Maybe I can't control the Boston College admissions board, my friends leaving, or even what will happen with my parents, but I can affect what happens between me and Alec.

I dress precisely and slip into school after homeroom, keeping my attendance off the radar. Alec has free study first period and I find him in his usual spot in the library. He's tucked into the over-stuffed chair that is hidden on two sides by obsolete card catalogs. The toes of his Converse peek out from where they rest on the ottoman just beyond the barrier. I steel my breath, brace myself against the wooden wall of Dewey for strength.

I can't do this. I hate eyes on me.

But then. No, I need to do this. Because I can't imagine what my life will be like if I don't do this.

The librarian's desk faces the nook where Alec sits, but she has her back turned, her attention focused on her file cabinet. Then she gets up, disappears into the records office.

I pull my coat tighter around me and move into Alec's space. He looks up, his face opening with surprise before his features withdraw into the memory of why he's mad at me.

I stand, wordless. I raise my fingers to the top button of my pea-coat, unbutton it with a twist. Then the next button and the next.

My coat falls open. I tug at one side, pull it down slowly. I let my coat slip along the length of my arms, its wool weight collapsing to the floor at my feet, exposing me in an enormously tiny black dress, every curve outlined. I steady, step out of the pool of fabric, stride toward him, making sure to rub my knee against the knob of his. He swallows hard, speech humming on his lips.

"*Shh*," I hush. He obeys, tucking his words into silence. I am next to him now, our thighs pressing together, the heat intoxicating. My mind fills with danger and fear, not knowing if my plan will work, or what will happen if it does. I settle slowly onto his lap. The dark hem of my dress rises over my bare thigh, an exposure he registers.

Wordlessly, he runs his hands up my thighs, raising my skirt higher until his hands cup my bottom. He yanks me closer on his lap and heat soars through me as we silently hold one another's gaze. I squeeze my legs hard around him, lean into his ear, and whisper, "Tell me you won't throw me off."

"That would be impossible."

"So then you'll hear me out, about how sorry I am, how you're the only guy I could ever want?"

His gaze trails the tight cloth over my hip, into the cavern where my stomach dips and then up to my cleavage. "Full disclosure?"

I nod, biting my lip.

"It's a little hard to concentrate with you"—he waves his hand along the length of my body—"like this."

"But I want to apologize. I need to make you see."

His eyes widen. "All I can see is this dress."

"Then maybe I need to take it off." The offer stuns even me.

Alec drains of color except for a darkness that films his eyes, making him look distant and alert all at once. "Are you saying what I think you're saying?"

No. Yes. I know only one thing. "I don't want anyone else."

"I want to believe that, but how can you be sure?"

"It's the only thing I do know. I love you." My heart waits to beat, braces for rejection.

But he doesn't reject me. He moves his mouth onto mine and our tongues meet with the fury of regretted absence. His hand slips to the scoop of my neck, and his thumb dips over my bra, wakes the skin around my heart. My body lights to the heat of his touch and the promise of more.

I pull away, whisper, "Get a pass for the bathroom. Meet me at my car. Upper lot."

"How are you getting excused?"

"I'm not even here as far as Sudbury's concerned. I just came to kidnap you."

"Why does that totally turn me on?"

I stand, pull down on the hem of my skirt. "Come on."

He runs his fingers through his hair, gets up and walks to the librarian's desk. He requests a pass and it is done.

I take a deep breath, proud for staying true to my plan, prouder still for not blushing during its execution. I pull on my coat and leave through the rear door, disappearing into the empty hallways and out to the upper parking lot where my trusty Volvo still holds heat.

Within minutes, Alec jumps in the car joined by a burst of frozen wind. "Does it count as kidnapping if I come willingly?"

I thrust the Volvo in gear. "Technically, no, but it's a minor detail."

"Well, your proposition was better than anything the library could offer. Where are you taking me?"

"My house."

"Then please, drive on." Alec lowers his head onto my lap and trails my thigh with a thousand bird kisses. I fight to focus.

When we arrive at my house I'm relieved the locked door buys me time. Turns out, I hadn't fully thought through the protocols for taking Alec back to my place.

"Can you get the key?" I point to the fake rock that sits inside the urn of pine boughs.

He hands me the ring. "High tech."

I laugh, open the door while Alec returns our security system to its not-so-incognito existence.

In the kitchen, I can't locate the bold feeling I had in the library. "Do you want something to drink?"

"No. That's not what I want." He peels my coat from my shoulders, then his hand slips into mine and he leads me to my bedroom. He closes the door behind us.

Alec plops onto my bed, folds his hands behind his head. "Stay there. I want to look at you."

My blush returns but I obey him for the endless minutes he gathers my bits into memory.

"So what's all this talk about an apology?"

"I made you a promise and I broke it. I shouldn't have gone over to Gregg's without telling you."

"That's a start. Now unzip the back of your dress."

"I'm sorry?"

"This is how I think this should work. Every time you make a compelling argument for my forgiveness, that unnecessary dress should get closer to the floor."

"So you're making the rules in my apology?"

He teases a smile. "I'm trying to restore trust between us, Zephyr."

I laugh. "Oh, is that what you're doing?"

"I hope so, yeah."

And isn't that what I want? His trust. Restored. I reach my fingers to the zipper along the back. I notch down the metal teeth slowly, air painting my skin with its invisible bristles. I stop at the base of my spine. The top of the dress loosens, the fabric bunches with the release.

"Now. What else?"

"I promise I'll always be honest with you. I don't ever want to fight with you."

"I don't want to fight either. I never want that, Zephyr." I pull my arms free of the fabric and stand before him in my new crimson bra. Alec stands quickly, gathers me to him.

"I'll do anything to make it up to you."

"You have, believe me. This is huge. What you were willing to do for me." He kisses me so softly then. He steps back, pulls off his shirt. The muscles in his stomach ripple and I feel a hunger inside. He pulls me in tight and we press our bodies against each other. "Trust goes both ways."

He lowers me to my bed and gathers me in his arms. I feel his hardness and my breath darts.

His fingers trail down to my hip and the fold of dress that rests there. My skin rises to his touch. "It killed me, you know. Not calling you."

"It killed me. Not hearing from you."

"It won't happen again. I don't want to be that guy."

"What guy?"

"You know how I told you my father's pretty much always gone?" I nod. He continues. "What I didn't tell you was how my mom constantly accused him of cheating. I don't think she ever trusted him. And I think my father probably is cheating. In fact, it wouldn't shock me to discover he has a whole other family. That's how crazy things are between them. But the craziest thing is that I think he cheated because my mom was always riding him about it. I think one day he figured, why not, you know, I'm catching shit for it anyway."

"I didn't know."

"I've never told anyone before." His fingers rake at my curls. "I think I have trust issues because of my parents' bullshit, but I don't want that for me. I want to know I can trust the person I love, that we'll always treat each other with respect." He twists my hip, flipping me to face him. My chest presses against his bare skin. My heart thunders with the rush.

"I don't want to do anything to lose you." He kisses me, butterfly wings sweeping. "I'm just so afraid of being a shitty girlfriend. What if I mess up again?"

"You won't."

"You can't know that. I could screw it all up like I almost did."

"We'll be okay."

"Yeah, until the next time. I've never done any of this before, Alec. Not really. I mean, not seriously."

"Done what?"

"All of it. Love. Sex. Dating someone this seriously. I've never met anyone who mattered the way you do."

"It's okay. I get it."

"You do?"

"Of course. Why do you think this fucked with my head so badly?" He pulls away, lies on his back, stares at my ceiling.

"I wish I were more experienced. Or better at this or something."

He props onto an elbow. "That's crazy talk. You're perfect, Zephyr."

"Not even close."

"Well, we'll figure out the imperfect parts together. And we'll wait until you're ready. Go as slow or as fast as you want. No pressure."

"I'm not sure I want slow," I say, and that distant darkness burns deep in Alec's eyes again.

He kisses me hard then, his hands roaming over my chest, until he stops, whispers in my ear. "I made myself nuts this weekend imagining you with Slice."

"I told you it's not like that."

"I believe you, I do." He moves off me. One finger trails a line across my skin, bumping into the soft hollow of my belly button. His touch, there—it steals my breath. "But I need you to prove it. This is important to me. Like I said, I've got trust issues. It's my baggage and I own it, but I couldn't handle losing you. I just couldn't."

I couldn't either. I don't ever want to feel like I have these past few days. "You have me. We have each other. I won't break your trust again. You'll see."

"So you're cool not hanging out with other guys? Slice included."

I roll toward him, covering my breasts with my arm. "But I told you—"

"I need to protect myself."

I see that. The way he needs to keep his heart safe. The same way I need to guard my own. "Okay."

"Okay?"

I nod. I want the two of us locked together. No outside world. No people. No pressure. Our own paradise.

"I'm enough for you?" he asks.

"More than enough." I reach out, stroke my hand down the hard cut of his chest muscles.

He glides his hand over my bottom, pulls me to him. "You make me happy."

But I am the happy one. With him, so close. Even closer when he admits his weaknesses. He holds me and I'm grateful for our openness, our willingness to negotiate all the terms that will keep us safe.

"Now that we're okay again, we probably don't need this dress, right?" His shy grin plays at his mouth.

"Probably not."

Alec moves on the bed, slips my dress from my waist. My heart races. He kisses a trail up and then down my body, guiding my underwear off my hips. I twist to cover myself as he stands at the end of my bed, unbuttons his jeans. His look asks, *Is this all right?*

Is it?

Am I ready?

I nod, holding my breath. He slides his jeans off his hips and they fall to the floor with a dull, weighted *whoosh*. Then he pulls down his boxers and I don't hear them drop. I can only process Alec, stripped before me, every inch of him exposed. Fear and excitement intertwine in a rope inside me.

Alec slicks up the length of the bed, links his bare leg with mine. My stomach flutters. My skin craves the blanket of him. And fears it.

"I can't," I say.

"I know. I want your first time to be special. More than special."

Relief hisses from my lungs. "I want that too."

"But that doesn't mean we can't enjoy making up." He presses his body into mine and the rush is so fast and sweeping that his hands build a white light in my head that threatens to explode.

He whispers in my ear, "I'm glad you like the way I touch you."

I hear myself answer from some faraway existence. "I like it so much."

There is a new sound coming from within me, a sound that denotes pleasure.

But when I hear it again, I realize it's coming from outside of me.

A small whimper.

A dog's whimper.

Chapter 20

"How long has he been behaving like this?" The veterinarian feels for Finn's pulse.

Finn lies listless on the exam table, his breath short and too fast. His tongue dangles from the side of his open mouth, as if he doesn't have the energy to wrangle it back into position.

"Just today, really," I say, hating myself. How could I have been so focused on Alec—no, on *me*—that I completely missed the fact that Finn didn't greet us at the door when we snuck home from school?

Alec rubs reassuring circles across the small of my back. The motion holds me upright. "The last time I saw Finn he was fine. I guess that was . . . what? A week ago?"

The vet looks at me through her glasses, slid halfway down the bridge of his nose. "True?"

"Yeah, but he was really tired the other day. I thought maybe he'd gotten into something in the woods." I wish Mom was here to say what she's noticed, but I couldn't wait for her to get home from work.

"Did he vomit?" the vet asks.

"No. I-I don't think so. Not that I saw. But he could have. I found him outside and he seemed disoriented."

"What's wrong with him?" Alec asks.

The veterinarian shakes her head. "Not sure yet. But he'll need to stay here. We'll hydrate him, observe him. And I'll let you know if we find anything conclusive in the blood work."

I don't know why her words aren't more urgent, why she's not hydrating him right now. Drawing blood. Making him feel better.

A sob rattles my skeleton. "He'll be all right, won't he?" I am nine years old again, helpless in the moments after Buttons was hit by the car that never stopped.

"We'll do everything we can," she tells me.

I press a kiss into the top of Finn's head wishing I could pour my good health into him. "I love you, boy." Grief crackles and divides my words. "More than anything."

The vet adjusts her stethoscope. "I need to know if you want us to place a monetary cap on his treatment."

"You mean . . . like stop fixing him if it gets too expensive?"

She nods.

"God no." But then I realize I'm not the one to make this call. I have no real idea about my family's finances lately.

"Give him the best care," Alec says. "I'll make sure the bill gets paid."

"Alec, no. You can't."

"I can, Zephyr. Money is so not something you need to worry about right now."

"Thank you." My words are not big enough.

"We'll do everything we can," the vet says. Her promise without a guarantee.

"Please be okay," I whisper to Finn.

Alec rubs my shoulders. "Zephyr, he's in good hands."

The vet lets go a small smile. "You're lucky to have so much support."

I am. I press my head to Alec's chest and he wraps me in his arms.

It's hard to concentrate at school the next day, so I don't. I keep checking my phone for an update on Finn, but there's nothing.

At least I have Alec back. That's almost everything.

When I meet with my guidance counselor, she informs me that two more students at Sudbury have heard from Boston College. That's everyone who applied early but me. Neither of them got in. It's another blow in a shitty day. I check the Boston College website even though I know early decision letters are sent by mail. It says so, right on my screen.

"I think it means you're in," Lizzie tells me after school. We're at the hockey rink, waiting for Alec's game to start. Lizzie's balancing a paper box of hot fries on her knees. "They're saving the best till last."

"I'm not so optimistic." Finn's being sick feels like a tiding of bad things to come. "I don't know what I'm gonna do, Lizzie. I lied about having a backup plan." I dip a fry into ketchup, but abandon it in the box.

"Plans are overrated."

"Easy for you to say; you're all set."

"You're letting Boston College's admissions board run your life, Zee. You can go anywhere in New England for marine science. The Earth won't stop spinning if you don't get in that exact college."

"I'm not so sure."

"Whatever happens"—she points a long, drooping fry at me—"I'll be here to remind you of how crazy incredible you are."

Her reminders will have to come long distance because we both know she won't be here for much longer.

"You'll hear soon, Zee. You have to. It's the way this stuff works."

"I hope so." I rub my hands together as the teams slip onto the ice. The crowd around us stands, pulls us upright.

When the puck is in play Lizzie asks, "Do we have to stay for the whole game?"

"Yes. I promised Alec I'd be here." The way he's been here for me.

"You two have been attached at the hip all week. Don't you need to come up for air?"

I wonder if Lizzie can remember the days when Jason was her air.

I hear a referee's whistle screech at the exact moment I see the red jersey take a dive across the ice. A collective moan rises from the crowd just as my phone barks. It's the vet's ringtone. I frantically rip off my mittens and dig my phone out of my pocket.

"Hello?" I say, just as the stadium hushes eerily.

"This is Atlantic Veterinary Clinic. We're trying to reach Zephyr Doyle."

"That's me. Is Finn okay?"

"He's ready to be discharged but the vet would like to see y—"

"I'm on my way." I grab Lizzie's arm and tug her down the bleachers, her fries spilling.

"What's up?"

"I need you to take me to the vet. They're waiting for us." Lizzie knows how much I despise the idea of any animal being locked in a cage, and my heart breaks for Finn, how he must feel so abandoned. I'm only vaguely aware of the crowd forming at the Plexiglas sides of the rink as we exit for the parking lot.

On the drive over, I gnaw two of my fingernails down to the

soft, fleshy skin underneath. I leave Mom a message on her cell phone and even though I know she has court today, I resent that she can't be here the way she'd promised.

Lizzie and I reach reception and an older woman I don't recognize greets us. "You can take a seat there, dearies."

We do and the wait stretches out in front of us like a desert highway.

My phone rings. It's Gaga: *I'm gonna run right to, to the edge with you.* Lizzie looks at me, her sideways glance asking, *Why is Alec calling you in the middle of a game?* The same question takes up residence on my tongue.

His reason: "The game had to be postponed."

"Why?"

"I'll explain in person. Where are you?"

The urgency in his voice causes a tiny earthquake to shake the building. I steel my nerves. "I'm at the vet. Waiting to see Finn."

"I'll be there in ten." He hangs up.

I give my phone—and then Lizzie—a puzzled look. "Strange."

"Things are weird," she says ominously. "Do you feel it?"

I feel it like a haunting.

Maybe that's why neither of us posits theories about why the hockey game was postponed or if Finn's ailment will be permanent, or worse—shorten his life.

The vet tech emerges from the back room with Finn's leash and I grab for Lizzie as I stand. "Where is he?" His lonely leash hangs listless from her wrist and I swallow back fear.

"He's in the exam room, anxious to see you. Come with me."

It is only when I see Finn greet me at the door that I start to breathe again. His tail wags feverishly and he presses his head to my thighs, forceful enough to push me over. His strength feels like a miracle. "Oh, I missed you so much, boy." He pushes past me, toward the closed door. I laugh at his determination, his personality fully recovered. "I know, buddy. I want to go home too."

"The vet will be right with you," the tech says before disappearing through the back door. I sink to the floor and bury my head in Finn's neck, scratch deep into his fur. He makes a seat of my lap and Lizzie's flash pops.

"For posterity," she tells me, approving the photo on her phone. "He looks really good, Zee."

He does. I am grateful.

The vet joins us in the exam room carrying Finn's chart. "Ah, Finn. One of our success stories." She smiles at me, at Lizzie.

"He's okay? What was wrong with him?" I ask, my words running so fast.

The vet makes a notation. "It's hard to say. There was nothing in his bloodwork and his energy seems to have returned to normal. It's possible he may have eaten some spoiled food."

"But I'm so careful."

She pulls the clipboard to her chest, looks sympathetic. "These guys are tricksters. They can get into things we'd never expect. The good news is that we found no signs of an external wound so he should be just fine."

"Thank you." I stand and latch Finn's leash to his collar.

"Keep a close eye on him for the next couple of days. Call us if anything changes."

"I will." She leads us out of the office and Lizzie's hand comforts my shoulder. "Thank you for coming with me," I tell her.

"Of course. Anything for the Doyles." We walk Finn to the reception desk. Across the room Alec stands, jogs to me.

"Is he okay?" I nod and Alec sighs a gigantic sigh. "I'm so glad."

Alec takes my hand, lifts it to his mouth, and kisses the skin below my knuckles. His lips are warm, soft, familiar. Lizzie clears her throat and Alec releases me, takes an apologetic step back.

"What was the matter with him?" Alec asks.

"They don't know. Maybe spoiled food."

"Yeah, like a half-dead squirrel served on the forest floor," Lizzie says.

"That's good though, right?" Alec sounds as relieved as I feel.

"It is. I feared way worse," I say as the receptionist slides a multipage invoice in front of me. My eyes drop to the total: $1,075.17.

Shit. Mom gave me a check this morning, but told me not to spend over five hundred dollars out of this account.

"I've got it," Alec says, snapping a silver Discover card onto the counter.

"What? Alec, no. That's way too much."

"I told you I'd help and I'm helping. I want to do this for you, Zephyr."

Lizzie lets out a low whistle. "That's a whole lotta helping."

"Lizzie's right. I can't let you. I can't accept that."

The receptionist arches her gray, untamed eyebrows.

"Zephyr. This is a gift. Take it."

"But it's too much."

"You can consider it a loan if it makes you feel better. Pay me back when you're thirty."

The elderly receptionist approves. "You've got quite a gent there, dearie."

"Seriously, Zee," Lizzie chimes, pushing on my elbow to just accept his generosity already.

"Thank you," I say, and know my words will never be enough.

The receptionist looks at me and then at the credit card, quirks one brow. I nod permission. She takes Alec's card, swipes it, prints the signature slip, which he signs before we all walk outside and load Finn into the backseat of Lizzie's car.

Alec locks his hand with mine, lowers his gaze to this connection. "Zephyr, I didn't come here just to help you with Finn."

A tingle along my spine. A warning. "What's happened?"

Lizzie sidles close.

Alec lowers his head, his voice. "Slice had an accident on the ice. He's over at Eastern General."

Lizzie gasps.

My bones melt from my body. "Is he okay?"

"He was talking when the EMTs loaded him into the ambulance. Coach said that was a good sign. But none of us knows. Not for sure. I came here to take you to see him."

I look to Lizzie. "I have to go."

"Yes, of course," she says. "I'll take Finn to your place, get him snuggled into your bed. Promise me you'll text what you know when you know it, okay?"

"Of course. Thank you." She wraps me in a hug four times the size of her.

"Call me if you need anything. If anyone needs anything."

And then I am in the car with Alec on the way to the hospital. The roads through Sudbury turn inside out. We drive through this alternate universe, one in which Gregg isn't the strongest person I know. A twisted around world where Gregg is vulnerable—a world I can't control. I press my two palms flat against my stomach trying to hold in all the sick that bullies me from inside.

My throat opens, croaks. "What happened?"

"It was the craziest thing." Alec's worry draws out his words;

they are stretched with disbelief. "One minute he had control of the puck and was skating so fast down the length of the ice—" He breaks off and my heart lunges over a cliff.

"And the next minute?"

"He just fell forward, Zephyr. Like a cut tree."

"But hockey players fall all the time." It's the nature of the game.

He shakes his head slow. "Not like this. I've spent my whole life in a rink and I've never seen anyone fall like that."

These are the words every athlete fears. They are the gateway to the end. Spinal injury. A concussion you don't return from. Fractures and breaks that keep you out the whole season—if you're lucky.

"Thank you for taking me."

Alec reaches for my hand, squeezes it. "Of course, Zephyr."

"No, I mean . . ." And I'm almost too fearful to say more because I don't want to start a fight or remind him of our last. "Thank you for taking me to see Gregg. I know this can't be easy for you."

He stops at a red light, turns to me. "This isn't about me, Zephyr. Slice is my friend too. All that jealousy stuff doesn't matter now. This is different, bigger than us, bigger than my stupid insecurities."

The light turns green and Alec moves us forward, closer to Gregg, closer to knowing something, anything. "I'm not a monster."

"I never said you were."

"No, but you were thinking I wouldn't want you to visit your friend when he's injured."

It was exactly what I was thinking. Fearing.

When we check in with hospital reception, we are directed

to the trauma wing. I push against the assaulting smell of bleach and worry and see Mrs. Slicer first. I run to her and she cocoons me under her mothering arms. Just a few feet away I see Mara clinging to Anna's leg. She doesn't storm at me. I can't imagine the weight of this moment that anchors her four-year-old body into stillness.

"I'm so glad you're here." Mrs. Slicer pulls me tight enough to join our heartbeats. "Gregg will be pleased."

"Can I see him? Is he okay?"

She nods, her eyes shadowed with anguish. "He has a concussion, Zephyr, and they want to monitor him for twenty-four hours, but he can have visitors. You can go in when his dad comes out. As you can imagine, we're all in shock. But grateful it wasn't anything more serious, of course. So grateful."

My relief is obvious. "I'm so glad. I was so worried."

She pats me then, the way I do with Finn, and I feel the depth of love in the simple gesture before she returns to her little ones. I have never seen the Slicer siblings so still. Muted. Like they can't pull themselves inside right again, even though Gregg will be okay.

I know how they feel.

Alec and I take a seat on the hard plastic chairs that line the hall. My leg bounces frantically, my nervous energy unable to leave me even now. When Mr. Slicer enters the hallway, I jump for my turn. Mrs. Slicer waves me in and I round the door to Gregg's room.

Gregg takes a moment to register. I think it's the concussion, making him slow until, "Hey Zipper." His smile a flower opening. "I thought you weren't allowed to see me. Isn't that the rule?"

I want to laugh at his sarcasm because it feels like a miracle that it's intact, along with his memory, his recognition of me.

Everything. "Alec brought me here. He's the one who came and found me, told me what happened."

Gregg adjusts to sit higher in his hospital bed, the thin cotton gown straining against the spread of his shoulders. "Huh. I guess all I had to do was get concussed."

"Not funny. Don't ever scare me like that again."

He laughs. "Sorry to inconvenience you."

I give him a light tap on the arm and he draws in his limb, wincing with pain.

"Oh my god. Did I hurt you?"

"Nah, just playing with you." He nods to the bag of clear liquid hanging above his bed. "They've got me on the good stuff. Everything looks pink. And swirly."

I smile. "Pink and swirly, huh?"

"Except you, Zeph. You look like shit." He webs his fingers with mine and I feel his beating pulse there. Strong. Reliable. "You know . . . if that were possible."

"You scared me, Gregg. I-I don't know what I would have done if . . ."

"Hey, no bringing down the half-dead guy."

I smack him on the arm and he laughs.

"You know I'd never do anything to hurt you, Zephyr."

There are promises, apologies, confessions that fight for the chance to be heard, but a faint knock on the door silences me. I turn and Alec lifts his eyebrows, asking permission to enter.

"Come in, man," Gregg says, his tough guy athlete voice joining us in the room now. Gregg drops my hand, positions himself even higher in bed.

They exchange the manly secret handshake of locker rooms and Alec tells him, "You had us all worried."

"So I hear."

"What happened out there? One second you were fine and then . . ."

Gregg shakes his head, trying to pull up the memory, but I watch it swim away from him, lost to the river of pain medication.

"Coach told us it was a problem with your skates," Alec says.

I turn to him, this news new. "That's why the game was postponed? Because—"

"The coach suspected sabotage," Mr. Slicer interrupts. I turn see him at the doorway, his hands clasped behind his back, his face looking like this is the last news he wants to share.

"Sabotage?" I scramble for the meaning of the word because Mr. Slicer can't possibly mean it in the traditional sense. The treacherous sense.

"The blade on his skate was bent. By a machine. I just got word." Gregg's dad shifts his feet, and I can feel how restless he is.

"This is crazy," I say. "Why would anyone do that to Gregg?"

"Probably because he's the best." Alec says. "Maybe Hamilton wanted to guarantee a win."

"That's beyond messed up," Gregg says.

"We'll see what the Division Board and the police find out." Mr. Slicer is all authority. "We'll know more soon, I'm sure. For now, Gregg should rest." Today is the first time in years I've heard Gregg's parents call him by his first name, which cements the gravity of this situation. "Alec, would you let your teammates know he'll be fine in no time? Most of them are downstairs, clogging up the waiting room. You can send Coach up. And Zephyr, thank you for coming. Tell your mom and d—" He lets the word hang.

"I will." I move to Gregg and kiss him on the head, in that place where Rachel Slicer always kisses me.

On my way home, Alec holds my hand as I call Mom and fill her in on Finn and Gregg. Just bringing her up to speed propels me into a new exhaustion, but I'm glad the news for both of them is ultimately good. At home, Alec holds me for a long time before I get out of his car. "Everything will be all right," he tells me. And I want to believe him. I find Finn in my bed and snuggle him so tight our bodies warm one another.

My fingers play with my phone, my thumb hovering over Dad's number. I want to make good on my promise to Mr. Slicer. I want to share the news that Gregg will be okay. And I want Dad to know about our scare with Finn.

And I would call him if we could only talk about Finn and Gregg. But I can't make room for the other stuff we need to talk about.

When Finn falls asleep, I go to my closet and pull out the Box of Dad. Inside, there's a handful of *Classic Car* magazines and his acrylic paintbrushes. And the picture of me he kept on his desk, the one where I'm on a slide and Dad's shadow stretches out in the photo so I know he was the one ready to catch six-year-old me. I gathered these things when he left because I didn't want to lose all of him. Then. And still.

When the phone rings I reconnect with Alec and his comfort. His safety.

Chapter 21

Alec drives the familiar roads of Sudbury but it's a secret as to where he's taking me. We stayed up too late on the phone last night, unable to break our bond after a day twisting in our combined worry over Finn and Gregg. But there's no room in the simmer of my excitement to feel tired now.

Alec turns onto a wooded dirt road, his lights catch on a giant white sign: FUTURE HOME OF APPLE BLOSSOM LUXURY VILLAGE. He drives carefully over the rutted road. "I'm not buying a condo, in case you're wondering."

I chuckle. "Good to know."

He leans closer to his windshield, peers out. "Construction stopped out here a while ago. My mother's the developer and she put things on hold because of the economy."

"You come here a lot?"

"It was my secret place before I met you."

"What's your secret place now?"

His eyes flicker. "Don't laugh?"

"What?" I say, too much laughter in the word.

"Nice," he mocks.

I straighten my face, my posture. "Okay, try again. I'll be good."

"You," he says.

"Me what?"

"You're kind of my secret place now."

I stare at him. "Oh."

"Yeah."

We drive in silence down the narrowing dirt path until we are face-to-face with an abandoned front loader. It waits against the tree line, its headlights and front bucket looking like a giant yellow smile. But when Alec cuts the engine, the machine disappears and darkness drapes over us like a villain's cloak.

"We're here."

"We are?" There is no *here* here.

Alec rotates to face me, raises his hand to my cheek, caresses my jaw line. I feel his calluses, rough and bumpy against my smooth skin. He turns on the cabin light, casting away the darkness of this secluded place. "I'm glad it's just you and me tonight. No more drama. Everyone's going to be okay and we can just be. Here together."

"I'm glad too."

"Good. Because I hate sharing you."

"I know what you mean." My voice is low now, the tone made for Alec. It's my voice, but filled with steam, a low, bubbling heat that syrup-coats my words.

Alec smoothes the run of my collarbone with his thumb, rubs the length of it, his eyes fixed on its confident rise. "Even though I see you every day it's not enough."

"It's the same for me." The night ticks soft around us. There are no people. No cars. No emergencies. No sounds. Just me and Alec in this tucked away space.

Alec's lips move closer to my ear, his breath hot and quick. My neck warms, my insides twist in a spiral. "You're pretty much all I think about."

There is a rush of something like gratefulness for my love protected in his safe hands.

"Wait here," he says.

"Where are you going?"

"Just outside for a second. Promise."

A short, nervous laugh arrives. "Isn't this how, like, every horror movie starts?"

He cracks his door open. "Trust me," he says before exiting the car. He wrestles with something. A coat? A blanket? He pops the hood and I can't see in front of us. My mind races until I see Alec at the tree line, the dark too dark to make out his movements. Then Alec opens my door, his beautiful face smiling for me. "Come outside." He ushers me toward him with the sweep of his arm.

Relief waterfalls through me as I take his hand. But then, a shiver ripples. "It's freezing out here."

"Not for long." Alec walks me to the edge of the forest and that's when I see he's spread a quilt onto the dropped pine needles. Two pillows rest at the top of the blanket. A bed in the woods. Alec lifts the quilt and invites me to tuck in. I'm surprised when my hands find heat.

"Is this . . . ?"

"An electric blanket." I hear the grin stretch across his face.

"How do you have an electric blanket out in the middle of nowhere?"

"It's a nerd trick I learned in shop. I jimmied the extension cord to run off the car battery. Get warm. I'll be right back." I watch him go to the trunk, drape another blanket over his arm. When he returns, he layers it over me and the weight is a luxury. He sets down the familiar picnic basket, takes off his coat and burrows in beside me.

"Ever moon-gazed before?"

"Not like this."

"Good. I'd hate to be redundant."

"I don't think that's possible."

"It's full, you know. The moon."

I look above the trees, find the white round, its paper skin. It sprays its light over us, as romantic as candlelight. "It's beautiful."

"Like you." I pull his hand up, press it to my chest. He leans against the place of my heartbeat and studies my features, memorizing me. "I'm really glad I could be there for you. You know, with Finn and Gregg."

"Me too. I can't even tell you how much." I smile under his stare and a new kind of warmth fills me. I hear a horn beep somewhere out on the road but it's as if the sound comes from a different dimension. Like Alec and I are hidden in a pocket of forest made especially for us. "I couldn't have gotten through it without you." I trace the soft swell of his cheek.

He pushes into my touch. "I want it to be like that always. I want you to come to Michigan with me."

My heart trips. "What?"

"I don't want to be without you."

I can't stay here without him, but go to Michigan? "I can't go to Michigan."

"You haven't been accepted to Boston College yet, right?"

A twist in my core. "No."

"Promise me you'll think about it then. You know, as a back-up plan or whatever. All I know is that the next four years will suck without you."

Four years. It's a lifetime.

"We're good together, Zephyr. Maybe we shouldn't leave that behind."

But I'd be leaving other stuff behind. "I've never even considered going to college anywhere else. I visited the campus when I was a freshman and it was like I knew I belonged there. That it was my future. Have you ever felt that way?" I don't tell him that shortly after Dad left, I toured the campus and had a panic attack walking into the library. How since then I haven't felt totally big enough, strong enough, to claim my future. Until I met Alec.

He flattens his hand over my heart. "That's kinda how I feel when I'm with you. Like, I don't know . . . like it's where I belong."

"Yeah?"

A laugh tickles at his words. "I guess you could say you're my Boston College."

"Careful. That's a bold statement."

He smiles. "I know."

Oh.

Alec moves on top of me, his body slicking with the precise grace of water.

His chest hovers over mine, our hearts building a staccato rhythm. And when he fills my mouth with his kiss, I want our heartbeats to sync. I want to forever be connected to this person. All at once he feels like my now, my future, my everything.

He unbuttons my coat and I wriggle free of it. He raises my shirt, his callouses skating across my flesh. He cups my breast and I arch closer to his touch, his warmth. He presses his kiss deeper into my mouth and I move my tongue against his.

He fumbles for the lip of his shirt and I tighten. Is this it? *The It?* I tense.

"Are you okay?"

"Yeah. I don't know."

He kisses me softly. "It's all going to be okay. I promise."

The blanket slips to his waist as he draws his shirt over his head, lifts off his T-shirt. His torso flashes naked to the night, his flesh almost golden in the moonlight. "Man, it's cold!" A shiver shakes along the length of his body.

"I kind of like it," I say, even as a bolt of cold convulses my spine.

"Do you? Hmm." He disappears under the blanket and pulls off one of my boots, cradling my heel. Then, the other. He tosses my boots behind him with a playful gesture that helps cut through my anxieties.

Alec pulls off my socks and my toes wriggle. He massages the arches, and I'm shocked by how good it feels. Then he slides his hands along the length of my legs until he reaches my waist. He pops the button on my jeans with an impossibly smooth motion. My hand flies to my stomach.

"It's okay, Zephyr. We'll go as slow as you need."

"You're sure?"

"Surer than sure."

I lift my bottom and he slides off my jeans, abandoning them somewhere in the vicinity of my socks. The freezing December air rushes into our makeshift bed and shocks me with its intensity. I have never felt so alive. I wear my skin in a way that is truly mine for the first time. All because of Alec.

He undresses down to his boxer shorts. My breath quickens. His shoulders rise, a white crest against a dark wave. He crawls into our sleeping bag and folds me in his arms. He kisses my mouth, my neck, my jaw.

Then he stops. I hear the hollow snap of the elastic waist of his boxer shorts. "Would it be all right if I took these off? They can be quite cumbersome, you know."

"Is that so?" A nervous laugh tickles the corners of my words.

"Seriously, Zephyr, it's your call. I don't want to do anything you're not comfortable with."

He locks eyes with mine for moments that suspend time. I think we will freeze out here, that they'll find our frozen bodies in the spring thaw. But there is a current of heat, too. Just between us. Keeping us warm.

"It's okay."

"Positive?"

I nod softly. The gesture is fear and want coiled into one rope of movement.

Alec maneuvers out of his boxers, freeing one hip, and the next. I catch glimpses of the cut of his chest, the column of his hips, the flesh of his thighs.

"Now you. Sit up."

I do and Alec reaches around me to find the clasp of my bra. Alec watches me, his eyes steady and transfixed. Slowly, he twists the clasp and the fabric releases. I move to hold my bra in place.

"It's just us, Zephyr."

I look around and he's right, there is no one else with us. Only something. This thing between us that might happen tonight. That we talked about happening tonight. It crowds the space between us, this huge thing. But it also promises to erase any space between us.

I bite my lip as I peel aside the blue lace cups. I'm still self-conscious about my body, this new bra, the way he watches me like an eagle hunting prey. The way my flesh rises to the cold. But he accepts me with his eyes, the way his gaze lingers.

Alec leans back, his breath catching. "You"—he swallows hard—"look amazing."

My breath buckles. I want to be beautiful, sexy, all the things he wants. But I need him in order to be any of these things.

He strokes my face and then my chest. I could stay like this for years. My breath trembles. Above me, a maze of early stars blaze white and I am alive.

"Tell me." He nuzzles his face into the nape of my neck. "Tell me how much you like being here with me."

"I don't want to be anywhere else." And it is the truth, even if I am petrified of all that could happen between us out here, under this blanket of moonlight.

He kisses me and I fold into him. His strong arm tucks me under the covers where we become heated, together. Outside our blanket, the world is another place, not our place, something separate from our two entwined bodies.

He raises my arms. One by one, he pins them onto the cold pillow. He kisses me deeply, warmly, his entire body coiled, inseparable from mine. My body becomes liquid beneath him, melting into his touch. I disappear in his breath, his heat, his fingers tracing my every inch. And then there is the quick rustle of plastic and then . . . an unexpected pinch on the inside of my flesh.

My body stiffens. My brain fires with fear. I can't do this. I don't know how to do this. Am I ready to do this?

He breathes calm into my ear. "Shh, it's okay, Zephyr. You can trust me."

But I can't. Not now that this is *the moment*. My mind swirls with every sex conversation I've ever had with Lizzie, every *Cosmopolitan* article I blushed over. And I don't feel prepared for what is happening *right now*. My hips speak instinctively, twisting away from his. I close my legs.

He pulls back, strokes my hair away from my face. "I love you, Zephyr."

He kisses my forehead. "I want . . ."

He kisses my nose . . . "to feel . . ."

He kisses my lips . . . "all of you."

My heart catapults.

"Don't you love me?"

A rasp. "Of course." I force my body to relax.

"Then be with me, Zephyr Doyle."

"I'm scared."

"There's nothing to be afraid of." Alec kisses me and my pulse quickens. "You know I'd never hurt you, right?"

"I do. Of course."

Alec moves slowly on top of me and I trace my fingers along the hard ridges of his back. I watch and listen, trying to capture every sound and smell. The way a few defiant leaves rustle on the limbs above us. Alec's mouth hot and cavernous. The wink of star-light above. The pressure inside me building.

Alec kisses the cove of my neck. I shake off the fear that's rising in my brain and listen to what my body wants, what my brain trusts. The way my heart beats: *Al. Ec. Al. Ec. Al. Ec.*

His eyes meet mine. "Are you okay?" His words are whisper soft, a private language.

Am I? It's hard to know in this cyclone of nerves and fear and love. My tongue answers when my brain can't. "I am." I wrap my arms tightly around him, my thighs pulling his hips closer. Slowly. Slowly. *Slowly.* He watches my face as he fumbles under the covers. For an instant, I think he will change his mind, tell me he can't, that he doesn't really love me. That none of this is real.

Until I feel that pinch, stronger this time. My entire body clenches and I gasp.

The pain grows. Becomes excruciating. A knife of lightning across a still, dark sky.

"You are perfect." Alec's gaze hangs distant and fogged under his flopping bangs. Then he moves gently. Joins me. Fills me. As if disparate parts of me connect as one whole for the first time. Alec kisses my lips. We lie interconnected like that for a minute, an eternity.

He and I moving together, in a new kind of forever.

"I need you, Zephyr. I want you at Michigan. With me always."

I need you too, I want to say, but words are beyond reach as I fall into his need . . .

the motion of his body . . .

the promise of us. . . .

Later that night, I lie in bed not moving. From the record player, Joan Armatrading's honey-slick voice bleeds love into the very air around me.

Oh the feeling, when you're reeling.

There's more beauty in you than anyone.

The memory of Alec cocoons me. Protected. Secret. Mine.

I don't call Lizzie. Trying to put tonight into words would erase its magic.

I hold tight to Finn, tell him the way my heart has found wings.

Before I close my eyes, I get a text from Alec: In ur dreams tonight, imagine me with u.

Me: As if I have a choice.

My eyes draw heavy while staring at the ceiling, trying to press every minute of tonight into a sacred scrapbook of memory.

Just before I fall asleep the air shifts slightly, as if it also knows that everything has changed.

Chapter 22

I wake in someone else's skin. Or mine, but different.

Finn lies spooned into me, his breath steady and so beautifully normal sounding. He stirs when I sit up. I watch him jump down to wait at my door like he'd never been sick at all. I let him out and he pads happily down the hall as I make my way to the bathroom.

In the shower, the spray hits me like Alec's touch, awakening me everywhere. I swab my neck gently with my loofah sponge because I don't want to fully wash him from my skin.

When I make it to the kitchen, Mom's hunched over a cup of coffee at the island. I register her spacey stare, how it's not even slightly focused on the newspaper opened before her. Then I panic. I hadn't thought about Mom. Can she smell the sex on me? Does it linger on your skin like scented body wash? Just as I'm about to pivot on my heels and bolt back to my room, Mom looks up.

"Good morning, Sunshine."

"Morning." I wonder if my voice is different now too, if she can *hear* some indication of sex.

She picks at the edge of the newspaper.

"You okay?" She doesn't look so okay.

"I just got off the phone with Rachel."

The room stills around us. The windows are shut tight against the winter so there is no breeze, no rustle of leaves, no birdsong. I am trapped in the airless space of my selfishness. I've barely even thought about Gregg. "Is Gregg all right?"

"Rachel called to say that he's home, resting. I was hoping you and I could go visit him later today." Mom's worry flinches her shoulders.

"Did she tell you he's going to be fine?"

"She did. It just hit too close to home. I couldn't help thinking what if it had been you."

"It wasn't. I'm fine. Gregg's fine. Rachel will be fine once Gregg's back at school." I'm not certain if my words are aimed at reassuring her or appeasing my guilt.

"When do you want to go?" I fill a bowl with Cheerios. "If we head over around lunch we could grab him a Slice Special from Fernalds. It's named after him. Because it's his favorite."

She closes the newspaper. "I'd like that. And we can pick up some penny candy for the little ones."

"Sure. Give them all a sugar high. Rachel will love you for that."

Mom winks. "What kind of aunt would I be if I didn't spoil the girls?"

I open the fridge, grab some milk. "A lame one."

"Exactly. I can't have that."

I bring the milk to the table but don't pour it. "So, does Dad know about Gregg?"

Mom tries to hide her surprise, but I can tell I've caught her off guard. "He does. I told him last night. Why?"

I'm relieved. This feels like something Dad should know

about, even if I couldn't make the call. "I guess I'm just wondering how much you and he talk or whatever."

"We talk a lot, Zephyr. Really talk. In a way we didn't for a long, long time."

"That's good. I mean, if that's what you want."

She reaches for my hand, blankets it with hers. "I think I'm still trying to figure out what I want. Parents don't have all the answers, you know. Just because we're older doesn't mean we're always wiser."

"But you forgive him?"

She leans back in her chair, contemplates. "I think forgiveness is a process. I'm not there yet. I don't think I'll ever be okay with the way he left, that ridiculous letter and his disappearing."

"But you let him back in."

"I did. Because I love him, Zephyr. I always have. And we both made mistakes. Some big. Some smaller. I'm just trying to figure all this out, same as you." She cascades her finger over the ridges of mine. "One thing you learn by the time you're my age is that life is made in the mistakes. It's impossible to get it right all of the time. And in a weird way, I admire your father for doing what needed to be done."

"How can you admire him?"

"I know it sounds crazy. Believe me. But the split has allowed us to come together even stronger. Your dad and I let a lot of things get between us, push us apart. When he was here, I didn't want to see it. When he was gone, it was all I could see."

Mom's face softens as she talks, veils with peace. "I didn't know."

"We haven't enjoyed each other's company like this in a long time."

"I think it's great you're happy, Mom."

"And I want that for you."

"I think maybe I have more questions than you did. I want to know everything. What he felt like before he left and for how long. How many years he'd been planning this."

Mom laughs. "I'm still not done asking him questions."

"Really?"

"Your father spent our first few meet-ups like a witness on the stand."

I'm surprised by my laugh and the connection I feel with Mom after knowing she badgered him the way my mind's been badgering me. "I've been thinking of calling him." Since my fight with Alec showed me that forgiveness can be a gift.

"I think I've made my argument clear on the subject of regret." She taps my hand, stands. "And it's okay to give him hell, Zephyr, if that's what you need. Tear into him, yell at him. Whatever works. Just don't keep it bottled up. That's how your dad and I got here in the first place."

"I'll think about it."

Mom pushes in her chair. "Clock's tickin'."

"But no pressure, right?"

"Not from me."

Gregg doesn't even appear an inch sick when Mom and I enter his room. His face glows. He's embroiled in a game of NHL15 and his sister Courtney looks relieved to have the interruption. She throws down her defeated controller.

"I'm going to get snacks," Courtney tells him. "You cheat anyway."

Gregg laughs. "Six girls in this house and I get exactly zero sympathy."

Mom goes to his bedside, kisses him on the cheek. "It's nice to see you looking so healthy."

"Don't tell my mom, but she's making a way bigger fuss about this than is necessary. I feel fine."

"I think your mother has the right to be scared about a concussion."

"Athletes get them all the time."

"Yes, and their moms worry all the time."

"Fair enough," Gregg tells Mom.

"Well, I'm glad I came. I can see you're on the mend and I'm no good at video games, so I'll leave you two to catch up."

When Mom leaves the room I climb onto the end of Gregg's king-size bed and sit cross-legged.

Gregg nods toward the bag in my hand. "That smells suspiciously awesome."

I hand it over and he sniffs deeply. "A hand-delivered Slice Special? Why Zephyr Doyle, whatever did I do to deserve your attentions?"

I flick him in the leg. "When are they springing you?"

"Doc says I can go back to school tomorrow, but no hockey for at least a week."

"Ouch."

"Yeah, I have these headaches that come and go. She tells me that's normal."

"Still."

"I know. How will my adoring fans cope?"

I flick him harder and he rubs the spot.

"Seriously though. What's with all the attention? Is your presence here Alec-sanctioned?"

"Don't."

"It's not my fault the kid's got issues."

"We all have issues."

"Too right. So I can't bag on him for being a jealous ass?"

"No, you most certainly cannot. You may have been too doped up to remember, but Alec was the one who brought me to the hospital."

"The last thing I want to hear is how he's your knight in shining armor."

I blush. "No armor, just shining."

He studies me then. "What's different? You're looking very girlie in this moment."

My smile spreads until I think maybe he can see the sex on me.

"Don't tell me you really like this guy."

"Would that be so wrong?"

"Yes. I thought you coming here to fawn over me was a sign that you were ready to declare your love for me."

"Funny."

He laughs. "I wasn't trying to be funny."

"And yet here you are, being hilarious."

"Hmm. Deflection. Nice technique." He nods toward his bed-side table. "Rummy?"

"Sure. If you can take an ass kicking in your condition."

"Hah! Now look who's the funny one."

I hand Gregg the cards and he shows off with a fanning Vegas shuffle. "Have you had many visitors?"

"A few. All girls, of course."

I smile. "Of course."

"Has Lani been around?"

"Look at you all curious about my love life."

I roll my eyes. "Forget I asked."

"I will since there isn't much to tell. So, gin rummy or five hundred?"

"Five hundred."

"A vintage favorite." He deals the cards. "Just like the old days."

And that's exactly how this feels, being here with Gregg. Safe and simple and just like it's always been.

Chapter 23

The following night, I knock at Alec's door. He opens it quickly, pulls me in with his smile. "It took you too long to get here."

His front room has stockings hung over the fireplace, complete with roaring fire.

"Come upstairs."

My body warms. Remembers.

Alec leads me to his bedroom with its dark blue walls and light wood furniture. He stops at the side of his bed, pecks at my neck.

"You're sure your parents aren't coming home?"

"Dad's in the Far East. My mom's at book club. Don't worry." He puts his hand to my hip, fingers the skin above my jeans. Anticipation floods my veins. "I'll always watch out for you."

He could never know how deeply I need to believe his promise. "Always?"

"And more." His unwavering commitment flicks a switch somewhere deep inside of me, somewhere I didn't know existed until Alec. A place where love can last an eternity. A place the two of us can protect if we love hard enough.

He begins to undress me, taking care with every piece of clothing. When I wear nothing except my bra and underwear, he lays me across the bed and *tsks*. "When will you learn not to wear these silly things?"

I smile, my body on fire. He pulls the underwear from my hips and slides them over my bare legs. His hand reaches for the drawer of the bedside table, drops my underwear inside. He drinks me in, inch by inch, and I let him. Though the shade is drawn, it's still light in the large room and I watch his every expression, how his jaw tightens with longing. How his eyes survey me with need. My skin goosefleshes under his delicate touch. I rise to him.

He kisses my toes, his eyes cut to mine. He sees my body arch with pleasure. And then we are wrapped in his comforter, lost to civilization. We kiss with our bodies pressed into each other, me trying to crawl into him, him into me. When our tongues become violent, he pulls away, finds my gaze.

He fumbles with something in the bedside drawer. The top of a cardboard box pops. The wrinkle of a condom follows. Alec lies next to me, touches me to him. He is hard in my hand and something else. Pulsing. Like a heartbeat.

"I can't think of being without you," he tells me.

My breath hitches. For him. "I'm not going anywhere."

He pulls away. "So you've changed your mind?"

His sudden distance surprises me. I prop my head onto my elbow. "I'm lost."

"You said you're not going anywhere. That means you'll come with me to Michigan."

"That's not what I meant."

Seriousness draws over his features like a mask. "Are you playing with me?" He sits up, the blankets slipping. I can't help the way my hand reaches for the middle of his chest, where his muscles slope together. That place just over his heart.

"No, of course not. It's just that I can't."

"You can't or you won't?"

Can't? Won't? "Both, maybe . . . I don't know."

He lifts away my hand and instantly my skin feels cold. "So then what are we doing?"

I sit up, gathering the comforter to my chest. "What do you mean?"

"I mean, what's the point of this"—he gestures over our bodies entwined on the bed—"if it won't last?"

"Why can't it last?"

"Because you insist on going to Boston."

"Insist? That's been my plan since—"

"Since before you met me, I know. I'd go there too, Zephyr, I swear I would, but I've already accepted Michigan's offer, or my mom has anyway. If I'd met you earlier it could all be different. But it can't be, not for me."

"We can make it work."

"Everyone says that. I've seen guys from school try to keep girl-friends at home. Long distance never works."

The air turns colder, as if someone's opened a window, as if a December breeze is taunting us. "Do we have to think about all this now? I don't even know if I've gotten into Boston College yet, so I can't really make plans."

"But you'll consider it?" he asks hopefully.

"If I don't get into Boston College, I'll have to consider it."

"Good. That makes me happy." He leans in to kiss me and then quickly draws away. "Except I'm the asshole boyfriend now, aren't I?"

The word "boyfriend" still makes my heart dance. Even now. "How so?"

"Because I know how important Boston College is to you and I'm wishing you don't get accepted."

"That is shitty." I raise my brows, teasing. "Supremely shitty."

"See? Told you." He slides next to me. "If you're not with me next year, I can't do this." He disappears under the covers and kisses me between my legs until my head spins and my skin boils, a screaming, screeching tea kettle for his touch. Then he kisses my stomach, looks up at me with pleading eyes. "You wouldn't want that, would you?"

My head shakes. My body trembles.

"Or this." His fingers explore me now. My breath is short, hitching. I want more of him, all of him. I want him to love me again and again. And in this fog of pleasure I can't imagine being without him next year. Or ever.

This time I'm the one who reaches for the condom in the drawer. My fingers search greedily for the coin.

"So forward," he teases. "I like the way you think."

His movements are hurried and powerful and beyond exhilarating. This is so not our first time. My body gives over to his pulses, begging him for more even as he gives me everything.

When we separate, my body is still shaking. He finds my hand under the covers, lifts it to his mouth and kisses each finger. "Even your fingers turn me on."

I wiggle them playfully.

That's when I hear the metal crash. A pan dropping hard against a tile floor. I bolt upright. Alec dashes out of bed, throws me my clothes. "Go into the bathroom. Get dressed." I scramble out of bed, clutching my clothes against my private bits, and tiptoe the few steps into the hall and then the bathroom. I lock the door and fumble my jeans over my legs, my shirt over my head.

In the mirror, I see my hair is a mess. Bed head. Sex hair. Oh shit.

I grab a hair tie from my back pocket and rake my curls into a ponytail. I run water, splash it over my face in an attempt to erase the red splotches on my cheeks. Then a voice from the lower hall, calling up the stairs.

"Alec?" His mother. Oh shit, shit! I press my ear to the door.

"Up here!"

Her footsteps sound impossibly loud as she climbs the carpeted stairs. "Whose car is out front?"

"I thought you were at your book club."

"Becky got sick. We decided to try again next week." A beat of dead air. "Who's here with you?"

"Zephyr." Alec's voice is calm, casual. My ear melts into the door. My heart is about to pound out of my chest and he's as cool as if he were answering a question in French class.

More silence. I imagine Mrs. Lord at the entrance to his room, peering in, surveying. "*Just* Zephyr?"

"Yup."

"What were you two doing in your room?"

"She's helping me with French. I didn't think it would be a big deal."

"Where is she?"

Oh shit. Shit. Shit.

"Mom, relax. She went to the bathroom. Please don't embarrass her. She'll be out in, like, a minute. Can we just come down when she's done? She can probably hear you, you know."

Another drum of silence. I expect she's looking at the disheveled bed, but then she says. "Yes, of course, I just thought because of . . . Just come down. I'd feel better about you studying in the living room."

"Yeah, okay. No problem."

When I'm sure she's gone, I return to his room. The bed is meticulous, the shiny condom coin nowhere in sight. Alec's at his desk with his laptop open, Mrs. Sarter's Google page on the screen. He doesn't look fazed. At all.

"Oh my god," I whisper. "Is she going to kill you?" Hate me?

He looks at his laptop, at his bed, at the extra study buddy chair he has pulled up to his desk. It all looks perfectly innocent. "Everything's fine. I told you I'd always look out for you."

Relief feels like oxygen refilling my lungs. "What if we'd gotten caught? That was way too close."

Alec stands, strokes my ponytail. "It wouldn't matter to me. I want the whole world to know you're mine."

"But your mom? That's creepy."

"Then prepare to be creeped out. She wants us downstairs." Alec takes my hand, leads me to the door. My feet can hardly move. How can I meet his mother knowing what we were really doing? When she might know what we were really doing.

As if he knows what I'm thinking, Alec says, "You'll be fine. Take this." He plucks his French text from his shelf, hands it to me. "Props always make for good storytelling. Adds authenticity."

"Right." God, he's good.

Almost too good.

Mrs. Lord is filling a pot at the sink in the island when we come down. My nerves rattle as I white-knuckle the textbook that grounds me in the lie.

"Mom, this is Zephyr. Zephyr, my mom, Ellen."

I force eye contact, feign innocence. "Nice to meet you, Mrs. Lord."

"Please, call me Ellen."

"Yes ma'am." I want to kick myself. Where did *ma'am* come from? My brain is completely fried.

She laughs. "And you definitely are not allowed to call me ma'am." She transfers the full pot to the stove, wipes her manicured hands on a dish towel. She has kind eyes and an easy smile. It's hard to believe she's the same controlling woman Alec's described.

"I'm going to walk Zephyr out, Mom."

"So soon?" A silent language exchanges between them before Mrs. Lord forces cheer. "Well, it's too bad you can't stay. Will we see you again, Zephyr?"

Alec squeezes my hand, too hard.

"I look forward to it," I say.

Her gentle smile widens. "Merry Christmas, Zephyr."

"Merry Christmas."

Alec walks me to my car. "You okay?"

"Hardly. That was beyond awkward." I peer around him, looking for Ellen's face in one of the gatrillion windows.

"But nothing happened. Everything's so okay." He kisses me gently and my mouth responds obediently. "I wish you didn't have to go, though. I wish I could lie in bed with you forever."

"Me too. Without your mom home, of course."

"We could have that next year." When he opens my door, I slide onto the cold seat. He pulls a paper tube from his back pocket. When did he pick that up? He hands it to me. A booklet? A magazine? "I'm glad you'll think about it." He extends my seat belt over my front, clipping me in safely. I place the roll onto the passenger seat and it spreads open. A lapis blue brochure for University of Michigan. "Go Blue," Alec says.

I can't help but smile. "Subtle."

"Just hopeful."

He shuts my door and flattens his palm to the window. I reach up and mirror his touch, our good-bye that allows us to avoid saying the actual word.

Alec is my bridge across limbo. Protecting me no matter what. Loving me for me.

At the stoplight on Main, I glance over at the University of Michigan brochure and let myself wonder, what if?

But after only a few minutes, my mind attaches to the college catalog with the solitary girl on the cover. Is that student alone because her boyfriend is at another school? In another state? Does she miss his touch the way I know I will miss Alec?

I'm no closer to an answer when I arrive home and empty our mailbox of useless bills. The silence from Boston College is deafening.

Chapter 24

I'm at my locker the next morning when there's a tap on my shoulder. I twist to find Lizzie, hands on her hips.

"So glad to see you in person instead of on the side of a milk carton."

"Good morning to you too." I slam my locker too loud.

"I haven't seen you around much."

I duck my books into the crook of my arm. "Things have been crazy with the holidays. You know."

"I get it. It's hard to balance the boy and friends, especially in the beginning."

Beginning? Alec and I are so past the beginning. "Look, Lizzie. I know I've been lame."

She holds up her hand. "You don't have to say it. Alec's gorgeous. Who wouldn't want to spend time with him? I just miss you is all." She nudges her elbow into my side. "I did appreciate the updates on Slice, so you won points there."

"I'll be better. I promise. I'll even toss in some Junior Mints as an apology."

"Deal."

When the bell rings, we scatter in our separate directions. Just like we'll be doing next year.

Change haunts me as I fight to pay attention in classes. My mind drifts to all the unknowns of next year, nebulous and undefined, like a dream I can't quite remember. Except next year hasn't happened yet. And the dream I can't remember is really the future I can't articulate.

When I get home I go for a run, check the cavern of disappointment that is my mailbox and then spread my textbooks across the table in an attempt to plant myself in the now. At least that I can control. I'm surprised when I hear Mom's car in the driveway so early.

"What are you doing home?" I ask as she walks through the door.

"I forgot a case file." She takes in my spray of books. "I like seeing you buckling down. *Alone*."

"What's that supposed to mean?"

"It means you've been spending a lot of time with Alec and I know all too well how a boy can distract from schoolwork."

I wave my hand toward the empty rooms, showcase-style. "No distractions here." Under the table, Finn plants his chin onto my feet.

"Alone time is good for a girl your age. I don't think I got enough of that when I was young." She twirls her key ring around her index finger creating a quick, chaotic jingle. "Course, I had you." She smiles, bends to give me a kiss. "I wouldn't trade that for the world. But you'll have plenty of time to meet boys at college. You and Alec shouldn't get too serious."

Too late. I shift my feet, which makes Finn grunt with displeasure. "What time's court?"

"Just a meeting with the judge. Four o'clock." She looks at her watch. "I'm running late, but don't expect me home before seven. Judge Matheis can *talk*." She throws a wink and I laugh.

"Good luck."

"I'll need it. Or earplugs." Mom goes to her study and returns with a stack of folders she balances across her elbow. "I love you, kiddo." And then she is gone.

"Luf too," I call at the same time Finn snores out a soft whistle.

And in the quiet Mom leaves behind I should be able to focus entirely on midterms, but my head scrambles with invasive thoughts.

If Gregg's restless on home confinement and if Lani's with him, nursing him. The thought brings a bizarre jealousy that tastes bitter and wrong. Then there's Boston College not even bothering to send any communication. At all. And Alec being too far away next year while Dad's here and still so far away. I don't know which worry threads to drop and which to hold. I'm so wrapped up in my head I don't even hear the car approach.

Just the doorbell.

And I jump.

Finn too.

For a moment—or maybe much longer than a mere moment—I stand frozen, holding on to the back of my chair for support. It's my father. Mom told me he'd be coming around while I was at school, collecting more things from his studio. My heart pounds, the air feels too hot, too still.

Finn yelps out a loud, vicious bark.

I could pretend I'm not home. Disappear into my room. He wouldn't come looking for me.

Finn barks again, this time in rapid succession. He is determined, deafening. He crouches in front of the door and scrapes at the base with his claws.

This is stupid. I should just answer the door. Invite Dad in.

See him. Deal with this now since there will probably never be a perfect time.

But as my hand turns the doorknob I feel weak, like I've forsaken any control I might have.

I open the door a crack and turn to the table. I swallow hard.

Behind me, Finn barks louder, which pleases me since I want him on my side, not Dad's.

"Hello?"

That's when I realize it's not my father's voice. I whip around and see Alec in the doorway, holding a foil-wrapped dish.

"Alec?" I cringe at how I must look in my Boston College sweatshirt and ratty sweatpants. I'm wearing zero makeup and my hair is a rat's nest with at least one pencil sticking out of it.

"Isn't this the part where you ask me in?"

"Of course. Yeah. Come in."

He steps across the threshold, hefts the plate. "I owe you edible eggplant parm."

"You don't owe me anything." I peek down at Finn, who growls. "Be kind, Finn!" If Finn could only know how much Alec's done for him.

"He looks good," Alec says.

"Yeah, and I'm going to pay you back. I promise."

"The money's not important." He waves away my concern. "I wanted to help."

I blush, overwhelmed by his commitment. It's almost enough to forget I look like a horror show.

"I hope you're hungry." He peels back the foil from a corner of the plate. Steam rises. "Good. Still hot."

"You or the food?"

His eyes widen. "Both, I hope."

230

I chin-nod toward the plate. "The verdict's still out on the egg-plant."

He grabs my wrist, locks his gaze onto mine. He kisses me roughly.

I pull away, breathless. "Alec, we can't. What if my mother comes back?"

He rakes his hand through his hair. "She won't. I watched her pull out."

Panic nudges me. "Did she see you? Were you in the driveway?"

"Of course not. I waited on the street. Very clandestine."

"Stalker."

"Just being careful."

"Good. She thinks I'm studying."

"Not anymore." His wink causes a corkscrew of want to churn through me. How can I be expected to focus on Milton or qua-dratic equations when I have this boy in my life? He gives me a long, deep kiss, bolts his hips to mine.

When I can barely stand, he sets me into a chair, moves my books to make room for place settings. "I hoped you'd be home. I didn't want this meal to go to waste." He insists I sit while he fumbles around the kitchen for utensils. He opens all the drawers. Finds what he needs.

He places a serving in front of me and I pull in a deep, delicious breath. "You're spoiling me."

"You deserve it."

I scoop a forkful of eggplant and take a bite. It is soft and per-fectly spiced. "Oh my god, this is *phenomenal!*"

"You think so?"

"I know so." I chunk out another bite.

"You might be biased."

"Yeah, but this is reality show cook-off awesome."

"I need you to always believe in me."

I tap on the dish. "Feed me like this and I'll forever be your biggest fan."

"Deal." He smiles. "I have one more thing for you, Zephyr."

I lower my fork, setting it softly to the edge of the plate. "More? Okay, I'm officially spoiled."

A gleam jumps to his eye. "Wait here."

"I'm not going anywhere."

While Alec's outside, my mind stretches with possibility for what his gift might be. And then, too quickly, guilt invades for not surprising him with tokens of my love. I wish I knew how to be a better girlfriend. I wish all of this came to me as easily as it does to Alec.

Then I hear his car door slam and when he returns, Finn barks at Alec as if they've never met.

"Enough Finn!" I scold. He slinks to the living room.

Alec comes to the table with a stack of papers. Mail?

"I checked the mailbox for you on my way in. Hope that's okay."

"Of course!" My concentration slips to the one large white envelope. The familiar maroon crest peeks out from underneath the cable bill. I reach for the packet slowly. The seal comes into full view. Maroon and white letters. Boston College.

I look to the addressee: "Miss Zephyr Marie Doyle."

Breath abandons my lungs.

"It looks meaty." I hear his hope, louder than his words.

I rub the cool, slick envelope between my fingers. Would Boston College waste all this paper on a student they didn't want? I tear the flap and reach inside. There is a letter and a thinner version of my coveted brochure. My fingertips numb. My eyes cloud with tears, but I blink them away to read the first line:

"We are pleased to offer you . . ."

I gasp, then scream. Finn lets out two low, guarded barks.

My heart soars and calms in harmony, a tightrope of extremes. I am holding the end of limbo in my very hands. I own my future. My dream realized. My body floats weightless as I press the envelope to my chest. "I thought it would never come!" Alec's arm pulls around my shoulders.

When I slide out the brochure I half expect I'll see my picture on the front cover, my step caught in midflight, but of course it is that other girl. And for the first time I'm not jealous. She can have that floating step; I will have everything beyond. The classrooms, the dorm rooms, Faneuil Hall, the T, the Head of the Charles, and Boston Common.

"I'm so happy for you, Zephyr."

"Yeah?"

He collects me to him, locks my gaze. "Of course."

"But you're not . . . I don't know, upset?"

"How could I be?"

Because Michigan and Boston are so far away. Nine hundred miles to be exact. A $435 round-trip plane fare. "Because Boston College isn't in Michigan."

He smiles. "I could never be mad at you for accomplishing your dreams. No matter where they take you."

I snuggle against Alec. I breathe him in, the spearmint and sweat and this new, earthy smell we make together with our heat. I could close my eyes, fall asleep in his arms, and live in him forever. It's a dream, I know. But so was Boston College and I got that, didn't I?

He peels me from our embrace, stands to leave. "I should leave. You probably have a million people to tell. Call me later?"

"I will." I squeeze my letter to my core. "Thank you so much."

"For what?"

"For being you. For supper. For bringing me this letter. It's all just so perfect."

He gives me a small smile. "Perfect," he repeats and I listen to his footsteps, know the measure of his gait as he walks to the door. He turns. "I'm proud of you, Zephyr."

I go to my room and drop onto bed to reread the letter. About eight times. I imagine being a Boston College Eagle, playing field hockey on their lush grounds, college crowds cheering in a sea of maroon. Wind tunneling under my wings as I fly.

And for the first time since Dad left, I feel like I'm capable of anything.

Everything.

I'll decorate my dorm room. I'll buy that down comforter I saw online last week. And crates. Cool ones to stack books and shoes and records.

I read my acceptance letter again, committing it to memory. I read it aloud to Finn as he curls against the back of my knees. He coughs at one point, as if he's a cat trying to heave up a hairball. I'm momentarily worried, but he settles. "You okay boy?" He snuffles his reply.

I pat his head, kiss his soft velvet-fur temple.

I smile to myself. My excitement is too big to be crimped by worry or unexpected problems.

Orientation begins August 24. I'll have to choose a single or double room if I'm going to live on campus. I have to send back my commitment letter by December 15. Next week. It is a dream. No, better. A doorway to a dream. And I hold the key.

• • •

I meet Mom at the door when she gets home. I fall into her, let her squeeze all her happiness into me now since I had to give her the news over the phone.

"We must have cake!" She sets down her bags and goes to the freezer. Somewhere behind a box of hyacinth bulbs, she finds what she's looking for. "I froze this for when you heard. I had my suspicions it might be earlier than you were letting on." The cake is decorated with the Boston College crest and reads CONGRATULATIONS! around the edges in the same font the college uses on their sweatshirts and other official logos. "I told you Boston College would think you're as perfect as I do."

It's amazing the way Mom's been able to believe in me, even when I couldn't.

Mom tries unsuccessfully to insert a candle into the rock-hard frosting.

"Microwave," I suggest.

"You can't microwave a frozen cake. We can wait."

I'm through waiting. "If there's one thing my friendship with Lizzie has taught me, it's how to manage sugar." I set the cake into the microwave and cook it for one minute. When I take it out, the top is just soft enough to insert a candle, which Mom lights.

"Make a wish." Pride radiates from Mom's smile. Her joy makes me realize my acceptance into Boston College—the realization of my goals—is an accomplishment for her, too.

I wish for more of what I already have: this feeling of floating, of invincibility. I blow hard and the flame disappears.

"This is only the beginning," Mom tells me.

And I feel that. In my bones. Stitched into my every breath.

Chapter 25

I text Lizzie to meet me at my locker before school the next day.

"You look happy." She leans against my neighbor's locker. "I take it you have good news?"

I shove my textbook onto the high shelf and hang my bag. "The hugest news." I close the door, secure the latch.

"Alec asked you to marry him?"

"Hilarious, but no. I heard from Boston College." I beam. "Class of 2020." My excitement is a wild horse stampede, beyond my control.

"Ho. Lee. Shit!" Lizzie punches my arm. "I told you that stuffy institution would want a fresh breath of Zee."

"Hah. Seriously though, it's crazy." I want to tell her so much more. About Alec. About losing my virginity. Planning a future with him. But maybe this is the way limbo works. Maybe parts of me have already moved on without her.

"I think it's supposed to be crazy. Like, crazier than we can even imagine. That's the shit that keeps us mortals wanting more, no? The thrill of the emotional high." She throws her arm around me and the weight of her hug is so much more than just an embrace; it is years of holding each other up. Only now, we're holding on.

"Doyle!" A voice booms, forcing Lizzie and me to break apart. I feel lopsided without her. Lizzie eyes Coach as she storms toward me. "Maybe I should go." Lizzie winks. "In case she plans on reading you the riot act." Coach's specialty.

"Okay, I'll catch up with you in trig."

Coach reaches me and I take a step back, expecting her to shove her face in mine like she's been doing on the sidelines for four years. It's a surprise when she speaks with gathered calm. "I assume it was something important that kept you away from accepting our trophy." Alumni Weekend. God, that seems like forever ago.

Then guilt floods. For letting her down. For letting my team down.

"Your team missed you."

"I wish I could have been there."

"We all do. This was your team, Doyle." She rubs the whistle at her neck. "So this is it, huh?"

"You could come see me play in Boston if I'm lucky enough to make the team."

"I'm a homebody, Doyle. But I think you've got a shot if you keep training. I'll be here if you ever come back to visit."

"Thanks Coach."

"Can I give some unsolicited advice before you head off into your future?"

"Sure."

"It'd be a waste if you missed out on things at college because of a guy."

A protest hangs on my lips but she holds up her hand.

"Something to think about. One of many." She turns on her heels to leave, her sneakers squeaking.

Of all the reprimands I've received from her, this one is the harshest, cuts most deep. I exhale a huff for her invasion into my private life. Coach could never understand what Alec and I have and I suddenly feel bad for her. I can't imagine how bitter I'd be if I were her age and hadn't met a guy who made me feel the way Alec does. I'd probably choose a career in yelling too.

On the walk to homeroom, I pass Gregg at Lani's locker. He's got his arm slung so easily around her there's no sign he was ever interested in me at all. When Lani waves, Gregg stares at me, his face unreadable. Half of me wants to bound over to him, tell him about the letter. My future, confirmed. But the other half of me lowers my head in a secret smile. I've got all the time in the world to tell Gregg our dream of Boston next year has come true. I can wait for when he's ready.

Midterms sucked. I've never been so underprepared for any test. I even guessed at some of the multiple choice questions Mr. Barnes gave in lit class, and trig was a disaster. But I don't let any of that spoil the weightlessness of joy as I ready for my date with Alec, pulling on my Apology Dress the way he requested.

He picks me up and drives me to his house. When we pull up the driveway, I fantasize it is our house.

In the dining room, he pulls out my chair, gestures for me to sit. He ducks into the kitchen and then music seeps through hidden speakers, its buoyant tempo painting the air with a mellow rhythm. I recognize Joan Armatrading's soulful voice immediately. "Down to Zero." My favorite. Gratefulness builds inside me for the way he remembers all the details.

Joan pours her words into the air weighted with fragrant Christmas pine and the just-baked smell wafting from the

238

kitchen. I fidget my hands under the linen tablecloth because we are alone and there is so much I want to say and do but not nearly enough time. Alec's mother is in Boston, picking up his father at the airport; we only have a few hours. I don't want to spend them eating.

When Alec emerges from the kitchen carrying our plates, a linen cloth hung over his arm waiter-style, I laugh. His pumpkin-colored apron has a baby chick with a chef's hat perched on the pocket.

"Your dinner is served, *milady*." He sets my plate onto the placemat before me.

I stare at the breaded roll of meat, which looks a lot like Mom's chicken cordon blue. Hers is delicious, though sloppy. This one is so perfect I can't help wonder if it's takeout. "Did you make this?"

"Just for you." He takes the seat next to me.

"And the music?"

"Also for you."

"Would it be an insult to call you perfect? Because all of this is better than perfect."

"You should eat first. It's my first shot at cordon blue so it could be a disaster."

A light sauce drapes the sides of the roll, and I can see the wrap of chicken, cheese and ham in the middle. I pick up my fork, but hesitate. "It's almost too pretty to eat."

He gives me a shy smile and raises his glass. "To Zephyr, and all the pretty meals I'll cook for her."

He *clinks* my glass and I take a sip of the white wine, its warmth flowing in a river through my middle, settling in my stomach, making my head clear and confused all at once.

"I'm glad you're here." He crawls his hand to mine and gives it a squeeze before cutting into his meal.

We eat in silence, each mouthful sacred. I take another sip of wine and now want dinner to last for hours. I want to linger over every bite, this new feast for my senses, this new part of Alec to be savored. I drink more wine and the music fogs. It feels too good to let go of some control, give it over to Alec.

When we're through, I help Alec clear the dishes and he leads me upstairs to where a new hunger growls within me. My head spins with heavy indulgence. He walks me to the side of his bed, brushes the tips of his fingers over my cheek. I lean against him, already swaying under his touch.

"Someday we can do this every night," he tells me.

"I'd like that." And I'm certain we'll have all this someday because what we have is so much bigger than me or him or this moment.

When he kisses me we float to the bed together, already connected. We are slow with each other. Linked. I am transported on cresting waves, my senses heightened, my love intensified. I let myself get lost. In him. In us.

After, with our bodies entwined, our hearts struggle to simmer and cool. I press my ear to his chest, trace the ripples of muscle that track across his abdomen. Until reality invades with its axe, reminding me that we'll be too far from each other next year.

As if he knows what I'm thinking, Alec asks, "Do you know what you're going to do?" He strokes my hair, his fingers predictable in their timing.

I wrestle from my dream space and wish his question didn't break the silence, force us to talk about the issue consuming us both.

"Have you decided?"

There's never been a decision to make. "Yes."

"So, Boston College then?"

"We'll make it work." I lift my head from his torso. "I know you think long distance can't work, but we can do it. Maybe it's not too late for you to come to Boston—"

He presses a finger to my lips. "Michigan's it for me. The hockey coach is flying me out in February to watch a few games. There's no going back now." He brushes his thumb across my mouth. "You have to know I'd do anything to be with you. I'd have found a way to decline Michigan in a second if you'd asked. If the timing had been different."

"Really?"

"Of course, Zephyr, don't you get it? I love you. Love. You. I want to move in together, start a real life with you. But I don't have a choice. Not anymore."

But I do.

Boston College seemed like my only option for the future once, but that was before Alec, before *this*, before our lives intertwined, inseparable as reaching vines. My stomach dips for not being as sure as him, for not thinking of him first. He's always putting me first. He paid for Finn's vet bill without question. He gives me thoughtful gifts at random times. He overcame his jealousy to support me and my friend. He protects me.

What have I done for him?

It seems impossible to be uncertain over my acceptance when this is all I thought I ever wanted. But now there's Alec and I want him too.

"I want you to do what's right for you," he says.

But before I can even think what that is, his lips pucker against my neck, and then more. His breath trails heat all the way to my collarbone, to my chest. His mouth is everywhere and I soften under his touch. My head fills with his scent. My body quivers.

"You want me, don't you?" His words call to me from above the surface.

"Yes." The word is hot liquid, a volcanic burst.

"More than anything?"

"Yes." I close my eyes, my body heaved with anticipation. But his movements are off. His knee isn't coaxing my legs apart. Where is the weight of him blanketing me? I come up for air, the world crashing into me with all its colors.

He releases my arms and the mattress buckles. Is he sitting up? My head swirls. What happened?

He throws his legs over the edge of the bed, fumbles for his boxers, and stands to stretch on his shirt.

I sit up, clutch the sheet to my chest. "Is something wrong?"

He hands me the slink of my dress and then slips on his own jeans. "No." He sits on the bed next to me, hangs his head.

"Something just happened. What did I do?"

"You said you wanted me more than anything."

"I do."

He lifts his gaze then, his eyes red and stung. "Obviously, that's not true. If it were . . ." He rakes his fingers through his hair. "We shouldn't be doing this if we can't be together. It's not fair to either of us. I don't think you love me the way I love you and"—his breath skips—"that kills me."

I reach for his back, but it is rigid. He moves away.

How did we get here?

"Get dressed." He taps my knee. "I should drive you home before my parents get back."

In the tangle of sheets, I wriggle my dress over my head. I am a million miles away from him. No, I have *pushed* him a million miles away.

"Alec, please. I wish it could be different."

"You have to do what makes you happy."

God, he is such a better person than I am.

"Is it okay to tell you I love watching you dress? I'll miss that if . . ." He looks away, trails off.

He'll miss that . . .

. . . if I choose Boston over him

. . . if this is over for us now

. . . if I can't love him as much as he loves me.

If I stay with him, he wants to watch me get dressed every day. Share an apartment. A life. Make me dinner before making love. Make love before falling asleep. Wake next to me.

It's the same reality I dream of every day.

I find my bag and go to the bathroom. Staring in the mirror, my cheeks are still ruddy, flushed with want. How can I give this up? Alec is the best thing that's ever happened to me. Unexpected and perfect. Am I going to walk away because of bad timing?

He said it wouldn't even be a choice for him. That it would have been me over Michigan if he were the one who had power over his academic choices. I pull the acceptance form from my bag and stare at it.

All the power I do have. Plans change, right? People change. I've seen it with my own parents. How could I know Alec would change my world the way he has? Maybe the future isn't some distant dream but a series of changing choices. I flatten the paper against the vanity and sign the bottom, checking the appropriate boxes. I stare at the maroon logo one last time before licking the envelope. The paste tastes bitter, but there is something more — the excitement of the unknown.

"All set?" he asks when I exit the bathroom. He's in the

hallway, his blue fleece already on, another barrier between us.

"All set."

The car has trapped bitter cold air and when he turns over the engine every inch of me wants to be back in his bed, between the sheets, connected in the energy we effortlessly brew together.

We drive through the sleeping neighborhood in silence, my bag propped on my lap.

Alec turns onto the main road. "Can I tell you something?" Brake lights blink at us from a car up ahead.

"Anything." Always.

"I wish I were . . ." He hesitates. "I wish I were better or more than or something, you know?"

No. "What do you mean? You're incredible."

"If I could make you feel about me the way I feel about you. . . ." He slams at his steering wheel. "Fuck. I just don't want to think about losing you. If we're done, you know."

I break at the thought of being without Alec. "I don't want to be done."

"I don't want that either, but I can't see a way to make it work."

I stare at his features reflected in the low lights off the dash. It's not possible to imagine a reality where I can't see him every day.

"I don't think I can do this anymore." His hands grip the steering wheel hard, fixed. "I think it's easier if we end this before it's too late, before it's too hard."

Oh god. I struggle to get breath. *End?* He passes the grocery store that is fully dark now except for one spotlight above the automatic doors.

"Pull over." I point. "There." Alec looks at me sideways, but he maneuvers the car to the front of brick office suites, cuts the engine.

I pull the envelope from my bag and hand it to him.

244

I watch as he reads the destination address of the college. "Are you trying to make this harder for me?" His voice shakes.

"I would never."

"Then why—"

"I can't go." My words surprise me even though the ink is dry. "You were right. All that stuff you said about how you'd make a different choice if you could. Well, I can. I did." I point to the envelope. "I declined their offer. I don't want a future without you. I can't imagine it. I want you." I signal to the blue postal box a few feet from where we've parked. "Will you drop it in the mail with me?"

He leans close to me, filling my field of vision. "Are you sure?"

"I am."

A weighty gasp of relief escapes his lips just before he grabs my hand, kisses my palm. We scurry into the outside air, run to the mailbox. I grab the metal handle and the box yawns open. He hovers the letter over the black void.

"You're sure-sure?"

"Sure-sure." I have never been so sure.

Alec drops the envelope. I think I hear the faint rustle of paper as it hits the bottom. That small, impossibly slight sound speaks volumes.

Alec hugs me hard, kisses me harder. I smile and laugh, feeling a wave of recklessness and determination that seems long overdue. He walks me to the car, pushes me against the side. "I want you. Here. Now." His words are breathy and hot.

"You have me." His hand flies under the hem of my dress, yanks it over my hips. My breath hitches as I scan the parking lot. "Won't someone see us?"

"I fucking hope so." His words thick. Dangerous. "They'll see what they don't have, what they'll never have." I am liquid under his touch and he moves harder, deeper. My body melts.

My fingers scratch into his neck, feverishly pulling him closer. I feel the door open behind me and we fold into the car, stretching across the back seat. He raises his fingers to my face and traces the line of my bottom lip. "You are mine, Zephyr Doyle."

His words are a frightening and precious brand. A promise.

His lips fill my ears with *thank yous* and *I love yous* and *I would have done the same for yous*. I can't believe for a minute I questioned making a different choice.

We connect in our practiced dance, but this time things are different. Our bond is deeper. Something I could not have dreamed possible even yesterday.

And I understand what Alec means when he talks about sacrificing for someone you love, really love. How it proves your feelings in an exponential, inarguable way. In a way that words never could.

I just had no idea sacrifice could feel so good.

Chapter 26

A blue curbside mailbox—its mouth hinging open and swallowing up my certainty—is the new symbol of love. The world can have its paper hearts and glitter. I have my signature in ink, my future with Alec. And there is an atmosphere of difference between the me of yesterday and the me that has committed to a boyfriend in the way that I have. In this new reality, there is no rainfall, no doubt, only me and Alec and my deepest heart.

This push into a new world somehow manages to make even the jungle-like Sudbury High cafeteria less annoying. Like I'm physically here with Lizzie while the best part of me remains with Alec.

Maybe my spanning two worlds is the reason I don't see Gregg until he twists one of the chairs at our table, straddles it backward.

"What up, Five? Dizzy Lizzie?" Gregg scores an orange slice from Lizzie, pops it in his mouth as he tosses her a shiny wink.

"Noggin looks good," Lizzie says.

"Yeah, are you sure you even had a concussion?" I say.

Gregg taps on his head. "Nothing to slow me down."

"Can you play hockey?" Lizzie. Her finger forever on the newsbeat pulse.

"Verdict's still out, but I'll work my charms."

If anyone can charm doctors despite their infallible X-rays, it's Gregg.

Gregg raises his chin to a kid walking past, his signature silent hello. It strikes me as strange how I know all Gregg's gestures. Can you even unknow something? Someone?

Lani saunters over to our table and sits on Gregg's knee. She throws her arms around his neck and kisses his cheek with all the intention of a branding iron.

Lizzie clears her throat, kicks my leg. *Awkward.*

"What are you kids talking about?" Lani asks.

Gregg shoots me the briefest look and there's something distant there. It's too quick to identify fully. "I've got strict instructions from my mother to make sure Zeph is coming to Anna's wedding."

"Is she bringing Alec?" Lani asks Gregg, even though I'm sitting right here.

Gregg drapes that dark look on me again. A dare? "I doubt it. She's coming with her mom. They're family friends."

Only then does Lani drop a condescending pucker my way. "Well, I'm sure you'll have a swell time with your mom, Zephyr."

"Are you going?" I ask her.

Something uncomfortable exchanges between her and Gregg and she shifts off his lap. "Come on, let's go sit at our table." I interpret her nonanswer as a no.

Gregg rights his chair and tucks it under the lip of our table. A bolt of shock ripples through me when Gregg bends to my ear, so close. So unexpected.

"How am I doing?" His whisper almost disappears before reaching me.

"With what?"

The faintest response. "Acting like I'm over you."

A small metal marble pinballs within my chest, banging and clanging against all the routes inside of me. Setting off bells.

When Gregg stands, he bumps right into Alec.

They exchange the requisite jock fist bump and I see Lani staring at me. Like she's seeing me for the first time. Then she pulls Gregg away and Alec lifts me from my chair. He kisses me so hard he thrusts me against the windowed walls of the cafeteria. He presses me there, his body fusing into mine. I can't slip breath into the space between us, his hands locking my hips in the puzzle of his.

I raise my hands to his chest, try to push him back. But he kisses me harder and there is a slip of time before I hear the chanting, the swell of cheers for me and Alec to *Do It, Do It, Do It*. I pull my lips from Alec's and shove hard against him. The caf lets out a collective, disgruntled *Boo!* At our table, Lizzie's trying to keep her jaw attached to her skull, but then there's Gregg, watching. Except it is not Gregg. He has morphed into a boy built of smoke and fire.

"What was that?" I ask Alec.

He blushes, leans into me. "Um . . . a kiss."

My voice hushes with not wanting the entire G block lunch crowd to hear my frustration. "Was that totally necessary? Here?"

Alec steps back, searches my eyes. "You never had a problem with me kissing you before."

"Yeah, well. You've never used a kiss to basically claim me in front of the entire school."

Alec's face falls wounded and I see his insecurities. How he saw me with Gregg. A trigger for his own self-doubt. I reach for his hand but he shrugs me off. "I'll give you your space."

"Alec, don't."

But he is already turned away, heading toward the door.

"Damn," Lizzie says when I return to the table.

"The kiss?"

"No. The boys." She nods to the door where Alec's exiting and then back at Gregg's table. "You know you've got a problem there, right?"

I do. But it's not the one I thought I had.

I run through the woods, past the park, down the side streets of Sudbury where quiet families live in quieter homes. All the while, I'm chased by this new, darker version of Alec. The one who marked me with his mouth, his hands. For everyone to see. It is impossible to outrun him. And even harder to escape Gregg's words. Or the wild look he aimed at me.

It is late by the time I return home and so dark that the slice of moon is already pinned to dusk's canvas. The bright windows of our house beacon like a lighthouse and wash away the fog of boy haunting. My body cools as I walk the driveway. I walk past the mailbox without opening it and my thoughts calm under the weight of physical fatigue.

Inside, Mom has an entire bag of potting soil dumped onto the kitchen island. "Everyone's getting new nutrients." Her gardening version of hello. I know this potter's musical chairs. Plants in small pots get moved to bigger pots. Their roots find room to spread and grow. Tender shoots get rooted into the tiny pots and we end up with more green in the house, more oxygen in the air.

"Lucky them." I grab a water and she turns to kiss me, her dirt-stained hands never leaving their station.

"How was school?"

"Good," I lie. "I'm gonna shower."

"I'm not cooking tonight." She spreads her gaze across the island by way of excuse. "But we could order something. Thai food, maybe? We haven't done that in a while."

"Sounds good. After I get cleaned up." I resurvey her mess. "And you too."

"One should never outgrow playing in the dirt."

I laugh, but in the shower I try my hardest to wash off the dirt. The layer of dust Alec scattered with his too-hard very public kiss. The film of Gregg's words, clinging to me like sin.

I don't get dressed right away. I wrap myself in a towel and fall onto my bed. I focus on the tiny glowing stars glued to my ceiling. I remember the sixth grade versions of me and Lizzie pasting every sticker onto my indoor sky. I remember it like it was yesterday and it seems impossible how time refuses to follow rules. It claims to be linear, but it can bend and slip in too many ways. Parts of me want to be in sixth grade again, when things were easy. Next year was just next year and friends were friends. The past turns my head to the side, to the pictures of my friends from when time was predictable.

Gregg. Lizzie. My father holding me on my first day home from the hospital. My first field hockey uniform at twelve. My first visit to Boston College. The newspaper photo of me winning State. Finn as a pup. My eyes retreat. Return to the newspaper photo of me at State. It is graffiti-marked with the red strokes of a pen.

Thick red marker.

Four capital letters. Block letters. Painstakingly perfect.

And deadly.

SLUT

In the photo under this word, my post-win smile is smeared with the S of the word. S-L-U-T. My brain blurs the letters, wondering if

I've read them in the wrong order. Or maybe I've imagined them. I shake my head clear. But the letters remain. All four. Standing at attention. In their persistent order.

My chest fills with more air than it can hold, or maybe not enough. It makes my brain spin. Who would do this? And why? How? I look for the joke, want to see it, but instead I see my full name, my signature in the bottom corner. *Zephyr Marie Doyle*. Every floating curve of my letters, even the capital Z and the way I draw a line through the middle. My handwriting. Gregg's red sharpie.

I rip the clipping from my wall, the tack tearing a jagged line through the thin paper. I crumple it into a pea even as it grows to a boulder within my fist. And in the space I've just cleared, the collage photo under this clipping is the one of me and Gregg at Mara's christening. Summer sun freckles my face, Gregg at my side. Except only his hand remains. Gregg has been torn from the photo. Leaving me in a blue sundress and a smile too innocent.

Time stiches, distorts my reality. I don't know how many eternities have passed before I go to the kitchen. The island still holds a volcano of dirt, but Mom's hands are clean and she's putting on her coat. "I ordered our usual. I'm on my way to pick it up now. I'd ask you to come, but . . ."

I look to my middle, where Mom's trained her gaze. I'm still in my towel. "Mom, was there . . . did you see . . . did anyone stop by for me today?"

Her brow creases. "No, why?"

"No reason." I squeeze the pea of newspaper smaller in my grip.

"I'll be back in fifteen. Set the table?"

I nod and Mom's out the door with Finn, his whole body eager for the ride that holds endless possibilities. I wait for a beat before ducking out to check the key rock. The key huddles there, silver and small and completely unaware of its role in derailing my life. The cold outside is so cold that I want to stay here forever. Let the elements freeze my hair, then my blood, then my skin.

Instead, I scribble a note to Mom that I'm not feeling well, that I'm skipping dinner, that I need some sleep. The words smudge with dirt, mocking my illusion that anything in life is controllable. I crawl into my room, crawl into myself, a turtle retreating into its shell. I want to call Lizzie but can't imagine how to tell her what's happened. I can't show her the photo or the red devil ink that pierced "SLUT" onto paper. Talking about this with anyone would make it too real. Realer than the real of right now, and I can't carry that weight.

And I can't call Gregg to ask him why he'd hurt me like this. Did he come over here after he saw Alec kiss me in the caf? He knows where the key is. Finn would have let him in — been thrilled to see him, even. And Gregg used his red autograph Sharpie to make sure I knew it was him.

Gregg had to sneak into my house.

Slip into my room.

Brand his jealousy onto paper — a paper I signed and gave especially to him.

Pin it to my wall.

Know that it would crush me.

Chapter 27

When Mom comes to check on me I look half dead. Because I am.

She raises the back of her hand to my forehead, tells me to get some rest. I nod, slink deeper under my covers. But when I hear her bathwater filling, I sneak into the kitchen and grab my coat. I text Lizzie: Now

I slip outside and jog to the end of my driveway, where I've instructed Lizzie to meet me.

I'm halfway to my full escape when my phone buzzes. I study the small screen, the way the words are too fuzzy. Too jumpy. Untamable under my tears.

Alec: Where are you?

Gotta do this thing with L. It's a carefully selected portion of the truth.

See me instead.

Not tonight.

Why?

Because the tectonic plates of my world have shifted. Tomorrow. Promise.

Tonight.

Can't.

I see Lizzie's car and feel annoyed by Alec's persistence when there's something so much more important I need to do.

"Why all the clandestine?" Lizzie asks when I pull on my seat belt.

"I need to talk to Gregg." No, yell at Gregg. Sever this so-called friendship once and for all.

Lizzie looks at me sideways. "No offense, Zee, but you look like shit."

I rein in my anger, try not to give too much away. "Not really a major concern right now."

She eyes me suspiciously. "What's going on? Does this have anything to do with the lunchroom today? Am I missing something?"

I can't tell Lizzie where any of this came from or why. I only know who.

"Maybe we should talk about it. Before you see Slice."

"I appreciate the offer but this only concerns Gregg."

She hesitates. "Okay, if that's what you want."

"It's what I need." And I hear the darkness in my voice, how I'm losing the ability to control my emotions.

But as Lizzie drives I secretly hope she will get lost. That she won't remember her way to Waxman's. Then I won't have to confront Gregg. I won't have to admit to another person that I've been leveled.

I crack the window for air.

But there isn't enough oxygen on Earth. Not even as we walk across Waxman's lawn.

"Wait here," Lizzie says as we reach our tucked-away nook against the trees. "I'll grab you some water."

"I want a beer."

"Yeah, no." Lizzie heads to the house as I practice my words for Gregg on a loop in my head, never more thankful that I've chosen Alec. That I'll be hundreds of miles away from all of this bullshit next year. I can't even believe what the mistake of Boston with Gregg would look like. How much more devastated I would feel by his betrayal.

Sounds dart between my ears, arrow blades of indistinguishable noise. But then, clarity. My name. Through the trees. I turn and see Gregg. Looking too casual. Too normal. And I hate him even more for it.

My teeth clench, warping my voice into a growl. "How could you be such an asshole?"

Gregg stiffens. "Um, hello to you too."

I scoff. "You want me to say hi?" I force nonchalance. "Oh, hey Gregg. You good? Great. Good to hear. So glad you took the time to completely humiliate me. And in my own home, that was a nice touch." I give a twisted laugh. "Oh wait. Did I say hi? Wouldn't want to be impolite."

Gregg's face hardens with confusion. Still, he keeps his voice hushed. "*Me* humiliate *you*? Judging from that display you put on in the caf today, you're doing a fine job all by yourself, Zeph. You don't need my help."

I press my feet into the ground, stand firm. "I got your note. Your little message made it perfectly clear how you feel about me being with Alec."

"Zephyr, what are you talking about?"

"Are you such a coward that you're not even going to own what you did?"

"I kissed you, Zeph. I've already told you that I didn't mean to fuck everything up with that stupid kiss. And I shouldn't have said that thing today. That wasn't cool. If I could take both back, I would. Believe me."

The kiss? His words? I stare at him and see a lifetime in his gaze, the years we spent exploring the woods as pirate zombie adventurers, the sharing of Popsicles on a summer day when everything was quiet and we could ask each other anything we didn't understand. Like why the Dead were Grateful or how come jelly always took second chair to peanut butter. Those quiet times reach up from deep inside of me and pull me to the girl I used to be. Gregg's friend, his confidante.

Tears climb into my eyes, uninvited. I scurry after my resolve. I remember: S-L-U-T.

"Why would you even want to be friends with a slut?"

"You are making zero sense."

"The note you left in my room. You're seriously going to deny it?"

Gregg runs his hand through his thick hair. "Can we start again? I feel like we're having two different conversations."

"There's only one conversation, Gregg. And it's our last. I can't even look at you after seeing that note."

"I need you to slow down. Tell me what note you're freaking about."

"The one you wrote with your ridiculous red autograph Sharpie."

He reaches in his back pocket, pulls out the marker. "This?"

Seeing it makes my stomach wretch. "Nice. Want to throw anything else in my face? Now's your chance. You won't have another."

"When would I have left this note for you?"

"You broke into my room."

He lets out a laugh. "Broke into your room? Why would I do that?"

"Because you're pissed I'm with Alec."

He pulls back. "I'm bummed, not pissed. And this isn't news, Zeph. I wouldn't have to break into your room for you to know this bit of information."

My head swims. "I know it was you."

"Why? Because of a red marker?" He toggles it between his fingers. "You can pick one up at Staples." He pulls back his arm, hurls the marker deep into the surrounding trees. I can't hear the rustle of its landing. "That pen is meaningless, but you accusing me of breaking into your house is huge. Christ, Zeph, how is it that lately you don't know me at all?"

A weakness begins to build in my knees. My brain clogs with facts. "It was you. It had to be. You made me sign my newspaper photo at breakfast."

"Uh, yeah. And I still have it somewhere in my locker."

"So how is it pinned to my wall?"

"Look, I don't know what you think I wrote, or pinned to your wall or whatever, but you've got the wrong guy."

"Right. It just appeared there. My signature and all. Did the word slut magically appear over my image too?"

"How can you think I would call you a slut? Ever."

"You did. You wanted me to know it was you. That's why you used that photo. It was signed. You *knew* I'd know it came from you."

"Fuck. I don't know shit about that photo. It could have dropped out of my locker. I don't know." He lets out an exasperated sigh and I feel its depth. A canyon of regret. "How did I become the enemy?"

He reaches out, touches my elbow with his. I want to pull away but I can't. It's our secret code, the one we'd started when our parents were torturing us by making us watch boring documentaries that were supposed to broaden our view of the world. But we were nine and we dreamed of bigger things. Explorer things. So we'd touch elbows to communicate that we'd make it through the torment together. We'd come out the other side.

But now when he touches me in this way, the connection seems fragile. It's the first time I'm unsure if we'll be okay on the other side.

"Look, Zeph, I don't know how or why that note got pinned to your wall and I'm pissed it did, but it wasn't me. There isn't a part of me that could hurt you. Not on purpose. You have to know that."

Confusion spills over my thoughts. "So then how . . . ?"

He shakes his head. "I don't know, but I promise I'll find out. No one deserves that, Zeph, least of all you." He twists his empty keg cup in his hand.

"You swear it wasn't you?"

He reaches for my hand and I let him hold me. "You know it wasn't me, Zeph. You know me."

And I do. The Gregg standing before me is the Gregg I've always known, not the monster that note conjured in my head.

He gives my hand a gentle squeeze. "I always thought senior year would all go down so differently."

My throat is dirt dry. My nerves scattered. "Yeah."

He throws a quick laugh. "Something tells me you and I had different versions of how it would unfold, but I'm willing to overlook the details."

A small smile creeps onto my face. "Gracious."

"I just want this again." He strokes his finger across my palm. "Me and you, the way we used to be. Before I fucked up."

The way Gregg holds on to his uninvited kiss as the worst thing he's done makes me certain he couldn't have written that note. Makes me hate myself for believing he could. And that's when I know it had to be Lani. She must have heard what Gregg said to me in the lunchroom. I'd seen the way she hung her stare on me. I'd always known she was jealous of my friendship with Gregg. And then I threw it in her face, how she's not invited to Anna's wedding. She's pissed that I am. Or maybe she thinks I'm leading Gregg on—that I want Gregg *and* Alec.

The more I think of it, the more I'm sure. She would have ripped Gregg from his half of our childhood picture. She would have had access to Gregg's locker. She set him up. Wanted me to suspect him. So I'd back off, stop being his friend.

"I'm sorry," I tell Gregg, because I am. For too much.

"You're lucky I'm the forgiving type." His smile spreads easily across his face. It's the smile he's always had for me, the one that sits a little deeper in his cheeks than the smile in his press photos. Even deeper than his smile for Lani. She must see that too, the way he looks at me. I stare at his features, maybe a beat too long. Our eyes catch but we don't look away. I can't look away.

"Hiding in the bushes?" Lizzie says as she joins us. She registers me and Gregg holding hands and our fingers release simultaneously. Lizzie offers me a keg cup and I bring the water to my lips. It is cold, cleansing. "You two good now?"

"Fine," I tell her.

Lizzie eyes me with her need to know the details, but I'm thankful she doesn't press. She turns to Gregg. "I heard about Boston College wanting you to play for them."

A bashful look crawls over Gregg's features. "Yeah, looks like everything's going according to plan."

A sadness plummets then. For all our plans. Before.

Lizzie darts her eyes between us, craves the story that's not being told. My feet shift, restless and a little trapped. "I think it's incredible. Not that I ever had any doubts. About you or Zephyr."

Gregg raises his cup to her in a toast, but her gaze stays on me. A quiet interrogation.

When Gregg taps my cup with his, this small gesture is like a string between us, a pulley. I move to him and place my arm over his hard shoulder. His free hand rounds my waist and he draws me in for a hug. My arm wraps tight, pulling him closer as an apology. And a promise.

He knows what I am saying. Without words.

Gregg has always known.

I close my eyes as he holds me, suspended. I wish I could stop time. Let this moment between us erase all of my mistakes. I let the safety of Gregg's hug envelope me and a tear forms. For Gregg going to Boston. Without me. For not being able to have Alec and Gregg next year. I blink away the tear because I can't let more follow. That would be too much.

Gregg's arm relaxes and I open my eyes. The forest folds back into existence, sound rises to my ears. And something else. A figure in the distance. Too familiar.

Gregg puts me down and my feet stumble. He rights me and I hold onto his outstretched arm. For balance. For strength. But the scene beyond pulls me and I step away from Gregg's support, Lizzie, and the small pocket of our shared Earth.

I walk toward the figure, squint my eyes.

Lizzie's words are far away now. "Zee, where are you going?" Or maybe this is an echo in my head. My mind focuses only on the boy who looks like Alec.

I squint in the darkness, knowing my eyes are wrong. Praying they are wrong.

The way his body leans in against the house, the easy set of his hips. The way his frame seems to hover.

Over something?

Someone.

A shiver rattles through me. A surge of panic propels me forward, even as I want to shrink back.

Lizzie pulls at my jacket. "Zephyr, are you okay?"

That someone is a girl.

He's got one hand pressed against the house, his head tilting in. *What is he saying? What are the words he is listening to?*

I snap my coat free of Lizzie's grasp. I keep my eyes trained on the boy who looks too much like Alec. The boy who is about to kiss the girl leaning against the house.

So it can't be Alec.

My feet tread a steady beat, the Earth pushing back hard beneath each step. I pick up speed, while the party around me slows. The logs in the fire pit squeal and then pop as loud as a firecracker. My heart skips faster.

I'm closer. He's closer. She's closer.

The couple swims in clearer now. He reaches an arm toward the girl, tucks a strand of blond hair behind her ear. The gesture is so familiar it spasms my gut. But wait. I don't recognize his jacket.

That's not Alec's blue fleece.

The one I've pulled off his body.

The one that makes his eyes shine.

It's someone else. It has to be.

This is all a mistake.

Then Gregg is in front of me, jogging backward, blocking my

view. I stop. His eyes swell with a sadness I've never seen, not even after he saw me kiss Alec that day at the rink. This sadness is different. It's not because of me, I realize; it's *for* me. That's when I know the boy doesn't just look like Alec.

The boy on my horizon is Alec.

And the scene before me cuts deeper than any note Lani could write.

"Leave it, Zeph." Gregg reaches for me, but I slink him off. I clutch my cup so hard the plastic crackles in my fist, water slipping out over the side, shocking my skin with cold.

His free hand sits on her shoulder now, like it's made to be there.

Alec's hips sling closer to the girl's, his body almost covering her in that blanket. My blanket. My thoughts fog.

Her hand rising to his hair, just over his ear.

His lips move but I can't make out the words.

Her head lifts to his, her mouth inviting a kiss.

"Alec?" I whisper. The couple doesn't stir. Maybe I'm too far away for him to hear me. Maybe it's not really him. Loud music rushes into my ears. I step past the speakers, tuck behind the deck to listen.

He drops his head so close to her shoulder.

Is he kissing her neck? Asking her to go somewhere else? To be alone?

Her body pulling him in, so eager.

Lizzie and Gregg approach but I wave them away. I hush everything around me so I can hear this couple. And I hear them.

"You are really beautiful," he tells her. "Sexy."

I feel sick. The kind of sick I'll never stop being sick from.

"You cold?" He rubs her forearms.

"Not with you." Her flirt drips sugar.

"You want to go inside?"

Inside?

"Alec?" I blurt. The name I've held on my lips for months, the name that edged out Boston College.

He turns then, focuses on my face in the shadows. His hand drops from the twist of the girl's hair. He takes a half step back from the house. I can't read his expression. Is it satisfaction? Regret?

"Zephyr." His voice silks out my name while my world implodes.

Words strangle my throat. I feel my jaw drop open but I can't make sound. Who is this girl?

A million questions battle in my head but nothing catches. Confusion overwhelms me.

I bend into the stitching ache in my core. Lizzie says something behind me but her words are garbled, remote.

"What are you doing?" My question belongs to someone else. I cannot be here. This cannot be Alec.

Alec reaches for my wrist and holds tight. His grasp is a cold metallic restraint. I wrench my arm free.

"It's not what it looks like." His words are too simple, too regulated. Rage boils in me and he is so calm.

"It looked pretty clear to me," Lizzie says.

Pain scorches my middle. "What was it, then?" I find these words somehow.

"Zephyr, I had no idea." It's the girl now. Tiny, young. An underclassman.

"Do I know you?" I whisper.

"I'm Katie. I tried out for JV field hockey"—she slinks a step away from Alec—"I didn't know he was your boyfriend. Honest."

These words lash like a taunt: *boyfriend. Your boyfriend.*

Then Gregg ushers the girl beyond my sightline.

Next to me, there is the heat of Lizzie's body. "Zephyr, let's go." Anger spikes the edges of her words.

Alec grabs for me again, but I step away. "Look, it isn't what you think. Zephyr, you of all people should understand things aren't always what they seem."

Lizzie bristles. "What is that supposed to mean?"

He ignores her, steps toward me. "What you saw. I wanted you to see that."

Lizzie slaps Alec's face hard enough to hush conversations in the forming crowd. His hand darts to his cheek, meeting the sting. "You"—she thrusts her finger in his face—"Are. A. Piece. Of. Shit. You don't deserve Zephyr." Each word drops cleanly, sharply. Daggers.

Gregg positions himself between Alec and Lizzie until she backs down. She grabs the sleeve of my coat. "C'mon, Zee, we're leaving."

Lizzie's hand tugs at my jacket, but I don't move. I'm trapped in this spot, tortured by the reoccurring image of Alec and another girl too close. Had they already kissed by the time I saw them? Done more? And he *wanted* me to see? And what if I hadn't blurted out his name when I did?

"Zee!" Lizzie pleads.

Alec approaches me, wraps his arms around my waist. He twists me quickly, away from my friends. His head fills the sloped cove of my neck the way it has so many times. I smell mint and my body remembers. My knees weaken. But that girl must have smelled it too.

And how many other girls?

My head whirls. My brain stutters. "W-why would you want me to see you with another girl?"

Alec's fingers slip down my sleeve, web their way around my fingers. I feel the squeeze he gives my hand, but it's disconnected somehow, like I'm watching this happen to another girl.

His low words float to my ears. "Zephyr, nothing happened."

Somehow I manage to speak. "It did. Or it was about to."

"No. I wanted to prove a point."

That you have the power to gut me? "B-but you didn't know I'd be here."

"I knew."

"Zee," Lizzie urges from somewhere behind me. "Please don't listen to anything he says."

"Can we talk about this in private?" Alec asks.

"I've heard enough," I tell him.

"I did this for you. You'll understand once I can explain." He drops his voice so that only I can hear. "I love you, Zephyr."

Love? The word cuts quick, a whip sliced through flesh. How can any of this be love? "What I saw. You and her"—I huff out air, my head spinning—"you *wanted* me to see that?"

"I wanted you to know how it feels."

"I trusted you." And then, as pieces fall into place, as my mind and heart sync with the madness of this scene: "I changed my life for you."

"Don't, Zephyr, please."

"*Me* don't?" I say, but then I am torn from my spot. Lizzie. Pulling me from behind.

My body breathes without my permission for a swell of minutes. Clarity builds slowly. Oh god, what have I done?

Only feet from me, Gregg towers over Alec, their faces close. He threatens something I can't hear. Alec throws up his arms.

"We need to get out of here." Lizzie yanks me hard enough

to make me stumble. She bodyguards me through the crowd that splits with curiosity. We walk across the frozen ground. She sets me into the car, closes my door.

Alec had wanted me to see. Wanted me to hear.

He'd planned this.

Specifically to *hurt* me?

When we turn onto the crossroad, Lizzie asks if I'm all right. Her grip moves from the stick shift to my knee. The light, unexpected pressure feels foreign, as if I haven't yet returned to my body. I press my temple to the passenger side window while my brain replays every gruesome second of the past ten minutes of my life. I struggle to keep from puking but can't. I bark at Lizzie to pull over and open my door just in time to spray vomit onto the side of the road.

Chapter 28

My phone rings seven times on the way to Lizzie's.

"You should turn it off." Lizzie's eyes scan me as she drives.

But I don't. I squeeze my phone in my palm, hoping the pinch of skin will wake me from this nightmare.

In Lizzie's room, I collapse onto her mattress, let it absorb my weight. I hear the door latch softly before Lizzie kneels at the side of the bed.

"Can I get you anything?"

My tongue is too thick to answer. My head shakes out a small *no*.

"Zephyr, what was that?" Lizzie's voice fractures as if her words have taken on my pain.

"Do you think he . . . that they . . . you know?"

Lizzie tries to squeeze back a troubled look. "Honestly? It kills me to say this, but I don't know. Maybe. I'm so sorry, Zee."

My head clutters with Alec and that girl having sex at the construction site. In his bedroom. His car.

"I wish I could make this better for you, Zee." Lizzie's phone vibrates then and she reads the text, fingers a response. The phone buzzes again and Lizzie turns the screen to me.

Gregg: Are u with Zeph?

Lizzie: At my house.

Gregg: Take care of her Lizzie. I'm here. For anything.

The exchange mines tears from the deepest parts of my heart. Lizzie's protectiveness, Gregg's loyalty, all things I've never had to question. All the things I've taken for granted lately.

I press myself into the minutes of yesterday, how close Alec and I were. He'd promised me a future, given me a glimpse. I'd given him everything in return.

So why would he do this to me? Why did he want me to see him with another girl?

My phone rings: Maroon 5. "Sugar." *Yes please/Won't you come and put it down on me?*

Lizzie grabs it, flicks the screen to answer. "I think I speak for Zephyr when I say you can lose this number." She disconnects, chucks the phone onto the comforter where it jumps once softly before settling onto its face. It sings again almost immediately.

Lizzie catches my mournful stare. "Oh Zephyr, you cannot seriously want to talk to him."

"I don't know what I want." I brush a tear from the corner of my eye, biting back the torrent that's building. "He said he could explain."

"Explain why he was with another girl? What possible explanation would you accept?"

"I don't know, Lizzie." Tears lick my words. "I just can't figure out why he'd want me to see them together."

"It sounds like a bullshit line he thought would save his ass after he got caught."

His words repeat in my head: *You'll understand once I can explain. I wanted you to know how it feels.* Had he seen me hug Gregg? Or worse, did he hear Gregg whisper about not being over me? I suck in a quick breath.

269

"What?" Lizzie says.

I stare through the wall, at nothing.

"What is it, Zee?'"

A tear streams down my cheek, chased by another.

"Has he done this before?"

I shake my head. "No." And then, "Not exactly."

"Define not exactly."

My voice breaks as I tell her about that day on his stoop, how he'd made me feel so, so good, but then stopped, telling me he needed to be careful with me. That he was too insecure and I had the power to hurt him. And when I spent time with Gregg at Thanksgiving, how he's shut me out for days.

"Zephyr, that's not normal. It's Manipulation 101. You are such a smart person. How could you not see that?"

"It's not like that, Lizzie." My words hiccup. "I really love him."

"That's not love, Zee. Not when someone's forcing you to do it."

"He never forced me."

Lizzie's trying hard to control her frustration. "Love is a choice, Zephyr."

Breath rattles in my chest, struggling to pass in and out. "It's not that simple. There's . . ." But I can't say it. I can only grieve.

Lizzie's eyes beg. "What are you not telling me? *Please* tell me you're not pregnant."

"No!" I am grateful for that, at least.

"Thank *god*. Then what?"

I ball Lizzie's comforter between my hands and make a fist of fabric. I twist at it as I tell her about yesterday, about my perfect night with Alec, how it ended with my commitment to him over Boston College. I tell her about Alec's jealousy of Gregg and even though I know they are my words, they sound like they come from some other girl.

She looks at me like I am some other girl. "Zephyr, what were you thinking?"

I love him. He loves me. "Everything's different when I'm with him."

"I don't even understand. When did you become this girl?"

She couldn't understand. This is between me and Alec. He has an explanation for me. "I need to talk to him."

"What? *Why?*"

Because I'd been wrong about Gregg and I could be wrong now. The note, the word in red—it had all been a misunderstanding. One I couldn't see clearly before talking to Gregg.

And I know Alec wouldn't hurt me. He's the one to make everything better. That's what he does. But Lizzie can't know that. She can't know how being in his arms feels like the sky and ocean melting into one another, endless and lasting. "Because he said he can explain."

"What do you care what he has to say? This dude freaks about you spending time with your friends. Basically banned you from Slice. Made you give up your dream of Boston College for him—"

"Don't." I shoot her a look.

She throws up her arms. "Okay, maybe I don't know what I'm talking about. If you feel you need to hear his reasons for being an asshole, you do what you have to do. Just know I'll be here for you, Zee. However this turns out."

And the familiarity of this promise sends an itch squirreling along my skin. "I can't get the scene out of my head."

"It's a hard scene to forget."

"But Alec and that girl? It doesn't make sense. I should hear him explain why he would do that, right?"

"I think only you can answer that."

"I need to talk to him." I reach for my phone.

Lizzie grabs my arm. "Are you sure?"

"I-I have to know."

"But you know, Zephyr. I mean, you saw what I saw."

My mind strips away the physical pleasure I feel when I'm with Alec and shows me only his need. How he needed me to choose him over my friends, didn't want me around Gregg. But didn't I want that too? Time where it was just the two of us? I did. I do. I want it to be only us. Next year. Now.

"It wasn't what it looked like. It couldn't have been."

Lizzie turns away as I pull up his number.

Alec answers on the first ring. "Zephyr, I need to see you. I need to explain. If you hate me after hearing what I have to say then I'll go away forever."

Even after tonight, the thought of losing him rips darkness into my heart.

"Zephyr actually"—his pleading blurs the edges of my thoughts—"we can't do this over the phone. Please."

And I know then what is right for me.

Chapter 29

Lizzie parks in Alec's cul-de-sac. "I'll wait here. I don't want him driving you home."

I nod, my fingers already gripping the door handle. I hold on to it, wondering if I'll have the strength to step outside, confront Alec.

"I'm here for you, Zee. *Here* here. Whatever you need."

"Thank you." These are the words that come out of my mouth, even though the ones asking her to drive me home are the words searing my brain with their chant.

But then Alec's front door flies open and he's running to the car, opening the door for me. He guides me up and into his arms so fluidly I almost forget my confusion. "I'm so glad you're here."

The cold air morphs into a cloud of sweet mint and I take a step back, push down his arms. "Don't."

He gestures toward his house, the front door hinged open. "Come in?"

Even though the entrance is only steps away I gather all my strength for the journey. Because I have to know. If we're over. Why he'd hurt me so badly. "Only for a minute."

"I'll take your minute." He attempts a small smile and makes me recall a time when I had only ten minutes for him at Waxman's, what we'd done then.

A wave of nausea threatens my middle as I wonder how many other girls gave him ten minutes. Or more.

In the foyer, I catch a glimpse of the formal dining room where I sat only last night. How can the house still surge with the fresh, innocent scent of pine when the universe is exploding?

He leads me to his room and I stop short when I hear voices. "Are your parents home?"

"They're wasted. It's the only way they can stand each other." He takes my hand, settles me on the edge of the bed. Kneeling before me, he catches my chin so I see his eyes clearly. Wet as tidal sand. Full of sorrow.

The bed beneath me stirs both sadness and longing. "I can't stay."

His gaze pleads. "I wasn't with that girl, Zephyr. I need you to know that. I'm not saying what I did was right, but I didn't cheat on you. I would never do that."

"That's not what it looked like."

He hangs his head. "I know what it looked like. I wanted it to look that way."

"Why?"

"Because I'm an idiot." He brushes away a teardrop that creeps along his cheek. His eyes meet mine. "I wanted to show you how you hurt me."

"When have I hurt you like that? I've never even *looked* at another guy."

"See? You don't get it. That's why I needed to teach you a lesson."

274

My head kicks back, stung. "What lesson?"

"Sorry, no—that came out wrong." He squeezes my hand. One of us is clammy, but I don't care. "Last night was amazing. The best night of my life. You changing all your plans for me—for *us*, so we could have a future—blew my mind. I was insanely happy."

"So was I."

"You have no idea how glad I am to hear you say that."

"So how did we get here?" I pull my hand away, furious we have slipped so far from that perfection.

His fingers pull at his hair. "I was hurt. I wanted to celebrate with you more, be with you. When you blew me off for Lizzie tonight I was so bummed. I went to Waxman's, hoping I'd get to see you."

"It didn't look like you were trying to find me."

He holds up his hand. "Let me finish. I saw you in the cafeteria with Slice today. The way he was talking to you."

"That was about his sister's wedding. And *he* talked to me. I can't control what he does." I huff, shake out my frustration. "That so doesn't even matter."

"I know. I figured it was something meaningless and I didn't freak. But then you pulled away from my kiss in the caf. It was like you didn't want anyone to know you were with me but you didn't care who watched you talking to Slice. And then tonight, I saw you and Slice alone together and then he was hugging you. And then I saw *you* hug him, Zephyr."

"So?"

"I've told you how much it bothers me that you hang out with him and there you were. You two have years together and we'll never have those kinds of memories—so to see laughing, talking—I guess I felt like words weren't going to cut it; I needed to show you how it felt. Make you live it the way I do.

"You have no idea what you do to me. You make me crazy. I lost it. It was all to make you jealous. I thought if you could feel what I feel when I see you with Slice then you'd understand." His eyes beg mine. "I was selfish, I know, but I want to spend every minute with you and I felt like you didn't feel the same way. I thought"—he knocks his forehead with the heel of his hand—"I guess I thought if I made you feel the same way—second best or something, then you'd understand. You wouldn't choose your friends over me." He bites his lip, pleads at me with his stare. "I was stupid not to think it would backfire."

His explanation.

His apology.

His regret.

It's a lot to process.

"You did this because you were hurt?"

"Yes." Shame licks the word. "And because I love you. Too much. I've never loved anyone before, Zephyr. You make me beyond jealous and I know how much Slice digs you. I'd do anything not to lose you. It sounds totally effed up when I say it out loud, but that's pretty much all I ever think about."

"Really?"

"Really." I feel myself tipping forward. "I love you, Zephyr actually. I just never knew love would make me do such insane shit. But it will never happen again. Tonight when you wouldn't answer my calls I thought I'd lost you. It was the scariest feeling. I'll do anything to make it up to you. Anything."

My resolve softens and he senses it. Alec reaches up, brushes his lips against mine. The tender kiss calms me and excites me all at once. My insides are a jumble, but the kiss, the kiss feels right.

He rises and sits on the bed, pulls me onto his lap. He burrows his face into my neck and I feel the warm wet of his tears. "I swear I will never hurt you again. You'll see. Next year everything will be different. We'll be together always."

I hear the purity of that promise, that gift. "Alec?" He draws his eyes up to meet mine. "What if I don't get into the University of Michigan?"

"Of course you'll get in. You're brilliant and athletic. If Boston College wanted you, Michigan will too."

"But—"

He silences me with a finger to my lips.

"No matter what happens, we'll figure it out, just like we're doing now. That's what love is."

I see my parents then, fumbling through love even after twenty years. My dad, acting in the extreme. My mom finding space to forgive him.

"We'll get through it together. Just promise you'll forgive me for being a complete ass."

And when he kisses me I let my mind wash of everything but his lips. His tongue so familiar.

It's not until I get in the car that anger rises. It is the same kind of anger I felt after learning of Dad's note. Why couldn't my father or Alec talk to me about the way they were feeling? Why was their instinct to hurt me?

"You okay?" Lizzie says when I pull on my seat belt. "Did you forgive him?"

"Not totally."

"So you forgave him a little?"

"It'll never happen again."

Lizzie hangs her gaze on me too long.

"What?" I snap.

She lifts her fingers from the steering wheel in surrender. "Nothing. You're a smart girl. I'm sure you did what you thought was best."

"What would you have done?" I explain how Alec was hurt and wanted me to know what that felt like. How he was acting out of love. How he didn't actually do anything with that girl.

Lizzie is quiet for a long moment. "I don't know what I would have done, Zee. I've never had to deal with this with Jason."

They are the last words Lizzie and I exchange as she drives me home, and the stillness leaves enough room for uncertainty to creep in. Because I don't see the dark shadows of Ashland Drive as we drive down my road, I see Alec hovered over Katie, too intimate, too easy.

An endless haunting.

When I'm inside, I go to my bedroom and watch the clock tick numbers until long after midnight because it's easier to watch time pass than to replay that twisted scene on a constant loop. The image is tortuous and cruel and I wish my memory could forgive Alec the way my heart has. The way my body has.

I look to my collage, to Alec's cards. Proof of his love. He is the Alec who leaves me flowers, trusts me to know his quiet dream of becoming a chef. He is the person I can talk to about Dad and my future. That person would never hurt me. Not intentionally. It is this thought that carries me into a welcoming darkness and the reprieve of sleep.

And when I hear a knock, my brain mistakes it for the sound of a field hockey stick connecting with a hard white ball. My arm reverberates at contact but then the sound echoes and the lush green field fades from view. I am pulled to my bed, to reality. I look around my room, my closed door. Daylight sneaks in through the sliver between window and shade. The knock sounds again.

"Come in." I burrow under my down comforter. A warm chocolate fog enters the room and someone's weight depresses the end corner of my bed. Too tentative to be Mom. Lizzie? Gregg?

"Hungry?"

I pop from my covers and see Alec. "Alec? How?"

"Your mom let me in."

My hands fly to my hair in a taming attempt.

"I needed to see you, Zephyr." He places a mug on the table. "Last night sucked so bad."

"It did."

"I want today to be so much better." He holds up a brown paper bag. "Would breakfast in bed be a good start?" The scent of hot cinnamon bread fills my head. "Next year I'll make you eggs in our kitchen. Next year I won't be a complete idiot."

I want to believe that. But, "Smells delicious" is all I can say.

He opens the bag, flattens a napkin across my comforter and sets out two thick pieces of cinnamon nut bread.

"Did you make this?"

"Special for you."

A skip, a flutter. My heart can't help it. Alec leans over and plants an apologetic kiss on my cheek. When he pulls back I see the circles under his eyes, his drawn expression. "You look tired."

"I didn't sleep. I screwed up so badly. After we talked I kept imagining Lizzie telling you what an ass I was, trying to turn you against me."

"She's not like that."

"I'm glad. Because this is between us."

I raise my hand to his jaw, the angry raw line of purple I've just noticed. "What happened here?"

"Gregg." Just the one word, no details, no explanation. He bends toward me and our foreheads press together. "Say you forgive me."

I want to forgive him. I remember Lizzie telling me how love makes people do stupid things. And I see my mom, forgiving my dad. If his huge mistake wasn't enough to destroy their marriage, don't I owe it to Alec—and me—to try to find forgiveness? But I can't quite make the words *I forgive you* form. Instead, I say, "I do."

They are enough. Alec lets out a relieved sigh, nuzzles his head onto my chest. We stay like this for a long time, him listening to my heart, me combing my fingers through his soft hair.

But then I tell him, "You can't stay." He shifts off me, his heat a stain on my skin.

He questions me with sad eyes.

"I need to write my essays for Michigan."

He smiles, kisses me hard on the mouth before standing. "Call me when you're done?"

I nod. He kisses me again before slipping out of my room with a high step, almost a skip.

I go to my computer and log on to the University of Michigan's website. I research student life and academics and their field hockey team. And I can imagine myself there. With Alec. The version of Alec that has promised never to hurt me again. The version of him that made me choose to be with him next year.

The university accepts the common app, which I give them permission to view, and I enter in my references, same as I'd done for Boston College months ago. I spend the rest of the morning trying to focus on my essay. Trying to crowd out doubt. It's a relief to hear a knock at my door.

"Feel like decorating the tree?" Mom asks.

And it is the exact thing I want to do. Something simple and mindless and wrapped in the comfort of years.

I follow her to the living room, where Frank Sinatra croons the words to "Have Yourself a Merry Little Christmas" from Mom's favorite 1950s holiday CD. Hearing the lyrics makes me feel like a kid again. I'm suddenly grateful for the small things that will never change. Like the blue spruce tucked into the same corner as every year. This one is smaller than usual and Mom didn't drag out all the boxes of decorations, but these tiny changes don't make me sad now that I'm facing huge changes. Like starting an unexpected life with Alec.

Mom's untangling a string of tiny white lights but doesn't miss how preoccupied I am. "I didn't know teenage boys brought their girlfriends breakfast. Alec seems very considerate."

"He is."

"You're lucky."

"I am." I just wish last night didn't taint how lucky I feel.

"And that shiner on his jaw?"

Leave it to Mom to notice all the evidence. I pull at the corner of my lashes and the lie races off my tongue. "Hockey." I pray Gregg doesn't tell his mom the truth about any part of last night. So Mrs. Slicer won't tell Mom. The need to get farther away from all things Sudbury burns deeper than ever.

"Lizzie called the house earlier, said you left your phone in her car. She offered to drive it over if you wanted."

"What did you tell her?"

"That I wanted you all to myself to decorate the tree. And that I think you can live without your phone for a day."

"I can try." I don't tell her a quiet day at home feels exactly right.

Mom grabs a new mound of lights, tackles the untangling anew. "I thought we'd get a small ham since it's just the two of us this year. And Rachel asked me over for drinks Christmas Eve. You want to come? See Gregg?"

Oh god. I hadn't even thought about facing Gregg. "I'm good, but you should definitely go."

"Rachel says she misses you coming around."

"I'll see her at the wedding."

"True." Mom considers. "But no plans on Christmas Eve sounds lonely."

It was the same thought I'd had about my father. How he's not here sharing any of our traditions new or old. "I was thinking of calling Dad." If I can forgive Alec for the way his love made him act, I can try to forgive my father. At least take the first step.

Mom smiles a soft grin. "That's the best Christmas gift I could ask for."

We wrap the lights around the girth of the blue spruce and when I plug in the cord I have to stand back. The display is beautiful. So much light on the darkest day of the year.

Chapter 30

I use the house phone to call Dad while Mom's out last-minute Christmas shopping. It's not that she'd eavesdrop, but I need to be alone when I make the call. My nerves are untethered explosives, squealing in every direction. I pace the house, trying to give my whirling anxieties somewhere to go.

"Olivia?" When I hear my father's question, the world stops.

I summon my voice. "It's Zephyr, actually." This inadvertent string of words makes me aware of how much of my life my dad has missed.

"Zephyr?" I hear the way surprise nearly steals his breath.

"Hi Dad." A bridge.

"It's good to hear your voice. How are you? How's school. Merry Christmas." His sentences come rapid-fire. Like he doesn't know what to say and can't say it fast enough. "Is everything all right?"

"Everything's fine, Dad." It's a lie but I'm not sure how much I'm willing to share with him yet. I pace the kitchen, my thumb trailing along the island.

"You had me scared there for a minute."

"You're scared because I called you?"

"I guess you caught me by surprise." I hang on the cadence of his words, the depth of each syllable, and it is a relief that this part of him has not changed. His voice, here in the kitchen with me now, it fills me. "What really scared me, Zephyr, was thinking I'd never talk to you again."

"Same." Because it's always been that. Even when I convinced myself I was scared of running into him around town—even then I was more afraid of never seeing him again.

"You don't know how happy it makes me to hear you say that, Zephyr."

"Dad . . . I-I was wondering if you maybe wanted to meet up for dinner."

"Yes." An intake of breath. "I would love that."

We decide on a Chinese restaurant halfway between here and him. Neutral ground. After the holiday.

"I'm so glad you called." I hear the relief in his voice, feel it in my own chest. It is the first time in months that order feels like it could be restored. Or at least, redefined.

I curl up in front of the television with Finn and find a showing of *Miracle on 34th Street* before there's a knock at the door.

"Come in!"

Lizzie pops into the kitchen under a dusting of snow. She kicks off her boots but doesn't take off her jacket. She joins us in the living room, twisting her hands for heat. "You doing okay?"

"I'm good." I scrunch my legs, make room for her on the couch. "I called my father."

"No shit."

"Shit."

"What did he say?"

"We're gonna meet for dinner."

She leans back, lets out a surprised *hmm*. "I think that's great. What brought on your sudden change of heart?"

"I've been thinking about it for a while and it seemed like the right time. Christmas and all. I figured I won't be here next year so . . . time's running out."

"Because you'll be in Michigan."

I pet Finn, avoid Lizzie's gaze. "That's the plan."

"Is that your plan or Alec's?"

I cut her a look. "That's not fair, Lizzie. You don't even know Alec."

"I'm aware. You've had considerably less time for me since you met him."

"Why don't you just say what you came to say, Lizzie? That Alec fucked up and—"

"He did, Zee. What I saw last night was beyond fucked up."

"Agreed. He got crazy jealous and admitted what he did was stupid. And hurtful. We've all done stupid shit for the right reasons. There. Now, can we move past it? I have."

Lizzie throws up her hands. "No boy is worth losing a friendship over. I don't need you going to Michigan hating on me."

"I could never hate you, Lizzie. But I need you to trust that I know what I'm doing."

"Okay, if that's what you need." But even now I hear her doubt. "Listen, I can't stay." She gives Finn a quick pat. "Gotta do some stuff at the house before Saint Nick gets here. I just came by to make sure you were okay."

"I am."

"Good."

She stands and suddenly I don't want her to go. I don't want to be alone with my doubts. "Lizzie? Thanks for coming over. For checking on me. Last night too. It means a lot."

She nods, considers. "Course, Zee. Always."

Always. Since my father left, I've been consumed with redefining the word, but as she throws a wave from the door, I know Lizzie's definition of "always" remains unchanged.

I curl tighter against Finn and check my texts.

Alec: Call me

Alec: What r u doing?

Alec: Where r u?

And then one from Gregg: Are you around to talk? I read it a few times. My curiosity swells for how that talk would have gone.

Alec: Going for a drive. Text when u get this

Alec: Zephyr, I'm officially worried

Alec: Call me. Now. Please. Let me know ur okay

And one just after midnight: Can't even sleep I'm so worried about u

Then: Where are u???!!!

Six more from this morning, almost exactly the same.

And then another from Gregg: Talk. You know, that thing where friends exchange words. Sentences even.

I punch up Alec's number and he answers on the first ring. "Zephyr, are you okay?"

"Totally. I left my phone with Lizzie and just got it back."

"I was so worried."

I give him the number to the house phone in case he can't reach me again and tell him there's nothing to worry about. I only wish my friends didn't make me doubt my own words.

I go to my bedroom and dive onto my bed, my hip nicking the University of Michigan catalog from the edge of my desk. It flutters to the floor but I don't pick it up. Instead, I let my eyes roam to the acceptance letter from Boston College. It is tacked to my wall, among the photos and cards. Even from this distance, I see the maroon crest. It draws me up, until I am close enough to read the letter, and I remember how happy I was when Alec delivered it to my hands. It seems like a lifetime ago. I look to the date printed in the lines above my name.

I squint my eyes closed, shake off the impossibility. Then look again.

November 11.

Impossible.

I open my desk drawer, frantically dig in my file folder that holds all things Boston College. My fingers clasp the edge of the envelope. The one my acceptance letter arrived in.

In the corner, in eraser-red ink is the postmark date.

November 13.

More than a month before Alec brought me the letter.

An entire month.

I look at the date on the letter again. Two days earlier. It took two days for the letter to be sealed and receive a postmark.

So why did it take a month to reach me?

Did Alec have it before he gave it to me?

And then, the most awful suspicion: Had he been holding on to it? So he'd have time to convince me to hitch my future to his?

And as oxygen drains from my room and the scene from last night reemerges, I think it's possible.

Probable, even.

And that's when I hear Lizzie's words: *Manipulation 101.* And Gregg's: *The kid's got issues.* I remember the times Alec wanted to be with only me. The distance he wanted me to have from Gregg and Coach, even Alumni Weekend.

But didn't I want all those things too?

I do. I did.

I wanted Alec so much, the rest didn't matter.

And it is this realization that collapses me against the wall, sinks me into a blurred heap because I can't separate what is real and what is Alec and what is me.

Chapter 31

I knock on Mom's bedroom door even though it's open. She looks up from where she's reading in bed, beckons me in.

"I thought you were going to the Slicers." I can't keep my voice from cracking.

Mom removes her reading glasses and her eyes lock on mine. "Changed my mind." She pats the bed, makes room for me. "Zephyr, what's the matter?"

I fall into her arms and the deluge opens. I cry for Boston College. For lines being blurred. For doubting Alec. For believing in Alec. For forgetting me. For believing in the new me Alec made. I hate all of me and most of me and I don't know how to escape the skin I'm in.

Mom strokes my back. "Whatever it is will be okay, Zephyr."

She has no idea.

"Tell me what's going on."

Where do I even start? The day at the park? Sex in the woods? Alec bringing me dinner and the news of my future? These things are too beautiful and kind and exactly what I wanted, so how can I be questioning them now?

"I think Alec did something, Mom. Something so bad and I

can't know for sure but now I can't take back what I've done." I sob against her.

"Did he hurt you? Are you in trouble?"

I shake my head.

She comforts me, but then separates us. Our eyes are only inches apart, and I don't like the person I see reflected. "Then let's start with the facts. We'll go from there."

I nod, thankful for the rational side of my mom, the one that can help separate the truth from my suspicions. I drop my gaze as I tell her about my plan to go to Michigan with Alec.

She tries to hide the way shock deflates her, but I know she's calculating physical distance, the uncharacteristic reasons behind my decisions. "And now you regret that decision? Or did you two break up? Is that why you're upset now?"

I hand her the letter from Boston College and she surveys it quickly. "Look at the date."

"November eleventh."

"I didn't get it until a month later."

"You think it got lost in the mail?"

"Maybe. But, the thing is . . ."

"What?" Mom presses, her word filled with too much concern. "What is the thing, Zephyr?"

"Alec brought me the mail that day, the day the letter came."

"Okay."

"But I'm not sure that's when the letter arrived."

"What are you saying?"

That Alec may have orchestrated the biggest mistake of my life. "I think maybe he might have had it for a while."

"What possible motive would he have for that?"

"I think he waited until I was open to changing schools." And then it all sounds too calculated. A small laugh jumps out at the absurdity of my suspicions. "Oh my god, I sound like a crazy person."

"Zephyr, I'm not going to lie and tell you I approve of the plans you made to attend Michigan because of a boy, or let you off the hook without telling you how disappointed I am that you didn't talk to me about any of this, but you are not crazy and this is not the end of the world. You can still go to Boston College."

And the truth hammers me. "No Mom. I can't. I declined their offer. I sent the paperwork. It's done."

Mom goes rigid, the color erased from her face. "Please tell me that's not true."

"I wish I could."

"Oh Zephyr." Mom releases me fully then, sinks back into her propped pillows. "How could you let this happen?"

It is a question I can't stop asking.

I drive through town, intent on my destination. My knuckles whiten with the death grip I have on the steering wheel, but I can't relent. It's irrational, I know. But if I ease off the slightest bit, I'm afraid I will disappear. That I will be swallowed by all my doubts. When I reach the house, it is an effort to pull my hands free of the wheel and step out into the cold. But I do, because I have to. Mom's advice was dead-on. Do the thing that I can control. Fact check. Talk to Alec. And listen to my gut.

I can't separate out the timing of my letter from Boston College. The scene of Alec and that girl. Alec's jealousy. But then there is the Alec who set aside his jealousy when Gregg got hurt, the Alec who helped me with Finn, the one who keeps me safe in his arms, promises me forever. Confusion circles in my head on an unrelenting loop and spits me out in front of Lani's house now.

When she opens the door, she's as surprised to see me as I am to be here. She doesn't even bother with a greeting, just steps aside to welcome me in. Her look stretches beyond me, searching for Gregg before she closes the door behind us.

The house smells of apple pie. It's surprising the way I remember so much of this living room from when her mom was our Brownie troop leader.

"This is unexpected," Lani says, crossing her arms, judging me already.

"I know it's weird timing and it's lame that I'm interrupting you or bothering you."

"No bother. What's up?"

I fumble in my jacket, my fingers grabbing onto the swatch of newsprint. It is flimsy between my fingers, near weightless. And yet it is almost too heavy to exhume from my dark pocket. I fight its determination to stay hidden and haul it up, unfold the news clipping for Lani. "Do you remember this?" I don't look at the paper. Instead, I study her eyes, the way they dart bigger when she reads the taunt etched in red. There is a dash of horror, a spec of disbelief.

"No." She shudders.

My heart plunges because I know as I watch her reaction that this act of treachery was not committed by Lani.

"I mean, I remember when you signed it at breakfast that day, but that"—she nods toward the slur—"Zephyr, who did that?"

"It doesn't matter." It is the biggest lie I tell. I crumple the clipping and shove it deep into my coat pocket.

"You didn't think I . . . ?"

"I had to make sure."

"I might be envious of what you and Gregg have, but I would

never." She cups her hand to her mouth and her voice softens. "I'm so sorry this happened to you, Zephyr."

And in that moment I'm not sure if she's sorry "SLUT" graffitis my image or if she's sorry for me because I'm out here on Christmas Eve searching for the person who marked me. Either way, her innocence plays with the gravity around me, shifting it so I sway, my feet liquid. Lani reaches out to steady me.

"Are you all right?"

"I'll be fine." Another lie.

I manage to get into my car and drive down the road before tears rise up. I pull over and squeeze them back, keeping my eyes shut, seeing Alec bent before me, lacing up my skates with such tenderness, sharing his heat under a blanket in the woods. And I see his gifts. The carnation and the cards pinned to my wall.

Pinned.

My eyes dart open.

Panic sweats my palms.

I dial Alec's number, my hands shaking. I am too much of a coward to face him and, worse, I fear he'll be able to soothe away all my suspicions under his touch.

"Zephyr. Happy almost Christmas. I was just thinking about you." Alec's voice is cheery and light, a world away.

"A-Alec?" His name breaks over a sob.

"You okay?"

"No." Not in any sense of the word. My heart pounds too fast and too hard. My rib cage struggles to keep it all contained. I can almost see him there, at my wall. Pinning the news clipping onto my collage.

"What happened? What's wrong? Can I help?"

"I need to ask you something."

"Anything."

Did you play me? Did you betray me? Is any of us real? "Remember that day you delivered my acceptance letter from Boston College?"

"Of course, Zephyr. It was one of the happiest days of my life."

And mine. I force my words out, "Did you find it in the mailbox that day?"

Time buckles for the briefest instant. "What a weird question."

"You didn't get it before then; hold on to it so I'd consider Michigan?"

"Of course not. Why are you even asking me that? Tell me where you are. I'll come meet you."

"You can't. I'm not home. I'm out driving. Trying to process."

"Zephyr, you're scaring me."

I think of the irony. "And that press clipping. Did you write that word? Break into my house?"

"What press clipping? Why would I break into your house when I'm there all the time?" Concern builds in his voice. "Where is this even coming from?"

I hear the Alec from my arms, between my sheets, the one who promises and carries through.

"How could you ever think I could hurt you?"

"I didn't. It was the last thing I expected until I saw you with that girl." And there it is, in words. The hurt that has so much depth it feels bottomless.

"Zephyr, we've covered this. You know why I did that and I admitted I was stupid and wrong. Why are we still talking about this?" Anger reaches into the phone, frosts his words.

I still have too many questions about Katie, but that's not what worries me in this moment. "Alec?" Time bends. Mocks me. "I never told you the press clipping hurt me. How could you know that unless . . . ?"

"Zephyr, I can obviously hear that you're upset even if I don't know anything about some random press clipping."

Pieces scramble to fit together, make a whole. Alec knows where my house key is. Has always been crazy jealous of Gregg. Would have had hundreds of opportunities to take my signed photo from Gregg's gym locker. And if he was jealous enough of me hugging Gregg at Waxman's to orchestrate an entire scene of practically screwing a girl, what would he have felt if he'd heard Gregg's words: *Acting like I'm over you.*

Oh god. "I need to go, Alec."

"Don't do this, Zephyr. You can't call me all upset and then just hang up. It doesn't work that way."

And then a voice from deep inside, one that has been silent too long: "And you're going to tell me how it works?"

There is a loud bang. His foot pounding a hard surface. I yank my phone from my ear but still hear him yelling, so crisp, too clear. "Why are you doing this?"

"Good-bye, Alec."

It is the first time I say these words and they leave a bitter after-taste. We'd promised never to say good-bye, Alec always claiming the phrase was too harsh, too final.

Alec calls back immediately, but I turn off my phone. I don't have room for more than one voice in my head right now.

I break open, remembering every beautiful promise he made, and the girl he woke in me. But now I need to go to the only place I know that is truly safe. I drive home, where Mom's waiting for me in the kitchen, her face drawn with concern. "Are you all right? Did you see Alec? What did he say?"

"I called him. He denied it." The letter, that is. I don't bring Mom up to speed on SLUT and that added bit of humiliation. I can't let Mom know my failure is bigger than the one choice.

"Do you believe him, Zephyr?"

"I don't know what to believe anymore, Mom. Everything feels so out of control and I don't even know how to fix any of it." My lungs grow too small to hold enough air, my ribs strangle. How do I go back to the days before Alec? Can I undo the things we've done? Return to a person I barely remember being?

"Sit." Mom guides me to the kitchen chair. Her hand plants on my knee. "Breathe, Zephyr. There's a way through any problem. Let's take it one fact at a time."

I nod, wanting nothing more than her help, her clarity.

"Tell me one thing you want from this."

"The truth." Breathe.

She kneads the round of my knee. "There may be too many versions of that. I'm asking you what *you* want. What would you do if it were in your power? What would you change if you could?"

"Boston College." It is the one sure thing that bobs to the surface in this ocean of doubt.

Mom looks relieved. "Okay. And is that in your control?"

"Not anymore." Breathe.

"What if you went to the admissions board, withdrew your rejection?"

A light. Hope. "Is that even possible?"

"I don't know, Zephyr, but if you tell me you want my help I will do everything in my power. But you have to swear this is absolutely what you want; that you won't change your mind."

"I won't." If I could get Boston College back I'd never want anything more again.

"Then that's where we'll start." She pats my knee with this new optimism. "We'll contact the college first thing Monday, after the holiday break. But for now I think a cup of tea might be all we can do."

Tea sounds simple and good. And Monday sounds possible, the first step in a controlled, executable plan. "Yes. Tea."

"Chamomile or mint?"

The house phone rings and Mom stands to answer. "Hello?" A few seconds pass before she gives the phone a blank look, hangs up. "Wrong number, I guess." She holds up the two boxes of tea for me to consider.

"Anything but mint," I tell her.

I drink the hot tea with Mom, but it does exactly zero to settle me. The quiet of the kitchen, Mom's concern, my future unknown—again. It's all too much.

When I head to my room, I pull up the Boston College website and search the athletics staff contact list. I write an e-mail to the field hockey coach, telling her I've been accepted and asking her to meet with me. I detail Sudbury's 12–1 record, our state title. And I write about what it means for me to be on the field, part of a team. I don't disclose what I've done, what was in the package I mailed to the college.

I read the e-mail more than a dozen times, changing one word and then fifty. Finally, my nerves step aside long enough for me to press send.

And I wait.

Again.

Chapter 32

The ability to sleep abandoned me. Last night was too dark and too crammed with the best memories of Alec. I tossed in bed, plagued by his fingers skating across the flat of my stomach, his shape hovering over me in his backyard, my skin exposed to the dusk. The electric touch of his sneaker against mine. The shock of him inside me. The white light he'd build within me.

But the morning sun wipes away all those memories and sprays light on all my doubt.

If Alec did keep Boston College's letter from me, wasn't it because he wanted to be with me?

And the newspaper photo, the word branded there? There were fifty people in the caf that day and all of them dumb enough to think that would be a funny joke. Maybe the clipping fell out of Gregg's locker somehow. Maybe a million things could have happened that prove Alec's innocence and my paranoia.

Or maybe only one thing happened. The thing I suspect. And fear.

I lace up my sneakers and head out for a run. The sun is low over the trees, barely awake. Its gold light blankets the snow-tipped pines. There is no sound but my footfall crunching against the crisp snow.

The roads sleep with the soft of Christmas morning. There are no cars or distractions, only me and my brain working up the nerve to see Alec. And I will. I have to. But my feet have a different mission and I let them run for miles in the early cold. I jog under the umbrella of hush that softens the neighborhoods. No one stirs, not even a dog barking. It is as if time has stopped and I am alone. It is eerie the way Christmas has quieted all movements but I am hungry for this calm, the complete silence. And the power of my legs and lungs to propel me in whatever direction I want to go.

By the time I return to Ashland Drive, I feel strong enough to face anything. Alec. The truth. I slow to a walk and stretch my arms to the sky. I tilt my head back, relax my neck muscles. The sun bears down on my cheeks and feels almost warm since the wind can't build momentum through our thick stand of trees. I stop and draw the heat down. My breath slows. The world pulses quiet. Soundless.

Until a twig cracks in the forest and breaks my meditation. It is a deer, I am sure. Within seconds, another crack echoes in the trees, bouncing off the still limbs, the snow caked on the forest floor. It causes fear to bump along my skin. Because nothing is for certain.

I race home and into the kitchen where Mom's brewing coffee. "You were up early."

"I needed a run." Needed to think.

She moves to the island. "Did it help?"

"Yeah." The run was perfect. It's all the other stuff crowding my heart I could do without.

Mom crumples the note I left her before leaving the house this morning. "So, what are you going to do, Zephyr?"

"I don't know."

"I'd be willing to bet you do know, even if it seems like the hardest thing in the world right now."

And she is right. Of course.

I tug off my hat and scarf, unlace my sneakers.

Mom stirs cream into her coffee. "But none of that needs to happen in this very instant, so how about we try to conjure up some semblance of a normal Christmas? The rest can wait. Step by step, remember?" She gives a hopeful smile. "And those gifts aren't going to unwrap themselves."

"I could do with normal." Anything to keep my mind off Alec. And maybe Mom needs the same thing, to keep her mind off Dad not being here and all the disappointment in me she's trying to hide.

We go to the tree and I choose a medium box and tear at its wrapper. Inside is a Boston College sweatshirt and it steals my breath with all its maroon color and bold white stitching.

"I wasn't sure if I should still give it to you. But you said it's what you want."

I rub at the thick material, think about its journey from the bookstore on campus. "It's all I want." I lost track of that too easily. If Alec is innocent, I still want Boston College. I can have him and Boston College and it will work. "Would it be weird to put it on?"

"Not at all. It's important you visualize what you want. Maybe this will be a good sign for our mission with the dean."

I pull off my outer tee and stretch the sweatshirt over my head, poke my arms into its soft inner fleece. It's too big, but in that perfectly oversize way. I brush my hand over the front, my fingertips catching the embroidered seal. "Thank you."

Mom looks at me, so proud. "Don't thank me. You're the one who did the work to get there. And you'll do it again, Zephyr."

Mom's faith is so strong I almost believe a second chance is possible.

"Zephyr, I think your father deserves to know what's happened."

Shame visits me again, quick as lightning striking. "I thought you might have told him already."

"I wanted your permission first. And I wanted to suggest that the two of you talk about what's been going on with you lately."

"I don't know if I can, Mom. It's bad enough you know."

"Telling me was the best thing. And talking to your dad about it might provide new perspective. Maybe he can see through this problem in a way we can't."

"Maybe." Maybe. "Could you tell him? I think I'm fine to talk about it when I meet him for dinner; I just can't bring it up. I need to focus on talking to Alec first. One thing at a time, right?"

"Step by step," Mom says, and I can hear how she's trying to draw the stress from me, help me survive this.

We spend the morning opening gifts and baking cookies until I am stretched on the couch, lost in a sugar coma. It is dark by the time the doorbell rings. Mom calls to me from the kitchen, "I've got it!"

I stand and watch Mom put her hand to the doorknob and in that instant all of me wants our visitor to be my father. I want to hear his reasons for leaving me and why he wants me back. I want someone to show me that love is complicated and makes us do ridiculous things. And that it's okay to fall. And make mistakes. And forgive and come out the other side.

But it is Alec's voice I hear exchanging polite greetings with Mom as she welcomes him in. I meet him in the kitchen where Mom throws me an *is this okay* look. I nod. Finn barks.

Mom resumes the noisy work of loading the dishwasher so I invite Alec into the living room where A *Christmas Story* is too loud on the television and shredded wrapping paper litters the rug. I can't help remembering the first time I let Alec into my bedroom, my fear of him seeing anything out of place. Now, I don't even lower the volume on the TV.

"What are you doing here?"

Alec leans in. "It's Christmas." He kisses me on the cheek.

I recoil but he hands me a small box. "I wanted to give your gift in person and see if you were feeling better."

"Better than what?"

He grabs my chin, holds it softly. His eyes search mine and I cannot look away. "You were so upset yesterday. I tried calling after, but . . . did you turn your phone off?" Then he waves off his question. "Doesn't matter. I just hope you got the answers you were looking for."

I didn't. I don't know any more than I did yesterday. Not for sure.

He nods at the gift. "Aren't you gonna open it?" That's when I feel the box in my hand, so innocent, too much of what I wanted with Alec next year. Surprise. Kindness. Trust.

"It's just something small." He eyes the kitchen to make sure Mom can't hear. "To celebrate you coming with me next year."

I take a small step back.

"Us together next year. It's everything, Zephyr."

The word *everything* echoes.

And it is too much.

"Open it."

I unhinge the box to find a silver necklace. An artistic, sweeping heart dangles from the chain's center.

"Do you like it?"

I close the lid with a snap. "I can't accept it."

"And this." He ignores me, pulls a small holiday bag from behind his back. He shows me the dog collar inside, shiny, bright red.

"The material is reflective. So Finn will always be safe if he gets out again."

His thoughtfulness at the vet, his care of Finn. Him remembering how my first dog died.

But still. "Alec, we need to talk. Can you wait for me in my room?"

He smiles. "I'll always wait for you, Zephyr actually."

The pull of that nickname softens me. I go to Mom in the kitchen. "I have to tell Alec about how you're gonna help me get back into Boston College. He's in my room, waiting." I read Mom, how hard she's fighting not to judge Alec. Or me. "I just need a little privacy. Is that okay?"

She worries the dishcloth, tosses it onto the counter. "I won't listen, Zephyr, but I won't be far. Door open."

"Of course."

She nods, her face tight with concern.

Alec comes to me when I enter my room, takes my hand. "You freaked me out yesterday."

I pull back from him and sit at my desk chair. I need distance from his body and his mint smell that wakes such a deep wanting. I place the jewelry box on my desk.

He sits on the bed. "I think I figured it out. Why you were trying to blame me yesterday."

"Why?" I am desperate to hear any version of the truth other than mine.

"We talked about it before. How the first Christmas or birthday is the hardest. Your dad's always been here and you're angry that he's gone now. You just took it out on me. It's totally normal, Zephyr."

I'm not sure what I expected. A full confession? A string of irrefutable facts that would prove he didn't do what I suspect? But as I sit across from him now I realize neither of these things was a possibility.

"Next year your entire lens will be so different and you'll be the missing piece that returns home. Things like this get easier with time."

I steel my nerves, even though my stomach quakes. "We need to talk about next year."

"My favorite subject."

"I want to go to Boston College."

He lets out an exasperated sigh. "I thought we covered this. Besides, isn't it too late?"

"My mother doesn't think so."

"Your mother?" Alec stands. "So you told her."

I nod.

"Is that what this is all about?" He points at my sweatshirt like an accusation. "She's trying to keep you close."

"This isn't about her. It's what I want. What I've always wanted."

"What are you even talking about? You chose us, and Michigan. I never pressured you." He hears the way his voice escalates, and softens. "What about all our plans? What about me, Zephyr?"

"I think I need some space."

He crowds me. "What does that even mean?"

"I need to think."

"Think? About what? This preposterous idea that I hid your acceptance letter? You were the one who signed those papers for Boston College. Not me. I wasn't even with you when you did that."

I pull the defaced press clipping from my desk drawer, hand it to him. "What about this?"

There isn't even a shift in his eyes as he reads the slur and it makes me go cold. He crumples the paper, tosses it into the corner. "Zephyr, you think I wrote that? I would never."

Tears fill my eyes. The word didn't surprise him. He didn't ask about my signature or when I found it. He just cast it aside like it wasn't important now. "I so didn't want it to be you, Alec. Even after I knew it was you, I didn't want it to be you."

"Zephyr, you know me. You know how much I love you. Why would I do something like that?"

But I don't hear his words, only his tone. The same one he used to convince me the girl at Waxman's was for my benefit. That he needed to teach me a lesson. "I don't doubt you love me, Alec." I doubt his version of love. "But I think we need to stop seeing each other."

He reaches for my hand, squeezes. "Don't do this, Zephyr. It'll be the biggest mistake you ever make."

But he's wrong. I've already made the biggest mistake. "I feel like we need to take a big step back. Get perspective."

He discards my hand, too forcefully. "So you're dumping me on Christmas. Really classy."

"I didn't want this, Alec."

He turns on me quick. "Yes. Yes you did. Because you're the one who's doing this. Not me. All I have ever tried to do was protect you. I listened to you about your father, helped you when your dog got sick. And all those things you begged me for?" His eyes go sly now. "The way I made you feel. You wanted that. But now you're acting like a complete nutcase. No wonder your own father didn't want to stick around."

A serrated knife cuts through my heart, shreds me. "You should go."

He grabs at my wrist, too hard. I try to pull my arm free from his grip, but he tightens his hold. "Don't think for a minute that this isn't all your fault." When he finally lets my wrist drop, he grabs the gift box and punches the wall just shy of the light switch. The plaster buckles under his force. I hear a different Alec reach the kitchen, exchange polite good-byes with my mother, like nothing happened between us, like he didn't just level me.

Chapter 33

I drive the highway, grateful for the distance from Sudbury. I find the Chinese restaurant we agreed on and my father is already seated in a red vinyl booth. He stands when he sees me.

"Zephyr, it's so good to see you. I was afraid you wouldn't come."

"I thought about it." A lie to sting him. Because it only seems fair.

I take a seat opposite my dad and my brain clogs with all the questions I wanted to ask. About another woman. Another family. If he doesn't love us anymore. But I hear Alec's words above everything else: *No wonder your own father didn't want to stick around.* And the question that rises faster and stronger than all the rest: "Why did you do it?"

My father folds the cloth napkin from rectangle to square. "You don't want to order tea first? Get warm?"

"No." I hadn't meant to bring this much confusion to dinner, but Alec's words have me spinning. And I think my father is the only one who can slow me down. "I need to hear you say it. I need to try to understand."

He clears his throat, looks impossibly nervous. "I was feeling lost, Zephyr. Like I'd forgotten who I was."

My insides jolt. I lean in.

"I'd made all these promises and had all these expectations and they felt cumbersome. I fell into that cliché trap of wondering, what if? What if I could see the green on the other side? But then I did and it showed me was that all I've ever wanted to be was your dad. And a husband to your mom."

"You couldn't have figured that out without leaving us?"

"I wish I'd been smart enough to handle it differently." His hand reaches across the table for mine. I slink back.

"You really messed me up. Mom too."

"I know, and I'm sorry. You can't know how much."

"I've been thinking about this for so long. Wondering if sorry would be enough. If it could ever be enough." I accepted Alec's first apology. I gave him that. I fear giving away too much again, even to my father.

Dad's eyes search mine. "And did you reach a conclusion?"

"I'm not sure. I think sorry can only be a start. Like a place-holder." I straighten my fork against the knife, center them on the cloth napkin. Order, in miniature. I pull up the napkin, letting the silverware fall into a chaotic pattern. "Then we see what comes next, if sorry can stick."

"A start is good, Zephyr. And my apology will stick. I'm not going anywhere. Not unless you tell me to go." His gaze stamps with that promise.

The waiter breaks the tension, asks for our order.

Dad asks, "Our usual?"

I nod and Dad tells him we'd like cashew chicken with white rice, wontons, shrimp rolls, and tea. Our favorite dishes.

When the waiter leaves, I say, "You remembered."

"It was never my intention to forget."

"Then what was your intention exactly?"

"I don't know, Zephyr. I'm even more confused than I've ever been. But not about us. Our family. I want to earn a way back into your life."

"Is that why you're not lecturing me?"

"Lecture you? I'm the one who screwed up."

"You did, but so did I. Mom told you about Boston College, right?"

"She did."

"And yet no lecture?"

"I think you deserve a congratulations first. I wish I'd been there when you heard."

I wish I'd heard when I was supposed to. And for the first time I wonder if things with Alec would have been different if Dad hadn't left. If I hadn't felt the need to bond with Alec over our absent fathers—have Alec in my life to fill the void Dad left.

"Did Mom also tell you how I decided to go to University of Michigan. And why."

He nods. "Yes, and I'm here to help any way I can, but I think I have to earn back your trust before my opinion can really matter."

"But I want to know what you think." I want to hear it, need to hear him tell me I fucked up. Maybe it will make us both seem normal or human or something.

"I think you made a mistake and you're working to fix it."

No different than him.

Dad's simple honesty makes me reach into my bag then, pull out the three fall issues of *Classic Car* magazine and slide them across the table. "I've been keeping these for you."

Dad's face softens as he rests his palm on top of the small stack. "Thank you, Zephyr."

And I hear what he's really saying. How he's thankful I always knew there would be a time when I could give them to him.

"Dad, I need you to do me a favor." Or Mom a favor. As a thank you for her always being there for me. For her loving me despite my bad choices.

Dad searches my eyes. "Anything. Always."

"I'd like you to come to Anna Slicer's wedding reception. For Mom. I think it's something she'd really want."

"Will you be there?"

I nod. "I'll be there."

"Then I'd be honored."

And something forges between us then, me accepting him into Mom's life in this small way, one step removed from mine. We both honor the safety in this first step.

When I return home, I bring in the dress I bought at *Second Skin* vintage shop on my way back through Sudbury. I hang it over my door, far from my closet with all its false sense of order. I smooth the clear plastic over the dress, love how the claret color deepens in different light.

"Pretty."

I jump with fright, my hand leaping to my heart. Alec sits in the corner of my room, next to my record player.

"Is it for something special?"

"What are you doing here?" I step back, into the door's threshold.

"What? You're afraid of me now? Jesus, Zephyr, what went wrong?"

"Well, yeah. You're sitting in the corner of my room like a creeper. How did you get in?"

"The key. I needed to see you." He stands, pulls a carnation from behind his back. It's the one from my wall, the one he'd tucked in the grill of my locker, though it is dry and brown now, its crown fragile. He sets the flower on the desk like a peace offering. "I feel like we got lost somehow. Can't we start again, Zephyr? Be like we used to. We were so good together. You know that."

"You need to leave. My mom will be home soon. She can't find you here."

"Don't lie, Zephyr. I saw her note on the island."

The back of my neck goes cold. Did he watch Mom leave? The way he did when he brought me eggplant parm and the letter that changed everything?

"You used to like when I came over. Remember all the times you invited me into your room? The time you kidnapped me from school? I love you, Zephyr. I want that back. And deep down, I know you do too. You can go to Boston College. I don't care. I've always said that. I want you to do what you want to do. I just want to be with you. And I want you with me. Like before." He selects a record from the stack, empties it from the sleeve.

"Alec. What we had is over. Really over."

He eyes me, taunts me. "Don't say anything you'll regret." He spins the record around by its thin edge. Clockwise. Around and around. It is almost mesmerizing until he smashes the vinyl against his knee, the record snapping in half, shrapnel shards jumping into the space between us. He drops the pieces, comes to me. I back into the hallway and he follows. He presses his chest against mine, the same way he did at the rink that day. His breath hovers so close. "You'll figure it out soon enough. How much I love you. How I'd do anything for you." A finger strokes my jawbone, soft, knowing. "Hopefully, before it's too late."

He drops his hand to mine, squeezes my fingers. "I don't want this to be good-bye, Zephyr." He raises my hand, kisses it so tenderly. Then he turns to leave. I watch his back disappear around the corner and into the kitchen. I follow behind, locking the door as he lets himself out.

I wait until his car leaves before I pull my key from under its rock.

When I return to my room, my heart thunders as I literally pick up the pieces of my mess. And then I go to my collage, rip down everything Alec ever gave me. I shred his cards, cram their flimsy pieces into the wastebin. I stomp the trash down with my foot, trying to contain what feels like madness.

Chapter 34

I prep for the wedding, stepping into the dress I rescued from the consignment racks. It's a tight fit and I question my choice when I have to tame my boobs into place. I pin up my hair and finish my makeup just as Lizzie calls.

"Do you look like Cinderella?"

I look down at my unemptied trash. "Slightly less fairy-tale."

"Hah! We still on for tonight?"

"Still on. I'll text you when I leave the reception."

"Deal. And stop freaking about your dress. You have to own it." It strengthens me the way Lizzie knows and loves me fiercely, doesn't judge me despite everything. Even when I told her Alec's words; how it was *no wonder my own father didn't want to stick around*. They were difficult to repeat. Impossible to forget. Still impossible words to process.

When I meet Mom in the kitchen, her eyes widen. "You look gorgeous."

I try to be okay with the compliment. "Thanks. You, too."

Mom tucks her lipstick into her purse and snaps the butterfly clasp, nods at the two twenties on the counter. "Take that. In case you need anything or if they don't have an open bar." She cuts me a look. "For soda."

I tuck the cash into my purse and shake off the memory of sipping white wine with Alec, my whole body thirsty for him. It causes my skin to shiver in a new way now.

Mom wraps her heather gray cashmere shawl around her. "I decided to get a room at the hotel, but I still want to take one car. I'll get a ride home with Rachel tomorrow." Then, almost as an afterthought: "Lizzie's still sleeping over tonight, right?"

"That's the plan." All except for the part about Dad replacing me as Mom's date. That part is my secret gift to Mom.

She fixes her gaze at me. "A sleepover with Lizzie sounds nice. I like seeing you two hang out again. But no parties."

"I don't exactly need the headache on top of everything else."

"You'll get through this, Zephyr." Boston College. My breakup with Alec.

"I know, but it doesn't inspire celebration."

"It will. When you wow the admissions board at your interview."

"If we can even get an interview."

"You need to think positively."

"I'm trying. Believe me." I pull on my peacoat and Mom cringes. "You're not wearing that ratty jacket, are you?"

"So far you're not knocking it out of the park in the date department."

She laughs. "I guess I'm rusty."

The drive is slow in the falling snow and the church is full by the time we arrive. As we're escorted beyond the heavy wood doors, the heat of the space assaults me. The air is woven with incense and perfume. Organ music reaches out from somewhere high in the rafters. The tune is soft and low, as if the very church is inhaling and exhaling song. My eyes follow the white satin runway down the length of the aisle where Gregg stands at the altar in a black suit, a white carnation tucked into the lapel of his jacket. For a moment, I cannot move. I stand in the entryway, the cold air at my back and the warmth on my face. It's like being caught between two worlds.

Gregg is taller than the other groomsmen, his red hair softened in the yellow light. Responsibility and grace set in his stance as he anticipates the arrival of his sister. Still, I don't miss the small smile that lights along the edges of his lips when he sees me. The slight tip of his head.

An usher leads me to a pew in the back of the church, mere steps away. I am careful in these foreign heels. Mom slips in beside me.

She whispers. "Gregg's looking like quite the handsome man."

I *tsk*. "No impure thoughts in church."

She clucks, slaps gently at my thigh.

A new song begins to play from the hidden organ and the congregation stands. Within moments, Anna floats down the aisle, her fire-red hair pulled into a brilliantly slicked twist. Her smile spreads wide and bashful and dazzling all at once. And then she is past us, walking toward her future husband with a lithe, certain stride. I watch her reach the altar, join hands with her fiancé. But it is Gregg I study as prayers are read and vows are made.

Mom holds my arm for balance as we head back into the snow, the wind whipping at my face. We drive a few blocks to the hotel reception hall, Mom gushing about Anna's beauty and how she'll bawl uncontrollably when I get married.

In the reception hall, smooth light ricochets throughout the room, glowing from candles and white flowers. Lilting violin music sings from a lone musician in the corner.

Mom plucks a glass of champagne from the tray a waiter offers. "Let's find our table."

Within moments of taking our seats, the room hushes. Mr. Slicer stands at the head table. He *tinks* his silverware against his glass in wedding Morse code, making champagne flutes rise around me. I raise my water glass.

"I've thought about this day for a long time," Mr. Slicer starts, adjusting his tie. "When Anna was born, she was no bigger than my forearm."

Mom reaches for my hand and squeezes it like she's remembering when I was that little. She must have so many memories of me that I don't even have. Memories she shares with Dad. It's right that he'll take my place as Mom's date tonight.

Anna and her new husband tuck into one another as Mr. Slicer finishes his speech and toasts the room. The sound of clinking glass reverberates throughout the space. The air is electric with love, the promise of love, the anticipation of love. It sends a tingle onto everyone's skin, like love is possible for every attendee at this very moment.

And I remember its intoxication. Parts of me still crave it.

Until I recall all the bits that weren't love at all.

Music blooms in the room once again and then my father is walking toward our table. I watch Mom's face, how she lights with surprise.

"Jimmy! What are you doing here?" She stands, my father takes her hands, kisses her so gently. Like he's trying to get it just right.

"Zephyr asked me to come."

"He's my plus one," I tell her. Mom looks at me then, and

her joy fills me. She lowers her eyes in a soft *thank you*.

My father offers me his elbow. "Care to brave the dance floor with me?"

Dad and I are both crappy dancers, but that never stopped us from fooling around in the kitchen when I could still balance on his toes.

I follow him to the dance floor where Gregg's little sisters are doing a mash-up between the waltz and flailing. The sweetness of it climbs in me, settles there.

"You look beautiful," Dad says.

"I'm glad you came."

I let my head fall against my father's chest and close my eyes. The music swims in the room but all I can hear is his heartbeat. How it is reliable and here.

"Thank you for this, Zephyr." My dad's words are whispered, filled with gratitude.

I open my eyes, find his.

"Thank you for letting me back in, allowing me to earn your trust."

"It's just a dance, Dad." I tack a laugh onto my words, but both of us hear how the giggle is forced. Because both of us know this is so much more than a dance.

"You know how your mother and I have been going out to dinner lately?" Dad asks.

"I know. Date night."

"Date night." Dad laughs. "I like that."

"Well, I was wondering if it might be all right if I came to the house after one of our dinners? Just to see you and say hello. I won't stay long. Not if it makes you uncomfortable."

It wouldn't. "I think that would be okay."

"Yeah?"

"Yeah."

And there it is. A small pact, another small step.

When the song is over, Gregg walks to us, all shoulders and strut, like he's on the ice, like his steps are effortless. I move to give him a hug.

"Congratulations," I tell him.

"I didn't get married."

"No, but you got a brother-in-law. It's about time men started to gain numbers in your family."

He laughs. "I hadn't thought of it that way. Good point." He looks to Dad, shakes his hand. "It's nice to see you here, Mr. Doyle." He nods toward the head table. "You've made my dad happy."

Dad winks at Gregg and takes a step back. "I assume you'd like to cut in?" Dad says as he gives me a small bow.

"I would. May I?"

"Uh, I suck at dancing."

"I know. My toes still ache from prom. But you have to. I'm in the wedding party. I get whatever I want."

"Is that so?"

"That's what they tell me." It is the Gregg Slicer flirt on full beam and Dad gives a chuckle before heading back to our table.

"Okay. One dance."

I take Gregg's hand and he pulls me to him. "You've been avoiding me, Zephyr. No texts, no phone calls. I have to talk to Lizzie to know what's going on with you."

"I thought we were dancing."

"Dancing and talking."

"Okay. Let's talk about what Lani would say if she knew you were dancing with me."

"Lani and I broke up."

"Really? Why?" I've grown oddly fond of Lani since showing up at her house.

He shrugs. "She's not the one."

"If 'the one' even exists."

"That's a fairly cynical thing to say when you're dancing at my sister's wedding."

The word *sorry* hangs on my lips, but I pull it back. "Good call."

Gregg laughs. "You seem happy, like your old self again."

I want to tell him about Alec and how we've broken up but it doesn't seem the right time. Mostly, I don't want thoughts of Alec to invade this night. And then, I don't have to say anything because Gregg's face pinches with pain.

"How can someone with so much grace on the field be so clumsy on the dance floor?"

I laugh. "Lucky for my teammates, one thing doesn't have to do with another." It feels good to smile, spar with Gregg in the relaxed way I've always known. I find solace in these parts of me that are resurfacing, finding air.

I focus on my steps. The music is slow and the silk of my dress brushes my legs like wind. I lean my head against Gregg's chest.

"You look fairly passable tonight, Zipper."

A laugh bubbles in my chest. "You clean up pretty good yourself."

"High praise." Step. Turn. "I'm glad you came."

"Me too." Side step.

"Ours will be better." Step.

"Our what?" I raise my gaze to meet his. Side step. Hand squeeze.

"Our wedding." He leans down to kiss me, his lips tender, meeting mine. I watch it happen, as if standing outside of myself. The kiss occurs in slow motion. And I don't stop him.

The room melts away and it is only me and Gregg and his perfect kiss. I can't help but kiss him back as he holds the small of my back, pleasures my mouth with his.

This is not the kiss in the woods. This is not the hunger of Alec. This is something more. This is . . . safety . . . and forever . . . and scarier than losing myself to Alec.

I pull back. "I can't."

"You can, and you did. Splendidly, I might add." He shrugs then, trying to shrink the moment. "Write it off to wedding romance. I'm not trying to come between you and Alec. I just wanted to get it right this time."

He did. So right.

"It can be our secret," he says.

"I don't want any secrets."

"Fine. Tell the world, but just don't be pissed at me or stop talking to me. Deal?"

I nod, my feet unsteady.

"Good. I don't want to lose you again."

I don't want to get lost again.

My thoughts sway with the lights, the beautiful kiss. I dip my ear to his chest, listen for his heartbeat under the chorus of strings. I feel the race of his pulse and how mine responds.

As we dance I can't help wonder how much would be different if Gregg had kissed me like that back in October.

I practically stumble back to the table where Mom and Dad are huddled together talking. I sit to steady my nerves. Keep from running back to Gregg.

Gregg who is still on the dance floor, his arms outstretched, his feet platforms for his youngest sister's tiny dress shoes. My heart leaps for another chance at our dance. For another kiss.

I chastise the thought.

I should leave. I shouldn't be thinking about kissing anyone. Worse, I shouldn't be *liking* kissing anyone.

A waiter taps me on the shoulder and I jump in my guilt. Mom gives me a concerned look.

"Would you care for chicken or salmon?" the waiter asks.

"Nothing for me, thank you." Every inch of me wants—no, needs—to get out of here. If I could get outside to the ice-cold air my head will clear.

"Are you okay?" Mom asks. Dad is intent on my response.

"Sure. I was just thinking I might leave before the roads get bad."

"That's probably a good idea." Mom digs in her purse, hands me her keys.

I look at Dad and he gives me a shy grin. A year ago I would have thought my parents hooking up was gross, but now I find myself rooting for them. Hoping that forever is possible for some.

"Do you need anything?" Dad asks. "I could take you home."

"I'm fine," I say.

I see the way Mom's hand moves to cover Dad's. "She's fine," she whispers. Her reassuring words make me believe I will be.

"Okay, drive careful." Dad stands to give me a hug and I kiss Mom before ducking out of the room. I muster all my strength not to look at Gregg again.

As I walk to the car, my feet crunching snow, I breathe in the icy air. It makes me feel awake for the first time in a long time.

I am again that girl, walking across the Boston College campus, my future so clear.

I get in the car and start the ignition.

"Miss me?" The words reach me from the backseat.

Chapter 35

I jump, my head nearly hitting the car's ceiling. My heart thuds outside of my body.

"Miss me?" Alec repeats from the backseat. Through the rearview mirror, I see he's smiling.

Fear vines around my ribs. "How are you here?"

He leans forward. "Surprise is important in a relationship."

I adjust Mom's rearview mirror. "We're not in a relationship."

"You've made that clear."

"I'm not alone. My parents will be out any minute."

"Why are you lying, Zephyr? I saw your mom give you the keys."

He grabs the back of my hair and twists my head toward him. He gives me a quick, rough kiss, his teeth crashing against mine. I fumble with the keys in the ignition, calculate my chances of running across the ice and back into the reception hall, but it would be impossible in these heels.

"Drive." He pulls my hair tighter and I turn the key. "We need to talk."

"Alec. Don't do this."

"Please don't tell me what to do." His teeth are clenched. His anger brewing.

"Okay. I'll drive."

He climbs into the front, slips his hand into my coat. He thrusts open the flaps to study my dress. I feel his palm skate over my breast. He lets out a low whistle. "Your place."

I turn on the wipers and can see through the windows of the hotel, all the guests dancing. I hate putting the car in gear.

"So you had a good time?" He traces a circle into the cold windshield.

Fear erases everything before this moment. "It was okay." I catalog the whereabouts of my cell phone. Deep in my peacoat. My parents too far away. Gregg, oblivious. It is just me. Me and Alec.

I pull onto the road.

"I see your father's back. Looks like everything's working out for you, huh?"

"He was here for my mom." I adjust the wipers, fumble for control.

"That's cool. I like weddings. I like the commitment. How two people promise themselves to one another. Remember when we did that?"

"Alec—"

"Don't. We need to talk but not while you're driving. I want you safe, Zephyr, and the roads are bad." He turns up the music. I drive slowly.

When we reach my house, Alec follows me in. He takes off his jacket. I pull mine tight around me.

"Take your coat off, Zephyr. I need to see that dress."

"Alec, what are you doing?"

He moves to me, slips one shoulder free of my coat, then another. The air on my skin feels wrong, invasive. He drops my coat to the floor. His fingers trace the line of my collarbone, the length of my arm. Gooseflesh rises, but not the way it used to.

"Alec, you don't want to do this."

"Don't make the mistake of telling me what I want."

"You're scaring me."

He laughs. "I'm scaring you? You bailed on our future together. You don't think that's a little scary? To trust you like I did and then"—*smack*—his two palms slam together right in front of my face, barely missing the tip of my nose. I step back, stumble over my coat in a heap.

Alec catches me, his hand around my waist. "Do you have any idea how much I've done for you, Zephyr? How much I would still do for you?"

I slink away from him, move to the sink, brace my hands against its lip.

He drags his fingers through his hair. "I saw you dancing with Gregg. I saw him shove his tongue down your throat. I saw you *let* him shove his tongue down your throat." He lunges toward me then, grabbing my arm too hard.

"I don't know what you think you sa—"

"DO NOT lie to me!" His face consumes mine. He harvests a deep breath, makes a study of my cleavage before running a finger down the path from my neck, through my chest. "Look at you, practically naked. No wonder he thought he could fuck you."

"Stop!" I try to wrestle my arm free, but he only grips tighter.

"You said I could trust you. You *made* me trust you and now you're dressing like a whore and hooking up with someone who's wanted to get in your pants for years."

His fingers dig deeper into my flesh, redirecting blood flow. "You're hurting me."

324

"Hah! *I'm* hurting *you*? How do you think it felt to see you sucking face with Gregg?"

My primal brain orders flight or fight. I spy the knife block on the counter. "Let go," I say, and his hold releases.

He steps back, shakes off his frustration. "Christ, Zephyr, you make me crazy. Why do you have to do that?"

"I didn't do anything." I inch toward the knife set.

"See!" He jabs his finger at my words. "That right there. You're so good at playing innocent. And then I get nuts because I don't know what to believe." His step swallows the space between us. I smell the mint of his shampoo and I flash to that first day. Before I know it, his hands creep around my waist. "Forgive me," he begs. "I just want you back."

"Alec, this isn't good for either of us."

Alec caresses the cut of my jaw, the softness of my cheek. "You are so beautiful." His fingers travel along the span of my collarbone, up the tight angled curve of my neck. My body cringes. My breath comes shallow and rapid.

"You like that, don't you?"

I brace myself against the counter, inching closer to the knives.

Then the air pulses quiet for just a breath. His body releases from mine. Gone is his feather touch. There is only me and silence and Alec and stillness. I focus on Alec in this slip of time. How his arm raises, his elbow becomes a sharp point hovering. "So why would you leave me?" He drives his angular elbow into my skull. A hole is drilled somewhere above my ear. My head rings. Bells fill the hollowed-out space. I feel myself slipping down the length of the cabinets, my dress hooking on a drawer pull. I hear the fabric rip away from itself, a soft screech. I crumple to the floor, my head a basin filling with the rushing tide of terror.

A word sits on my tongue. *No? Don't?* I can't form my defense. The room kinks. Speech abandons me. My ears drum. I think there is no greater pain possible until a spike drives through my side, slamming my ribs. His shoe. The kick is a stake. Planted. Executed. I crunch into the agony, my brain crowded with all the words I cannot scream. A black rage erupts under my skin, under the footprint Alec has gouged into my side. I bite on my lip and taste the copper blood trickle on my tongue.

Words reach me. "You make me do this, Zephyr. You just couldn't love me enough to keep Slice's tongue out of your mouth, could you?"

The gravel of sound shakes free from my tongue, harsh as sandpaper. "Get out!" My skull explodes with pain. "Get out!"

His hands are on my arms then, propping me up. "I'm so sorry. . . ."

Blackness.

Then I'm in his arms, my head on his lap. "Talk to me, Zephyr. . . ."

Blackness washing.

"I love you so much." His voice strangled with fear.

I rock.

He's rocking me.

"I didn't mean to hurt you, but I have to protect you. We planned a life together, Zephyr. You can't give it away to another guy."

A deeper blackness.

I surrender.

Welcoming the way it swallows me and the pain all at once.

But there's a girl inside, too long silent. She wants a fight.

She raises my hand to my head and tries to press away the sharp ache, but it only makes me cry out in pain.

"Zephyr, let me help you."

"Leave. Now." My voice and her voice combine in a groan. Then she says, "I'll call the police."

And I am proud of her, a light of strength in this darkness.

Alec laughs, but looks confused. "It's me, Alec. Your future. Remember? What do you need the cops for?"

Her strength begins to leave me and I fear her absence. "Get. Out. Now."

He stands, stumbles back unsteady. "I'll let you get some rest. We'll talk tomorrow." And he walks out the door.

As if we've just ended a normal date.

As if I am not broken.

As if he has not shattered me.

I listen to the fridge hum for a thousand years. Shame drenches me. I am slick with stupidity. For throwing away my future for Alec.

I struggle to stand, carefully carrying the fireworks of pain. It takes too long to make it to my room, using the wall for support. Tears drain off my cheeks, a wet trail.

I shimmy out of my dress, hating it as it slides to my ankles. I burrow into a T-shirt and crawl into bed, every movement grueling.

I close my eyes and catalog my injuries. My skull. Ribs. Places others can't see. He was precise, and I am glad for the careful placement of my wreckages. So I don't need to show the world my shame.

Chapter 36

I wake to the smell of bacon and panic. Is Mom home? Is there blood on the cabinets? The night crashes back to me with too much clarity. I press my fingers to the golf ball pounding under my scalp.

Then Lizzie's voice.

So close.

"Zee, it's me. "I made you some food."

Her kind tone coaxes me to sit upright. I find I am in my room, surrounded by the familiar. Photos on my wall. My record player. Clothes. Lizzie.

And a tray on my bureau, with eggs and bacon and a small bowl of yogurt.

The smells turn my stomach as bits of Alec crash into my head. I reach for the water on my bedside table.

Lizzie leans in. "Just take it slow."

I take a sip and rest against my pillows. My side yelps.

"How bad is it?" Lizzie asks.

"It hurts." A squeak.

A song rises from the kitchen. Cee Lo. Faint, but Cee Lo. *I see you driving 'round town with the girl I love and I'm like, Fuck You!*

Lizzie gives a guilty shrug. "I couldn't resist."

My phone. Still in the pocket of my jacket. Is my jacket still in a heap on the kitchen floor? The way I was?

Lizzie strokes my leg. "Alec could have really hurt you, Zephyr."

"He did hurt me."

"You know what I mean."

I do.

"Do you remember what happened?"

I remember too much. "How did you know to come?"

"When you didn't text me, I called Slice. He said you'd left."

The wedding. The kiss. Alec waiting in Mom's car.

"Do you remember me coming over?"

I remember falling to the floor, Alec begging me to forgive him. I remember blacking out and coming to. And blacking out. "I remember something cold, and hearing your voice."

"I wanted to call the police, Zee, but you wouldn't let me. I still think we should."

"No," I say quickly.

The phone rings again. Alec.

Lizzie stands, paces. "Don't let him get away with this, Zephyr." She tucks back a string of her pixie white hair. "He beat you, Zee. For no reason."

"Not no reason."

A scoff. "Please don't tell me you think he was justified."

"No. Of course not. But I kissed Gregg. Alec saw us."

"I don't care if he saw you and Slice having sex. Nothing gives him the right to hurt you."

"I know."

"Do you?"

"Of course, Lizzie. It's just—"

"Please be careful how you finish that sentence."

The tears start now. Full and round, pooling in the corners of my eyes. The thoughts that tortured me all last night as I slipped in and out of awareness. "Shouldn't I have seen this coming? What is wrong with me that I let this happen? He was supposed to be perfect. I loved him, Lizzie. I gave him everything."

He reaches out to me again, my phone singing in the background.

Lizzie kneels at my bedside. "There is *nothing* wrong with you, Zephyr, and he's far from perfect. He's the asshole here, not you."

I pull my covers tight around my chest. "I can't have anyone know."

"You can't be silent about this, Zee."

"But I can't tell anyone, either. Then they'll know that I'm the idiot who fell for the wrong guy, and that I let him take too much. I can't, Lizzie. It's been hard enough admitting that to you and my parents; I can't have the school knowing." Tears conquer me. "Don't make me do that. I won't survive the shame."

"You have nothing to be ashamed of. This isn't on you." She stands quiet, thinking. "What's going to happen when you see him in school?"

"I don't know."

"How are you going to explain the fact that you can barely walk?"

I pull a tissue from the box, wipe my face. "I don't know."

Lizzie sighs out a long breath. "You're sure you were clear with him? That it's totally over?"

I swallow hard. "Yes. Of course. That's why he's pissed."

"Is there any way he thinks you'll forgive him again?"

Again.

It is a word.

An accusation.

My failure.

"No way."

"Okay, I'll stay quiet. I won't say anything until you're ready." She collapses into my desk chair, taps the top of the Boston College catalog. "You can recover from this, you know."

I thought I could, but now? "Can I?" I swing my legs over the side of the bed and the muscles around my ribs shriek. I push onto my feet. Lizzie half stands to help me, her arms extended, but I wave her away. I slip one foot in front of the other, my spine realigning, my muscles stretching into this newly reordered skin.

Lizzie follows me as I amble to the kitchen and swallow hard against every wrong decision I've made. Alec's constant calling is a soundtrack to my bad choices. I bend to my jacket, stroke its sleeve. When Cee Lo calls to me so close, I jump. As if the phone discharged an electric shock. Under my skin, scorching my bones. I pull out the phone, my thumb hovering over the irony of the word "accept."

I press.

"Zephyr? Is that you? Are you all right?"

The immediate push of his concern startles me but I gather purchase. "N-no. Not even close."

"What can I do? I never meant for that to happen, you just made me so jealous. See me. Let me apologize in person. Please, Zephyr."

"Alec." A beat. A slice in time. "This is over."

"Don't say that. I love you, Zephyr. Can't you see that's why this happened in the first place? Don't do this to me. To us."

I take a deep breath, stand. Steel my nerves. "There is no us."

"Forgive me."

A shudder mangles me.

"Give me another chance. Things can be perfect again."

Things were never perfect.

"It is so too late for that." I lean against the door, begging it for strength.

"Zephyr, don't do this."

My mind bends to the day on the swing set and then to the park. His car in the woods. The past. I press my thumb hard into the bump on my skull and a lightning bolt scorches, reminding me of the now.

"Don't come near me again." I flick off the call and there's an unyielding pain in my chest that has nothing to do with my bruised ribs.

A second later, Cee Lo. Lizzie grabs the phone from my hand, mutes the ring. "I was thinking you should come over to my place. Get your shit together before school tomorrow."

School? Tomorrow? Monday.

"You'll be safe there. Besides, I don't think you're ready to face your mom."

"Oh shit, my mom."

"I texted her from your phone last night. Everything's cool. She'll be back tonight around dinner."

She returns my phone and I see the seventeen missed calls. Seventeen voice mails. All from Alec. I block his number, delete the thread of our texts. It's not much, but it's a start.

"Get dressed. Eat something if you can. I'll clean up the kitchen."

I don't ask whether she's talking about the dishes from this morning or the chaos of last night. What I do know is that it's not her disaster to clean up.

"I need to stay here."

"Alone? No way. You were a mess when I got here and there is no way I'm leaving you alone so he can come over here and finish what he started."

"He won't, Lizzie."

She spurts disbelief. "How can you say that?"

"I know him. He flipped last night because of Gregg and the wedding, but he won't come back."

"I won't leave you."

"You can't stay with me forever."

"We're not talking about forever, Zee; we're talking about the day after your ex went psycho on you."

I peel my back from the brace of the wall. "I need some time alone. To figure shit out, get my head straight for tomorrow morning when Olivia and I call Boston College. I can't focus on anything else, Lizzie. I can't fuck this up again."

"Shit, Zee. That's tomorrow? Could it be worse timing?"

"No, it's perfect. It's exactly what I need. I need to move on. Put this behind me. Trust me."

She finally concedes. "But I'm calling every hour to check on you. Maybe every half hour."

"Deal."

Lizzie moves to hug me, wrapping her arms gently over me. She is careful with me, and not only because of my external bruises. "I love you, Zee."

"I know, and I'm sorry for letting you down."

"Never apologize. None of this is on you."

As Lizzie leaves, she tells me, "Keep your door locked." I do.

I bolt the door and humiliation's undertow drags me down. I slink against the wall and lower my core until my bottom connects with the floor.

I curl my knees up and hold them close, the position bringing comfort. And that's when the scene plays out. Me and Alec. Just a few feet away, in the opposite corner of the kitchen. Alec branding me a whore. His elbow jammed into my head. His shoe splitting my ribs. Him begging for forgiveness.

And before. How he loved me.

Cooked for me.

Brought me my acceptance letter like a gift.

Held me closer than I thought one person could wrap another.

Chapter 37

Mom and I sit at the island the next morning linked by a suspended hope. Me, too aware of my hidden bruises, determined to move beyond all my mistakes. Mom with her need to protect me, fix what went wrong—the parts she knows about, anyway. I want this second chance with Boston College so badly it hurts more than my physical wounds. We listen to the clock tick and neither of us talks about the wedding or Dad or anything other than this goal before us. And when it is five minutes past nine o'clock, Mom picks up the phone, dials the number printed at the top of my acceptance letter.

"Yes, I'd like to speak with the dean of admissions, please. Tell her Olivia Doyle's calling in regards to an acceptance packet my daughter received."

In no time, I listen to Mom go into professional argument mode. No blame, no presumptions. Just facts spread out between two adults. There's been a mistake, she says. We'd like to remedy it, she says. She's careful not to reveal why this mistake occurred, but so articulate in providing options, solutions. She is powerful and believable and I think she could get anyone to see our way. But it is the silence when Mom's not talking that kills me.

When Mom hangs up, she brushes the front of her wrinkle-free suit. "I think it's good. The dean asked that you come for an interview a week from Thursday." Mom sets the date and time in her phone and I do the same. "This will be your opportunity to reaffirm your commitment to the school." She studies me for that commitment. "She's doing you a huge favor, Zephyr. Most kids don't get one chance at this school."

"I know. You won't regret this, Mom."

"But don't count on anything, Zephyr. She said this is highly unusual and it sends up some red flags."

"I know."

"So we'll need to prepare you, no different than how I prepare a defendant. We'll get you ready to handle questions from any angle. You'll need to prove you're capable of the social and academic challenges Boston College will demand. And that you regret declining their offer of acceptance."

I do. "I will, Mom. I've never been more ready. I've already contacted the field hockey coach. I want to see her when we're on campus."

She pulls on her coat. "Good." She fastens her last button. "These are good first steps, Zephyr. Strong steps."

And I feel it, the tidal wave of Mom's help and how she reached the dean. Maybe before my packet did.

But as I drive to school, I almost bail a hundred times.

Because I can't see him.

I won't see him.

I inhale deep abdominal breaths and exhale through my nose, a calming technique Coach taught me that is having zero effect on my spiraling nerves.

But I can't run away. Can't let Alec take more.

I walk across the parking lot and through the halls, kaleido-scoping glances in every direction, searching through the crowds.

But it's not Alec waiting at my locker.

Gregg points to the slight limp in my gait. "You hurt?"

"Twisted my ankle running." Lie.

"Not dancing?" He winks.

"That I escaped injury free." Half lie.

"So are you going to tell me why you left the reception without saying good-bye?"

"Headache."

He looks at me hard, suspicious. "Feeling better?"

"Much." A lie trifecta.

"Can you hobble over there?" He signals toward the front lobby. "I want you to see something." I walk beside him, an imposter fak-ing health.

The red entry doors approach. I could leave. It is a bossy temp-tation. But I refuse to run.

Gregg halts in front of the award case. There's a new, three-tiered trophy, gleaming silver: SUDBURY HIGH SCHOOL FIELD HOCKEY STATE CHAMPIONS. A female figure stands on top, a field hockey stick in hand, the wind in her immortalized hair.

The playoff game meets me here. The lights. The crowd. The green of the grass. I search the team picture propped next to the trophy, me smiling with victory. I feel that girl in me still.

"Cool, right?" Gregg says. "That trophy should have your name on it."

"As if."

"Oh right. I mean, you're lucky your team let you sit on the sidelines while they brought home the championship."

I smile, try to play along with his joke. But it is just that, a joke.

The truth is that I played my ass off. For four years. And I want to be that girl again. "I'm not going to Michigan."

Gregg's posture bolts with the surprise.

"I'm going to try to play for Boston College. If they'll have me."

"I thought you said—"

"I did." I straighten, ignore the twist in my side. "It was a mistake."

"And what about Alec?"

"No Alec. No Michigan. It's Boston College like we always talked about."

"So did you guys . . . ?"

"Break up? Yeah."

"Damn!" Gregg looks all impressed with himself.

"What?"

He shrugs like it's nothing. Then, "That must have been some kiss at the wedding."

It's impossible not to laugh at his idiocy. "Yep, you got me. That's why we broke up. Oh, except for the fact that we split up before the wedding."

"Huh, so it wasn't because of me?" He winks.

"Not because of you."

"You doing okay?" Gregg asks.

"Are you?"

"Me? I didn't break up with Alec."

"No, but I think I owe you a million apologies. For pulling away like I did. I just didn't see it. I couldn't see it, you know?" I feel that lump rise in my throat, the unwelcome reminder of how much emotion I invested in a boy. The wrong boy. "That's not true. The truth is I didn't want to see how my relationship with Alec was driving all this distance between you and me. I never wanted that. I hope you can forgive me."

"Done." He bends to shove at my shoulder. He bites back on all the other stuff he wants to say and I am grateful.

"Let me make it up to you?"

"No need," Gregg says. "We're cool."

We walk to French class and I grab his forearm as we enter the room. "Sit with me."

Gregg claims his old seat and Alec never arrives. It adds a layer of torment, trying to calculate when he'll show.

Gregg nods toward Alec's empty chair. "Guess he doesn't want another shiner."

I can't think what Gregg would do to Alec if he knew the whole story.

But I don't tell him. I'll never tell him.

When class is over I shuffle off to English, my books already tucked under my arm in an effort to avoid my locker. My elbow forms a hard pointed angle and somewhere, somehow, Alec's blow hits me again. So hard I have to steady myself against the lockers. My breathing turns shallow and I wonder how long it will take until I forget. If I'll forget.

Someone asks me if I'm all right and I wave them off. I'll be fine, I tell myself. Just fine. And I will be. I can't doubt that.

I head to the bathroom and my phone rings. A number I don't recognize. I squeeze out a tentative, "Hello?"

"This is Atlantic Veterinary. We've been notified by the credit card company that a Mr. Alec Lord contested the charges for Finn Doyle so we'll need someone to come to the office with a check."

Anger rises in me.

But, then . . . maybe this is a good thing.

Alec's pulling away from me.

"I'll be by tomorrow." I flick off my phone. I'll talk to Mom about the vet tonight. Right now nothing matters beyond Finn being home safe, and me arriving that way too.

I splash water on my face. I can finish this day.

I rejoin the crowded halls and head toward English until I stop short, my lungs firing.

Because Alec waits at the stairwell.

I turn sharply to avoid him but he races to me, hooks my waist. Pulls me beyond the crowd.

"I need to tell you how sorry I am."

"You said that already."

"But you didn't hear me. It's killing me not to be with you, Zephyr." He ducks his head close to mine, whispers. "Yesterday was unbearable. I'd do anything to make you forgive me. Take me back, give me another chance."

"I can't."

"You can. I know you want to." His hand lowers onto the slip of my back. "Don't give up on what we had. I love you."

But I don't see love. I see the moment when my fingers calculated the distance from the knife set. My heart quickens, reliving it. Again.

And I think I won't survive months of this. Him skulking out of corners, tugging at my sanity. "If you come near me at school, I'll get a restraining order." I don't know if orders of protection are granted to teenagers but the threat is enough to make his hand drop away.

"Zephyr, please."

I leave him and his pleas in my wake, but I am still haunted by shadows.

In the library, I bury myself in the stacks until it's dark, until I know Alec's at practice. I call Lizzie when I'm in my car. "I'm heading home."

"You want me to come over?"

I buckle in, turn on the defroster. "It's been a long day."

"Call me when you get there."

"Promise."

I pull out of the parking lot and the dark asks me to remember the abandoned building site with Alec, our forest bed. I wonder how long flashbacks of Alec will bubble up. The good memories hurt more than the welts. I'm assaulted by all the things I wanted. All the ways I messed up.

And I wonder how a heart can hold so much pain when it is a fist of an organ. Yet it throbs. It *feels* torn and shredded. It hangs dense in my chest, remembering its wounds.

I turn off the main road and the Ashland Drive pole has a cap of ice at the top, like the snow cones Dad would drizzle with maple syrup. I slow, the road frozen and rutted. My car bounces over the deep channels, spaghetting my spine.

The forest is too dark for dusk, even for early winter. I lean forward suspecting one of my headlights is out. And that's when I see it. A mass of red fur curled in the road. I slow to a stop, switch on my high beams and squint into their spray of light.

"Finn?" I pop my seat belt, open the door into darkness. Cold air stabs me.

My heart reels as I kneel beside the lump of fur. "What's happened to you?" I gather his head into my lap. He is warm. His middle labors with the rise and fall of breath. I reach over his fur, under him. My hand returns free of blood. "You'll be okay." It is a promise I want someone to make me. "I'll get you to the vet. Come on." I cradle him in my arms, set him onto the passenger seat. He lets out a groan from the faraway place he inhabits. "Stay with me, buddy." I pet his head and something catches the dim interior light, throws it back at me like a knife's edge. Something that is not his collar.

It is shiny.

And sharp.

My necklace. The heart Alec gave me at Christmas.

It hangs around Finn's neck.

My own heart catapults, leaping my pulse.

The air swallows me, the woods scurry too close. I run to the driver's side and lock the door.

I can't go to the vet; that is what Alec wants. I try to imagine where he'd be waiting for me along the way. Fear propels me to the house where it is warm and bright and I can shut out the dark.

Chapter 38

I bolt the door behind me, swim into the light that floods the kitchen. "Mom?" I call.

I place Finn onto the couch, recheck the locks. I find the card for the twenty-four-hour emergency vet clinic and pluck it off the fridge.

"Mom!" Only stillness answers, reminding me it's Monday. Date night. I fumble in my pocket, my keys falling to the floor. I pat my jacket, my phone is in my car's console.

I pick up the landline, dial Mom's cell. It takes too long to connect. There is only the static silence of a dead line, and that's when I know I'm not alone.

I drop the phone onto its cradle and eye the door, my car keys on the floor in my path. In seconds I calculate how my body will need to scoop the keys as I run from the house. I move just as a metallic snap echoes from under the house.

The breaker.

In the basement.

Someone has thrown the main switch, pitching me and this house and my escape into blackness.

Fear roils in my blood. Becomes me. I kick around for my keys but with each sweep, I am losing time.

I reach for the island, my eyes adjusting, carving light into the shadows. The smell of spearmint bleeds through the air, through my memory, as my senses conjure the last time panic joined me in this space. And how my fingertips reached for the knife set even then. But the block of knives is gone now. The counter cleared. I open a drawer, rifle for utensils, scissors. My fingers meet with the smooth wood of inner drawer and nothing else. I fumble around the sink, but even Mom's pruning shears are missing.

The phone rings and I freeze from the impossibility of its sound. A second ring sears through silence. I wade across the black, remove the handset, place it at my ear.

I pray that it's anyone besides him.

Terror climbs the ladder of my spine. My voice, reluctant. "Hello?"

Silence.

Then the dial tone cries *beep beep beep* and I hang up, quickly dial 911. But he's quicker.

The line falls dead again.

He's in the basement, where the phone line enters the house.

But then, no.

He could be outside. At the junction box.

All at once the woods feel too hungry, haunted.

My body tells me I need to flee, protect. My brain tells me to fight, engage. I tuck into the forgotten corner of the laundry room, quiet as my fear, and wrap my hands around the butt of my field hockey stick. I hold it tight against my chest, a weapon.

I try to reverse my breathing. Make it soundless. Make it so I cannot be found. The darkness is a comfort, a cloak. I blend into it. For anonymity. For safety. There was a time when I feared darkness. As a child. Alone.

344

Not now.

Darkness doesn't have fingers that twist into my flesh. Darkness can't stalk me. It can't drive me into the shadows because darkness is fleeting. Not like the threat before me.

Then, impossibly, Joan Armatrading joins me. The familiar steel guitar notes creep over my skin, unseaming my flesh. Alec manipulates electricity now, just as he did in our forest bed. I grip the stick tighter and trace the music to my bedroom. I picture him at my desk then, a flashlight in hand. He will be so much more prepared. All of this carefully planned.

Does his beam of light scamper over my Boston College catalog? The faces of friends in photos? Does he see the absence of his tokens? How they are smashed into the well of my trash can?

I want to run for the door but can't drive without my keys. Still, I know the woods. Better than anyone. And I can run. I'll come back for Finn. I tiptoe one foot toward freedom, until Alec freezes me.

"Your favorite song."

His voice surges through the air, galloping my pulse. He is close. In the kitchen close. Inches away. I grip the neck of my stick tighter, silently retreat my foot. My breathing impossibly loud.

"You don't have to answer me, but you should. I know you're here. And you know I'll find you."

Then, Joan:

Oh the feeling
When you're reeling . . .

All those times I reeled from Alec. His touch. His promises.

"You know, this really isn't a love song." He raps his knuckles against the butcher block top of the island, a slow, dull metronome that lets me know he is patrolling its outer edges. "You should have listened more carefully, Zephyr. This is a song about rejection, something you know too much about."

She'll take the worry from your head

But then again, she put trouble in your heart instead

"I want you to hear it for what it is. You put trouble in my heart, Zephyr."

His voice tracks to the living room. I tighten my grip, plan my escape. Then, only Joan:

Can bring more pain than a blistering sun

But oh when you fall

How did I not hear the heartbreak in this song? How did I miss so much?

Alec calls over her lyrics. "Favorite song to hear again?" he asks the darkness.

The universe pauses. Joan sings.

"No? Nothing." Another pause. "I vote for a repeat. Let's play it again, shall we?"

I raise my foot, waiting to step, to escape. I wait for the shuffle of his footsteps on the carpet, his shadow skulking to my bedroom, toward the source of the music. I wait for Joan. A noise to locate him, any little sound that will buy the seven seconds I need to get a head start out the door.

But the room hangs motionless for a dozen eternities.

"Choosing to stay put, are you? Smart girl, Zephyr. You make the chase fun. You always have." The curtain in the living room draws back too quick over its rod. Metal scratching metal. He's searching. It's only a matter of time and he can't find me cowering.

"Oh, hello mangy dog. Not feeling so hot?" Finn. On the couch. The playfulness in Alec's voice distorts reality. "You know

346

it didn't have to be like this, Zephyr. I gave you every chance to come back to me."

His words bounce off the photos in the hall, the path to Mom's study. I move from the laundry room, marrying my back to the wall, my stick firmly in my grasp. The front door is within reach, its knob glistening in the dense dark. I step quietly, my feet barely touching the floor. I reach for the doorknob and that is when I find my keys. They clink underfoot, kicked by my creeping toes. The clanking is a bullhorn, a siren, the dull foghorn call of a lighthouse.

I grab the knob with lightning quickness, turn it, and pull.

But my fingers slip, clutching air. A hand grabs the back of my hair, yanks me away from the freedom of the woods. I fall to the floor. Crashing onto my hip. I writhe against the siege of pain as my body is stretched, dragged.

Then there is my scream.

The only sound in a sea of dead air.

He tugs harder on my rope of hair, uprooting me. "Quiet." His word is clipped, hard. "Be quiet and I'll let you go."

I have to trust his words. Mute mine.

Every follicle, every inch of my scalp screeches in protest. And then, my head drops, hitting hard against the unforgiving floor that blunts and swallows my cry.

A minute. Maybe two. Maybe a hundred.

He stands over me and there is a beam of light casting a dance of shadows around the room. A flashlight rests on the island. It is enough to illuminate his face. His eyes, the cut of his jaw. Malice makes the person tented over me unrecognizable. I work up a scream but then Alec's fingers are at my throat.

He straddles my waist, pins my arms under his knees. The

pressure of his weight on the inside of my forearms is too great to fight against. I cut my eyes to my stick, just out of reach.

Then, in an almost intimate gesture, he brushes back my hair, floats it onto the floor around me. "Such a beautiful neck." He presses against the tender cords hidden beneath. My throat becomes smaller, pushed into submission.

"Don't," I choke. "Please." Finn groans and my heart breaks.

Alec pushes harder, my voice box bruising. "I like it when you beg. Remember how you'd beg me, Zephyr? With that arched back? Your eager tongue? I know you still want that."

"Alec, don't."

"I will."

Cold rushes down my neck as he unfastens my buttons. I swim my fingers along the floor searching in vain for my stick.

He opens my coat, pins its sides under his knees along with my arms. His hand releases from my throat and I cough out the bruising irritation, my chest convulsing.

"Tell me you love me."

"Alec," I beg. "Please." I wriggle to kick, but he's pinned me fast.

"Yes, like that. Beg me." His hands pull at the bottom of my tee as if he'll rip it.

"Alec, don't!" I yell, but the words only find life as a whisper. "You don't want to do this."

He traces his finger along the lines of my lips. His skin tastes sour. "I didn't want any of this, Zephyr. I only wanted you to love me. I wanted to be there for you. After Finn got sick. After Slice was hurt. You made me do those things."

I gasp. The sound is thick, underwater. "What did I make you do?"

"It was nothing that would kill him, just some herbs to make him sick enough for you to need me. And Slice, well, you needed me then, too, didn't you?"

Gregg's skates. Finn's health. My future. Blue turns to black in this ocean under the ocean where no light can penetrate.

Then his lips are on mine, his tongue forcing its way into my mouth, pressing too hard, too fast. I twist my head to gasp for air. I heave oxygen into my lungs, panting.

"Alec, let me up. You're scaring me. I'll do anything."

"You'll apologize?"

"I apologize."

"Hah." A slap singes my cheek. The sting is vicious and rings across, under, through my skin. I twist my head, press it against the floor. "You don't even know what you're apologizing for."

"Please don't hurt me."

"Hurt you? Can't you see I love you? You're the one threatening to call the police. What am I supposed to do? Just walk away? I don't walk away from love, Zephyr. I'm not a quitter. We planned a life together. We planned it. You don't get to ditch that."

He stands then, towers over me. I scramble to sit up, a trickle of blood seeping into my mouth.

"Who do you think you are to dump me? You're lucky I even looked at you."

I used to think I was lucky. Now I wish I never imagined what Alec smelled like or what his skin would feel like under my fingertips.

Time slows. His foot leaves the ground. It moves back, away from me. Gains momentum. Too quickly. His shoe thrashes into my ribs and I double over from the pain firing up the side of my rib cage.

And there is a brilliant flash of light, from the pain or something else I cannot say, because I am being pulled. Up. Up. By my hair.

The pain is excruciating. Alec laughs, "I always like it when you wear your hair up." And then, release. I hit the floor hard and I am grateful. Until another kick smashes against the back of my thigh.

My brain screams, but I can't make a sound any louder than a moan.

"That's it, Zephyr. Moan for me. Tell me you like it."

Kick.

An anvil to my chest. I tuck myself into a small ball, bracing for the next jolt, fearing where it will land, how much it will hurt.

When I hear the sound of bone meeting bone I wince and tears squeeze out of my eyes. It takes a few seconds to realize the blow brought no pain. Am I numb? Is this the blessing of adrenaline? I scramble to the edge of the room, find my stick. I hoist myself to stand even though my entire body wants to give over to gravity and crumble. I try to see clearly, but the dark only sprays a heap of shadows.

I raise my stick, fix my grip.

There's a moan.

Someone yells a muffled *"Fuck!"*

The unforgiving ice of air joins us.

Knuckles crack, a body falls. Two bodies on the ground together. Wrestling. Grunting. Punching.

"Zephyr, get out of here." It is my father's voice. Impossible, but here. Oh god. He can't see me like this. He'll kill Alec. And go to jail for it. I can't ruin him too.

"Go to your car. Call for h—"

One figure rushes another. Strangles Dad's word. I grab for the flashlight, shine the light along the two figures. One has gone limp. It is my father, his strong frame wilted.

Alec scrambles over the threshold and onto the porch. He

comes for me and I drop the light. "Stay back." I raise my field hockey stick over my shoulder. I can see he's winded, that Dad slowed him. Blood trickles from his mouth, but I taste it on my lips. "How did you think this was going to end?"

He snickers. "You still don't get it, Zephyr. This isn't going to end." And I hear the promise in his voice. The way I used to.

He leans forward, lunging for my waist as I draw my stick back, back, back, over my shoulder. My muscles ripple with familiar momentum. My hands lock into the grip. My left foot plants forward, knows its place. I lean in. I focus on Alec's middle, the stomach. I can hit the wind out of him, make him choke on the airlessness. Then it is not my muscles that engage, but my heart, my memories—all of the want that Alec distorted rages inside of me and I ready.

One arm straight.

One elbow bent.

I fix my stance.

I swing from behind my ear and hear the *whoosh* of air as the stick cuts through the atmosphere. I bend my legs and arms, all to make contact with Alec's core. The place where I traced the cut of his muscles, the soft of his skin.

He collapses as he comes at me, one arm ducking into the fold of his waist.

I clench my grip, raise the stick overhead again. I watch my target. Alec. I want to hurt him, hurt him the way he's hurt me. I want to stop him from ever hurting me again. I swing my stick down hard and the force meets Alec's back with a focused whack. I hear the crack of bone, the screech of his pain.

I step over him quickly, my stick again at the ready. But he doesn't move. Only his lips. I hear it clear. The *I love you.*

Around me, the woods are silent except for a crow who caws from somewhere in the trees. I hear its mate answer. Their speech is a cold, desolate chorus.

And then there is the light that burns behind me, an approaching car shining its white glow over my father and Alec. Both slumped mere feet from my own. I drop to my knees and cradle my father's head, telling him everything will be all right.

And then my mother is next to me. And she holds us both.

Together, she and I promise my father that everything will be all right.

The New Beginning

I pull on my jersey, number 11. Twenty-three was available when I made the team. So was five. But eleven was the number of years it took Sudbury to win a state championship and that feels worth remembering, even now. I tuck my shirt into my uniform skirt and my fingertips float over the tiny scar on my hip. Small and thin. This raised wisp of flesh stretches out from the past. My fingers go to this abrasion often, purposefully. This line in my flesh, it will grow old with me.

Reminding me.

I lace up my cleats and walk out of the gym. My superstitions no longer with me.

Drums and horns from the Boston College band invite players to the field, spectators to the stands.

"Ones!"

I turn to see Gregg with his arm slung around a girl. And as they get closer, as I see her clearly, I scream. I can't help it.

Lizzie runs to me, arms open. We hug and she feels taller, grander. As if New York has stretched her, making Lizzie as sleek as the city. I pull away and even her face is longer, older. She wears her professionalism in her bones. "New York looks good on you, girl!"

Lizzie beams. "Yeah, well, I'm sort of head over heels in love with that smelly city."

It's been over four months since I've seen Lizzie, though we talk all the time. But to see her, here in the flesh, is huge. "How are you even here?"

She flicks her thumb at Gregg. "Ask Slice."

Gregg's smile creeps wide across his face. "First game of your college career, thought I'd bring in the big guns to cheer you on." He gestures to the stands. "Even Olivia and Jimmy are in attendance."

That I knew, but still. "You came all this way and I won't even get to play."

"So I'll watch you warm the bench," Lizzie says.

"How thrilling. The scoop of the century."

Lizzie lifts her hands, shows open palms. "I'm off duty. I'm here only for you."

Like she's always been. In the days after Alec's attack, Lizzie brought me information while my parents and the Slicers brought me comfort. Lizzie went to Phillips Exeter and met with Alec's ex-roommate. The roommate never had a girlfriend in his room, but there was a girl. A girl Alec liked too much. She ended up leaving campus, even after Alec was made to leave. I wish I'd known her. Before.

And I hope Alec's far away from both of us now, even though it's impossible to say for sure. When he disappeared from school, I wondered if he was sent to live in the Far East with his father. Mom's been convinced he's somewhere less exotic but even her legal connections can't pull the strings necessary to know if he's locked away. He was seventeen, his record sealed.

Mom convinced me to press charges against Alec. For assault. For battery.

Dad made his own legal claims without Mom's prodding.

Dad and I sat in the police station for hours that night, in separate small rooms. Mine smelled of burned coffee and stale air. That was the space in which I let go of my story, the story of Alec. Officer Lancel listened and never blinked. Made no judgments. She watched me as I wrote it all down on soft, yellow-lined paper. Watched me sign the bottom. My official statement.

I thought about the girl from Phillips Exeter as Officer Lancel collected my words. I wanted her to be with me in that moment. I wanted to know if she wrote it all down too. If she was as scared as I was.

If I'm being honest, I think about that other girl a lot.

I wish I knew her. Now.

I wonder if she has a mark on her hip. If she's safe. And I wonder if there were other girls before her, and if those girls had people who would listen to them the way I did.

I want to tell the girls it's not their fault.

I want them to tell me I'm not at fault. I want them to hear me say, "I know."

I know.

Coach blows her whistle for us to gather up.

"Good luck." Gregg cups my wrist with his hand, rolling his thumb over the sharp bones there. Then his thumb strokes again.

I lean into him. "Thanks."

"Give 'em hell, Ones."

I run to my team and take the bench with the other freshmen. Sweat thickens on my palms. Even now it's hard not to remember that night as I hold my stick. The way I hit Alec, broke his ribs. But when I think of all the other ways it could have ended, I'm grateful for the solidarity I feel with this length of wood. It has saved me, in more ways than one. Even in the days after Alec disappeared, it was everything to sleep with my stick tucked into my covers. Finn snoring at my feet.

The ref's whistle blows with another point for Boston College and we stand to cheer. When I sit back down, it is impossible to remain still. I lean forward, my elbows on my knees, my body wanting desperately to be on the field. I watch my teammates rack up points. They are quick and smooth and so professional, nearly shutting out the visiting university entirely.

When we enter the fourth quarter, Coach yells my name. "Doyle, you're up!"

I stand quick, shove in my mouth guard and run into position, my stick tucked across the span of my pelvis. I steal a quick look at the bleachers, how Mom and Dad stand together, in anticipation. I grind my cleats into the grass, knowing this spot on the field is a gift. Our team is so far ahead Coach can afford to send in her B string players. And I'm okay being B string. For now.

Above the crowd I hear Lizzie's ranch-hand whistle.

Gregg calling out my number.

And all that matters is the grass under my feet, the lights watching the field. My team around me, my parents with me.

And how good it is to feel worthy.

Acknowledgments

This book would not have been possible without the cheerleading of my oldest son, who has overcome unspeakable odds and still sees the world filled with love. Thank you for sharing your wisdom. Thank you for teaching me how to never give up. My heart strives to be as kind as yours. I hope that you always see magic in the world. You are mine.

Thanks goes to my youngest son, who is still so young but has taught me bravery nonetheless. You are joy personified.

An unimaginably huge thanks goes out to my husband, Keith. For sticking around. For never doubting. You are my North Star and the only person I'd want to hike beside in this world.

Thank you to my sister, Kerry, for believing in me. Thank you to my godmother, Patricia Collyer, for reminding me always of the healing power of deep, necessary laughter. And to Cousin Nicole for being the hippest girl evah. Thanks goes to Carol Brown and Tom Wright for quietly championing all that I do. And special, loving thanks goes to Lucia Zimmitti, the best writing wife any girl could ever ask for—the best person, really. Zephyr would not be in the world if not for you and your genius.

Thanks goes out to the venerable Anna Kathryn Senechal Rodgers, who has the unique ability to make me feel seventeen again. To Ellen McManus, Beth Renaud, and Melissa Gravois— my Saint Michael's College soul sisters and early readers of some ghastly trunk novels. And to Jennifer Crimi, who proved every day of her life that great things are possible. And to Daniel Murphy, whose joy is not forgotten. Thanks goes to Laurie Smith at SMC's English department for helping me hone my craft long before I understood writing was a craft. To Joshua Bodwell of Maine Writers & Publishers Alliance for having a big heart, and for corralling all of us Maine writers into a garden of community. To Mr. Leme for teaching me to see poetry in a drop of dew. To Sagamore Beach and its sandbar, flotsam, and restorative power.

To Patricia and Richard Warren for being tireless supporters of my writing, my parenting, and my choices. Thank you for gobbling up every page I write, but mostly for bringing my husband into the world, a monumental gift for which my words cannot convey my gratitude.

Thanks also goes out to beta readers of this and other works, including Elizabeth Sherfey, Susan Batchelor, Cassandra Marshall, Dennis Hilton, Kristen Graham, Laura Snyder. To Buddy at the Carleton Inn for making me hot meals during a blizzard so I could finish this novel. Thanks goes to Colette Grubman for loving this book, and for her tireless advocacy to end abuse. To the ladies of Sixteen to Read—thank you for every cheer, every laugh; I am humbled by your talent and grace. And to the debut authors of The Sweet Sixteens—thank you for showing me that all the debut crazy is normal.

Endless thanks goes to all the book bloggers who have championed this book since it arrived on the YA scene. In particular, Jennifer

Gaska, whose kindness should be cloned; Talina Roma, who made space for this story in her heart; Brittany Press, who took this book under her wing; Nori Horvitz, who is both sweet and sassy; and Rachel from A Perfection Called Books, a true blogger bae.

Thank you to my remarkable agent, Melissa Sarver White, who saw this story's potential before I ever could. And to my brilliant editor, Nicole Ellul. Thank you for taking a chance on me and championing this book. I've got a crush on you, girl! To Regina Flath and her mad design skills. Her cover is an iconic reminder that we are each entitled to our own unique voice. I am so deeply indebted to the team at Simon & Schuster who walked my story into a book. You are all dream makers.

Enormous thanks goes to Darcy Woods for her effervescent spirit, twelve-year-old sense of humor, and fierce friendship. I like you very much, Darzilla. Just as you are.

To Marisa Reichardt, a whip-smart woman and immensely talented author. Thank you for all your words, the ones we share in friendship and the ones you set down in your novels. You are a true and rare gift. You are treasured.

To my father for mistrusting every boy I ever dated.

And finally to my mother, without whom I would be nothing.

Author's Note:

I am often asked if *The Girl Who Fell* is my personal story, if I was the victim of the dating manipulation and violence depicted within its pages. The answer, for me, is no. However, I have worked with many teenage girls who had survived stories similar to Zephyr's. These girls fell victim to controlling partners who wanted to limit their movements, eliminate their friendships, and erode their sense of self-worth. These girls were strong and smart. But in their desire to feel loved, validated, and recognized, they sometimes couldn't see the dangers in their relationships. For some, they saw (and suffered) the dangers, but were too afraid to speak out.

It is my hope that readers will identify with Zephyr's strength in this story. Her worth. The value of her voice. It is my hope that readers will reflect on their own worth. The power and preciousness of their singularly unique voices. And perhaps this book will help readers to see that every girl is important and brave and worthy—and we need not sacrifice these things for the soft and precious gift of love.

There are resources to help those who may be struggling with similar issues as the ones explored in this book. The volunteers at these organizations will listen. They will not judge. So please reach out for help. For you. For your friends. Sisters. Loved ones. And remember that you are not alone. And love should never hurt.

Love Is Respect
loveisrespect.org
1.866.331.9474 | Text *loveis* to 22522

Break The Cycle (partners with Love Is Respect)
breakthecycle.org
1.866.331.9474

National Domestic Violence Hotline
thehotline.org
1.800.799.SAFE (7233) | 1.800.787.3224 (TTY)

Crisis Intervention for Sexual Assault
Rape, Abuse & Incest National Network
rainn.org
1.800.656.HOPE